D0777112

STAR STRIKER

GAME ON!

MARY AMATO

HOLIDAY HOUSE · NEW YORK

To my beautiful-game teachers—to Lucy Neher who first kicked it off for me (it's true, Lucy!), to Ivan who kept the ball rolling by stepping up to coach, to Simon and Max and all their friends and teammates over the years, to Howard Kohn, especially for the summer camps that have delighted and employed so many kids and teens, and to Karen Giacopuzzi and Bob Antonisse and all the dedicated coaches out there who teach kids to love both the game and the community with just the right spirit. Goal!

Library of Congress Cataloging-in-Publication Data

Names: Amato, Mary, author.
Title: Game on! / Mary Amato.
Description: First edition. | New York : Holiday House, [2021]
Series: Star Striker ; #1 | Audience: Ages 8–12. | Audience: Grades 4–6.
Summary: "Albert, a 7th grader, is abducted by aliens who recruit him to play Star Striker for their interplanetary soccer team, but it isn't until after he agrees that he discovers that someone or something is trying to kill him"—Provided by publisher.
Identifiers: LCCN 2021010213 | ISBN 9780823449118 (hardcover)
ISBN 9780823450329 (ebook)
Subjects: CYAC: Human-alien encounters—Fiction.
Soccer—Fiction. | Science fiction.
Classification: LCC PZ7.A49165 Gam 2021 | DDC [Fic]—dc23
LC record available at https://lccn.loc.gov/2021010213

ISBN: 978-0-8234-4911-8 (hardcover)

You can be a superstar; you just can't be one alone.
What you need is a star system: a constellation of positive,
authentic influencers who support each other,
reinforce each other, and make each other better.

— Shawn Achor

0.0

The day aliens abducted Albert Kinney happened to be the day he was trying out for his middle school soccer team.

Actually, it was the third and final day of tryouts; and, as Albert and the other seventh graders were warming up with a run around the track, his mind was racing. But it wasn't because he knew that a dangerous and extraordinary mission was about to bring him to the Fŭigor Solar System. Like the rest of you on Earth, he didn't know the planets in that system even existed. Albert's mind was racing because he was thinking about his soccer career. If he didn't get on the school team in seventh grade, he couldn't possibly make the eighth-grade team; and if he wasn't on the eighth-grade team, forget about playing in high school or college or having any hope for happiness.

That's the way life works for you, too. You think the most important thing in the world is that tryout or that math quiz or whatever—and you don't even see the huge tornado coming your way.

1.0

Eyes on the track, Albert jogged.

"Hi, Albert," Freddy Mills said, approaching him on his left.

"Hey," Albert said, immediately turning on the heat. Freddy was slow, which meant Albert's own pace must have fallen.

A kind of light-headedness came over Albert, and he wondered if he was having a panic attack. It's the final day of tryouts, he thought, and I'll probably pass out during the warm-up. He pushed through it, though, and increased his pace, catching up with Trey Patterson and his pack.

And then Trey pointed at Albert's yellow soccer socks and shin guards and said, "You got chicken legs, Kinney!"

It was a ridiculous, immature joke—who cared what color his socks and shin guards were?—and yet the guys actually laughed.

Trey Patterson. A year ago Trey would have been running by his side, not making fun of him. All their lives, Trey and Albert had been next-door neighbors and friends. Not heart-to-heart friends—they were too different for that. But they had grown up playing soccer together and had a great connection as teammates. First in Albert's yard, and then in the park down the street, and then as the two strongest stars in their recreational league, and finally, last year, as the stars of the same travel team. At the beginning of the summer, though, Trey left for a six-week soccer camp—the first camp experience that the boys didn't share—and he came back transformed. A growth spurt combined with new training changed not only Trey's body, but also his mind. He informed Albert that he was quitting their old travel team to play in a more serious league. That wasn't the surprise. Trey had always been competitive. The surprise was the condescension and contempt in his voice. Trey, for no good reason, had turned mean. And now, some of the other guys, impressed by Trey's bulked-up physique, were siding with him. And that was messing with Albert's mind.

"Bawk!" Trey called out, and the guys laughed again.

"Not funny," Freddy called from behind.

After five humiliating laps—each pass punctuated by bawking from Trey—the coach split the group into four teams for simultaneous scrimmages, and Albert's heart sank even more. His name was called for Team C. Trey and Raul and all the other skilled players were on Teams A and B. Honestly, Albert knew he had a better sense of the field than Trey or Raul. They were both strong, but Raul couldn't kick the ball with his left foot to save his life, and lately Trey hogged the ball and took risky shots for personal glory rather than seeing the passes that would pay off.

"It's over," muttered a player on Team D.

"Mr. Perez is crazy," Freddy, assigned to Team C, whispered. "Everybody knows you should be on Team A, Albert."

"Perez hates me," Albert muttered. Unfortunately, it was true. Right before school had started, the old coach left and tapped Mr. Perez to take his place. Mr. Perez had been Albert's history teacher in sixth grade and had been, in Albert's opinion, criminally boring. If Albert had known that he'd have to impress Perez this year, he would have tried harder last year. Yesterday, when they did drills, Perez praised others and didn't say a word to Albert, even though Albert knew he had done well.

When the whistle blew to start the scrimmages, Albert tried to shake off his anxiety and come out hot. He was playing center forward, his favorite position, and that boosted his confidence. In the first five minutes, he had three shots on goal and set up two chances that resulted in two more shots on goal—all of which Mr. Perez missed because he was watching Teams A and B. Still, Albert kept firing. In the ninth minute, he pressured Team D's left outside back to force a bad pass into the midfield. Freddy was actually in the right place at the right time and somehow delivered a solid pass to Albert. In the nanosecond before Albert received the ball, he glanced around. No defenders on either side. He took a couple of touches to the inside and ripped it.

Goal!

"Yes!" he yelled, hoping Mr. Perez would tear his attention away from Teams A and B to look.

His teammates cheered, and Mr. Perez glanced over. A quick, distracted nod was all the coach gave. And then he called out his announcement for the scrimmages to end and told them the last drill they'd do: shots on goal.

Albert felt his spirits lift. This was his final chance to show what he knew to be true, that he deserved to play for the team.

1.1

The dog, a muscular Ridgeback named Tackle that lived next to Albert Kinney and belonged to Trey Patterson, stood still, eyeing the furry thing in the tree. Oh, the thing looked like a squirrel, and it climbed like a squirrel and it jumped like a squirrel, but it didn't pee, didn't eat, and—

Tackle made a sudden dash, leaping up onto the trunk and barking at it sharply.

See? The thing didn't run, didn't even move. Tackle sniffed. Not a whiff of fear. He sniffed again. The scent it exuded was faint but detectable, a scent similar to the Pattersons' cell phones. *Grrr.* He didn't trust it. Didn't trust it for a second.

To be clear, Tackle was one hundred percent ordinary Earth dog. That you are witnessing his intellect in action here doesn't mean he came from another planet or had technologically enhanced abilities. Whether you're aware of it or not, animals think; you just can't always hear them. That said, there is a range of intelligence in dogs, just as there is in humans, and it can be safely said that Tackle's was above average.

Normally, he didn't bother with squirrels. Strangers, package-delivery persons, approaching storms, unusual vehicular sounds, changes in the way people smelled, an occasional rat, and one particularly aggressive neighborhood raccoon—these were his priorities—to protect not just the Pattersons but also the Kinneys next door. But, to be honest, this was work that typically used only a fraction of his brawn and brain to resolve. The four-footed furball in the tree? It was getting the better of him.

He began to pace. The squirrel-thing had arrived at some point before school started. Maybe two or three weeks ago. Tackle wasn't great with time, but he had noticed it right away and had been watching it ever since. Not just watching. He had tried to catch it numerous times since then, only to be outmaneuvered.

Now that school had started, the thing tended to perch in two favorite spots. One was the maple tree closest to the street, which it hung out in when school was in session. The other was a sweet gum tree on the side of the Pattersons' yard whose limbs reached over the fence to Albert's house. For some mysterious reason, the creature seemed to be obsessed with Albert. When Albert came home from school, it would settle itself on the limb of the sweet gum tree that was closest to Albert's bedroom window and perch like a statue.

Without success Tackle had tried to warn Albert and had tried to get Trey's help. Neither of the boys understood what he was barking about. Today he was going to show them. He stopped pacing and shook out his muscles, his glossy reddish-brown coat gleaming in the afternoon sunlight. Yep. Today he had a plan. When Albert came home and the thing jumped onto the fence top, Tackle was going to be ready. He would finally grab that freak in his jaws.

1.2

"Line up single file at the cone," Coach Perez said from the eighteen-yard box. "We'll do a one-two. You pass to me. I'll lay it off and you strike it."

Albert was fifth from the end, in front of Freddy.

Trey was first. One-two. Goal.

Raul, Mr. Perez's other favorite, was next. Another goal.

Jealousy began to gnaw at Albert.

Michael next. A good, hard kick. The goalie stopped it, but it was a solid strike.

"My sister said your sister got on the best team in the state," Freddy said to Albert as they moved up the line to take their shots. "She said that club is where all the future Olympic gymnasts train."

Albert kept his mouth closed. Yesterday the coach had yelled at Freddy for "chitchatting."

"My sister saw her over the summer at that exhibition tournament," Freddy went on. "She won, like, gold in everything. Did you go?"

"Yeah," Albert said quickly. "Shh."

"Kinney and Mills," Mr. Perez called out. "Cut the chitchat."

"Yeah, cut the bawking," Trey whispered to more laughter.

Albert's face reddened. He turned away from Freddy and tried to focus. Two more players and then it would be Albert's turn. The keeper was tall and strong, great at catching and blocking the shots that went to his right, but not as solid when it came to diving to the left, Albert noticed.

One guy's shot bounced off the goalpost; the other was easily caught. On it went, and then Albert was up. He could feel the eyes of the coach on him, the keeper's eyes, too, as he crouched, ready to spring.

Almost shaking with the desire to score, Albert passed the ball to the coach, who sent it rolling. Albert raced toward it, planted his left leg at the perfect angle, and fired his right leg forward, knowing in his bones that the connection between foot and ball was going to be perfect. But then—time seemed to shift into slow motion—at the exact same moment, dozens of black birds flew out of the trees just behind the goal, screeching, as if a huge invisible hand had struck the branches. Startled, Albert felt his upper torso jolt back and his plant foot slip out from under him. He fell with a thud.

A few laughs.

Albert jumped up quickly, hoping the coach would give him another shot, but instead the coach called out for Freddy to step up. Avoiding all eyes, Albert retreated to the back of the line, fuming.

It wasn't fair. He would have had that shot. He was perfectly placed.

After the last guy took his shot, the coach blew the whistle. "That's a wrap. Stretch and cool down, boys. I'll post the list by tomorrow. Good job, everyone." Just like that, he set his clipboard on the bench and started to collect balls.

Feigning the need to leave, Albert skipped the cooldown and grabbed his backpack from under the bench. The "yes" list on the coach's clipboard was easy enough to see. Trey Patterson's name was first and had the word *captain* next to it. Albert's name wasn't on the list.

For the next few minutes, he tried to focus on getting home. One foot in front of the other. His phone buzzed in his backpack. The sixth text from his mom since school had ended:

How did tryouts go? Your sister's practice is almost done. She was flawless on beam. Bars to go.

A grim heaviness came over him. His soccer career was over.

At the end of the summer, his mom had called a family meeting to discuss the fall schedule. Erin's new opportunity on the most competitive gymnastics team in Maryland was going to make after-school and weekend schedules complicated. As a single parent, his mom couldn't get Erin to her new team's practices and get Albert to his travel team's practices, especially since Trey—their carpooling partner—was no longer playing on Albert's team. At that time, Albert had assumed he would spend the next six years of his life playing soccer for his schools' teams, and since those teams routinely took state and attracted recruiter attention, he had agreed to drop out of the travel league.

He couldn't believe what was happening now. He was losing what he loved most.

Another buzz. Another text.

When you get home, let me know how Nana is doing.

This is what I have to look forward to, Albert thought bitterly. Failure, humiliation, and checking up on my grandmother.

Deep in this vortex of anger and depression, he walked up his driveway. As he headed toward the side door, he could see between the slats in the fence that Trey's dog, Tackle, was running toward him at full speed. Albert's anxiety level rose instantly. For three weeks now, Tackle had been aggressive, jumping and barking and scaring the heebie-jeebies out of him, and he couldn't understand why. Now, Albert saw the squirrel out of the corner of his eye and, with horror, watched the dog leap up, slam against the fence, and grab the poor squirrel between his teeth with a sickening crunch.

Startled, Albert jumped, dropping his backpack.

Then, in an even worse development, he watched Tackle rear back and fling the corpse over the fence. It landed with an appalling thud at Albert's feet, and Albert staggered back. "Tackle, what's wrong with you?"

The dog jumped on the fence, barking and baring his teeth, drilling into Albert with his oddly intelligent eyes as if he were trying to tell him something.

"Stop it!" Albert yelled at the dog. He didn't say what he was really thinking, which was that it was bad enough to lose Trey as a friend, but Tackle's sudden aggressiveness was driving him crazy.

In the next second a dozen birds from the oak tree across the street flew up, and the dog's posture changed radically. His head jerked up, and he jumped back and froze, looking skyward.

Albert felt it then—something was above him. He looked up, expecting to see a bird hovering over him, but the sky was blue and clean.

Tackle, able to see ultraviolet wavelengths that no human could see, watched a patch of UV light appear high above Albert's head and grow rapidly larger, as if the light were a flame burning a hole in the fabric of the sky. Emerging from the hole was a sphere of small, tightly packed shapes, like shimmering snowflakes that created a sound like the crackling of a fire in a frequency no human could hear.

Perplexed, Albert watched the dog snarl at what looked to him like nothing above his head. Front limbs stiff, tail erect, hackles raised, his lips pulled back as if a mortal threat were descending from the sky.

"Tackle, what is it?" Albert asked, anxiety morphing into fear.

The dog let loose a bone-chilling growl; and in the next second, the sphere of shimmering shapes plunged from above, hit the top of Albert's head, and burst like a soap bubble.

Albert felt first an icy prickle at the crown of his head and then a ripple of prickles across every inch of his skin, as if an invisible net made of tiny icicles had been dropped over him.

Run, he said to himself, but the ground snapped away from under his feet. His body grew warm, the prickles melting instantly, and then he began to slide upward, as if it were possible to fall up instead of down. He marveled at the sensation for a split second, and then he was yanked up violently. Everything turned black.

1.3

For twenty seconds Albert lost consciousness as he was teleported through the threshold. Silence. And then he blinked several times as his eyes adjusted to the light.

He was sitting inside a small...aircraft? Rocket? Whatever it was, it was rumbling. Dim, with a sloped ceiling, the chamber was about seven feet high and maybe twelve feet across, with a control panel in the front that he couldn't comprehend. Above the various levers and buttons and wheels was a rectangle that Albert presumed was a window, although it was pitch-black.

A smell that oddly reminded him of pine trees seemed to emanate from the walls or the air or the floor. And then from the shadows and into the orangish-violet light of the center of the small vehicle, an object emerged at eye level. A yellowish drone, about the size of a loaf of bread, with four snakelike arms, hovered for a split second and then flew toward Albert.

As adrenaline flooded Albert's body, he tried to move but found that two shoulder belts had been activated to keep him in place. The drone zoomed in, hovering in front of his face, emitting a hum as well as a metallic odor, and then one of the arms reached toward Albert's mouth with a spoon-sized tool, a metallic stick with a coin-sized swatch of fiber on the end of it.

Albert's heart pounded. He tried to turn his head, but the chair's viselike headrest held it in place. In the next moment, one of the drone's other arms leaped forward, suction-cupped Albert's chin, and pulled it down. Before he knew it, the spoon-sized tool was in his mouth.

A strange woolly taste. He gagged, the tool withdrew, and he clenched his jaw tight. The drone turned abruptly, zoomed to a panel on the opposite wall, and slipped the tool into a port.

A screen appeared and a number of incomprehensible words began to scroll.

Albert was barely breathing. He wanted to try bargaining for his life, arguing to whoever or whatever might be present that there must be some mistake, but he had clenched his jaw so tightly after the probe, he was having trouble opening it. A strange image floated into his mind—his mother and sister and grandmother at his funeral. Trey was there, too, trying to look sad. And then Trey turned to Albert's mother and offered to help with the chores around the house, and everyone was amazed by how perfect he was. Albert tried to shake the scene out of his mind, realizing how ridiculous it was for him to be thinking about Trey Patterson at a time like this.

A sound emerged from the control panel, and one phrase blinked into place on a large screen:

Although he was still strapped into the chair, the vise holding his head released. From behind him came a disconcertingly familiar voice.

"Welcome, Albert Kinney. You can call me Jessica." A figure stepped into the light.

Albert stared. Here was his classmate since fourth grade, Jessica Atwater. She was slightly taller than him, dressed in her usual T-shirt, skirt, leggings, and boots. She was a girl you couldn't help noticing because of her upbeat energy, a girl who had nothing to do with him, a girl who, this year, was in his Spanish class and friends with both Trey and Raul. Here she was standing in front of him, with one hand on her hip, smiling at him.

And yet she wasn't Jessica Atwater. She was...a robotic version of Jessica Atwater.

"An apology for your discomfort, Albert."

Instinctively Albert began looking around—for an exit or a weapon, he wasn't sure. At the same time, he was kicking himself for having left behind his backpack, which contained his phone, assuming, incorrectly, that it would be of use.

But then the robotic Jessica slapped her hip, and he was startled to watch what happened next. With a ratcheting sound, her knees bent and she lowered into a sitting position of perfect posture—without a chair in sight. "You look pale, Albert. Not a good choice for my appearance?" the thing asked. "Based on my research, this body-form was determined to be one that you'd enjoy."

Albert flushed, speechless.

The thing continued. "I observe that you are, as they say,

13

freaked out. Perhaps you desire to see the body-form menu." She opened her forearm to reveal a panel.

Albert stared at the mechanics. "Are you…are you a robot?"

"Yes. I am an intelligent robot with smart-skin body-form technology that can be made to resemble any life-form. Assuming you would prefer human, I have been constructed with one head, two arms, and two legs, so I am limited in appearance. However, I can transform to generic female, male, or gender-neutral. Which would you enjoy?"

The black-eyed stare was intense.

After several seconds of stunned silence from Albert, she said, "No decision is, in fact, a decision, Albert. Remember that. Generic female it is." She pushed a button on the panel embedded in her arm and then snapped the panel shut. As the orangish light around her seemed to wrinkle, the human clothing, skin, and facial features of Jessica Atwater evaporated, revealing a somewhat old-looking female-form robot of scratched and dented metal.

"In the saving of time, I won't ask you for a name preference. You may call me Unit B33QX920J63434. Or abbreviate to Unit B, if you must." The robot abruptly spun around and began tapping a large control panel with slender metal fingers. "Connecting to Zeeno."

Before Albert could even process what had happened so far, a large video image appeared on the screen. Albert found himself staring at a dozen aliens who were all crowded together, staring back at him. They appeared somewhat human, each with two legs and two arms that looked muscular yet flexible; but, instead of the ranges of skin tones that Albert was accustomed to, the color of the aliens' skin was a luminous swirl of multiple tones of browns and greens. As for their faces, they had no noses that he could see, but they had recognizable mouths for speaking and breathing and—Albert noticed with immediate relief—for smiling. Their eyes were slightly larger than human eyes and either forest green or pale violet in color, remarkably clear, glittering with excitement.

"Team Zeeno, please meet Albert Kinney," Unit B said.

First, the tall one in the center bowed. "I am Kayko Tusq, team tactician," she said, "and on behalf of the team and planet, I extend our greetings." The other Zeenods stood and straightened and bowed, not quite in unison, although they had intended to be.

Unsure, Albert froze.

"Bow in return," the robot whispered, reaching over to release Albert's shoulder belt.

Shakily, Albert stood and bowed, and then they all resumed sitting. The look on their faces astounded Albert. It wasn't the shock and fear that he knew was radiating from his own eyes. It was the excitement of seeing a celebrity.

1.4

Although the desire to stay with Albert would be understandable, it's essential to pause for a moment, peer into a new window, and meet another important player in this drama: a botmaker.

He was a Zeenod nicknamed Mehk, which meant "overtime" in the Zeenod language. In his early twenties by Earth standards, he was painfully thin, not by choice or by genes, but rather because he frequently forgot to eat.

At this moment in time, he was at the creature-fabrication facility where he worked, staring intently through his smartgoggles at the next project on his desk—a new line of robotic ahda-bird pets. But he was only pretending to be interested. Secretly, he was watching the video footage of his squirrelbot's demise and Albert's abduction, via an encrypted channel in his goggles. He had rigged them so that when he lowered them down to the tip of his nose, the footage would project onto the interior of the lens, where he could view it while appearing to be working.

After replaying the scene three times, he tapped the side of his goggles to stop. A part of him was relieved that, even though his squirrelbot was mangled, the surveillance camera embedded within it continued to operate. Another part of him hated having to watch the video. With trembling hands, he opened his log and began to type his thoughts, translated here for convenience.

```
Distressing news. Kinney has been teleported and this
phase of my mission was thwarted by a dog! What a fail-
ure! You idiot! Why didn't you—
```

He paused. Self-loathing. Not helpful. An idea popped into his head. Excited, he resumed typing.

```
I could create a microbot to detect self-loathing that
delivers a small neural shock to disrupt it. This is
brilliant! I wonder—
     Stop. Do not become distracted!
```

He hit himself sharply on the side of his head.

Return to the subject.

Yes, you have experienced a setback. But remember, Kinney is an Earthling. Weak. Insecure. Even without the insertion of the negative thought-loop, Kinney will probably say no to the team. If Kinney does accept, you can get him to change his mind before the Opening.

Remember that your masterpiece is in place! Focus.

1. Initiate remote diagnostic and self-repair of squirrelbot.
2. Determine if the microbots housed within the squirrel are operational.
3. Continue with plan to deploy negative thought-loop microbot when Kinney returns.

He paused to think about the dog. Did the canine interfere deliberately? Could the canine sense the szoŭ?

Canines are not intelligent. You underestimated the animal's drive to hunt, that's all. The dog thought the squirrel was real. Ha! And you didn't even program it to have a mammal aroma or to perform bodily functions. Ha!

He paused and touched the ticklike bump on the back of his neck, the positive thought-loop microbot he had devised that sent a code to his mind...not an audible voice, but a silent yet comprehensible thought that repeated over and over:

Believe in your brilliance. You will succeed.

1.5

As Albert watched, a short Zeenod, unable to contain himself, jumped toward the camera. "It is the genuine Albert Kinney!" he exclaimed, waving with a wide smile. "Albert Kinney! Hello!"

The aliens laughed, and the mood of the meeting shifted from formal politeness to exuberant enthusiasm. Most of the others joined in, waving and calling out their greetings. Something about the way they were smiling and bouncing made Albert relax just enough to take in his first full breath since his abduction.

"Are these guys my age?" he whispered to Unit B. "Who are they? How do they know me?"

"We can hear you." Kayko smiled and gestured for everyone to hush. "We have much to explain, but yes, we've been watching you. We are the official Fŭigor johka team from planet Zeeno. Johka is a sport, like your soccer. I am what you call the coach. These guys, as you say, are approximately thirteen Earth years old. I am nineteen Earth years old."

A thin-faced Zeenod sitting on Kayko's left interrupted, whispering something to Kayko in a language Albert couldn't comprehend; Kayko nodded appreciatively and then turned back to the camera. "A warning about errors in our speech before we start. We use translation implants to speak in English. Language is complex and what we receive in our brains may not capture perfection, so we make a gift of our apology to you in advance."

The entire team stood and bowed again. Not sure how to respond, Albert bowed and said, "Your English is amazing. Thank you."

They sat back down, looking relieved.

Unit B's head swiveled to face Albert. "The Zeenods' translation implants and the translation software in my own system are self-learning." Her eyelids blinked. "The more we converse with you, the more our ability to speak your language will improve."

Kayko turned to the same thin-faced player who had whispered to her. "Feeb, why don't you begin?"

With a quick nod, Feeb rose to his feet. Albert had noticed that he had been silent earlier, when the rest of them had been laughing. "Feeb is my name. I am the team statistician and a defender. For questions about regulations or records, I will be at your service." He sat back down.

Before Kayko could tap another player to go, the short smiley one jumped up and again waved at the camera. "I'm Doz!" he said. "Center midfielder. I am crazy to meet you."

Most of the players laughed again. The serious Feeb said, "Doz, please wait until Kayko tells you to speak."

Kayko smiled. "We forgive excitement when no harm is done, Feeb. Ennjy, why don't you speak next?" she said to the player on her right, a Zeenod with a gentle face and violet eyes.

All this time, Albert had been catching glimpses of the odd physical features of the aliens. Each Zeenod had a circle of skin speckled with tiny gill-like dots on the sides of their heads that contracted and expanded slightly when their mouths were closed. He guessed that this was a secondary breathing mechanism to take in and let out air. More dramatically, each had a capelike thing on his or her back, a thin, wide, almost fabric-like sheet that began behind their shoulders and draped down to their lower backs. At first, Albert had thought it must be part of their outfits. Frankly, the tight-fitting official-looking uniforms they were wearing looked more like superhero costumes than athletic clothes to him. But when Ennjy stood, Albert realized that the capelike thing, which was the same luminous swirl of colors as their skin, wasn't a part of their clothes; it was a part of their bodies. As she spoke, the thing moved of its own accord. It was an appendage! With muscle! The way it hung but also moved reminded Albert of an elephant's ear.

"I am called Ennjy. I am the team ahnuru, and I play forward."

Albert could hardly listen, he was so hypnotized by the subtle movements of her appendage, the way the bottom edges of it were shifting and lifting as if it were a living creature on her back. On the other Zeenods, the thing had hung inertly. But hers was active, as if it were listening. He wanted to ask about the appendage and its purpose, but he didn't want to interrupt.

One by one, team members introduced themselves, including a set of identical twins named Beeda and Reeda, and then after they were done, many of them started talking to Albert at once. Kayko interrupted, speaking to them in their language. As they quieted down, Unit B translated the obvious. "The team is excited. Kayko is telling them to be of calm minds."

The team hushed, and Kayko straightened up. "Team Zeeno invites you, Albert Kinney, to join us for the next Fŭigor Johka Tournament. As tactician, I have prepared a contract translated into your language. We hope with our hearts that you will sign."

Kayko nodded at Unit B, who tapped a second screen. In English, a document appeared.

As Unit B started to go over the contract, Albert tried to focus. Under an official Fŭigor Johka Federation seal, seven paragraphs laid out dates for practices and training sessions and tournament games, as well as information about providing "technologically and biologically appropriate" gear, translation devices, and breathing apparatuses.

"Did they say johka is like soccer?" Albert whispered to Unit B, feeling utterly stupid. "Are they actually asking me to play on a team?"

"Yes, Albert," Kayko said. "On your planet the sport is known by many names. *Fútbol, futebol, football, voetball,* and *fodbold* are a few examples. Your country calls it soccer."

"All of these terms are descendants of johka," Feeb explained, "which originated in the Fŭigor Solar System approximately ten thousand Earth years ago and is still the most popular sport in the entire Milky Way Galaxy. Our ancestors brought the game to Earth about five thousand Earth years ago and—"

"Please wait, Feeb," Kayko said, nodding. "Too much information makes for overwhelming. We can explain more of the history later. For now, Albert, you should know that johka and Earth soccer are related, with important differences that you will discover. But the first thing you should know is that in our solar system our professional players are not adults; our professionals are ages twelve to sixteen Earth years old." Kayko smiled at her team. "These are professional johka players. As I said earlier, I am the old coach."

Albert tried to imagine what it would be like to tune into the FIFA World Cup and see guys his age playing. Not just guys, actually. All genders together. Amazing.

"Every year, the top four teams progress to the Fŭigor Johka Tournament," Kayko continued. "For the tournament, each team is allowed to recruit a player from any planet in the galaxy."

Doz leaned in. "We want you, Albert Kinney, to be our Star Striker."

Albert looked at the contract and then at the aliens staring back at him, waiting for his response. "You want me to play striker on your team?" he asked.

21

"We do," Kayko said.

"In a tournament on a planet called Zeeno?"

The entire team nodded.

"Clarification," Unit B said, and turned to Albert. "You won't only play on Zeeno. You will play on Zeeno for the first game, but other games are played on other planets."

"We will not only share in enjoying johka, we will also show you the secret beauty of Zeeno, Albert," Ennjy said. "With your help, we can usher Zeeno into a new age."

"Please sign the contract!" Doz said.

"Wait." Feeb leaned in. "Albert, please witness the secrecy clause in paragraph six. If you sign the contract, you cannot discuss the tournament or the Fŭigor Solar System with any human while you are on Earth."

"Our last Earthling player did an excellent job," Kayko said.

"There were others who did this?" Albert asked.

"The last to play was the favorite," Doz said with a huge smile.

"Lightning Lee!" the twin Zeenods said in unison.

"A kid like me?" Albert asked.

Kayko nodded. "Seventy-five years ago."

Doz cracked another huge smile. "We won."

"Lee was much loved. Is much loved," Ennjy said.

Albert looked at the document's secrecy clause. As he tried to read through it, Unit B pointed out that he also had to agree to participate in something called the Opening, which was to occur on a planet called Zhidor a week from tomorrow.

It was all so official. A contract. Dates. The reality of the invitation was sinking in. He, Albert, was being invited to play interplanetary soccer. He looked at the robot sitting next to him.

She stared back. "A thought is occurring in your brain."

"I'm not good enough," he whispered.

She popped open a panel on her forearm and tapped a button. "Shawble Code 17A."

"Wait. What does that mean—"

But before Unit B could answer, Kayko stepped forward so that her face filled the screen, and the mood changed yet again. The color of her eyes transformed from a clear green to a warm gold; and, although Albert knew no facts about the physiology of the Zeenods at the time, he instinctively knew that whatever Kayko was about to say was serious and important.

"Albert, as Ennjy mentioned earlier, for us this tournament has extraordinary meaning. Seventy-five years ago, shortly after that year's johka tournament was played, Zeeno was invaded by planet Tev," she explained. "We lost that war, and the Tevs took over our planet. Many Zeenods died. Many others fled to other planets. But some stayed on Zeeno and tried to keep our ways alive. This year, for the first time since the war, we formed a team and petitioned to play in the regular season. And to everyone's surprise, we advanced to the tournament. By playing, we hope to unite Zeenods everywhere."

The rest of the team looked at Albert, their eyes all now transforming to that warm gold color, radiating an intensity that enabled Albert to glimpse deep sorrows as well as determined hope.

A complex mix of excitement and anxiety rose in Albert's chest. He glanced at the robot, who merely blinked. "B-but...," Albert stammered, turning back to the video. "I'm...it's just... Why me?"

1.6

Tackle ran to the steps by his front door and howled, instinctively sending out an alarm, although he knew that none of the Pattersons were home to hear it. After that, he ran back to the fence, charging through the flower bed, well aware that this was a "bad dog" action. Protecting flowers was the least of his concerns. This was an emergency.

Grrr. He thrust his snout between the fence slats and sniffed. Somehow, Albert had been taken by that light that came from the sky, and somehow the light had left a residue of aroma on Albert's backpack and on the concrete of their driveway and on the body of that squirrel-that-wasn't-a-squirrel that Tackle had thrown over the fence. Light didn't have a smell. Yet, he was smelling something. It was as strong as the plume that always spewed out of the school bus's exhaust pipe and clung to the bushes by the side of the road.

Tackle had to get over the fence and give the residue a good sniff, and he had to get a closer sniff of that squirrel-thing. Wincing at the ache in his shoulder, he reared back and then flung himself at the fence for the fourth time in the past two minutes. *Thwack!* The boards vibrated but didn't break. Solid as a rock, the dog thought, stop throwing yourself at it.

That squirrel-thing had to be related to whatever had happened just now to Albert. He felt it in his gut. Well, and between his teeth! When he had bitten down on that thing's neck, his teeth hadn't met with flesh, his teeth had met with metal! A machine, the dog realized. That was what it was. The squirrel was a machine.

Thwack! He tried breaking through the fence again. *Thwack!*

He should have inspected the machine before flinging it over to Albert, but in the moment it had seemed critical that Albert see it. Big mistake. It had freaked Albert out. Even worse, Tackle's attempt to scare off that light from the sky had failed, too. His mission, his reason for being, was to protect, and yet a boy had disappeared right in front of him! *Grrr.*

He stopped and shook out his muscles. For weeks he had been on edge. The squirrel was to blame, sure. But also, his routine was completely off. He wasn't getting the kind of exercise he desperately needed to manage the stress of his near-constant vigilance. Trey had come home from camp changed. He had lost interest in taking Tackle to the park, lost interest in running with him, lost interest in wrestling with him. He was almost never home, and when he was, he locked himself in his room. Just at a time when Tackle needed an ally and needed to exercise, Trey was not the Trey he could count on. *Grrr!*

And then, a movement in Albert's driveway caught his attention. The "squirrel" had twitched. Cautiously, he crept closer to peer between two slats. The mangled body twitched again. Tackle didn't move.

The squirrel's tail flicked. A blue glow emanated from the gash Tackle's teeth had made in the fur of the neck. In the next second, the thing leaped off the ground and landed on one foot, balancing, as its head teetered awkwardly to the side. Another blue glow from the seams, and then, with a shudder, the head snapped back onto its neck and the entire thing rebalanced itself on two feet. Before Tackle had time to react, the squirrel-machine raced up its side of the fence, jumped onto the tree trunk, and scampered up to a safe branch.

1.7

"We have been watching and researching, Albert. You are our first choice." Kayko smiled. "Our ahnuru, Ennjy, believes you have the qualities we need."

Ennjy nodded. She leaned forward and looked closely at Albert. The bottom edges of the capelike appendage on her back lifted slightly and drew forward. She had a different way of looking at Albert than the others, a different way than anyone he had ever met. She seemed to be not looking at him, but rather listening to him, even though he wasn't talking, listening to him with her entire body.

No one spoke for a moment, and none of the Zeenods showed any signs of impatience. And then Ennjy spoke.

"Inside you, two Alberts are having an argument," she said. "*Say yes,* one Albert whispers, *and become a part of this team. Say no,* the other Albert whispers, *and avoid failure and disappointment.*"

Albert blinked. She had nailed it.

"Focus on our words," Ennjy said. "We *want* you to spell out the yes, Albert Kinney." She looked at her teammates, and they all looked at the camera and said in unison, "We *want* you to spell out the yes, Albert Kinney."

Albert glanced at the contract. "But how would I do all this—"

Feeb spoke up, his businesslike manner making him seem more lawyer than soccer player. "A complete set of regulations and guidelines will provide all the needful information. All you have to do is arrive for each practice and then for the games. Your robot will take care of all else."

"Clarification," Unit B said. "The use of the phrase *your robot* by Feeb could be misleading. I am not Albert Kinney's robot. I serve in the capacity of chaperone on a temporary basis."

26

"Correction noted." Kayko smiled. "Albert, the ITV, that's the vehicle you're in now, is orbiting in a cloaked manner near your home location. Unit B will pilot the vehicle. We have a Z-da for you to use for communication."

Unit B handed Albert a pendant. It was an oval metal disk, gold, with a mouthpiece and four holes, that was suspended from a loop of black cord. It reminded Albert of a smaller version of the palm-sized clay whistle called an ocarina that his grandmother had once brought back from a trip to Peru.

"This is your Z-da," Unit B said. "Your breath activates a series of internal sensors that provide different services for you. Cover the top left hole and breathe and that will signal me that you are ready for the szoŭ."

"The szoŭ is the process of being transported from Earth into the ITV," Kayko explained.

"Your sci-fi films call it beaming," Doz said with a grin. "Beam me up!"

"Wait. You watch Earth sci-fi?" Albert was astounded.

"For entertainment and to learn of customs, we watch films from many other solar systems," Feeb explained.

Another Zeenod leaned in. "The inaccuracy of the science in your sci-fi films creates much laughter for us."

"Ha ha, dude," Doz said.

"Doz enjoys the *slang* setting on his language-translation implant." Feeb rolled his eyes.

Unit B interrupted. "Regarding your Z-da, if you breathe once while covering the top right hole, you will activate the holographic tournament guide. There are more features, but that's enough for now. Go ahead and activate the guide. Top right hole."

Albert covered the right hole with his finger and blew into

the mouthpiece. A holographic screen appeared in front of him. Written in English were tournament rules, the schedule, the team assignments, field diagrams, player bios and pictures, and much more.

Unit B showed him how to progress through the guide by swiping left.

"Swipe right to close the program," she said. "Oh. And a copy of your contract is included in the appendix for review."

Albert reached out his hand and brushed it to the right and the hologram disappeared. "This is so unbelievably cool," he whispered.

"Before you make a decision, you may take the Z-da and read through the entire guide," Ennjy said. "Reading about the troubled history of our planet will help you more fully grasp the stakes."

Kayko nodded. "But we will need your answer by—"

"I'll do it," Albert said, surprised by his own voice.

The team looked at each other and then broke into cheers.

"We will release the news!" Kayko said. "This will cause much interest throughout the entire solar system! We can't wait to meet you in person at the Opening, Albert Kinney!"

Doz stood and thrust his arms in the air. "As you say, jolly goodness!"

The Zeenods erupted again, this time in song.

"The Zeeno anthem," Unit B explained as they sang. "You will need to learn it, too."

Their joy was infectious. Albert felt his own smile beaming back at them.

"Your signature here." Unit B pointed at the glowing line on the screen. Only after he signed it did he notice a phrase in the final paragraph.

Acceptance of Risk. My signature below verifies a full understanding of the possible danger of long-term psychological
effects as well as the possible danger of physical injury,
including but not limited to: limbs, spinal cord, major and
minor organs, and brain, any or all of which could result in
permanent impairment and/or death.

"Congratulations!" Unit B said.

The team applauded again and they began to say their good-
byes, using every English goodbye phrase that their translation
devices were feeding them, whether formal, informal, or botched.

"Farewell!"

"So long!"

"Super best wishing!"

"See you on the flipping side!"

"Until our roads meet!"

"Cheerios!"

"Wait!" Albert said. "What's—"

"Please utilize the guide on your Z-da to review all documen-
tation and instructions," Unit B said as she lifted the Z-da from
his hand and placed its cord around his neck. "We will see you at
the Opening a week from Friday at eleven forty-seven p.m. East-
ern Standard Time. Protocol indicates that unless we hear otherwise, we use the same location coordinates."

"But—"

Everything went black.

1.8

Frustrated beyond control, Tackle paced under the sweet gum tree, trampling the flowers planted around it. The squirrel-machine was up there on its favorite limb facing Albert's bedroom window as if nothing had happened. Ever since the remarkable resurrection, the thing had remained sitting in the tree.

Tackle's ears pricked. *Sniff.* There it was again...that aroma the light had brought. Whatever had come for Albert was returning! Flooded with adrenaline, the dog began to tremble. In the next moment, the birds that had been in the top of the tree startled and flew off.

The hairs on the dog's back rose and his head snapped up. In the sky, the ultraviolet light and the shimmering sphere appeared again. The sound of crackling came next and then, in the exact same location where Albert had been taken, Albert reappeared, looking stunned.

The air fizzed into silence and the sky became cloudless and blue.

For a moment, the boy stood still. And in that moment, Tackle thought he might have imagined the whole crazy episode. Albert looked normal, looked whole. But then a new smell hit the dog's nose. Pine trees? Albert smelled like pine trees. Why? Tackle lifted his snout to take it in, and the strange smell of the squirrel-thing also hit his nose. The squirrel opened its mouth and a beetlelike thing flew out and zipped purposefully toward Albert.

Tackle jumped on the fence and barked, his claws scratching furiously at the slats. But Albert didn't look up. In fact, he turned his back on the dog and lifted up an object that he was wearing on a cord around his neck, a gold-colored metal disk; and while he was looking at the disk, the bug landed on the side of Albert's head! Unaware, Albert began to walk toward the side door of his house. Tackle had to get that new thing off Albert!

The dog's nostrils widened, and a movement on his right caught his eye—a real squirrel scrambled onto the Pattersons' picnic table, leaped over the fence, and landed on a tree branch on the Kinneys' side. Tackle almost ignored it, but then comprehension flickered through him. The picnic table! Tackle had climbed onto the picnic table before and knew that when he was standing on the table, the tops of his ears were level with the top of the fence. He also knew that, with a running start, he could jump over anything his own height. Maybe with a running start, he could use the table to clear the fence. Why not? Was he less powerful, less agile, less of a risk-taker than that puny squirrel? No, he was not. He shook his muscles loose and took off running. If he could just get enough momentum…C'mon, dog! *Aiyeeee!* He bounded up and off the table, sailing over the fence…he was doing it…What a beast! What a hero!

With a crash, he landed on the Kinneys' big plastic garbage can, which tipped, sending him with a second crash onto the ground.

Halfway through the door to his house, Albert turned.

The smell of chicken scraps wafted from the split garbage bag just inches from Tackle's nose, and—*Yum!* He thrust his snout into the bag, rummaging past the wilted lettuce and onion…Stop it, dog! Don't be distracted by spilled scraps! You have a job to do!

He leaped out of the mess and jumped on Albert, who hit the side of the doorway and fell. This knocked the bug off Albert's head, and it landed in the center of the driveway on its back, legs in the air.

Before Tackle could make his next move, the fierce old one they called Nana rolled up the sidewalk from her trip to the park in her wheelchair. "Tackle!" she shouted at the dog. With one arm, she propelled her wheelchair up the driveway; with the other arm, she hurled her knitting bag, striking Tackle's rear with surprising force.

Nobody understands me! Tackle barked. *I'm a protector! Look! That thing was on Albert's head.* Just as Tackle caught sight of the bug flipping itself over, the grandmother's wheelchair rolled forward at breakneck speed. With a satisfying crunch, one wheel rolled over the bug.

Quickly, Tackle dove forward to sniff the dead body, but all that was visible on the pavement was a powdery film. In the next second, a whisper of wind blew the particles away.

1.9

"Albert, are you okay?" Albert's grandmother screeched to a stop in front of him.

Albert picked himself up, his mind spinning, and quickly tucked the Z-da under his shirt.

"What's going on?" Trey's voice called out next; and as Albert and his grandmother turned to see Trey approaching, the dog took off to meet him, barking all the way.

"Sit, Tackle! Sit!" Trey yelled. "Bad dog!"

"It's okay," the grandmother called out. "I think Tackle's over-stimulated. Albert is fine. Aren't you, Albert?"

Mortified, Albert muttered that he was fine and hurried inside. Through the open window, he could hear Trey apologize over the dog's continuing barks, and then the sound of the barks receded and turned into whines, and Albert guessed that Trey was forcing Tackle home.

The sound of Nana rolling inside sent Albert running to the first-floor bathroom, where he locked himself in. A few seconds later, there was a knock on the door.

"You okay, Albert?"

"Yeah," he called out, trying to make his voice sound normal. "Just taking a shower. I stink," he added, trying to make a joke.

"I saw that you scraped your hand when you fell."

Albert noticed his bloodied hand, which was just now starting to sting. "It's fine," he said. "I don't know what's wrong with Trey's dog. He's against me for some reason."

"I'm sure he isn't against you, Albert. Make sure you wash that well. Lots of soap."

"Got it." Albert turned on the hot water.

"I've got your backpack," she said. "You left it in the driveway."

"Thanks."

"Your phone must be in here," she said. "I can feel it buzzing."

He forced a laugh. "It's Mom. Can you just text her and let her know you're fine and that I'm home?"

"Got it. I'll leave your backpack here," Nana said, and then paused. "And I'll be in the den if you want to talk about anything."

"Thanks!" He turned off the water and heard her roll down the hall. He loved Nana but was grateful that she was leaving him alone. The quiet privacy was a relief. His mind was about to explode, and the last thing he wanted to do was talk about soccer tryouts or school or what they were going to have for dinner.

Carefully he removed the Z-da from around his neck and set it on the counter. Then he hopped in the shower. The back of his hand was fine. Quickly he soaped, rinsed, hopped out, wrapped a towel around his waist, and stared at himself in the mirror.

It was insane.

He had just been abducted and DNA-swabbed and then had met a bunch of aliens who'd recruited him to play in their interplanetary youth soccer tournament. His mind was brimming with questions. Why did Kayko mention that whole war thing between Zeeno and that other planet? And why did the Zeenods think he could help them win the tournament? Who did they think he was? And why did the robot say that Jessica Atwater was the "body-form" he'd "enjoy"? Thinking about that made him feel almost nauseated with shame. He had no possible connection to Jessica Atwater. Why would a robot from another planet think otherwise?

After bandaging his hand, he picked up the Z-da and sat on the edge of the tub. The necklace's metal was silvery and smooth. Was it real gold? The kind of gold that, on Earth, would be worth a lot? On the slightly domed side were the four tiny holes and the small mouthpiece; embedded on the flat side was a painting or photograph—a miniature landscape unlike anything Albert had seen.

He rummaged in the medicine cabinet until he found a magnifying glass, and he used it to take a closer look at the picture.

Lush, blossoming trees, a mountain covered with flowers, a flock of multicolored birds in the air, and what looked like multicolored, natural fountains shooting up from the center of a valley. Zeeno, he wondered? A real place he was actually being invited to see? It had to be. He was holding proof, right? He turned the device over and over in his hands, his mind buzzing, and then he put the cord around his neck.

The top right hole activated the official tournament guide. Gingerly he covered the tiny right hole without accidentally covering any of the others and blew, and the hologram appeared again: a glowing screen suspended in midair.

Official Guide to the Fŭigor Johka Tournament
EARTH/ENGLISH EDITION
1,336 pages

1,336 pages?!
He slipped out of the bathroom and locked himself in his bedroom. After getting dressed, he climbed onto his bed and began to read.

Prepared for Albert Kinney, Zeeno's choice for Star Striker in this year's Fŭigor Johka Tournament.

He stopped and read that first paragraph several times.

Tournament Structure
Round One
Gaböq vs. Jhaateez on Gaböq
Zeeno vs. Tev on Zeeno

Round Two
Tev vs. Gaböq on Tev
Jhaateez vs. Zeeno on Jhaateez

Round Three
Jhaateez vs. Tev on Jhaateez
Gaböq vs. Zeeno on Gaböq

Final Game
The two top-ranking teams play against each other.
Victory Parade and Closing Ceremony

Albert would be playing at least three games on three different planets. He could hardly believe it.

Unlike the other planets in the Milky Way Galaxy, Earth, a technologically inferior planet, does not know of the existence of the Füigor Solar System or our neighbor, the Saynar Solar System. For their safety, Earthlings must remain ignorant of our existence.

Albert thought about his fifth-grade science teacher, Ms. Holly, an astronomy nerd, with NASA posters all over her room. He also remembered the guest astronomers from Goddard Space Flight Center that she brought in to speak to them. How astounding that he was learning about things right now that they knew nothing about.

Typically, no one from the Füigor System is allowed to visit Earth or communicate with Earthlings. However, an Earthling can be recruited as a Star Striker, and then all Fŭigor Johka Federation regulations must be followed. The szoŭ process must be kept hidden. If, through carelessness or an error of judgment, the recruit allows a szoŭ to be witnessed by another human being, the recruit will be expelled from this or any future FJF tournament and have his/her/their memory wiped. Furthermore, the recruit must not share knowledge or information about the FSS or the FJF during or after the training and tournament with any other person on Earth, including family members and close friends. Breaking this rule results in one or all of the following:

1. Expulsion from this or any future FJF tournament.
2. Complete memory wipe.
3. Permanent relocation of recruit to appropriate location.

Albert stopped. Okay, he thought, complete memory wipe? Permanent relocation of recruit? Extremely serious.

According to the FJF bylaws, all players must be DNA-based life-forms. No robotic players. No technologically enhanced players.

To ensure fairness, the FJF will provide Interplanetary Transportation Vehicles and training equipment and gear.

After the Opening, training begins. Three practices per week on Zeeno as well as remote training on Earth are the goal.

Much is at stake. We will be playing our first game against Tev, the aggressive planet that invaded Zeeno seventy-five years

ago and has been occupying our planet ever since. For the sake
of Zeenods everywhere, we must win.

Albert stood up, inadvertently swiping the holographic guide
closed.

The Zeenods had made a mistake. There had to be another
Albert Kinney that they were looking for. An impressive athlete.
A daredevil. A junior astronaut or something.

He moved to his desk, opened his laptop, and launched an
online search of his name. There was an Albert Kinney who was
an actor in Toronto. A *dead* actor in Toronto. Also named Albert
Kinney were two more dead guys, an alive banker, a plumber, a
violinist in Dublin, the owner of a café in Los Angeles called Kinney's Kitchen, and a convicted thief writing a blog from prison
called *Time to Think in the Clink*. He'd had no idea there were so
many Albert Kinneys.

Albert opened his closet door and peered at himself in the
full-length mirror. The Z-da hanging from the black cord around
his neck either made him look interesting, like a world traveler, or
made him look ridiculous, like a wannabe cool dude. He wasn't
sure. He tried to look cool and stood taller, but he was still short
for his age. He had his nana to thank for that. She always said she
had been the shortest in her grade.

His phone in his backpack buzzed again. He fished it out and
looked at the text.

Erin just won first on bars. Home soon. How were tryouts?

The remarkable strangeness of what had happened that afternoon grabbed Albert by the throat. He didn't reply.

38

1.10

The botmaker was seething. Over and over Mehk had watched the video that had been captured by his surveillance squirrel, the footage that showed first the successful release of his beetle-shaped microbot and then the dog's leap and the destruction of it underneath the wheelchair.

As soon as his shift ended and he was out of the building, he found a private place to record an entry in his log.

```
When I think of how long it took to create that
negative-thought-loop microbot, the risk it took to get
the materials to make it, how much I was looking forward
to watching the effect on Albert Kinney's brain...And
there are only eight days until the Opening.
    You idiot! You should have eliminated the dog!
    Self-loathing. Stop.
```

He began to hit himself and stopped. He closed his eyes and listened for the positive thought-loop he had planted in his own mind. *Believe in your brilliance. You will succeed.* His breathing slowed. See? It was helping. Thinking more clearly, he reminded himself that the loss of the negative-thought-loop microbot wasn't the main issue. That was one of his newer inventions, and one he was eager to test on Albert Kinney, but his main goal was so much bigger.

```
Don't write down what you didn't do. Write down what you
did do...and what you are going to do! You have eight
full days to come up with a new plan.
```

1. Learn as much about Kinney's psychological and
   physical weaknesses as possible.
2. Continue spying in case Kinney breaks the secrecy
   rule. If he does, you could show the video to the
   FJF—anonymously—and he would be expelled, according
   to contract.

Mehk paused, wondering if he should simply remove or eliminate the dog now. Temporarily? Permanently? He would make a list of advantages and disadvantages.

1.11

When the Kinneys' car pulled up in the driveway, Albert peeked out his bedroom window. Trey was picking up the garbage that Tackle had tipped out of the can, and as his mom got out of the car, he explained and apologized.

Albert's ten-year-old sister, Erin, was staring at Trey with that look Albert couldn't stand. Because her gym had done a team photo shoot, she was wearing the three gold medals from her last competition around her neck. And when Trey noticed her medals and looked at them more closely, her smile made Albert's blood boil. Trey was still nice to Erin. Albert didn't understand why Trey had stopped wanting to be friends with him.

Albert's family came inside and a few seconds later, he heard his mom call up. "Albert?"

"Coming," he called down. He couldn't stay in his room forever. Glancing at himself again in his mirror, he slipped the Z-da under his shirt, told himself to pretend that he hadn't just returned from an encounter with aliens, and walked out.

His mom, Erin, and his grandmother were in the kitchen. Nana was working on her laptop and his mom was busy getting dinner on the table. Erin was standing by the refrigerator chugging down a glass of juice, her three medals around her neck.

"Albert, why didn't you text me back? How were tryouts?" his mom asked.

He froze for a moment, and then he heard a lie come out of his mouth. "I decided not to try out."

"What?" All three of them looked at him.

His grandmother's face grew worried. "I thought something was up."

"What happened?" his mom exclaimed.

"Nothing happened," Albert said, straightening up. "I just decided I wanted to focus my time on something else."

"On what?" Erin asked. "Soccer's your thing, Albert. Everybody knows that."

"On playing…" Under his shirt, the Z-da felt solid and cool against his skin. "On playing the clarinet," he said on impulse.

"The clarinet?" his mother asked.

"You tried that for, like, three weeks in the fourth grade," Erin said. "And then you quit."

Albert shrugged. "I'm going to give it another try."

His grandmother nodded. "I've always liked the clarinet."

"But you love soccer, and you're not going to be playing on

41

the travel team…," his mother said, her face clouding with what Albert knew was guilt. "Let me talk to Trey's mom one more time and see if there's a way to get you on his—"

"Mom," Albert snapped. "Don't do that. It's fine. All I used to do was soccer. Now I'm going to try something else. I can always go back to soccer."

The whole family was silent.

"I feel like this is my fault," his mom said. "What about trying to get you back in your old league?"

"Mom," Albert said. "It's not your fault. It's my choice. Just drop it."

"Are you sure?" Nana asked.

Albert nodded.

"Well," his mother finally said. "If that's what you've decided, I can talk to the counselor and get you into band."

"Band." Nana brightened. "That's a wonderful opportunity to become a part of a team."

"Um…" Albert forced a smile. "Band? Right. That would be great."

2.0

Albert's clarinet squeaked.

"Mom," Erin groaned. "Can't we make a no-clarinet-at-breakfast rule? Why can't he only practice after school when I'm at gymnastics?" She glared at Albert through the doorway.

Albert called from the living room to the kitchen, "I don't complain about the fact that you play your music all the time and your gymnastics stuff takes over the whole house, the whole garage, *and* the backyard." He plucked one of his sister's hair bands off the carpet, shot it at her, and resumed practicing.

"My routine music sounds good," Erin said. "What are you supposed to be playing? 'Twinkle, Twinkle, Little Star'?" She laughed.

"Erin, that's enough!" their mom said. "Be encouraging."

"It's not 'Twinkle, Twinkle.' It's an exercise," Albert insisted, but it did sound like that stupid song. While he squeaked away he thought about all the pressure he was under.

Eight days had passed since he had been recruited, and tonight was the Opening, whatever that was. Albert was both terrified and excited.

For the past seven days, he had kept the clarinet pretense going, making sure to play in the morning so that his after-school time was free. His mother, never a person to put off any tasks on her to-do list, had marched into the school office and changed his schedule from art to Beginning Band, which met right before the Jazz Band; so now, on his way out of the music room, Albert had the pleasure of having to walk out as the Jazz-Band players—including both Trey and Jessica—walked in. Trey made a point of smacking him on the arm each time and saying something insulting, like "Have fun learning a new note, Albert."

The after-school time was his opportunity to lock himself in his room and study the johka tournament guide before dinner and homework, easy because Erin was at practice from three to seven every school day. The amount of time-consuming Spanish homework he had on a daily basis was the worst.

Twinkle, twinkle, little star, how I wonder what you are.

"Keep playing a little every day, Albert. It's the only way to learn something new," his nana said, rolling past him into the kitchen. "You have to be bad at first."

His sister laughed. "See, I'm not the only one who thinks you sound bad."

"I said that's enough, Erin," his mom whispered. Then she stuck her head into the living room. "You do have to wrap it up now, though, Albert. Eat some breakfast."

Albert jumped up. "Not hungry," he said, and zoomed to his room. He packed his backpack, looked at himself in his closet mirror, and touched the Z-da hidden under his shirt.

In his mind, he repeated the instructions for tonight's adventure one more time. At 11:47 p.m. Earth time, he would initiate the szoŭ by covering the top left hole of the Z-da and blowing into the mouthpiece. He learned from the guide that nothing would happen at first, but that in thirty seconds, the szoŭbeam would lock and lift.

Albert touched the Z-da again and then checked the second backpack he had packed, the one he planned to take tonight to the Opening. He wasn't sure what he needed. The guide had described the Opening as a ritual at which guests were greeted, so he figured it was some kind of preparatory team meeting. Assuming they might kick the ball around, he was bringing cleats, shin guards, a change of clothes, three energy bars, an apple, and a water bottle. Now he made a mental note to remember to bring his cell phone. He wasn't sure if it would work, but he would feel better with it.

At school, his morning classes crawled by, and he was reprimanded so many times for not paying attention that Freddy Mills noticed and stopped by his table at lunch.

"Hi, Albert!" There was something about Freddy's face that always made Albert slightly uncomfortable, a kind of trusting openness. Freddy seemed to assume friendship, which was sweet, and which was exactly the problem. Sweetness was an elementary school thing, not a middle school thing. Being sweet in middle school was like wearing a sign that said PLEASE RIDICULE ME.

Albert barely acknowledged Freddy, but Freddy stopped at his table and chattered on, holding his hot-lunch tray with both hands. "Not sure if you know, but Coach said I could be manager for the team. I was thinking, you know, maybe we could split the job. Or maybe you could be our videographer or ball boy or something."

Coming out of anyone else's mouth, it would have been a put-down, but Freddy was genuinely trying to rescue Albert from the pitiful existence he assumed he lived, and that felt even worse to Albert. Adding to his discomfort, Trey walked by.

"Hi, Trey," Freddy called out.

Trey continued without stopping or acknowledging either of them, and Albert felt heat rise to his face. His confidence evaporated, and, in that moment, he wondered if the whole Zeeno experience had been a dream. But then he felt the weight of the Z-da against his sternum and he took a breath.

"Are you coming?" Freddy asked Albert. "I can talk to Coach."

"I can't come to any of the games," Albert said, and then he added loudly, "I'm playing for another team. I was recruited, actually."

Trey stopped, which was clearly what Albert had wanted. But the instant the words came out, Albert knew he had made a mistake.

Freddy's eyebrows went up. "Oh, that's great. What team?"

Trey turned around.

Shut up, Albert told himself, but the lie tumbled out. "It's a travel team. It's awesome. I'm their star striker."

Trey smiled. "Which team?"

Albert thought about the "permanent relocation" punishment for breaking the secrecy rule.

"A new league." Albert quickly collected his lunch and stood up.

"Which team, Kinney?" Trey called out, but Albert was already making his escape.

2.1

Tonight is the Opening! I am prepared!

Mehk paused, made sure that none of his coworkers or superiors were watching him, and then resumed typing his thoughts into his personal log.

Regarding the canine. I believe the dog will be more useful alive than dead. My recent research has made me appreciate canines. I'm embarrassed that I had assumed they were such simplistic creatures. But in my defense, the sense of smell is not on the radar of most Zeenods. Anyway, just as Tevs, for example, have superior abilities when it comes to vision, it seems that dogs have superior abilities when it comes to smell. 100,000 times more acute than humans! Could the dog smell something emanating from the squirrel that caused alarm? The triphenylphosphine oxide coating on the robot's chips?

Programming robots to be able to detect scents has been a difficult problem to solve. When this mission is over, I will fully download the dog's neural data to learn more. In the meantime, tonight I have a simple plan in place that will make excellent use of the dog!

A grin spread across the botmaker's face.

Believe in your brilliance. You will succeed.

2.2

The half-moon was as white as a boiled bone, and Tackle couldn't sleep.

All week, his dog door had remained locked. Except for short, on-leash walks to do his business, he had been kept inside as punishment for tearing up the flower beds.

Totally not fair. He hadn't damaged the flowers on purpose. He had been trying to protect Albert and the entire hood. The Pattersons should have been grateful. Danger was out there. If only he could get somebody to understand him. If only he could talk with Albert, let him know that he was a witness, that he knew something was going on.

Tonight, they had finally unlocked his door. Earlier, he had done a perimeter check. Had peed on the sweet gum tree and on the fence to show that squirrel-machine who was boss. All week he had watched it through the window. Then he had gone in and made the rounds inside the house, checking each human, checking each door, okay, stopping to drink out of the toilet, but then checking each window. Why? Because that was him. Committed. Loyal. Vigilant.

Now he ventured out again.

The night air smelled fabulously musky and damp. He took off for a quick run around the house at full speed. A chance not only to see if any danger was lurking but also to stretch his muscles. In the old days, Trey would have snuck out and the two of them would have played a little late-night tag, had a wrestle. It had been a long time and—

Tackle stopped by the gum tree and looked up. Sure enough, the dark shape of the squirrel-machine was up there, but its posture had changed.

Now, a sense of foreboding took hold. Although every cell in his body told him to bark and run to that tree, he kept quiet and stayed away from the newly planted flowers. He had to keep his cool, stay calm. Which wasn't easy. The vigilance was wearing him out. His nerves were beginning to fray. He was startling at every whiff, every twig snap and—what was that?

The side door of the Kinneys' house creaked open.

Tackle's head swiveled. Hmmm…what was this?

Noiselessly, he crept toward the fence.

Footsteps and then silence. Tackle thrust his snout between the fence slats and sniffed. Albert's smell wafted over. Between the slats, he could see Albert's overall shape, although it was dark.

Tackle sniffed again.

The boy was breathing heavily, exuding another powerful smell. The acrid smell of anxiety? Fear? Or was it excitement? Sometimes Tackle had a hard time distinguishing between human fear and excitement. Types of meat and fish he could easily identify. Types of animal urine? No problem. Human emotions he sometimes muddled.

Gold light flashed as the boy lifted an object to his lips, and then something happened. This wasn't anything the dog could hear or see or smell, but the gold object emitted an energy that hit him in the marrow of his bones.

Instinctively, he looked up, thinking he would see the strange light.

A smell grabbed his attention and he turned to the squirrel. The machine's mouth opened and another buglike object flew out, illuminated by the light of the moon. Like the first one Tackle had seen, this one began to fly toward Albert, but then it dipped down and headed straight for Tackle's own snout! He jumped back, and then it zipped up and over the fence. Through the slats, he saw it zip over Albert's head and then...the dog couldn't quite see...did it land on Albert's back? Clearly, Albert didn't notice it.

Tackle howled. The Pattersons had moved the picnic table so that he couldn't use it to leap over. Unable to control himself, he barked and flung himself at the fence—*Thwack!*

2.3

"Go away, Tackle!" Albert whispered, unable to believe his own terrible luck. He hadn't anticipated that Tackle would be outside this late at night. Now that he had activated the szoŭ, he had thirty seconds before the szoŭbeam would lock on him and lift him up. He wasn't sure if he had to stand still in order for the beam to locate him, or if he could move. To be on the safe side, he planted his feet on the ground right where he had experienced the szoŭ before, hoping the dog would shut up, completely unaware of the new bugbot attached to his backpack.

Tackle barked even louder, and, above them, the light in the second-floor window facing the Kinneys' house switched on. Uh-oh, Albert thought. Trey's bedroom.

The bedroom curtain opened and Trey's head appeared silhouetted in the window. Albert's heart thumped and he began to sweat. The moonlight was bright enough. Surely Trey could see him standing in the driveway. If he looked when the szoŭ occurred, he'd see Albert disappear. Through carelessness, the secret would be revealed, and Albert would be expelled.

As if the dog could smell his fear, Tackle became even more aggressive, throwing himself against the fence.

Trey's bedroom curtain dropped. Through the slightly open window, Albert could hear the voice of Trey's dad. A moment later Albert could see a light in the Pattersons' upstairs hallway flick on. They were coming to see what was going on.

"Tackle!" Albert whispered to the dog. "Go away!"

Tackle growled.

The only hope was to get Tackle to run to the other side of the Pattersons' house. Trey and his dad would follow the dog and miss the szoŭ entirely. If the Pattersons didn't see anything strange, they'd most likely take Tackle inside and go back to bed. And he'd be safe.

With fifteen seconds to go, Albert picked up a stick and threw it over the fence. "Go fetch, Tackle!" The stick sailed over and struck the Grangers' tree on the other side of the Pattersons' house, but the dog didn't move.

Ten seconds.

Think fast. Albert opened the trash can and the smell hit. His mom's tuna casserole from three days ago. He reached in, grabbed the bag, and heaved it as hard as he could.

As the bag flew over the dog's head and toward the Grangers' house, the seeping aroma pulled like a magnet on the animal's snout. Tackle took off running. At the same time, the Pattersons' front door opened and Mr. Patterson stepped out. The bag landed in the Pattersons' yard, and Tackle tore into it.

"Tackle!" Mr. Patterson shouted. "Bad dog!"

As Mr. Patterson focused on restraining Tackle, the light appeared. And in the split second before Trey and his mom stepped out to see what was going on, the shimmering sphere descended, and Albert Kinney was sucked into space.

2.4

Travel is always a tiny bit less stressful if you've been there before. So, when Albert beamed into the ITV after teleportation, his heart pounded at a reasonably fast rate rather than threatening to break free from his chest as it had done the first time around.

But then the robot, Unit B, turned to face him, eyes flashing. "This is a fully reserved ITV, sir," she said angrily, pulling a device that looked like a gun from a compartment in her hip. "Exit now or I'll be forced to liquidate—"

"But it's me. I'm—I'm—" The blood drained from Albert's face.

"Ha," she said, putting her device back. "That was a joke, Albert Kinney." Her face broke into a smile.

Albert exhaled and took off his backpack. As it thunked to the dark floor, the bugbot slid off and scuttled, unnoticed, to hide in the shadows.

Unit B picked up the backpack. "What did you bring?"

"Just things I thought I'd need. My phone—"

"Ah. Is the power on?"

He nodded.

A nod in return. "You will need a new one."

"What? Why?"

"We set the parameters of the szoŭ to protect biological matter and Fŭigor-based technology from harmful effects of teleportation radiation, but not Earth cell-phone chips. The one that drives your phone is now beyond repair."

"What? You should have warned me," Albert said. "Cell phones are expensive. My mom is going to kill me."

"Kill you?" Unit B opened a panel in her left forearm. "Your mother must be stopped before—"

"It's a saying. It means she's going to be angry."

Unit B nodded. "I will make a note of that." She swiveled to the main control panel and began tapping a series of commands. "Heading to Planet Zhidor, which, I'm sure you know from reading your guide, is a neutral planet, home of the Johka Federation, and home to many Zeenod immigrants. Zeenods everywhere will receive boosts of energy to see the team and to see you, Albert. Given the data we collected on you, I calculated an eighty percent chance that you would be a no-szoŭ." She paused and looked at him. "Kayko, in particular, will be happy you showed courage to arrive. As tactician, she is responsible for your nomination. I, for one, argued against it."

"Wait," Albert said. "Was that a joke?"

"No."

"Thanks," Albert said.

"You are welcome." Unit B peered more closely at him. "The joke I played about liquidating you was hilarious, right?"

53

Albert rolled his eyes. "Hilarious."

"My operating system detected your discomfort on our previous trip and Kayko heightened my sense of humor as a constructive strategy," the robot said.

In the rear of the spacecraft, a small round window showed the blackness of the sky and the small blue Earth shrinking away. How odd, Albert thought, that he could be having this experience and no one on Earth knew about it.

"I suggest you enter your hygg," Unit B said. "I can wake you when we reach Zhidor's orbit."

"Hygg?"

"Hibernation chamber. Although we'll be taking a shortcut through the Ceejek Space Warp Tunnel, the trip will take approximately four days and—"

"Four days!" Albert leaped up and began to pace. "My mom will think I've been kidnapped."

Something like a laugh came out of Unit B. "Hilarious joke."

"It's not a joke."

"But you will not be gone for four days on Earth, Albert. Page eighty-seven of the guide. We have the ability to time-fold. Regardless of how long we're away, we can place you back at the szoŭ coordinates twenty-seven Earth minutes after the pickup. Did you read the guide?"

"The guide is one thousand, three hundred, and thirty-six pages! I'm reading it, but I have homework, you know! My Spanish teacher gives, like, five times the amount one teacher should give!"

"I detect an emotional response to my factual statement about the guide, Albert. This is unnecessary." The robot lowered herself into that midair seating position that looked so odd to Albert. "I can explain the relativity physics behind time-folding if helpful, although the realities are different from what you Earthlings have theorized. Shed all you have learned and full me your attention, and we can see how much progress we can make in the next four days."

Activating a presentation on the screen, Unit B began her lecture. Albert tried desperately to concentrate; but after an hour, when his eyes began to close, she gave him a pinch.

"Chop-chop. Hibernation it is," she said, popping into a standing position. After a quick glance to make sure Albert was awake, she pulled a lever on the wall, and a locker-sized door opened, revealing a cold, empty space that was lined with icy spikes. "In you go."

Albert stumbled back. He had made the astounding mistake of trusting a robot with his life, including but not limited to limbs, spinal cord, major and minor organs, and brain.

"Just kidding," Unit B laughed. "That's the refrigeration unit. Follow me." She walked behind the chair that Albert had been sitting in and pulled another lever. A panel in the ceiling slid to the side, and from above, a volume of purplish silk floated down and then snapped into the form of a one-person tent that floated about two feet off the floor.

Unit B held the flap open. "Your hygg."

Tiny twinkling lights inside were golden and calming, and a cloud of warm mist with a lovely smell wafted out.

"It smells delicious."

"Zeenods have no sense of smell," Unit B said. "But it is known that Earthlings are influenced by aroma. We chose to synthesize the aroma of your favorite dessert to make your hygg as comforting as possible."

Albert took another inhale and grinned. "That's it. Oatmeal

chocolate chip cookies." He crawled in and stretched out, loving the way the thing bounced slightly. "Unbelievable," he said. "I've never felt anything so soft."

"According to the records, Lightning Lee enjoyed the hygg as well and was given the aroma of toasted garlic bread."

"Do you know Lee?"

"I was constructed before Lee arrived, but our paths did not cross."

"I like garlic bread, too," Albert said, "but this is perfect."

Two minutes later, Albert was sleeping like a newborn.

Ever since starting middle school, Albert had experienced trouble getting to sleep. Hibernating in a hygg was another thing entirely. *Delicious* was the word Albert used for the smell, but the word suited the entire experience for him. It was delicious. First, there was the material of the mattress, designed not just to conform to his body, but to oh so gently massage the connective tissue between the muscles and tendons. The mist not only carried the pleasing aroma, but also provided continuous micro-hydration to Albert's skin cells. And there was one more bonus— one that even Unit B was not aware of. One of the neurochemicals in the mist happened to have a unique side effect for humans: it activated memories, but only those that had humorous content. So, while Albert was massaged and watered in his slumber, he was treated to reruns of the funniest moments of his life.

At the very end of the trip, while Albert dreamed on, Unit B activated full autopilot, plugged herself into the computer, and put herself into sleep mode to do a quick recharge before it was time to land. The ITV had successfully taken the detour around the last of the pesky asteroid cluster, and Unit B knew that the rest of the journey should be uneventful.

And that was when the bugbot climbed out of its hiding place and flew up to the ITV's ceiling.

The small machine was the size and shape of an ordinary *Halyomorpha halys*, otherwise known on Earth as a stinkbug; but, instead of two eyes on either side of its small head, it had what looked like only one eye protruding from the end of its head—the camera lens. As soon as the bug settled into the grayish seam between two gray ceiling panels, its camera began to record.

2.5

Consolation: stinkbug spybot was not detected by the robot or by the ITV's sensor system and is fully operational. I am the master of deception! While this is welcome news, I'm still reeling from the fact that Kinney diverted the attention of the Pattersons with that trash bag right before the szoŭ. I thought for sure that the Pattersons were going to witness the szoŭ and that I would have the video needed to get Kinney removed.

A great pang of disappointment struck the botmaker. The thought that he did not, could not, control for every element of a plan—no matter how hard he prepared or studied—brought on a kind of nausea. An image of himself as an imperfect being began to rise in his mind like a specter, and he instinctively hit himself hard on the side of the head as if he could knock it away.

"Mehk is self-destructing again," a coworker passing by the botmaker's work space said with a chuckle. "Time to clock out, Mehkie."

Fuming, the botmaker snapped back. "I shouldn't even be here! I'm—"

"We know. You're smarter than all of us Z-Tevs combined. Blah dee dah!"

Mehk's superior, overhearing the conversation via surveillance monitor while sitting in her glass-walled station on the other side of the huge room, adjusted her microphone and said, "Do not write another letter demanding a transfer, Mehk. Your file is full of them. You're lucky to be here."

The coworker laughed and continued on his way, giving Mehk's shoulder a nasty little flick with his fingers.

Mehk hated his bosses and coworkers—Z-Tevs all—and had an overwhelming desire to stand—no! to jump on his desk!—and to scream: *While you've been making playthings, I've been creating a masterpiece! It's ready and waiting and when I finally get rid of Kinney, I can unveil it, and everyone will be astounded by my genius!*

He took a breath and listened for the positive thought-loop and pushed the impulse down. He had screamed before, and he had been told that this type of action plus the quality of the many letters he had written had done nothing to remove the label *unstable* that was in his file.

Quickly Mehk pretended to turn his attention to the project on his desk—an ahda-bird hatchling that was supposed to emerge from an egg. He knew exactly what improvements needed to be embedded in the chip inside the egg to make it crack in the most gloriously realistic way, but he purposefully programmed it with an inferior code, a code that was just good enough. Long ago he had made a promise to himself: he would not give his secrets or his best work to the system that devalued his genius. He had made the mistake once, inventing one of their most popular products— a robotic gnauser—and the Z-Tevs had taken credit for it. Well, he wouldn't give them any gifts now.

As he continued to "work," he replayed every moment of what had occurred on Earth. The actions and abilities of both the canine and Albert Kinney had caught him off guard. He had underestimated both. Lessons to be learned.

2.6

As the ITV was humming along on its trajectory to Zhidor, auto-pilot set, Albert was blissfully asleep in the misty, buoyant cocoon of his hygg, the corners of his mouth turned up in a relaxed and peaceful smile. At the control panel, Unit B was sitting, as per usual without chair, her biopolymeric eyelids closed, receiving the last three percent of her recharge.

That was when the alarm went off.

"Warning. Code 8X. Incoming DRED."

Unit B snapped to attention. It only took a millisecond for her to comprehend the warning that was being voiced by the computer as well as blinking on the control screen.

A dedicated remote explosive device, a DRED, was approaching.

"Warning. Code 8X. Incoming DRED," the alarm repeated. "Complete destruction in sixty seconds. Chance of survival: zero percent."

2.7

On the verge of hyperventilating, the botmaker watched the footage of the drama unfolding.

> Surprising development. Someone is trying to kill Kinney!
> I'm watching the video. A DRED is on its way. Who's behind this?

Secretly watching while at work was technically easy—thanks to the way he had rigged his smartgoggles—but trying to process what he was witnessing was too much. He fired off a message to his superior that he was feeling ill and ran to the restroom. He *was* feeling ill, actually. He always felt ill when something was happening that was beyond his control. He had wanted to remove Albert, yes. But in his own way.

2.8

"Warning. Code 8X. Incoming DRED. Complete destruction in fifty seconds. Chance of survival: zero percent."

"I heard you the first time," Unit B said, looking at the blinking DRED icon—a small red hexagon—that had appeared on the navigation screen. She steered the ITV sharply to the right and the blinking red icon followed.

"Computer, run complete diagnostic," she commanded. "This is peaceful territory with zero percent chance of attack. Perhaps the approaching vehicle is not a DRED?" She dipped the ITV to the left and the DRED followed.

"No software or surveillance malfunction," the computer announced.

"How is the DRED locking onto us?" she asked. "As an FJF-approved vehicle, this ITV is made of metal that is designed to resist DRED tracking."

"The approaching DRED cannot track the ITV," the computer replied. "However, it has been programmed to track the molecular signature of the ITV's smart-skin coating."

"Clever."

"Deactivating hygg hibernation," the system's secondary alarm announced.

"Stop!" Unit B said, trying and failing to override the command, knowing the boy would be a distraction.

A moment later, the hygg flap opened, and an oblivious Albert hopped out with a huge grin. "Wow. Wow. Wow," he said, laughing and dancing around the tight quarters, stretching muscles that already felt limber. "That was amazing! I love that hygg thing. I feel fantastic!"

"Warning. Code 8X. Incoming DRED. Complete destruction in forty seconds."

Albert froze. "What?"

Unit B did not look up. Her fingers were flying over the control panel, tapping into manual override.

"What's happening?" Albert forced a laugh. "Oh, I get it. Complete destruction. A good one."

"We are under attack." Unit B turned the vehicle and Albert's stomach at the same time. As he grasped the back of his chair, she continued in a calm voice, her eyes locked on the screen. "Early on in my career, I served as an interplanetary emergency responder trained to deal with dedicated remote explosive devices." Again, she forced a sharp turn, and again the DRED followed. "Please activate your seat belt."

Albert climbed into the chair and stared at the blinking red icon on the screen. "Did you say explosive device?"

"It has locked onto the smart-skin coating of our vehicle. What you would call the exterior paint."

"Warning. Code 8X. Incoming DRED. Complete destruction in thirty seconds."

Albert's heart began to pound. "What—What are you going to do?"

Ignoring Albert, Unit B asked the computer to run through three possible scenarios and calculate the likelihood of their success.

The computer's voice rang out. "Zero percent chance of survival if attempting to outrun the DRED. Zero percent chance of hitting the DRED at this distance with the defensive weapons currently on board. Zero percent chance of survival if DRED is allowed to approach close enough for defensive weapons to be deployed."

"This can't be real." Albert ran to look out the rear window. In the darkness, a speck of light glowed. "That's it? That little light?"

Unit B's eyelids closed. "I am accessing my own records to obtain a possible alternative." After a moment, she turned and headed into a field of asteroids at full speed.

As the speck of light following them grew larger and larger, huge rocks began to appear in the distance outside the window. Albert turned to face the front of the spacecraft and saw more.

"Sit and activate your seat belt, Albert." Deliberately choosing the densest path, Unit B began the difficult task of dodging the asteroids, trying to stay as far ahead of the DRED as possible. "With luck, an asteroid will destroy the DRED before either destroys us."

"That's your plan?" Albert asked as he managed to climb back into his chair and activate the seat belt. The navigation screen was filling up with the icons of incoming asteroids, as well as the ever-blinking red icon.

"Warning. You have entered the Guig Asteroid Belt. Likelihood of collision: ninety-three percent. Warning. Code 8X. Incoming DRED. Complete destruction in twenty seconds. Chance of survival: zero percent."

"My plan is two-pronged," Unit B said. "Take over. I need to relinquish control for three-point-five seconds." She popped into a standing position.

"Take over?" Albert almost fainted. "What are you doing?"

An asteroid blew so close, it rocked the vehicle.

"Take the wheel, Albert," she said.

Before he could move, she lunged to the rear of the spacecraft, grabbed four cans of smart-skin coating from the cabinet labeled MAINTENANCE and threw them into the compartment marked EJECT.

Then she pressed the lever for the chute and ran back to regain control of the vehicle.

"Complete destruction in ten seconds," the computer announced. "Count down commencing. Ten, nine…"

Another asteroid rocketed past their window, grayish and shaped like a torpedo, close enough for Albert to see the pocked surface close up. Albert looked back. The DRED was now close enough to see, too, a sinister hexagonal pyramid flying toward them, pointed tip glowing red. He felt a scream rising in his throat.

As the cans ejected out of the rear of the spacecraft, Unit B returned to the controls and made a ninety-degree turn, a turn with such force that Albert would have been slammed against a wall—maybe even killed—if he hadn't been belted.

Off they zoomed at the highest possible speed, the vehicle's engines roaring.

Albert twisted to look out the back window. The DRED had locked onto the higher concentration of smart-skin coating in the cans and was now headed toward them.

The simplicity and intelligence of Unit B's plan became apparent as the distance grew and then—*Boom!*—an asteroid took both the DRED and the four cans out at the same time.

The explosion shook the spacecraft, propelling it forward at such a high speed, it set off every other alarm.

Calmly, Unit B flicked off the various alarms as she steered past three more asteroids and zoomed out of the belt.

"We made it?" Albert asked, stunned, looking at the calm, clear space ahead.

She pulled back on the speed and the loud rumble inside the craft normalized. "We did."

"That was real. We almost died."

"Yes."

Albert turned to look at her, and then he said, "I think maybe I should quit."

2.9

Hiding out in a restroom stall, the botmaker grinned. Keeping an eye on the footage that was still projecting on the interior of his goggle lenses, he typed an entry in his log.

```
Another dramatic turn! Albert Kinney lives—and will
resign. I must admit, I'm happier with this outcome.
Resignation suits my purposes better in the long term.
I wanted to be the one who caused Kinney to quit, but,
after all the work I have put into this mission, I'll
take this.
```

Mehk stopped, realizing that underneath his excitement was a surprising emotion: admiration for Kayko Tusq's skill as a robotics engineer. He hadn't dreamed the Zeenod's robot would outsmart the DRED. Quite impressive. Kayko and her young assistant Giac did remarkable work, especially given how little they had in the way of resources. Like him, they were primarily self-taught. Like him, they were oppressed by the Z-Tev government. They had superior brains. Clearly. Not as superior as his, but still. A ridiculous fantasy popped into his mind: he and Kayko standing around a worktable, sharing notes while munching on a nice bag of warm roasted paranj seeds. And then, perplexed by the thought, he forced himself to snap out of it and turned his attention to his log.

Kayko's robot isn't that impressive. The speech is so stilted! Absolutely hilarious! If I'm not mistaken, "Unit B" was supposed to be programmed to be as human-like as possible to comfort the Earthling. Ha! My communications and language algorithms are light-years beyond theirs.

I'm dying to find out who's behind the DRED and—

Stop. Focus.

The FJF will be announcing the news of the Zeenod Star Striker's resignation soon. Maybe even at the Opening? What a shock this will be!

The second phase of my mission is soon to be initiated. The Zeenods will waste no time calling upon the alternate to take Kinney's place. It's happening!

2.10

Unit B tapped a button on her forearm panel and spoke into it: "Reorder four cans smart-skin coating."

"You're just going to go back to business as if everything's fine?" Albert yelled. "Did you hear what I said?"

"*I think maybe I should quit* is a weak sentence construction requiring no action on my part," Unit B said. "You are pondering whether or not to quit, and—"

"Fine. I quit," Albert snapped, his face growing noticeably hot, the smoldering stress of the last sixty seconds leaping into flame. "I'm very, very, very, very grateful that you got us out of that alive, but—" Albert released his seat belt, gripped his stomach, and doubled over. "I think I'm going to throw up."

"Are you physically harmed?" the robot asked.

"What? No."

"Are you psychologically traumatized?"

"Yes!" Albert said.

"There exist two possible options. I could accept your resignation, notify Kayko, and begin exit-processing, or—"

"Or you could turn around and take me home," Albert muttered.

"Or I could initiate a single memory wipe. If you were unable to remember what just happened, you would have no desire to quit."

Albert looked up, queasier by the second. "What?"

"According to Regulation 32209785A, I am allowed to wipe a single memory that occurred en route if three conditions are met: if the time period to be erased lasted less than three minutes; if what caused the memory to be erased is not a threat; and if the erasure is for 'security or medical purposes.' The experience lasted less than three minutes and the DRED has been destroyed and—"

"Someone tried to blow us up. How can that not be a threat?" Albert cried.

Unit B tapped a code into her forearm. "Shawble Code 99F. Interrupting speech is a symptom of poor listening and can—"

"This is insane. You're insane!"

"My logic is rational. Earthlings are known to sense emotions in their stomachs and are prone to a weakness called *nightmares*. Although Regulation 32209785A is meant to be employed if an Earthling were to accidentally see an image en route that could cause psychotrauma, such as the severed beings in the floating gravespace near Gaböq or the haagoolts of Tev, it is rational to use it here."

Albert didn't know anything about the detailed regulations of when and how memory wiping could occur, but he instinctively knew that to mess around with anybody's memories had to be serious business and to consider a bomb no longer a threat just because it hadn't hit them didn't make sense. From the fog of nausea, a reasonable idea rose up, which was that they should call Kayko and tell her what had happened. She was calm and knowledgeable. But before Albert could suggest it, Unit B activated the football-sized medical drone that Albert had met on his first trip and chose the correct code sequence for a specific memory wipe.

"Wait." Albert stiffened. "I don't like that thing."

Immediately, the drone flew to Albert and swept a laser quickly across the left side of his head.

Albert was stunned for a few seconds, and then he blinked.

"How do you feel, Albert?" Unit B asked cautiously. In her entire career, she had never initiated a memory cleanse on a human.

He blinked again, then grinned, and then hopped out of the chair. "Wow. Wow. Wow," he said, dancing around exactly the way he had done earlier. "That was amazing! I love that hygg thing. I feel fantastic!"

Unit B nodded.

"Usually, I can't get to sleep or I wake up in the middle of the night and can't go back to bed," Albert went on. "It's terrible."

Unit B nodded again. "Yes, Albert. You have primitive sleep arrangements on Earth." She reached out and squeezed Albert's shoulder.

"Ouch. What was that for?"

"It was a comforting gesture," she said.

Albert laughed.

"It wasn't comforting?" Unit B said. "Give me three-point-five seconds to do more research." Her body went rigid. After a few seconds, her mouth opened and out came the song Albert's preschool teacher used to sing at circle time. *"My happy friends are all around. We play and learn and never frown."* A perfect eyebrow rose. "Was that comforting?"

Albert laughed. "That was just creepy."

Unit B changed her focus and opened another compartment. "We will arrive shortly. You should uniform yourself."

"I wasn't sure what I should wear," Albert said. "I brought soccer gear and—"

"Uniform," Unit B said, and gave him a folded outfit. "To ensure that no team has technological or psychological advantage over another in terms of gear, the FJF gifts all team players with official practice and game uniforms and cleats. Game uniforms are worn at the Opening."

Albert unfolded the six-foot fuzzy yellow onesie and held it up. "Wait. This is a joke, right? Ha, ha, right?"

The smart-skin of her forehead crinkled. "No, Albert Kinney."

"I can't wear this."

"You must," Unit B said.

As Unit B prepared for landing on Zhidor, Albert climbed into the suit and zipped it up. Even without a mirror he could tell that he looked ridiculous, like a toddler wearing a giant bunny suit.

"Can I have another size?"

"That is your suit."

"It doesn't fit." He tried to push the sleeves up. "It has to fit. I can't meet my teammates looking like this."

Unit B gave him a surprised look. "Why would your outside appearance matter?"

Albert stared at the robot. "You don't understand."

She tapped a button on her forearm panel and spoke into it: "Shawble Code 47A."

"You keep doing that. What does that mean?"

"I am programmed to keep track of your shawbles."

"Shawbles?"

"Page four hundred sixty-seven. Your...there is no exact translation for *shawble*. 'Spirit challenges' is deemed to be the closest in meaning." Unit B snapped the panel of her forearm shut.

"Spirit challenges?"

"Shawble 47A is an unhealthy need for external approval."

"What? Any normal human being would be humiliated by this suit," Albert said, already sweating. He sniffed a sleeve. "Why does everything smell like pine trees?"

"You will learn how to make adjustments. The next step is Oxygen Membrane Implantation." She activated the medical drone, which flew toward Albert while pulling some kind of filmy white tissue from its side compartment.

"Wha—" Before Albert could utter another sound, one arm of the drone shot the tissue into his mouth.

"Inhale," Unit B said.

The tissue flew to the back of Albert's throat, and for a moment, he was certain he would suffocate. He grabbed his throat and gurgled and stomped, eyes begging Unit B for mercy; and then a warmth spread through his throat and neck, as if the film were melting, and he felt breath reaching his lungs.

"Inhale again," Unit B said. "This ITV is fully pressurized to deal with your need for oxygen; however, you need the implant to survive once our vehicle doors open on Zhidor."

Trying to steady himself, Albert breathed in.

Unit B went on. "The membrane sends nano–oxygen concentrators into the tissue of your lungs. While all planets in the Fŭigor solar system have different percentages of oxygen in their atmospheres, none have enough for your physiology." Unit B leaned back. "Standard Fŭigor technology."

Just as Albert was getting accustomed to the new sensation, the drone shot two more smaller tissues into his nostrils.

"You should have started with the nose," he argued. "That was way better than the throat."

"Seat belt activation. Five seconds to landing."

As the belt pressed Albert into his chair, he tried to gather his thoughts. Hopefully, Kayko would be there first to meet him. He could explain that Unit B had given him the wrong size uniform and Kayko could help him find another uniform before taking him to meet any of the other team members. He was probably arriving in a place like an airport where no one would be paying attention to him. And then they'd go to a place like a soccerplex and kick the ball around. No big deal.

The ITV landed with a thud. Unit B opened the ITV exit hatch and deployed a short staircase. "Enjoy the Opening."

The seat belt retracted. Albert didn't move.

The robot peered at him. "You are experiencing fear."

"No."

She clamped his thumb between her thumb and forefinger and watched a sensor on her thumb turn purple. "A lie." She tapped a button on her forearm panel and spoke into it: "Shawble Code 62." Snapping it shut, she asked, "Do you wish me to inform Kayko and—"

"What was that? A lie detector? And stop announcing my shawbles. I don't have any shawbles, whatever they are."

She popped her panel back open. "Shawble Code 10A."

"What are you talking about?"

"Shawble Code 62: denial of one's own emotional state. Shawble Code 10A: denial of shawbles."

"I'm not afraid and I'm not in denial," Albert said. "I'm mad! And I have a right to be. You're judging me and it isn't fair. I'm acting perfectly normal."

Unit B was about to tap the button on her forearm panel, but she stopped. "Recalculating best response." There was a split-second pause and then she said, "Time is limited. Are you ready?"

"Fine," Albert said, horrified by the shakiness of his voice. Shuffling in his giant yellow suit, he walked to the doorway of the ITV, looked out, and nearly collapsed.

They had landed on the field of a beautiful stadium, every seat of which was full. Thousands of faces, faces of all colors and shapes, were staring at him.

2.11

It was evening on Zhidor, and the sky was pitch-black except for the glow of three moons, each a different size and shape, and an enormous illuminated banner floating in the sky over the stadium.

Fŭigor Johka Tournament

Unit B had landed the ITV on one end line facing the field, so Albert had a view of three-fourths of the entire stadium, which was well lit and set up for a ceremony rather than a game. At the halfway line stood a large gleaming stage with a podium in the center emblazoned with a logo that Albert recognized from the guide, the FJF logo, a gold soccer ball swirling in the black center of the Fŭigor Solar System. The field itself looked quite similar to a professional soccer field on Earth, except the grass was a deep burgundy instead of green.

Tentatively Albert peered out the door. To his right, three other ITVs stood next to his in a gentle arc, their stairs deployed.

Just as Albert was trying to figure out what to do, a musical sound blasted throughout the stadium and four FJF officials, all Zhidorians, approached the four ITVs. Identical in appearance, they were tall, fluid beings, each bearing two heads and two tentacle-like arms. Albert remembered seeing pictures and reading descriptions of them in the guide and had thought they looked cool, but seeing them in person was dizzying. The alien who came to the base of Albert's stairs looked at him intensely with the eyes of the right head while the gaze of the left head was busy doing an observational sweep of the area; at the same time they reached an arm up to shake hands with Albert. Stunned, Albert took the plump, warm tentacle in his hand and gave it a squeeze.

The audience was silent, riveted.

"What's happening?" Albert whispered to Unit B.

"We were the last to arrive," she whispered back. "Now that all four Star Strikers are here, you will be given FJF-regulation language-translation devices and then introduced."

The four Zhidorian officials unfurled their tentacles toward their respective players, releasing four beetlelike objects into the air. One of those beetles flew up the stairs toward Albert; and before he could even raise a hand in protest, it burrowed into his left ear.

Even though Albert had already experienced swabbing and membrane implantation, he couldn't help panicking. Screaming, he tried to claw the thing out of his ear. Then he leaned his head toward the ground, jumping vigorously, in a vain attempt to get Zhidor's gravity to assist.

Deep inside the cochlea of his ear, the object exploded and sent millions of nanorobots through the stereocilia and the auditory nerve to the brain. And within a second, the feeling in his ear returned to normal.

Albert took a breath and returned to a standing position, mortified.

"Translation devices are harmless," Unit B whispered. "No need for panic."

"You could have warned me," Albert snapped back.

Another musical sound blared, and a huge johka-tournament flag unfurled behind the stage. The FJF director, a Zhidorian, was standing at the podium with the presidents of Tev, Gaböq, Jhaateez, and Zeeno, seated next to them. The director leaned one face toward a microphone and raised one of their tentacled arms: "With pleasure, the FJF announces the Procession of the Teams."

The language spoken wasn't English, but the device in Albert's ear enabled him to immediately understand it.

A thundering roar came from the crowd as uniformed players streamed toward the stage from four different directions. Jhaateez in purplish blue, Gaböq in red, Tev in silver, and Zeeno in gold.

After the players took their places in rows in front of the stage, the trumpetlike instrument blared and the director said, "The Introduction of the Star Strikers."

Albert's heart pounded as every gaze in the stadium turned toward the four ITVs.

"Playing for planet Jhaateez, Linnd Na from planet Liöt."

A cheer from one section of the stadium. Albert leaned out of the threshold and looked to his far right. A tall, thin figure with heronlike legs, winged arms, and pointed hands bowed and then began to walk down the steps of the first ITV.

"Playing for planet Gaböq, Xutu Nhi from planet Yurb."

Another huge cheer, this time from a different section of the stadium, and the figure from the second ITV bowed and began to emerge, this one as powerfully solid as a rhino. He had a wide lump of a head with three alligator-like eyes, arms reaching down to the ground, and one centered leg instead of two.

"Playing for planet Tev, Vatria Skell from planet Sñekti."

Albert leaned forward again to see better. Although this player, like the Zeenods, was somewhat humanlike in appearance—two arms, two legs, one head—her eyes were twice the size of theirs: two in front, and one in the center of the back of her head. Slightly taller than Albert, she was all muscle, wearing a sleek full-body uniform that hugged. She had the ears of a bat and grayish skin; her face had a large, square jaw and looked slightly tigerlike, with two bold, symmetrical striped markings extending from above each huge eye, moving down, and winding around her mouth.

"Playing for planet Zeeno, Albert Kinney from planet Earth."

A wave of nausea hit. Albert managed a quick bow and then grabbed the doorway of the ITV to steady himself as sweat trickled down the side of his face into the neck of his suit.

"Descend," Unit B whispered, but Albert's feet wouldn't move.

A glance to the right and Albert saw the other players waiting for him on the ground, each different in terms of body type and features, yet each standing majestically in their perfect-fitting gear. It was clear that they would all be walking toward the left to the stage, which meant that Albert would be at the front of the line.

The strength flooded from his knees, and he was sure he couldn't move, when a solid push from Unit B sent him stumbling down the stairs.

He caught himself before he fell and then looked up.

The player to his immediate right, Vatria Skell, sneered. She seemed delighted to see her opponent trip down the stairs in a bunny suit.

Mind spinning, stomach churning, Albert did his best to follow his two-headed, tentacled chaperone up the sideline, feeling the eyes not only of Vatria Skell and the two other players, who were walking behind him, but also of thousands of spectators in the stands.

As they approached the platform, Albert looked at the four teams waiting near the stage. Dignified in their matching uniforms and formal postures, they were all watching the four new arrivals. Albert winced, almost unable to look at the Zeenods, who were, unfortunately, closest to the sideline. They knew he was an imposter, he thought. They knew they had made a horrible mistake.

And then he was close enough to see Kayko and the Zeenod team, their lean athletic bodies, their luminous skin, their surprisingly familiar faces with their large bright green and violet eyes, and those odd capelike things on their backs. Kayko's eyes, the brightest, caught his attention. She didn't look disappointed. She looked determined to communicate a message to him. She was pressing the top of her left shoulder with a kind of urgency, and then he noticed that the other Zeenods were doing the same, repeating the gesture over and over while nodding their heads at him. Instinctively, Albert reached up to his left shoulder with his right hand, and when his fingers found a button, he pushed it. Instantly, the fabric of his suit contracted and formed to his body and head, turning gold in color and making microadjustments that tickled, until it hugged every centimeter of his body with a perfectly supple yet strong fit.

Kayko caught his gaze and smiled.

Albert glanced back at the figure of Unit B, standing in the doorway of the ITV. I'm going to kill that robot, Albert thought. She had known how to activate the smart-materials property of the suit and hadn't told him.

One by one, the four players were greeted by the four presidents and asked to stand, shoulder to shoulder to the left of the podium, spotlights on them. The better-fitting suit gave Albert a boost of confidence, and he tried to let it show by standing tall.

Each president gave a short address, interrupted often by applause. And then the FJF director announced the creation of the four johkadins, which translated in Albert's head as "holographic poster, similar in some ways to twentieth-century Earthling baseball cards."

Xutu Nhi was called forward first to stand center stage in front of a camera-like machine, his back against a screen. The Gaböq crowd—huge, rhinolike beings—rose to sing along with their anthem, their wide three-eyed faces breaking into jagged grins. Xutu, similar in size to the Gaböqs, showed off his unusual muscular, tail-like leg by slamming it to the ground and rearing up to balance on it. A flash ensued, and then on large screens that appeared throughout the stadium, a posterlike image of Xutu appeared, dramatic against the dark sky, with his name, the name of his home planet, Yurb, and the name of the planet he was representing all juxtaposed on a background that Albert correctly guessed was a scene from planet Gaböq. When a roar of applause went up, especially from the Gaböq and Yurb sections, Albert thought it would trigger an earthquake.

As the Jhaateezian anthem played, Linnd Na was called forward. For her johkadin pose, Linnd lifted powerful yet graceful arms to unfurl their sail-like wings, and her fans from both Jhaa-teez and her home planet, Liöt, cheered.

A chill ran down Albert's spine as Vatria was called and the Tev anthem played. A sound—a deep wailing from an instrument—came. No words. No chanting. Just dead stillness from the crowd as the eerie tune spread over the stadium like a stream of smoke. As the muscular striker took a position for her johkadin, the one eye in the back of her head blinked and pivoted to look directly at Albert, sending another chill down his spine. An eye staring at him from the back of an opponent's head was disconcerting enough, but the color of her iris was reddish orange and the pupil was a jagged rectangular shape that zigzagged down the fiery landscape of that iris like a black lightning bolt.

She took a running position and held her face stern and gave a nod. The stage lights went completely dark and everyone and everything disappeared from view—except, in a dazzling show of bioluminescence, there was Vatria, in her pose, glowing. When the camera flashed, her huge eyes reflected the flare of light so powerfully it appeared as if beams were coming from within. Tevs and Sñektis throughout the stadium responded by drumming their feet, and when Albert looked out, he could see them, even the ones in the highest part of the stadium, because they were glowing, too.

The lights returned, and as Albert's own name was announced, his throat went dry. He took his place center stage and looked out at the Zeenods, with no idea how he could follow any of the performances he had just seen. And then the Zeenod team stood and began singing their anthem. It began softly, but as they sang, a handful of Zeenods in the stands to the right stood and began to sing with them. And then a few more in a section farther up. As more joined—although not nearly as many as the fans of the other teams—his teammates reacted with surprised elation.

The color of his teammates' eyes transformed to gold, and Albert knew that something important was happening. He didn't understand the meaning of all the words, but the melody entered into him and made him feel completely alive. Filled with a rush of gratitude and the desire to make them proud, Albert surprised himself by jumping into a power pose, feet spread wide, chin raised, and two fists pumped in the air.

The camera flashed, his johkadin appeared, and the Zeenods leaped to their feet. Ecstatic, Albert beamed at the crowd and then glanced back up at the image of himself, larger than life, on the screen.

When all four images were glowing on the screens around the stadium, Albert noticed with a thrill that the scene representing Zeeno on his johkadin looked the most beautiful. Whereas the others looked harsh—one icy, one hot and dry, one cloaked in fog—the Zeeno landscape had those same blossoming trees, fountains, and clear pinkish skies dotted with colorful birds that were engraved on the back of the Z-da.

Another official appeared on the stage with a robot who delivered to each player their regulation cleats, the most high-tech boots Albert had ever seen. He remembered reading something in the guide about how the computerized shoes had a built-in energy-charging system, and he made a mental note to read up on that when he got home.

Next, the new Star Strikers and their teams were assembled on a different part of the field to take more formal photos with their planets' presidents, which was exciting; but Albert's favorite part came after that, when he finally got the chance to connect less formally with his fellow teammates in person.

The most enthusiastic one, Doz, turned to him first and fist-bumped him and then laughed. "We studied your fist bump, Albert!"

Beeda and Reeda jumped in to fist-bump him next. "This is how you say hello!" they said in unison. "It's craziness!"

They all had to fist-bump him and then fist-bump each other, and they couldn't break their habit of bowing, either, so it was a hilarious round of bumping and bowing.

"Kayko," Albert whispered, looking around. "Is Lee here? Can you introduce me?"

"We all agree that it will be easiest for you to uphold secrecy on Earth if you do not meet before the tournament."

Before Albert could respond, Doz pulled him toward a group of fans who had already downloaded the johkadins to their Z-das. They wanted his holo-autograph, and Doz showed him how to tap on the projection twice and then sign his name on it using the tip of his finger. Thrilled, Albert began to revel in the attention.

The other Star Strikers were similarly surrounded by their teams and fans, and as Albert took in the scene, he could clearly see why Tev, Jhaateez, and Gaböq had chosen their strikers. Not only did all three guest strikers share physical characteristics with the aliens from their host planets, a fact that would have to be helpful on the field, but also the guests seemed to be the new and improved versions. Xutu from Yurb looked like a stronger version of the rhinolike Gaböqs. The Liötian Linnd could pass for a Jhaateezian but had longer, birdlike legs and a bigger wingspan. And as for Vatria from Sñekti, her limbs looked stronger and her eyes were larger.

He turned to Doz. "Can I ask you something?"

"Now and whenever!" Doz said.

"You picked me, and you've picked Earthlings before. So, why us?"

Doz patted Albert on the back. "Even though you're technologically inferior, we have great affection for Earthlings!"

Ennjy smiled, overhearing, and the other teammates began to listen in.

"But why?" Albert asked. "Are we, somehow, alike?"

Ennjy nodded. "Like us, Earthlings are, how do you say, built for loving cooperation."

All the others cheered, and Albert tried to hide his shock. First of all, if any seventh grader ever said the words *loving cooperation* with a straight face out loud in front of a bunch of other guys... well, it wouldn't happen. Second, *humans* built for loving cooperation? No way. The horrible world history outline that Mr. Perez had made them copy in sixth grade flashed in Albert's mind: war after war after war. Through history, he thought, humans basically had destroyed each other and now were even destroying the planet. Albert considered telling his team that they were mistaken, but he didn't want to break the spell, didn't want this opportunity to disappear. Ennjy's *loving cooperation* phrase was probably a translation error, Albert told himself. Whatever the reason, he, Albert Kinney of Earth, had been chosen.

After more reveling, the closing was announced, goodbyes were said, and the Star Strikers were told to begin the ritual walk back to their ITVs. As the sound of the cheering crowd intensified, Albert stopped to soak up the energy and to wave at his team and fans one last time.

Vatria Skell, the Tevs' Star Striker, stepped up to him and leaned in, perhaps to share her excitement, Albert thought.

"Albert Kinney of Earth," she whispered, her voice a low growl, her breath hot and moist against the side of Albert's face. "My vision is superior. Do you know what I can see right now?"

Albert was too stunned to speak.

The tight gray skin around her mouth stretched into a smile. "I can see that you are weak. If you want to survive, quit now."

2.12

Outside the facility window, the botmaker could hear revelers. The entire solar system had watched the Opening in bars and restaurants, at parties, and on huge screens in the streets. Those, like him, who were working overtime had listened in, too, at their desks. He pulled out his log.

```
Kinney is officially a Star Striker, honored and cele-
brated when he should have been slinking back to Earth in
humiliation. I saw what happened en route to the Opening.
Fearing for his life, he had resigned! My masterpiece
should be taking his place right now. My Star Striker has
not one single shawble.
```

Their robot, also, showed a serious flaw in initiating a memory wipe! I have no doubt that Kayko Tusq would
have wanted the robot to report the DRED and Kinney's
response so that the context of the entire situation
could be analyzed and discussed. If I had designed that
unit, the cognitive reasoning would have been perfect.

Mehk stopped typing and glanced out the window. From where he sat, he could see the street-screen projection of an advertisement to buy all four new johkadin holograms. Anger began to rise, and he turned away and closed his eyes. There it was: the soothing loop of words.

Believe in your brilliance. You will succeed.

From his satchel he pulled out his robotic gheet, Zeeno's version of a tarantula and one of the creatures most despised by Z-Tevs. During his first year at the creature-fabrication facility, he had been assigned to create gheets to be sold as gag gifts for a Tev holiday, Haagoolt Eve. At the time, he had secretly coded the gheets to release a noxious chemical that slowly caused skin rashes. Mehk's company had to discontinue the line, never knowing he had planted the intentional flaw. Ha. Having the last laugh, he had kept one of the gheets for himself and had tweaked it into perfection. Initially it was his constant companion—he had programmed it to peek out of his pocket, which never failed to scare Z-Tevs away—until last year, when, thinking he should grow up, he had shelved it. Just yesterday, he had begun to carry it around again and found that having it nearby calmed his nerves.

The golf-ball-sized arachnoid crept onto the worktable, turned around, looked up at him, and purred softly. Mehk petted its hairy little head, and down it sat to keep him company. His comfort robot.

He returned to his log.

1. Continue spying.
2. Take strength from the fact that your masterpiece is still functioning beautifully—without detection—and will be ready.
3. Consider the possibility that whoever programmed the DRED will strike again.

2.13

"Blood pressure and oxygen levels are down. You are dehydrated, as well," Unit B said as she swatted away the medical drone and handed Albert a smoothie. "Drink this, change out of your uniform, and hibernate. Exhaustion is yours."

Although nothing sounded more welcome than a smoothie and that hygg, Albert bristled. The Opening, which had been a thrill but which had also been stressful and exhausting, would have been much easier, Albert realized, if Unit B had helped him prepare. "I'm not thirsty or tired," he said icily, setting the smoothie in the chair's cup holder.

Unit B snapped open her arm panel. "Shawble Code 62B—denial of physical weakness."

"Stop that!" Albert shouted. And then, "You did it on purpose, didn't you?"

"To what are you referring, Albert?"

"You didn't show me how to activate the smart-materials setting on my suit so that I would be humiliated." He stared at her glossy black eyes.

"Why would your outside appearance matter, Albert?"

"You know what matters? What matters is being nice to people!"

"I will note that," Unit B said, pulling the lever to pop the hygg into place. "Give me your Z-da."

"Why?"

"An update is required to include the johkadins created at the Opening."

Albert handed over his Z-da, sucked down the smoothie, changed back into his regular clothes, and crawled into the hygg. Within seconds, he fell into a deep sleep.

When Unit B woke him to get ready for the return szoǔ, they had an argument because he wanted to take his cleats to Earth and she insisted he keep them stored in the ITV along with his uniform.

"These are not just shoes, Albert," she said. "The piezoelectric polymers in the foam of the soles, sides, and toes convert mechanical energy through each of your kicks, jumps, and steps into electrical energy that recharges the shoe's battery, which, in turn, powers the shoe's sensors. Those sensors record data on your performance, which is collected via the shoe's optical port—"

"I know how cool they are," Albert snapped. "That's why I wanted to bring them home. I said that I'd keep them under my bed and—"

Unit B snapped open her forearm panel. "Shawble Code 5C."

"Oh come on! How is it a shawble to like your cleats?"

Her face turned to him, her eyelids narrowing slightly. "Albert Kinney has been chosen above all others to be a Star Striker. Albert Kinney has been a guest of honor at a ceremony where he received the adoration of thousands of fans. Albert Kinney has been given numerous gifts of technology to help him in the quest for victory. And instead of expressing gratitude, Albert Kinney expresses a desire for more. That sequence reveals the shawble of ingratitude."

Albert closed his mouth.

Unit B moved on, informing him that he could be beamed up and down from any location and asked if he wanted to be beamed directly into home. Imagining his mom, or nana, or sister seeing him materialize in front of their eyes, he thought it would be safer to choose outside. The backyard instead of the driveway.

Thankfully, the return was uneventful. No sign of Tackle. No lights on in either the Pattersons' house or his. Quickly, he snuck into the house and under the covers of his bed and then glanced at his clock and finally allowed himself a smile. He had left at 11:47, and it was now 12:17. Thirty minutes. Calculating that it must have taken him sixty seconds to get into the house, he realized that the time-folding, whatever that was, had worked. Although he had spent a total of eight days traveling to and from Zhidor, he had only been gone from Earth for twenty-nine minutes. Remarkable.

He took a breath and let it out.

Yes, the suit thing had been embarrassing, and yes, Unit B was annoying, and yes, Vatria's insult gave him the heebie-jeebies, but all in all the whole experience had been astounding and he was grateful, despite what Unit B thought.

The only problem, he realized, sitting up: he wasn't going to be able to sleep. He didn't feel the slightest need to. After all, he had just arisen after a four-day nap.

He activated the guide and searched for the johkadins Unit B had downloaded. There they were, along with all the Star Strikers that had ever played. He stared at each of this year's Star Strikers. Linnd Na had wings. Xutu Nhi had a...tail? Vatria Skell had those eyes, one in the back, too, and that bioluminescence. He wasn't sure what any of those had to do with johka, but he imagined that each trait gave them an advantage on their home planets, advantages he certainly wouldn't have. Scrolling back, he looked at each of the Star Strikers who had played in the past.

Kayko had said that the last time Zeeno had played in the tournament was seventy-five Earth years ago, so as he scrolled back, Albert made a mental note to try to read up on the history. And then he stopped. There was the johkadin for Lightning Lee. The striker's body was small but strong, completely covered from head to foot in a gold uniform with a gold helmet and black visor. The image, a bit old-fashioned-looking, surprised Albert until he remembered that Lee had played seventy-five years ago.

He called up his own johkadin and stared at his pose, pleased by the power stance he had jumped into. Who was this Albert, he wondered? What trait could he possibly have that the Zeenods would desire?

3.0

"Good boy," Trey said mechanically. He threw the tennis ball again, and the dog took off after it. Tackle knew exactly what was going on. This trip to the park, the solid half hour playing catch, the praise. Trey was exercising him and showering him with positive attention—at the command of Mrs. Patterson—in the hopes that he'd calm down and stop barking and digging holes and jumping fences and getting into their neighbors' garbage.

Mrs. P was right about one thing, the dog thought as he snatched the ball in his jaws. He did need the exercise and attention. Trey used to give it, but ever since the boy's body grew and his voice deepened and his smell changed, his priorities had changed, too. Now Trey was all about Trey. Too busy playing soccer on faraway fields that dogs weren't even allowed to run on. Too busy with the school team. Too busy working out alone. Too busy staring at his phone. Too busy locking his bedroom door. Right now? The boy's heart wasn't in it—look—on his cell phone again.

Instead of racing back to drop the tennis ball at Trey's feet, Tackle zoomed off in a huge circle around him. How would you like it if you had to be fenced in, huh, Trey? You think I like it? Two revolutions and Trey didn't even notice. On the third, Trey put his phone away and called out. "We're supposed to be playing catch. Give me the ball!"

Oh, you want me to play with you now, do you, Tackle thought. Chomping down on the ball even harder, he ran another lap. Trey not exercising him enough wasn't even the main point. The main point was that danger was under their noses, and only the dog could smell it.

The Pattersons didn't have a clue. Something had again happened to Albert last night, and he had failed to stop it. Stupidly, he'd allowed the smell of that trash to lure his attention away, and by the time he turned back to look, Albert was gone.

Grrrr.

The Pattersons had dragged him inside, thinking he was protesting because he wanted a bone in the garbage when what he really wanted was for them to see what he could see. Danger.

"Are we playing or not?" Trey called.

Tackle ran back and dropped the ball at Trey's feet.

"Good boy," Trey said, and gave the top of Tackle's head a pat before throwing the ball again. A pat on the head. What was that? He deserved a full rubdown.

The running did feel good, and he loved this park, the one

with the hill and the field and the duck pond rimmed with maples and oaks, even though it wasn't a far walk. As he sped up to catch the ball before it hit the ground, he appreciated the way his muscles stretched and contracted. The release of all that pent-up energy was more than welcome. Last night had been the worst—after the garbage fiasco, they'd locked his dog door and all he could do was look out the windows. When he saw Albert return, he tried waking up the Pattersons. And for that all he got was grief. Mr. P put him in the basement, where he had whimpered until he fell asleep. This morning he had woken up cold and angry and cramped.

But the park…this was what he needed. The Pattersons should know how important it was for him to stay fit, to be ready, especially now.

After a few more runs, Trey gave him another pat and pulled a treat from his pocket. Yes! How nice to be appreciated. But then Trey jumped up and held the treat high. "Up! Come on, boy! Up!"

Tackle put his head down. Lately he couldn't just be given a treat. No. Trey was making him sit or beg or jump or play dead.

The boy tapped the treat above his nose. "Come on, boy! Up!"

Reluctantly, the dog sat on his hind legs and put his front paws in the air.

"Good boy!" Trey threw him the biscuit.

He wasn't a good boy. He was a beast—clearly the fastest, strongest, smartest dog in the park. He could be even faster and stronger and smarter, of course, if the park were a part of his daily routine—and if he didn't have to waste his time doing tricks to get a treat.

As he crunched on the biscuit, he thought through the best plan. Stay out of the flower beds. Stop attacking the fence. Keep the barking and howling to a minimum. And maybe the Patter-sons would reward him with more of this. They would think they were just preventing "bad" behavior at home; but really, they'd be giving him the chance to build his muscles and get a good look at the greater area so that he could be ready to attack whatever it was that was coming from the sky.

"Let's go." Trey slipped the leash on and stood.

I am ready, Tackle thought, feeling that deep calm that comes after a workout.

And then, about forty yards from where they were, a young man happened to be walking home from the downtown area, where he had just purchased a new bottle of Deep Forest Pine cologne. It was Saturday and he had a first date that night. As he walked, he decided to test it out, spritzing the scent onto his neck. A light breeze brought the mixture of lemon, cloves, bergamot, and pine toward Tackle and Trey. The smell of pine, in particular, hit Tackle's nose like an alarm.

What the—

In the next second, the dog lurched, yanking the leash out of Trey's hand and bounding off.

The young man leaped onto a bench, cursing loudly.

The dog could feel Trey trying to catch up behind him, shout-ing, too, but that smell was too much. Tackle jumped up and snatched the bottle right out of the terrified man's hand.

3.1

"Text Nana and see if she did her physical therapy," Albert's mom said as she pulled out of the phone-store parking lot. "And tell Erin to be ready for practice."

"Mom, you don't need to text everybody on the planet every five seconds to make sure they're doing what they're supposed to do," Albert snapped, putting his new phone into his pocket. The Saturday late-morning trip to get a phone had taken too long, eating into what little time he had to study. This Monday, he was going to attend his first practice on Zeeno, and he desperately wanted to spend every possible minute reading the official guide.

"Nana's accident was extremely serious, and if she doesn't do her physical therapy, she—"

"Are you kidding me? Nana is totally on top of it, Mom. She's doing her exercises, and all her work for her school online, and she taught herself to knit!" He stared out the window. "You don't have to text me every day, either, to make sure I'm practicing the clarinet or doing my homework or chores or whatever."

"But that's my job," his mom argued. "Speaking of chores, you could do some yard work to pay for your phone."

He had told his mom that he had left his cell phone in the school library at lunchtime and it had been stolen. She insisted that, since he had been careless about leaving it, he would have to do extra chores to help pay for it.

He looked back out the window. "Nana isn't texting me every day. She hasn't texted me once the whole three months she's been here, except when you've made her. She assumes I'm a capable human being who can get from school to home without getting hit by a bus. And besides—" He was going to continue, but then he remembered something Nana had said the other day about looking at people when talking with them, so he turned to look at his mom and was surprised to see sadness sweeping over her face.

He closed his mouth.

Her eyes almost teary, she returned her gaze to the road. "I worry," she said softly. "I'm sorry, Albert. It's what I do. I worry because bad things can happen. I don't know how to stop."

They were silent for a block.

Bad things *can* happen, Albert thought. Look at what happened to Nana.

Three months ago, his eighty-seven-year-old grandmother had come for her annual weeklong visit from New Zealand, which was where she lived and taught at a school she had founded. On the second day of this trip, she had taken the Metro train from Silver Spring, where the Kinneys lived, into Washington, DC, to go to a new museum, and, as she was walking up the stairs of the Metro station to exit—she liked to take the stairs instead of the escalator or elevator in order to get her exercise in—she said she had a "bad" feeling, and she stopped and turned to look behind her. At that very moment, about ten steps below, she saw a man in the act of taking a wallet from a woman's purse as he walked up the stairs on her left. Nana and the man locked eyes. If he turned and ran back down toward the Metro, she could call out for people to catch him and a Metro officer would stop him before he could even get through the turnstile. His best bet was to run up and out; so, he charged up. She yelled, "Thief!" and tried to block him from passing her, and he pushed her down the steps.

A black eye, numerous contusions, bruises, sprains, and

a broken hip requiring two surgeries, the last of which she had just completed, were her reward for trying to help. At the doctor's suggestion, she was staying in Silver Spring until she recovered.

His mother had gotten a phone call from the hospital on the day of the accident when they were driving in this car on this very road.

And, although he had been too little to remember clearly, Albert knew that it was his mother's phone that had also rung nine years ago with the worst news imaginable. His dad, Thomas, was on a solo trip, visiting his mom, Albert's nana, in New Zealand; and when the phone rang showing his dad's ID, Albert's mom thought it would be cute if four-year-old Albert said hello first. But instead of his dad's voice on the line, it was Nana's voice, and she was crying. When Albert's mom saw the confusion on Albert's face, she took the phone from him and had to hear the news. An undetected heart malfunction had caused Thomas Kinney to have a massive, fatal heart attack. Bad things can happen. Their little family was proof of that.

They turned onto their street, the silence between them heavy.

"You're probably right about not having to check on Nana," his mother admitted, and tried to smile. "For someone her age who has been through what she's been through, she's doing amazingly well."

"There's only one problem," Albert said. "The sheep of the world are all going to be bald."

His mom laughed. "She's knitting a lot, isn't she? I can't believe she taught herself so quickly."

"It's because she can't sit around doing nothing."

"Being in that wheelchair would be hard for anybody, but especially for her," Albert's mom agreed.

"She'll probably teach herself how to play the banjo next," Albert said, and then his mom pulled into the driveway, and they both had to laugh because the garage door was open and there was Nana, in the garage, doing her physical therapy with Erin's exercise bands.

"Go, Nana," Albert said, and he was about to race into the house to barricade himself in his room and read the guide when his mom stopped him.

"Albert, thanks." She smiled. "That was a nice moment. I'll try not to text as much." She sighed and pressed her hands against the wheel. "Okay. Tell Erin to come out and to make sure to bring the lunches I packed for us. The chauffeuring never stops."

He nodded and rushed in. Erin was in the kitchen putting the lunches and her water bottle in her sports bag. "Good! I thought you guys were never coming," she said. "I'll get killed if I'm late."

As he raced past her, something caught his eye on the kitchen table.

His Z-da!

She saw him notice it and they both lunged for it at the same time. She grabbed it, laughing, and took off running.

"That's mine!" he shouted.

She ran through the open door into the garage. "I found it."

Chasing her, he shouted, "You found it in my dresser! Give it back."

Erin ran past Nana into the driveway. "Finders keepers."

At that moment, Tackle and Trey appeared, returning from their walk to the park.

"What's going on?" Nana asked as Albert lunged past her.

"Give it back, Erin!" Albert grabbed Erin's arm as she tried to open the passenger door of the waiting car.

She fought back, tightening her grip on the necklace. "Who gave it to you? A girl?"

Tackle was barking like crazy, and Trey looked curious as he restrained him.

Albert yanked on the arm that held the Z-da with such force that the Z-da went flying out of Erin's hands.

"No!" Albert screamed as it sailed toward Tackle and Trey.

Up jumped the dog, yanking his leash out of Trey's hand and snatching the Z-da in his mouth.

3.2

Tackle had known he would be rewarded. Stand guard, be ready, and something is bound to happen.

The new thing in his mouth was a prize. He could tell by the shrieks. Without hesitation, he took off, bursting through the unlatched gate of his fence, racing around to the backyard.

The thing was cold and smooth, tasting of metal. He wanted to set it on the ground and smell it, but he knew he didn't have time. Instinctively, he started to dig a hole with both paws, a small loop of the distinctive black necklace cord falling out of one corner of his mouth.

"Give it back!" Albert yelled, racing into the yard with Trey following.

Both boys wanted it, and Tackle was confused. He didn't understand what he had in his mouth or who should have it. Safest thing was to keep it. The dog turned to dig again, and suddenly Albert's hand was on his collar pulling him back.

Tackle kept his mouth closed, pressing the thing against the roof of his mouth with his tongue, trying to learn what he could about it, as he kept trying to dig.

Mr. and Mrs. Patterson were coming out of the house now.

"Give it!" Albert was going crazy, pulling at his collar.

"That's my dog," Trey said. "Back off."

"He's got my necklace!" Albert yelled.

"Everybody back!" Mr. Patterson crouched down, eye level. "Tackle. Tackle. Look at me. Tackle."

The dog looked at Mr. Patterson.

"Drop it, Tackle. Whatever it is. Drop it right now."

Completely unfair. His owner should be praising his quick reactions, not scolding him. Clearly this thing in his mouth was important, and, thanks to his quick actions, he'd caught it. Caught it! He jumped and caught a flying projectile in midair. That takes skill. That takes readiness. That takes—

"Tackle. I said, drop it right now."

Grrr.

A horrible position to be in. If they could only understand that he was protecting them. Grudgingly, Tackle bowed his head and, in a slurry of saliva, let the thing fall from his mouth. It barely hit the ground before both boys reached for it.

With an insanely fast lunge, Trey snatched it up and looked at the tiny holes and mouthpiece. "What is it, Albert? Is it something you, like, play?" As Trey lifted it to his lips, Mrs. Patterson, disgusted, swatted it away.

"For heaven's sake, Trey—"

Albert grabbed the necklace and ran.

3.3

Albert locked himself in the bathroom, shaking. The Z-da was wet, but after carefully cleaning and drying it, he could see that there was not one dent or scratch. He tested it by opening the guide, and when the holographic image appeared he breathed a sigh of relief. Still, he was furious. Yes, before they had driven off, his mother had made Erin apologize and promise not to "borrow" things that weren't hers; but all that was too little too late, in Albert's opinion.

His nana knocked on the door. "You okay in there?"

"Yes," he snapped.

"You have a right to be angry, Albert," she said. "Erin was way out of line."

"Thank you," he said, hoping she wouldn't ask where he got the necklace or why it was so important to him.

Silence for a moment, and then she said, "Why don't you go to the park and blow off some steam?"

"Thanks," he said again. "Good idea."

He put the Z-da in his pocket and left the house.

Next door, Trey and his parents were getting into their car, Trey in his new travel team's uniform. A game, no doubt. Pretending he didn't see them, Albert ran and didn't stop until he was at the park, out of breath. He missed this. The physicality of running hard.

There were a bunch of guys warming up on the field, old guys, mostly, in their thirties and forties, passing the soccer ball back and forth in twos and threes, dribbling, juggling, stretching. For years, this pickup game of soccer had been going on every Saturday around noon. When he and Trey were younger and would come to kick the ball around, they would often watch the guys, who were surprisingly good.

Today, there was one younger player, maybe high school age, who was passing the ball with a man who looked like the guys' father. Albert walked by slowly, so hungry to play he felt he might scream, and then their ball came flying out of bounds on his side. Instinctively, Albert raced toward the ball and stopped it with his chest. Ordinarily, he would have passed it back and kept walking. But the feel of that ball triggered something in him that he couldn't repress. Taking off, he dribbled the ball around two other players and took a hard shot on the goal. A beautiful curve. The keeper dove, but the ball zipped through his fingertips and hit the back of the net.

"Got your cleats?" one of the guys asked. "We're a man down."

"I could run and get them," Albert said. "My house isn't far."

"Go for it."

Albert's heart leaped as he took off again.

4.0

Although the botmaker was at home, he continued to use his smartgoggles as his primary viewing tool, one which allowed him to pace and watch easily at the same time. Multitasking even further, he began to dictate an entry into his log.

```
I've reviewed yesterday's video ten times. I was hoping
that the fact that both Kinney's sister and the Patter-
sons had seen the Z-da were grounds enough to call it a
violation of the secrecy clause. However, based on the
behavior of everyone present in the footage, I believe
that no one knows what the Z-da is. A close call, but not
in my favor.
```

If I could get my hands on the resources I need, I could create a new negative-thought-loop bot and—

Stop. You cannot risk stealing more resources. Use what is already in place.

Think about how weak Kinney is. If the memory wipe hadn't happened, it would have been game over. You don't need a DRED, you just need Kinney to believe that you have a DRED.

A false threat? Yes! Hack his Z-da. Why not? Introduce a code that would send a clear message...a frightening hologram? Take a page from the Tev playbook and make it 100% intimidating. Ha! But how to get my hands on the Z-da in order to introduce the hack? That won't be ea—

He paused. An idea occurred to him. One that required only his brilliance and materials he already had. He couldn't put it into place before Kinney's first practice on Zeeno, but he could deploy it when the practice ended. No doubt, FJF-regulated protection would be surrounding Kinney and the team, but this was exactly the kind of challenge Mehk relished.

5.0

On Monday morning, Albert woke up thinking about revenge. Nothing major—he didn't have time for that—just a little reminder to his sister that he had not forgiven her for stealing his Z-da. After breakfast, while she was in the bathroom brushing her teeth, he drew a cartoon of a braggy post from Erin's main gymnastics rival, the frenemy on her new team. Erin had complained about Brittany ever since joining her team and often said that Brittany's Instagram posts made her want to throw up. Their mom said it was ridiculous for Brittany to have an account at her age and wouldn't allow Erin to download the app yet. But, like scratching an already-irritated bug bite, Erin would look at Brittany's posts whenever she borrowed Albert's phone. He folded the cartoon and hid it between the cheese and the bread in her sandwich.

Delighted with the thought that his little surprise would eat away at his sister's self-confidence, he headed off to school with his Z-da safely in his pocket. He wanted to wear it—he liked the way it felt when he did—but he needed to keep it hidden, at least for today. Trey was dying to know why he was so "in love" with a necklace and wanted to see it.

First period was Spanish class and with it came another moment of panic for Albert. He had forgotten to study, hadn't even cracked open his Spanish binder all weekend; and now Señora Muñoz was beginning the class with her favorite game, one she called *Siéntense, Perdedores,* or Sit Down, Losers.

"You know how to play," she said, and clapped her hands. "Up, up! *¡Levántense! ¡Levántense!*"

Trey and Raul, fans of the game, both jumped to their feet.

"Game six," Raul called out to Trey. "This one's mine."

Trey laughed. "You need it, bro. It's three to two in my favor."

"Raul, you should win no problem," Jessica Atwater said. "You grew up speaking Spanish!"

"Excellent point, Jess," Trey said, beaming a smile at Jessica. "I should get extra points."

Albert wanted to vomit.

"*¡Levántate, Alberto!*"

Reluctantly, Albert stood by his desk. One by one, Señora Muñoz called out an English word to each student. Students who gave the correct translations in Spanish could remain standing. Students who failed had to sit down.

The first few words were from last week's unit: *school, man, cat.* Easy words that Albert knew. *La escuela. El hombre. El gato.* Of course, he didn't get picked to answer those.

"Alberto," she said. *"Peanut."*

Peanut was new, probably from the lesson that he should have studied this weekend. He was about to sit down in defeat, but then the correct translation simply popped into his head. *"El maní,"* he said.

"Correcto," she said, and moved on.

Unfamiliar word after unfamiliar word. *Brick. Eraser. El ladrillo. La goma de borrar.* Without having studied, Albert knew them all. As he remained standing and the game continued, he realized why he was having such success. The translation device in his ear—his souvenir from the Opening!

The rounds continued, and as the number of students standing decreased, the speed of the rounds increased. Each time Albert received a word, he fired back the correct translation. Then it was down to him, Trey, and Raul.

"You have some competition today, dudes," Jessica said.

"Itch," Señora Muñoz said to Raul. "The noun."

Instinctively, Albert reached down and scratched the back of his knee.

"I know this," Raul said. "Don't tell me. I'm drawing a blank, but I absolutely know this!" After five seconds of unproductive memory searching, Señora Muñoz made him sit down. Now it was Albert versus Trey.

Albert knew that he had never heard or seen the Spanish word for *itch,* and yet he said, *"Una picazón."*

Raul slammed his hands on his desk. "It was on the tip of my tongue, man!"

"*Una picazón. Correcto*," the teacher said. "Good job, Alberto. We're out of time. Between Trey and Albert, whoever says the next word first wins. The next word is *cow*."

"*La vaca*," the boys said at the same time.

Señora Muñoz smiled. "A tie! *Felicidades*, Alberto Kinney! I am overjoyed that you studied so hard over the weekend."

Albert smiled. Without any effort on his part, he had become a Spanish speaker. *Bien*, Albert thought. *Muy bien*.

To Albert's surprise, Jessica reached over with her easy smile and her chocolate-brown eyes to give him a fist bump. Him.

"What about me?" Trey asked.

Jessica laughed. "You always win, Trey."

After Jessica had turned back around, Trey threw Albert a hostile glance, and Señora Muñoz went on with class.

As the morning inched by, Albert found it difficult to focus. Finally it was time to activate the szoŭ. Albert put everything in his locker and hustled to the least busy of the boys' bathrooms, the one in the dead-end science hallway farthest from the cafeteria, trying to rev up for the adventurous risk he was about to take.

After the ceremony on Friday, he and the Zeenods had talked briefly to consider their practice schedule, which would be every Monday, Wednesday, and Saturday. Consistency of time was best, they said, and after discussion had decided that noon Earth time would be it. On Saturdays, his sister and mom would be gone for Erin's gymnastic practice. That would be easy. School days would be a little trickier. On Mondays and Wednesdays he had his lunch period from noon to 12:30. The middle school cafeteria was always chaotic; no attendance was taken, and no one would notice that he was gone. Students were allowed to use the library during lunch, so if anyone did notice he was gone, they'd assume he was in the library—he often preferred hanging out there anyway. As long as he was back in time for his first afternoon class, which started at 12:34, it would work. In fact, it would be nice to have a break from the lunch zoo.

Since the Zeenods had explained that he could be beamed into the ITV from any location—even indoors—he decided he would do it in the boys' bathroom and return there as well.

"Hello?" Albert peeked under the stalls.

Empty. Perfect.

He looked at himself in the mirror, straightening his spine and lifting his chin. "Albert Kinney, Star Striker for Planet Zeeno, reporting for practice." He forced a smile and held it for a few seconds. And then the smile gradually became genuine. The whole experience was amazingly cool. Shaking with excitement, he pulled his Z-da out of his pocket and put it back around his neck.

Top left hole, single breath.

Wait!

He checked to make sure he didn't have his cell phone in his pocket. He knew it was in his locker, but still, it didn't hurt to check. The last thing he needed now was to blitz through another cell phone.

Okay. Top left hole, single breath. Careful…Done. Thirty seconds until lift-off.

Heart pounding, Albert took the power pose, pumping his fists in the air. "Goal for Zeeno!"

And then the door opened, and in walked Freddy Mills with his lunch bag in his hand. Delighted to see Albert, he chirped out his hello.

Under pressure, Albert acted on the first idea that came to him. "Uh…Freddy! Go get the nurse!"

"The nurse?"

Albert brought one arm to his chest. "I'm—I'm having a heart attack!"

"A heart attack?" Freddy yelped. "But we're only in seventh grade! We can't have heart attacks."

"I—I—" Albert clutched his chest. "I was born with a heart malfunction."

"Heart malfunction?" The color drained from Freddy's face and his lunch bag hit the floor. Freddy Mills, a classmate of Albert's since preschool, knew something about the Kinney family that Albert had forgotten he knew, that Freddy had forgotten he knew until just now. "Oh my God. A heart attack. Your dad—"

Shame hit Albert like a tidal wave. What had seemed like a good idea had taken a dark turn, but he was in too deep. "Just go, Freddy!" he muttered.

As a terrified Freddy ran out the door, Albert stood, reeling with regret, wishing he could stop the clock for a moment to collect his thoughts.

Then, three…two…one…

The bathroom glowed a color that was invisible to his eyes and crackled with a sound that was inaudible to his ears, and Albert was beamed up.

5.1

Albert was silent on the trip to Zeeno, responding to Unit B only when necessary. He had been told that the president of Zeeno and news reporters would be at the practice facility to greet him. He tried to imagine a youth soccer tournament on Earth being so important that the president would show up to launch the first practice.

The hibernation in the hygg helped ease his tension a bit, and so did the appearance of a new set of practice clothes and cleats. This time, he knew enough to activate the smart-materials fabric of the suit to conform to his body.

As they neared Zeeno, he found himself more excited than scared and went eagerly to the window. At that moment, Unit B activated a blackout screen.

"According to regulations, visitors are not allowed to see Zeeno upon approach," the robot said.

"Why not?"

Unit B's eyes rolled, an action that had been programmed in to make her appear more lifelike. "Did you fail to read about the situation between Zeeno and Tev?"

"I read something. It was called the Great Fusion."

"That's what the Tevs called it. To the Zeenods, it was an invasion."

Albert glanced at the back window and saw that it, too, was covered with an opaque screen. "Can you just give me the summary?"

Unit B blinked. "Seventy-five years ago, the Tevs invaded Zeeno by force but told the rest of the solar system that it was a peaceful 'fusion.' Tev soldiers were sent to control the planet, and then Tev citizens were sent to colonize the planet. Tevs living on Zeeno became known as Z-Tevs. The Z-Tevs have mistreated both the Zeenods and the planet and have hidden their crimes. To keep others from seeing or hearing the truth, the Z-Tevs control what is seen and heard by others. Visitors must approach by navigation coordinates and are only allowed to land in approved zones. Z-Tevs insist the rules protect their technology from being stolen; however, the Zeenods on Zeeno know the truth."

"But wait," Albert said. "Zeeno has a Zeenod president. I saw her at the Opening. President Lat. So why doesn't she tell the solar system what is happening? Why doesn't she protect Zeeno?"

"She does what she can, but President Telda Lat has very little power. The rest of the government and the police and the military and the media are all run by the Z-Tevs."

"Why doesn't the rest of the solar system do something about it?"

"The Tevs have allies. As for Zeeno's old allies, many don't know how desperate the situation has become. Z-Tevs insist that the relationship between Zeenods and Z-Tevs is fine."

"If I were the president of Zeeno, I'd make sure the truth got out there."

"Zeenods who speak against the Z-Tev government have a ninety-nine-point-nine-percent chance of being found guilty of a crime or of dying accidentally. The last Zeeno president spoke harsh words about Z-Tev rule and died in an ITV accident. President Lat's objective is to gain resources for the Zeenods without threatening Z-Tev order."

Albert looked at the robot. "This game—the whole tournament—it's not just about winning a trophy."

"The short-term objective of the Zeenods is to use their success in the johka tournament to reveal their plight. The long-term objective is to regain control of Planet Zeeno." Unit B turned abruptly to the flight controls. "Arrival in twenty seconds."

When they landed and the hatch finally opened, a chill came over Albert. The ugly rooftop parking lot was nothing like the lovely, colorful scene that was pictured on both his Z-da and his johkadin. This backdrop was bleak. The city streets below were lined with rows of cubelike gray buildings and crowded with vendors as well as ground vehicles. More Z-Tevs and robots than Zeenods were visible, he noticed. In the distance, a hostile-looking rock of a mountain stood, and the sky was crowded with ITVs instead of those beautiful birds pictured on his Z-da. And this was the zone the Z-Tevs wanted visitors to see, Albert thought, realizing that the other zones must be even worse.

A small staging area was set up and a group stood waiting for him, including a Z-Tev news anchor, Kayko, President Lat, President Tescorick of Tev, and a tentacled, two-headed Zhidorian FJF official. Behind them was the prettiest splash of color, the rooftop garden of the capitol building across the street, which boasted the only tree Albert could see that reminded him of the scene on his Z-da: a graceful tree with pink-and-white blossoms. The cameras, all of which were operated by robots, were set up to face the staging area, which meant that the tree and gardens would be the backdrop of the videos, making it look as if that were what could be seen in every direction. Across the lot, a large silver spacecraft with Tev insignia was parked.

"I didn't know the Tevs would be here, too," Albert whispered.

Unit B nodded. "The Tev team arrived earlier. They have already been welcomed and are currently practicing."

The Zeenod team was waiting on the side in their practice uniforms, and when Albert glanced their way, many of them smiled or nodded.

Albert took a breath and walked out.

The Z-Tev reporter, a robot, spoke first, addressing the camera and introducing the leaders as well as Kayko and Albert. President Lat was asked to speak first. She was tall for a Zeenod and the colors of her face changed rapidly as she spoke, as if a hundred emotions were coursing through her. "On behalf of Zeeno, we welcome Star Striker Albert Kinney to the first practice of the tournament, and we thank tactician Kayko Tusq for leading the team to this qualification."

She bowed to both Kayko and Albert and smiled at the cameras.

President Tescorick, massive and fit, towered over them all. He looked young for a president and was handsome by Tev standards, but the bumpy grayish skin on the top of his bald head, which was glistening in the Zeeno sun, reminded Albert of the top of an alligator's head. "The Tevs and Zeenods have been enjoying a long and fruitful partnership here on Zeeno ever since the Great Fusion," he said in a booming voice. "On behalf of the Tev team and all the Tevs on Tev, as well as the Z-Tevs here on Zeeno, we were delighted that Zeeno decided to form a johka team again." He turned and smiled at Kayko and the team. "What took you so long, eh?"

The Z-Tevs and Tevs on the rooftop laughed, and President Lat managed a thin smile.

President Tescorick went on. "Now that both teams have qualified for the tournament, we look forward to a vigorous game against our fine friends."

Thanks to the little history lesson Albert had just received from Unit B, he knew that both presidents were playing a political game. Albert wanted to look at Kayko to see how she was responding, but he was afraid to move.

The Zhidorian spoke next. One head was laser-focused on speaking with intense eye contact, while the other head acted as an observational scout. "On behalf of the FJF, we also welcome you. I am here, according to regulation, to verify that the planet is providing an appropriate and safe FJF-approved training facility." The official turned to President Lat. "The facility passed inspection."

President Lat bowed. "The safety of Albert Kinney and all the players is of the utmost importance. Let the first Team Zeeno practice begin!"

The team gathered and more photos were taken with the officials; and, as the news team left and President Tescorick and the Zhidorian official returned to their vehicles, Doz whispered to Albert, "What took us so long? Zeenod teams have tried to play for years and Z-Tevs held us down."

"Shh," President Lat hissed. She addressed the team, lowering her voice. "Since the FJF official inspected the area, we can be sure that there are no Z-Tev surveillance devices in place. But there are eyes watching. Stand for an inspection of uniforms."

As the robotic chauffeurs, vendors, and guards on the rooftop went about their business, the Zeenod president pretended to inspect the team and their uniforms. Then she whispered, "Kayko, your request for funds to purchase supplies for the game one halftime ritual and for the on-the-field victory celebration has been approved."

"What?" Kayko asked, clearly in shock. "How did you manage?"

"I explained that the fans coming from all over the solar system will be expecting the home team to provide a good show and that it would look strange if Zeeno were not able to do so."

Kayko grinned. "Excellent!"

The entire team broke into smiles.

The team's keeper, a Zeenod named Toben, spoke up, albeit quietly. "But the ahda birds are extinct, and that's one of the few vacha trees left." He pointed to the tree on the capitol building's rooftop and then whispered. "My apologies for speaking so freely, President Lat."

Ennjy whispered an explanation to Albert: "The releasing of vacha blossoms over the stadium at halftime and ahda birds at a victory were both traditions of Zeeno."

"It's true that we can't offer blossoms and birds that no longer exist," President Lat whispered. "But for the first time in seventy-five years, we will have a team playing in the johka tournament on Zeeno, and at least we will be able to afford some kind of celebration for the fans."

"And that will help build support for Zeeno," Kayko whispered, and then she said loudly, "Yes, the uniforms and cleats are all in excellent condition. Thank you for fulfilling your responsibilities, President Lat. We will do our best to represent the planet."

"Please report directly to me if you require assistance," the president added under her breath. "That is the safest way to assume the message will be received."

After the president left, Kayko led the exuberant team across the lot to the building's entrance, which was manned by two armed Z-Tev guards.

"Finally!" Doz said to Albert with a huge grin. "The true excitement begins. Let's play some johka!"

Kayko pushed the doors open; and then Albert couldn't quite believe what happened next. As they walked in, the Z-Tev guards smirked and began muttering a string of obscenities at them under their breath about why they were such losers and how entertaining

114

it was going to be to watch them fail. Albert stopped, but Ennjy quickly put her hand on his back and gently encouraged him to ignore it and keep moving. "This is what they do," she said.

As they walked down the long corridor, Albert's mind was racing. It was disturbing to experience that kind of disrespect for even a brief moment. Albert couldn't imagine having to take it from the Z-Tevs for seventy-five years.

Passing by a team of robot custodians, they reached a set of double doors that led to their indoor practice space, and the team became exuberant again. "Normally, we don't have access to this practice space," Kayko explained. "It is special."

"Come, Albert. We need to heat up, man!" Doz said.

Albert smiled. Heating up was just as good as warming up.

The doors opened into a facility that looked to Albert like a gym, but it was another sight that froze Albert's feet to the floor.

One wall of the large space was glass, and on the other side of that glass the Tev team—the first opponents they would be playing against—were in an identical training room in two perfectly straight lines doing insanely difficult leg squats. Behind them, a row of robots were setting up weight-lifting equipment. Tall, with almost identically muscular arms and legs, the Tevs and robots were difficult to tell apart. The Tev's Star Striker, Vatria Skell, the one who'd told Albert he was weak, was the only one in their entire group who turned her head to look at them through the glass, a distraction that caused her to break timing.

Their team's tactician yelled a string of obscenities at Vatria in the Tev language; and, although Albert knew his translation implant was powerful, he was still shocked to be able to immediately understand the meaning of each curse word.

Calmly Kayko walked over to the glass and tapped a button.

The Tev tactician turned around and looked surprised to see them. He gestured for the players to begin the exercise again and walked over to his side of the wall and tapped a similar button.

"My apology," the Tev tactician, a meaty brute named Hissgoff, said. "The wall was set to 'share mode' when we arrived. We didn't realize you were arriving, or we would have changed the setting."

"Apology accepted," Kayko said, and pressed another button, causing the wall to turn completely white, effectively making the other team disappear.

Doz exploded. "That was, as you would say, Albert, a bunch of bull donkey! They knew we were coming. Hissgoff purposefully set the wall to 'share mode' to intimidate us."

"They did the same to us when they came here for their assigned practice during the regular season," Feeb added.

"Vatria wasn't here at the time, so she didn't get the message that she was supposed to stay focused," Ennjy said. "She won't make that mistake again."

Albert's mind was spinning—he wondered if he should back out now. But then Kayko put her hand on his shoulder and called for the team to gather. "We are excited to be here, but we have two important tasks today. To introduce Albert to what makes us Zeenods: the ahn and the zees."

In his mind's eye, Albert could see that long section in the holographic guide on the history between Tev and Zeeno and another long section on the ahn and the zees. He wished he had found more time to study. The translation device was telling his brain that a zee was an eruption and that *ahn* had multiple meanings. Not exactly helpful.

"Ahn first," Kayko said. They spread out to form a large circle with about two feet of space between the players. "We connect with each other through a kind of hum we make with our breath called the ahn. You can join us—"

"Wait. Hum…like, sing?" Albert felt more out of place than ever.

"No. Not exactly," Kayko said. "*Hum* isn't quite the right translation." She looked at Ennjy. "Ennjy, will you attempt to explain?" She turned back to Albert. "Ennjy comes from a long line of ahnurus and has the gift of ahnic clarity and strength."

Tiny Ennjy focused her violet eyes on Albert. "Your word *meditation* is closer than *hum*. We focus our minds on a vibration that we make with our breath called the *ahn*. When we do this correctly, we receive a boost of energy that makes us stronger, faster, sharper, more perceptive—"

"Hold on," Albert said. "You hum, or meditate, or whatever, and that actually makes you better athletes?"

"Better everything!" Doz said.

Ennjy nodded and touched her throat. "The physiology of our vocal folds enables us to generate the ahn through our breathing. It's like we are instruments and can make the ahn sound. Yet, it's not a sound you hear. It's a vibration you feel, and it's a vibration that feeds you with more energy when you align it with the vibrations of others."

"I can explain!" A Zeenod that Albert hadn't noticed before stepped toward him.

"This is Giac," Kayko said. "She understands how many things work."

The compact Zeenod with a friendly face nodded. "Our central nervous system, unlike yours, contains a multitude of nanogenerators that convert ahn signals into electrical energy," she said. "It's vibrational harvesting at the nanoscale. Those signals go to our megahno nerve, which is the longest and most important nerve that connects our bodies and minds. The nerve transmits electrical impulses to every part of our body; so, yes, the ahn gives us performance-enhancing energy."

"Giac is joyful at explaining," Doz said, patting his friend on the back.

Giac smiled. "We increase ahnic energy when we synchronize our individual ahn waves with the ahn waves of others." She turned slightly so that Albert could more clearly see the odd capelike appendage that hung between her shoulder blades and draped down from her upper to her lower back. "This is called a bem. It's like an ear that picks up and conducts ahn waves that are coming from others."

"I've been wondering about that. It reminds me of an elephant's ear!" Albert said. "Do you know what elephants are?"

The Zeenods all looked at the goalie, the big-limbed, normally quiet male called Toben, who said, "I do. My parents and grandparents are what you call zoologists."

"He knows about animals all over the universe," Doz said to Albert, and then he turned to Toben. "Do you have anyone with you today?"

Toben smiled and made a clicking sound, and from a little hiding spot underneath his bem, a mouse-sized creature with long floppy ears scampered out, climbing up to his shoulder and then down his arm into the palm of his hand. "This is a gnauser," he said, and the creature sat on its hind legs and licked its paws.

"A real live one," Doz added.

"Because many animals—pets included—have become extinct on Zeeno, robotic pets have become more common," Toben said.

The gnauser's nose twitched, and Albert grinned. "It's like a very tiny version of an animal we have on Earth called a rabbit."

"Correct!" Toben said, and gave the creature a little pat. The gnauser scampered back up and perched on his shoulder. "I've never felt an actual elephant ear, Albert, but I've studied their properties and I believe the texture of our bem *is* similar to your elephant's ear," he went on. "Feel it. You can't damage it." He turned so Albert could touch his bem.

"It's warm and fuzzy like a blanket but it has strength. It feels alive," Albert said.

Toben nodded. "Our bems have different purposes than elephants' ears, though. Your elephants use the blood vessels in theirs to release heat and scare away enemies. We use our bems to pick up vibrations and also as a stabilizing mechanism when we must balance."

"Through the vibrations transmitted via our bems, we feel the ahn of others," Giac continued. "But in order to get a boost from the ahn of another, we need to synchronize the phases, or cycles, of our individual ahns into a kind of perfect ahn chorus, and that takes focus."

Kayko nodded at Giac. "Good job. It's complicated." She turned to Albert. "When we synchronize our phases, the energy boost is—"

"As you say, awesomely!" Doz exclaimed.

Albert smiled. "So, matching up your humming with another person's humming makes you all have more energy?"

All the Zeenods nodded.

"But I don't have that thing on my back—the bem—or that megahno nerve or those vocal folds or whatever, so how am I supposed to do it?"

"Through past experience, Zeenods discovered that human beings are influenced greatly by ahnic energy," Feeb said.

"Like us, your psychological and physiological states are completely connected," Ennjy said. "You know this."

"I do?"

Kayko nodded. "If you are collaborating with someone whose energy is negative or low, it requires more energy for you to perform well. If you are collaborating with someone whose energy is positive or high, your own energy level is positively affected."

Ennjy leaned in. "This mind-body connection can be an advantage. But in order for it to be used productively, we must deal with our shawbles, our obstacles."

Albert tried to take it all in.

"Pardon me," a thin Zeenod named Sormie said nervously. She, Albert noticed, always seemed to be nervous. "Are we talking too much?"

Doz laughed. "Look at Albert. His brain is about to zeerupt."

"Sormie is right. Let us show instead of explain," Ennjy said. She turned to Albert. "Join us."

The circle of players gave Albert encouraging nods, and then the group settled into silence and closed their eyes. Albert kept his open. Nothing seemed to be happening, but after a minute or two Albert noticed that the Zeenods were now breathing in unison. As Albert copied the pattern of inhalation and exhalation, he noticed that his hands were clenched, his breath was shallow, and his shoulders were tight. He was afraid of making a fool of himself, of not being able to do whatever he was supposed to do.

They looked peaceful, breathing in unison, the gill-like circles on the sides of their heads expanding and contracting slightly, their bodies relaxed but engaged. And then, in front of Albert's eyes, their bems extended, draping all the way down to touch the ground. Albert gasped. He couldn't help staring. It was as if each player were wearing a cape made of living fabric.

He tried to steady his breathing. What Ennjy had said did make sense. Psychology was important.

The old soccer team on which Albert had played with Trey in the town's rec league had been full of team spirit. The coach and the core of players, including Albert and Trey, all had a way of inspiring each other. They called it "getting into the flow," and Albert had become a star along with Trey on that team. He and Trey had experienced times during their best games when each seemed to know what the other was thinking without saying a word. He had been excited when he and Trey had "graduated" to the travel team last year, but that coach and those other players—kids from other schools around the county—didn't have that connection, and he'd ended up missing his old league.

He closed his eyes. After a minute or perhaps more, he felt something. He wasn't sure what it was. A tiny sensation...that hum?

He looked around. No one seemed to be emitting anything other than breath. Was he supposed to be hearing something?

After a few more breaths, he closed his eyes and allowed himself to let go. Settling into silence, he began to feel something again. He could swear that he was feeling a sound, even though his brain was telling him that wasn't possible. But there it was... a shimmering thread of sound, a vibration of harmony that was somehow coming from someone in the circle and attaching itself to him. But no, *attaching* was the wrong word.

Albert stopped trying to figure out what was happening and allowed himself to simply be in the moment. And then it came... a sensation of energy from each player in the circle to him, energy streaming into him that seemed to both lift him and hold him steady at the same time. He felt centered and held by invisible bonds, and yet he felt as if he were on the verge of leaving his own body behind.

After a few seconds of increasing intensity, there was a loud, long whoop from Ennjy, and the players jumped forward into a huddle, throwing their arms around each other's shoulders, gently pulling Albert with them, all eyes open, all eyes gold. A current of electricity seemed to flow from player to player to player in the circle, every player radiating joy. As they stayed connected for a few seconds longer, it was so comforting and energizing and supportive and warm to be a part of the bond, so different from what he had been experiencing lately on Earth, that gratitude welled inside Albert and tears came to his eyes.

Ennjy stood and broke the spell, and Albert quickly brushed his face dry.

"Were you weeping?" Sormie asked. She quickly looked at Ennjy. "Maybe this was too much Zeeno for him?"

"No, of course not," Albert lied quickly. "I felt... I felt..."

"The ahn," Ennjy said, eyes shining. "I knew it!"

"This is why we chose you, Albert. You will learn to send as well," Kayko said. "Both are equally important."

Doz gave him a clap on the back. "Awesomely, man!"

"And now," Kayko said, "let's play some johka."

5.2

All was calm in the parking lot, and while Albert's first practice was occurring, Unit B was proceeding with her assigned task of downloading the training tutorial that Kayko had designed to Albert's Z-da. As she was finishing, an alert came through the ITV's computer. She paused to check it out and was satisfied to see that it was a routine battery-charge notice. The ITV's battery was at seventy percent, which would be enough of a charge to get Albert back to Earth, but since her calculations indicated there was time before the practice session ended, she stepped out to initiate charging via the external optical port.

About two dozen other vehicles were parked on the rooftop, including the two larger ones that transported the Zeeno team to and from their homes in Zone 3 and the Tev team to and from Tev. Enterprising vendors often landed on various rooftop lots to offer their products, so Unit B was not surprised to see a seed vendor selling roasted paranj seeds from a small hovercart to a Z-Tev driver as well as a security guard.

Because security cameras were everywhere and because the ITV battery-charging process had a 99.99999999999 percent chance of success, Unit B's vigilance level was automatically reduced to save energy for riskier actions.

Perhaps if it hadn't been, she would have noticed the small winged bug that lifted off from the cap of the seed vendor. About as small and round as a ladybug, the microbot darted through the air, successfully whizzing past not one, not two, but four security cams and three sensor beams. The seed vendor—Mehk—held his breath and pretended not to watch. Only the thinnest of smiles escaped his lips when the bot zipped inside the open doorway of

Kinney's ITV. Satisfied, he picked up a bag of seeds from the cart he had borrowed and popped a handful into his mouth.

5.3

When Mehk returned the borrowed hovercart to the real seed vendor, the vendor was playing with a robotic gnauser, enjoying the tickle as the tiny bunnylike creature scampered up and down his arm.

Glancing first at the mound of roasted seeds, and then at the paltry sum flashing on the account screen embedded in the handle of his hovercart, and then finally at the botmaker, the vendor asked, "That's it? You're already done?"

Mehk returned the vendor's official ID clip and nodded. "It's all yours."

Quickly the vendor protected his hold on the gnauser. "A deal is a deal, though. You said I could keep the pet if I loaned you the cart for—"

"We're even!" Exhilarated, the botmaker grabbed a bag of the delicious seeds and hurried back to record his thoughts in the privacy of his room.

Ha! No detection, despite the vast number of surveillance mechanisms. Further proof of my skill! With the

code-hacking microbot successfully deployed, now I
wait. How fun it will be to watch this plan unfold.
See...I would never have done this if I had succeeded
earlier. Failure forces creativity! When I can finally
reveal my accomplishments, this will impress.

5.4

Tackle swore the squirrels knew his dog door was locked. A real one stood right on top of that picnic table, with an acorn in its paws, nibbling away without a care in the world. Tackle had barked at it and pawed the window for a good five minutes. It didn't budge. The squirrel-machine in the tree was still there, too.

Everything was out of whack. It was a school day. The house was empty, and normally he could come and go as he pleased, but lately the Pattersons were restricting his outdoor access because of what they called "bad behavior."

If the dog could have understood them completely, he would have been even more upset to hear Trey laughing about both the cologne incident and the necklace incident and saying he only wished he had been able to catch them on video because funny dog videos could go viral.

At noon, a car pulling into the driveway sent him to the front door, where he barked and pawed until he heard the lock click.

"Stop barking, for heaven's sake," Mrs. Patterson said, entering quickly and closing the door behind her. "We're going to make this quick. I've got to get back to work. I don't understand any of this. You used to be a good dog." She grabbed his leash from a hook by the door. "Don't tell me you're going through puberty, too. Trey is already driving me crazy, and now you."

Roughly she attached the leash to his collar without so much as a single head rub. Rude. But he couldn't dwell on that injustice now. Finally, he was going to get out that door! After the long morning, the thought made him almost dizzy with desire. He wanted to chase the squirrel and pee on the fence and—

"Tackle." She paused with her hand on the knob. "Look at me, Tackle."

He looked up. Her face was heavy, seriousness pulling her mouth down on the corners.

"Be good. Hear me?"

He blinked.

Be good. Couldn't she see how double-edged that was? To be good should mean to protect against whatever was making Albert disappear and appear, to patrol, to dig, and bark, and pee. He needed to show whatever force was out there, which right now was manifesting only as the squirrel-machine in the tree, that he was on guard.

Her finger pointed at his face like a dagger. "Stay! Stay!"

Slowly, she opened the door. The smells were intoxicating.

Every cell of his being wanted to leap forward, but he felt the tightening of his leash and heard the repetition of her command.

Hold on, dog. If you control yourself, your dog door will get unlocked. That's what you need. Another morning like this one and you're going to lose your mind. She doesn't want to lock that dog door. It means she has to come home at lunch and walk you. Show her what she wants to see and get her to unlock that door. You can bark at that machine and pee on the tree when she's back at work.

With great effort and pride at being in such control, the dog walked out the door and into that realm of a thousand temptations with fierce calm.

5.5

Kayko led the team through another set of double doors to the regulation johka field, assuring Albert that the Tev team had already had their practice time on the field and that now it was their turn. The team fanned out on the field and began to kick the ball around, jubilant to be out.

"We love our time on the field," Ennjy said.

"I wish we could live here," Doz said, racing by to get to the ball. He took a kick on Toben, the keeper. The ball bounced against the net pole and began to sail out of bounds. This would be the point where someone would usually have to run over and get it or else go get another ball; instead, miraculously, the ball stopped itself in midair, flew back, and came to a quick but gentle landing on the field.

"What?" Albert yelled.

"Smart-ball technology," Giac said. "The ball's processor is powered by a capacitor and a superbattery. It knows when to stop and return, when to inflate or deflate, and has intelligent recharging capabilities. The electroactive polymers—"

"Thanks, Giac." Kayko smiled. "You can tell Albert about the science later. Now it's johka time. As you know, the game is similar to your soccer, Albert. But remember, each planet has its unique set of geologic features that provide different challenges. We have zees, and we use them in three different ways on the field, if we get the chance. We never know when a zeeruption will occur." She turned and called out to the players. "When one comes, let him feel it first and then we'll show him the bounce-off. Be ready, everyone."

After a few minutes of warming up with passes, Doz pointed and cried out: "There!"

Albert smelled it first. That odd scent of pine. Then he looked ten yards away and saw a zeeruption on the field. About two feet in diameter, a column of beautiful multicolored liquid was rising—not high, just about four feet. It was a much smaller version of what Albert had thought was a fountain pictured on his Z-da and his johkadin.

"Come quickly, Albert!" Doz yelled. "Put your fist in it."

Albert ran over and stuck his fist in the liquid, which was continuing to rise. Fluid, but with substance, like cake batter.

"Now step back and watch," Kayko said, pulling Albert back. "Initiate the kick, Doz."

Doz kicked a johka ball at the zee. Albert expected it to get gooped, but instead, the ball bounced off the geyser and then zoomed in a curve toward the goal with a speed unlike any kick Albert had ever seen.

"Whoa!" Albert cried out. "How did you do that?"

"I didn't." Doz grinned. "We did it. When we work together it isn't hard. It's a piece of cookie!"

Albert laughed. "That doesn't look like a piece of cake *or* cookie!"

The zee collapsed back into the ground and the scent dissipated.

Kayko smiled. "That was our first way of using the zee, to kick the ball off it, which is called the bounce-off. And you're right, Albert. It isn't easy."

"Why didn't the ball just go into the liquid?" Albert wiped the zee liquid from his hand onto his uniform.

"A zee is both a liquid and a solid, depending on how you interact with it," Kayko explained. "You might not have noticed it because it happened so quickly, but when Doz kicked, we all focused our ahnic energy toward him. Our support enabled him to synchronize his energy with the zee so he could send the ball with good force. When the ball hits the zee with good force, the liquid becomes not only a solid, but a solid that acts like a springboard to give our ball momentum."

Giac ran over. "That's because zee particles are rheological! Rheological particles can make a substance that is either liquid or solid depending on how you interact with it."

"The important thing is that you can't do it alone," Doz said. "Everybody sent me their ahnic energy, and when I connected with that, it gave me the support I needed to synchronize with the zee."

Albert took a step toward the spot on the ground where the zee had erupted. "Is it going to erupt again?"

"We never know. In five minutes, a zeeruption may occur over there, or there, or there." Kayko pointed around the field.

"They just happen?" Albert asked.

Giac jumped forward to explain and then stopped and looked at Kayko. "Apologies!"

"No. Continue," Kayko said.

Giac took a breath. "In pockets deep, deep in the ground, the vibration of the planet becomes concentrated, and when that happens in certain places, the vibrations travel upward, and when the vibrations interact with particles on the surface of Zeeno, it transforms into a zee. They rise up about three to five feet in the air and last from ten to thirty seconds."

"Why do zees smell like pine trees?" Albert asked.

Blank looks came over his teammates' faces.

"We don't have a sense of smell," Kayko said.

"I'll research this and get back to you, Albert!" Giac said. "Perhaps something in Zeeno's crust contains the same chemical compound that is in your pine trees, and it is released during a zeeruption. I will enjoy discovering this!"

"Zees are much more frequent in this location," Kayko explained. "Which is why our great-grandparents built the training facility here. The Z-Tevs took it over after the invasion and kept it for themselves until now. When our petition to play finally reached the FJF, the FJF stepped in and said the Z-Tevs must allow us access to the facility, just like any other team."

"It doesn't matter how much the Tevs practice," Doz said, grinning. "They still can't learn how to use the ahn or the zees. They can't connect with each other. On the field, they try to avoid—"

Albert noticed the smell again.

"Zee!" a player at left midfield yelled.

"Let's do the jump-over!" Kayko said. "Ennjy!"

As Ennjy took off running toward the zeeruption and the rest of the players focused their attention, Kayko explained to Albert.

"The jump-over isn't a ball move, it's a running move. Sometimes we need to get down the field fast and we use the zee as a springboard. This takes more focus…"

Albert noticed everyone's bems, those capelike appendages, extending as Ennjy sprinted toward the zee. When the zee was about three feet off the ground, she jumped on it and was propelled forward like a gymnast about ten feet, her bem fluttering; and then she landed gracefully back on the ground and kept running as her bem retracted.

Albert gasped. "That was amazing!"

Kayko called out to the team, "Beautiful job, everyone!"

Albert noticed it then, a shift in the energy of everyone present, and it made something buzz in the center of his chest. With wide eyes, he looked at them.

"You're feeling it?" Kayko asked.

"I'm feeling something," Albert said.

"Because we all connected with the ahn, we all receive the boost I was telling you about earlier. Ennjy receives the direct boost of energy from the zee, but it spreads from her to all of us."

Ennjy, normally quiet and reserved, continued sprinting around the perimeter of the field, as if the only way she could cope with her added energy was to blow off some of the steam. "It *is* amazing, Albert!" she called out.

Albert looked at all of them. "I really want to learn how to do that."

"Kayko," Toben called out. "Let's show him the ride-up."

The entire team began to clap and chant. "Ride-up! Ride-up!"

Kayko smiled. "When the time comes, we will try." She turned to Albert. "In the meantime, let's heat up with our regular skills."

Much like Albert's other coaches, Kayko gave the team

instructions for a passing drill; and for a happy ten or fifteen minutes, Albert had the chance to pass the ball around with his new teammates, getting a feel for the ground, which had a firm but spongy quality, as well as the high-tech ball.

Then, just after Albert smelled the scent of pine again, the twins called out that a zee was erupting, and all the attention focused down the field.

"Kayko!" Doz yelled.

As Kayko ran for it, Albert felt everyone focus on her and noticed the bems extending again.

The stunning move that happened next was over in a matter of seconds. Instead of using the zee like a springboard, Kayko hopped on top of it and rose five feet above the field with it, balancing on that column of energy the way a surfer rides on a surfboard, her knees slightly bent, her arms out, her bem extending beautifully behind her.

Although it was happening swiftly, Albert could feel the power in the atmosphere on the field. As all the players were focusing their energy on Kayko, Sormie kicked the ball high up to her. At the same time, Kayko used the zee like a trampoline and jumped upward, propelling herself above the approaching ball. In midair, she kicked the ball and landed back on the zee as the ball rocketed across the field. It sailed so forcefully that every player in its path, including the goalie, had no choice but to duck.

The team cheered as the ball hit the net, the zee collapsed, and Kayko returned to the ground.

The entire team began jumping and dancing around and whooping.

Albert grinned, unable to help feeling as giddy as they looked.

"When we synchronize with a zee, our cells have a party!" Doz exclaimed.

Albert laughed.

"You can see how advantageous this can be," Kayko said. She was jogging in place, shaking her limbs, beaming, her eyes bright gold.

Albert looked around. All their eyes were bright gold. "You all look…I don't know how to describe it."

"It's the ahnic boost," Giac said. "Our muscle and tissue and organ cells have been given a boost of ahnic energy."

"Okay," Albert said. "I really, really want to do this. How did you go up rather than forward on that zee?"

Kayko tapped her head and jumped up and down a few times. "You have to think up, and your body will work with you. Your mind is more powerful than you know."

Everyone began jumping, their jumps higher than he had seen. Albert joined in, but his jump was normal in comparison.

During the next two-hour period, whenever a zeeruption occurred, Albert was given the chance to try a bounce-off. To his chagrin, every ball he sent plopped into the zee-liquid instead of banking off it. Although he hated each failure, it was entertaining to watch the gooped ball rise up and rotate like a top to fling off the zee-liquid and then return, clean, to the ground.

Even though he didn't master the bounce-off, they insisted that he at least try a jump-over, even if just to understand what it felt like to fail.

He silently hoped that the field would have mercy on him and no zees would erupt for the rest of practice. But then, a zee blew and Kayko encouraged him to run for it.

Heart pounding, he took off, eyeing the column of rising multicolored liquid.

"Feel the ahn," Kayko called out.

When it was about two feet off the ground, Albert jumped. Instead of propelling off it like a springboard, he splashed down into its pine-scented goopiness, slipping and falling onto his rear.

Humiliated, he crawled out and stood up, trying to fling the stuff off his legs and hands and arms.

"Don't worry," Giac said. "Most of the liquid will evaporate in a minute."

Albert guessed that a trace of the scent would be left behind. At least he liked the smell.

With great enthusiasm, his teammates kept encouraging Albert and assuring him that improvement was possible. But after practice was over and Kayko was escorting him back to the ITV lot, Albert wrestled with the worry that the Zeenods had made a horrible mistake in choosing him and that he had made a horrible mistake in saying yes. "I think I should avoid the zees," he said. "That's what the Tevs do, right?"

"Typically," Kayko said. "But we'd like you to embrace the zees."

"I'll understand if you don't want to play me much," Albert said. "Or don't want to play me at all."

Kayko stopped. "Training will prepare you, Albert. You will improve."

Albert recalled reading about an alternate in the contract, and he felt a sudden surge of angst, wondering if their choice for alternate would be better than him. "But, in case things don't work out. You have an alternate, right? Someone...I mean, maybe that person..."

Kayko put a hand on Albert's shoulder. "Every team has an alternate striker chosen in case the first striker is injured or disqualified or quits. I can't tell you who our second choice is because of security regulations, but…" Kayko leaned in. "You are our first choice, Albert. Is your inner voice telling you to quit?"

"What?" Albert blinked. "No."

Kayko's eyes softened. "Self-doubt and self-loathing are common shawbles, Albert. The moment you failed at your first zee, your inner voice spoke failure. You can learn how to use the ahn and the zees—but to do so requires addressing your shawbles. Unit B has downloaded the training tutorial to your Z-da. Practice the first three lessons over and over. They are designed to help. We all have shawbles, and we can learn to deal with them. Be kind to yourself, Albert Kinney. Learning is difficult."

A lump grew in Albert's throat. He still didn't understand exactly what Kayko was talking about, but the compassion was obvious and for that he was grateful.

"All the Zeenods are so good at using the zees," Albert said. "We can easily beat the Tevs, no matter what I do, right? The fact that they glow can't really help them here, right?"

"You're right in that the bioluminescence of the Tevs and Sñektis does not give them any advantage on Zeeno, but it will give them a great advantage on the other planets, as you'll see. And our game against them here will be difficult to win. Even though the Tevs avoid the zees, they have advantages over us. That third eye in the back of each head enables them to quickly see both ends of the field. But that is not all. They have a critical fusion frequency that is much greater than ours or yours. Giac could explain it better than me, but essentially, they take in more visual information per second and this enables them to navigate faster, much like the way your Earth birds can fly through a thicket of tree branches quickly. They often see a zee before we do, which means that even if they don't want to use it, they can send their defenders to surround it and make it more difficult for us to use. In addition to all that, they have remarkable endurance."

They had arrived at the parking lot. Unit B had the door of the ITV open and was waiting on the threshold. Kayko bowed. "Farewell until the next practice. You will not be disqualified if you have to miss a practice, but we hope you will attend as many as possible."

"Thank you," Albert said, "Of course."

Kayko smiled and left.

As Albert headed to the ITV, a harsh voice behind him caught his attention. He turned to see Vatria and Hissgoff, the tactician of the Tev team, at the threshold of Vatria's ITV. Vatria stood, head bowed, eye on the back of her head closed, as a stream of insults poured out of Hissgoff's mouth. Albert couldn't pick up every sentence, but there were threats and the word *honor* was said a number of times. "Do you acknowledge your failures?" the tactician yelled.

"Yes," Vatria said.

"Hands out," Hissgoff ordered.

Vatria held out her hands and Hissgoff pressed something against them, sending a jolt through Vatria's arms.

The tactician turned and left.

Albert looked away, stunned. He recalled reading in the guide that the Tev culture was a "factory" for johka machines; players were sent to camps to train without concern for their well-being. The contrast between this treatment of Vatria by her team and how Albert had been treated at practice by the gentle, ahn-loving Zeenods was jarring to him, especially given how badly he had performed. Vatria was a Sñekti, not a Tev. Perhaps she hadn't known exactly what she was getting into. Yes, Vatria was obnoxiously competitive and the insult she had whispered to Albert didn't exactly show good sportsmanship, but maybe the bravado was her way of trying to build herself up, and no one deserved to be punished for not being perfect on the first day of practice.

Deep in thought, Albert was about to head up the stairs of his own ITV and greet Unit B, when he changed his mind. He walked over to Vatria. He wanted to say something in the Sñekti language and wasn't sure what to say or how to do it. She had turned and was watching him approach with the large red-orange eyes on the front of her face. At the top of the stairs of her ITV, her robot chaperone was waiting. While his mind was thinking about what to say in English, the foreign translation came out of his mouth: "Hey…Vatria, right? Those zees are insane, right? Any tips?" He tried a smile.

Straightening, Vatria looked at Albert and then moved closer to him, her eyes flashing. Her voice, barely a whisper, sent another chill through him. "A player with more intelligence would know when to keep his mouth shut. You are playing with danger, Albert Kinney, and you can't even see it." She leaned down and spat. When she turned to walk into her own ITV and yet was still watching him from the eye in the back of her head, a wave of nausea came over Albert. He looked down and there on his beautiful shoe was a glob of saliva. He kicked it off and headed toward the impassive Unit B.

His own failed performance at practice, the intensity of the competition, the cruelty of the Tevs, and the hate directed at him from a player who didn't even know him sank in, convincing him that he was in way over his head.

The return trip home was long. Unit B had much information to share with Albert, including instructions about the training tutorial now installed on his Z-da. The program contained a collection of lessons that he would need to copy from the Z-da to his phone at home so that he could view or listen to them more easily without detection. But Albert found it difficult to concentrate. On top of all this, he was realizing that the szoŭ would return him to school and to all the pressures of what, to everyone else, would be an ordinary day. Because of the time-fold, only twenty-seven minutes would have passed, and the thought of this made his stomach feel queasy. He wanted to climb into the hygg and sleep for a year.

As these thoughts were rumbling around in Albert's mind, neither he nor Unit B was aware of the newcomer on board, the bug-sized microbot on the floor, just inside the door. The microbot, however, had been programmed with both sound and motion detection. When Albert finally did get the chance to hibernate and Unit B sat at the main panel with her attention on the flight path, a sensor in the bugbot signaled activation.

Up the bugbot flew, moving as if by a magnetic force toward Albert's Z-da, which was hanging on a hook with Albert's Earth clothing. Hovering over the Z-da, the underbelly of the bugbot snapped apart to reveal a nanolaser, which transmitted code into the Z-da through its optical port. Once the mission was complete, the microbot self-destructed, evaporating in a tiny inaudible puff. The stinkbug spybot still embedded in the ceiling, of course, captured it all.

5.6

The moment Albert returned to his school's bathroom, he heard the commotion in the hallway outside.

Cautiously, he opened the door, hugged the wall, and walked closer. At the end, where the science hallway spilled into a bigger corridor, a small group had gathered: the science teacher, the school principal, the school nurse, Freddy, and a team of paramedics.

Albert hid behind a display case of science-fair trophies and listened.

"Albert's dad died of a heart attack when he was little!" Freddy was saying. "This is so, so serious."

"Did you call the mother?" the principal asked the nurse. "Maybe Albert called or texted her."

"She was in a meeting. I left a message," the nurse said.

With dread, Albert realized what had happened and knew, of course, that his impulsive fake heart attack had been a terrible mistake. Mortified, he eyeballed the emergency exit at the other end of the science hallway and fantasized about making a run for it, but he imagined his mother returning from her meeting and getting the message and knew he had to come clean. He stepped into the hallway, and Freddy cried out the moment he emerged.

"There he is!"

The entire set of faces turned to stare at him, and Freddy's face jumped into a relieved smile that sent another arrow of guilt through Albert's heart.

"You're okay! Where were you?" Freddy asked, running up to him. "I got the nurse and then we couldn't find you."

The science teacher pulled a stool over for Albert to sit on, as if he might faint or collapse, and they gathered around him. One of the paramedics set down a large black bag and began pulling out emergency response supplies just as the passing period ended and students began to fill the hallways. Trey approached from one corridor and Raul and Jessica and a handful of other students approached from another.

"I'm fine," Albert said, feeling almost sick with panic, racking his brain for some way to explain what he had done that wouldn't be totally humiliating. "I don't need all this. I'm fine."

Trey walked up and said with fake sincerity, "What's going on? Is Albert okay?"

"Albert told me he was having a heart attack," Freddy said.

Albert looked at him and a way out became horribly clear. He hesitated, hoping a more courageous Albert would appear and stop him, but then he spoke. "What are you talking about, Freddy?"

Freddy blinked. "What do you mean? You told me you were having a heart attack. You said—"

"I wouldn't have done that, Freddy," Albert said. "I said I wasn't feeling great and that I might go to the nurse's office. I never told you to go all dramatic."

"Go all dramatic?" Freddy screeched. "But—"

"Freddy, calm down," the principal said.

"It was probably something I ate," Albert went on. "I *was* feeling bad. So I stepped out the emergency exit to get some air." He looked at the principal. "I'm sorry. I know I shouldn't have done that. But then I realized I felt okay, so I came back in and everybody was freaking out." He glanced at the principal and the three paramedics. "I'm really sorry. But I don't need an ambulance or anything."

By now Raul had approached and hit Freddy on the arm. "Way to exaggerate, Freddy."

Freddy's face reddened. "But—" He looked at Albert with such hurt in his eyes that Albert had to look down. To admit that what he did was wrong was too much for Albert to bear in the moment, so he pushed down his guilt and turned to the nurse with a big smile. "You don't have to call my mom. I should get to class."

Freddy walked away.

"Let's do a quick vitals check before dismissing these guys." The nurse nodded toward the paramedics. "Just to be on the safe side."

As she lifted her stethoscope, Albert's hand flew to his chest. The Z-da! After his hygg on board the ITV, he had changed into his Earth clothes and had put the Z-da back around his neck. Quickly, he pulled it over his head, hoping to get it out of sight without calling attention to it, but Trey exclaimed loudly, "Cool-looking necklace, Albert! Where's it from?"

"It's nothing," Albert said, stuffing it into his pocket.

The principal glanced back, noticing Trey and the others who were still hanging around, and turned to face them. "The bell's about to ring," he said. "Everybody hit the road."

Albert's classmates walked, but he knew what was coming. Trey would tell Raul and Jessica about the incident with Tackle and how crazy Albert had acted when the dog got ahold of his pendant. *Albert's got a necklace!* They were going to give him a hard time about it later, Albert knew, in front of everybody. Jessica would probably tell her friends, and girls would tease him, too. *Albert's got a necklace!* As if it were any of their business. That was how it worked in middle school. Dare to change anything about yourself, and everybody had to comment.

His heart rate *was* high, not dangerously, but higher than average. And to Albert's dismay, because of the "family history," the principal insisted on calling his mother on the spot with his cell phone, and she picked up immediately.

"Please tell her I'm okay right away," Albert said, and the principal did. But at the mention of "high heart rate," she panicked.

"Can I just talk to her?" Albert asked, and the principal handed him his phone.

"Mom—I'm fine—"

"Albert, what's going on?" Her voice was shaking with fear.

Albert closed his eyes, wishing he could go back and undo everything. "It was a misunderstanding," he said. "Freddy Mills overreacted when I said I was feeling bad. That's all."

"Feeling bad how?"

"Just a little upset stomach, Mom. I'm fine. Probably something I ate."

He managed to calm her down, but she insisted he go to the nurse's office and wait for her. She wanted to come and take him to his pediatrician. The paramedics left, and then the bell rang for the next period to start.

In the school's sickroom, the nurse asked Albert to lie down on a cot, and she checked his vitals a second time. "Nice cologne," she said.

"What?" Albert blushed.

"Very piney." She smiled. "Most middle school boys pick something terrible."

The smell that emanated from the zees must have clung to his hair. "Um…thanks," he said, and tried to smile back.

"I'm glad you're feeling better now. But I think a check-in with your pediatrician is a good idea," she said. "Your heart rate *is* high."

Yours would be, too, if you'd just returned from outer space and betrayed someone who was trying to be nice and almost gave your mother a heart attack, he thought.

She felt his forehead again. "You don't look super great, either."

"Thanks," Albert said darkly.

She smiled. "A little depleted is what I meant. Anything you're anxious about? A test? Homework? Peer stuff? Anxiety can sometimes bring on all kinds of things—stomachaches, racing heart."

"I'm not anxious about anything," Albert insisted.

She nodded and told him to rest.

After fifteen minutes, his mom swooped in, relieved to see him. While she called the pediatrician, he was sent to get his phone and backpack in order to leave for the day.

On the drive, his mother told him that the nurse thought the higher heart rate could be the result of anxiety. "Are you feeling anxious, Albert?" She glanced over.

Instinctively, Albert felt his pocket to make sure the Z-da was still there. "No."

"I have to be honest. You do seem anxious." She glanced at him again. "It's okay to talk about it. Everybody feels anxious from time to time. The nurse said you went out the emergency exit to get some air, which sounded to her like a panic attack."

"It wasn't a panic attack. Yeah, I was feeling a little anxious, I guess, and that's why I went out. But I'm okay now."

"Well, when you *were* feeling anxious, what was it about?"

Albert tried to think of the least complicated thing to say. "Just the clarinet."

"The clarinet?" She was surprised.

"Um, yeah. I'm not improving. It's getting kind of frustrating. You know, the whole band thing. There's this concert in November and I'm just feeling way too stressed out—"

For a second, Albert thought this new lie was genius. He could switch out of band and back to art. He wouldn't have to see more of Freddy, who would probably be furious with him for the rest of his life; he wouldn't have to see Trey and Jessica walking out of Jazz Band; and he wouldn't have to spend time practicing. A win-win-win.

"I've got it! We'll get you private lessons!" his mom said, tapping the wheel with excitement.

Albert's heart sank and he geared up to protest, but then she was pulling into the parking lot of the doctor's office and asking him to call Erin to let her know that, since Mom was taking the afternoon off, she could pick Erin up from school.

When Erin started screaming at him on the phone for hiding the cartoon of her gymnastics rival in her sandwich, he ended the call. The universe was probably paying him back for that unkind deed right now. Dr. Jarvis was going to see the alien implants in his ear and his nose and send him off to the CIA, and then the FJF would hear about it and beam him to some kind of prison on Pluto.

Trying to hide his anxiety, he went in, smiling at the receptionist and the nurse, and then he was in the blue-and-red exam room with his mom and Dr. Jarvis was pulling out her otoscope to look in his ear.

"You don't have to do that!" Albert exclaimed nervously. "My ears are fine."

"It's like checking under the hood of a car, Albert," Dr. Jarvis said, peeking into the right ear. "I like to make sure all the parts are working. That one looks dandy. Turn your head a little." She stuck the scope into the left ear, and Albert held his breath. A few seconds passed, and the room seemed to grow hot.

"Wait…I think I see something…," Dr. Jarvis said, peering closer.

A prickle of sweat appeared on Albert's forehead.

"Your brain!" the doctor said, and set down the scope with a laugh. Albert's mom laughed, too.

Albert exhaled. Hilarious.

"Catherine, remember when you brought Albert in with nasal congestion when he was four?" the doctor asked as she picked up another scope.

"I do," Albert's mom said, and started laughing again.

The doctor smiled at Albert. "I looked up your nose, Albert, and found an entire almond!" She laughed. "I asked you how it got there, and you said very calmly said, 'My nose likes to eat.'"

Albert gave her an obligatory smile as she continued the exam.

When she was done she gave him a pat on the knee. "Healthy as a horse," she said. "But thanks for keeping me in business."

6.0

That night, Albert couldn't sleep. In the morning, he woke up with an actual stomachache, and his mom told him to stay home.

Albert had heard that stress could lead to stomach ulcers, which sounded horribly painful, and he thought he might be developing one. Knowing that stress increased the risk, he tried to stop thinking, but that only made him more stressed out. There was absolutely no way to win, he thought sadly.

At around 10 a.m., Albert's door opened with a bang, and his grandmother rolled in.

"Time to get up," she said, bumping into his bed with the footrest of her wheelchair.

"I'm sick," he said, keeping his eyes closed. "Stomachache."

She was silent for a moment; then she said, "Look at me, Albert."

She had a round face with thin lips and heavy lines that he noticed more when she was serious. Her cheeks—two pink knobs on either side of a pudgy nose—flushed easily. Albert wasn't sure how long her silvery hair was because she always wore it in a long braid that she wound into a bun pinned on the top of her head.

"There are all kinds of reasons why a person gets a stomachache," she said. "Food poisoning, viruses, ulcers, tumors—"

"This isn't making me feel better, Nana—"

She leaned in. "And then there's fear. It travels to the stomach, but it lives up here." She tapped a finger on the side of her head. "And it's important to recognize when it's kicking up a rumpus."

He blinked. "I'm not afraid of anything. I just have a stomachache, really."

Again, a pause.

"I know your mother told you to stay in bed, but often what the body needs is a bit of shaking up." She nodded at the window. "Get out there."

"Are you telling me to go outside?"

She shrugged. "Fresh air. A bounce or two on your sister's trampoline."

"A bounce or two? With a stomachache? What do you want me to do? Throw up?"

She smiled. "An experiment. If you throw up, I'll eat my hat." She reached into her knitting bag and pulled out a little orange beanie. "Actually I just finished knitting one!" She tossed him the hat and gave his foot a squeeze through his blanket.

"I'll get up," he said. "But I'm not jumping on that trampoline."

Still in his pajamas and bare feet, he walked into the

backyard. The September morning had that bright, breezy, you-should-be-in-school feel. He sat on the bench at the edge of their patio and turned his attention inward. His stomach did hurt, but maybe it was fear. Was fear a shawble? If so, he had a lot of it.

Fear that he wouldn't be able to balance school homework, clarinet practice, the extra chores to pay for his phone, and all his responsibilities to the Zeenods, including three practices a week on Zeeno, plus the new training tutorial lessons at home.

Fear that he wouldn't be able to find a truly safe space at school for the next szoǔ, which was supposed to be tomorrow.

Fear that he would make a fool of himself at the next practice and never master the ahn or the zees.

Fear that the Zeenods would discover that they had meant to choose *Alfred Kenney* instead of Albert Kinney and that *Alfred Kenney,* whoever he was, would find out and be furious with him for not confessing that he knew they had the wrong guy.

Fear that Trey would find out that he wasn't on any travel team and tell the world what a liar he was.

Fear that Vatria would destroy his confidence.

Fear that Vatria would destroy *him.*

Fear that he would quit and have to go back to being a nobody.

Fear that he would play and lose, sending Zeenods everywhere into a horrible depression.

He stood up and began to pace, wondering about Lightning Lee. Had Lee gone through this? Maybe the situation hadn't been as hard back then because Zeeno had its freedom. But still, the tournament was a big deal. Had Lee been plagued by fears? Albert understood the reasoning behind Kayko's decision that he should have no contact with Lee, but he wished he could get some advice.

The sliding glass doors to the patio opened slightly and his nana called out. "Set yourself a goal for the day, no matter how small. If you're not going to exercise, then practice your clarinet."

"Why bother?" he muttered, sitting back down. "I'm practicing every day and I'm not getting any better."

"That's because you keep playing that same song."

"But that's the only song I can play that sounds okay."

"Exactly. That's the problem, Albert," she said. "You have to practice what you *can't* do, otherwise it isn't practice." She closed the door and then opened it. "Set a goal," she added, and then Albert was alone again.

My goal for the day, Albert thought, is to figure out how to use the Z-da to get a message to Kayko that I'm quitting. Whoever they picked as their alternate Star Striker could have the job.

A sound came from the back of the Pattersons' house, one that Albert knew well: the dog door opening and Tackle bounding out. Albert could hear the dog stop near the fence, and then the barking began.

"Shut up," Albert said, getting up again. For the lack of anything better to do, he climbed through the trampoline's safety net and hoisted himself up. Once there, he stretched out on his back, looking up at the clouds and feeling the vibrations of the springs through the canvas under him.

The dog howled.

Albert howled back.

A second of silence, and then the barking resumed.

Albert focused on the warmth of the sunshine on his face. It felt good. After a few seconds, he stood and tried a bounce. His feet slipped out from under him when he landed, and he fell onto his back.

When his mom had first bought this trampoline, it was for both him and Erin. His sister was only five at the time, but she was better than he was and had made it look so easy, he had immediately given up. Now, he thought about his grandmother's admonition: *practice what you can't do, otherwise it isn't practice.* He got up and started jumping again, finding it hard to keep from stumbling on the return.

Each time he popped above the fence line, the dog looked up at him with surprise. The barking shifted from loud and constant to one bark when he was at the top of each jump.

"This is actually good zee training," he said to the dog, trying to keep his balance at the top and remain in an upright position all the way down. "Okay, my goal is to get at least one good jump in twelve tries."

After a dozen attempts, he started to improve. Each time he imagined that he was bouncing on a zee, and his body started to work with him instead of against him. Head up. Chest up. Use the arms. Bend the knees. He jumped a few more times, tightening his stomach muscles and breathing more heavily, the dog's bark at the top of each jump providing a kind of rhythm for his work-out. He tried to do what Ennjy had suggested, to send energy. At first, he wasn't sure how to do it. Then he imagined that his Zee-nod teammates were standing around the trampoline and that they were sending energy to him, which stabilized him without restraining him, supporting him as he jumped. Instead of letting his mind wander or criticize, he focused on sending energy back out to his invisible team.

"If you would stop barking," he said to the dog, "it would be way easier to focus."

6.1

Grrr. Tackle stopped barking for a moment and stared at the squirrel-machine in the tree. It was perched on that high branch, facing the Kinneys' property, and its head had swiveled toward Albert when he had first emerged into the backyard and had stayed locked on him ever since. The dog thought for sure that when Albert began bouncing, Albert would notice the thing. After all, his bounces were bringing him closer and closer to the machine's height. Finally, an opportunity for Albert to discover what the dog knew: danger was present.

Up Albert bounced. Either leaves were hiding the machine from Albert's view or Albert was too focused on his exercise.

Albert, the dog barked. *Man… if only you could understand.*

6.2

"Sounds like Tackle is frustrated about something," Nana said, rolling out onto the patio and gazing toward the Pattersons'.

"I wish he would stop," Albert said, continuing his jumps. "But look. I'm already jumping better."

"Fabulous!" Nana said. "Nothing like practice!"

"I feel better," Albert said, slowing his jumps, thinking about

Erin's springboard and vault in the garage. "I'm going to start working out more. I want to get stronger and more coordinated."

"Good goals."

Albert spotted a soccer ball by the bench. "Hey, Nana, I know this sounds totally weird, but will you throw me that ball? I want to see if I can kick it in midair. You know, just for fun," he added.

"Sure. Fun is good. Fun is important."

As she rolled over to pick up the ball, Albert realized it would be hard for her to throw the ball over the safety net from the wheelchair. "Sorry," he said. "I'll come out and get it."

"No! This will be good for me. I'm supposed to develop my upper-arm strength." She scooped the ball into her lap and positioned her wheelchair. Then she lifted the ball over her head and heaved.

The thing sailed over the trampoline.

"Whoa, Nana!" Albert watched it slam against one of the branches of the sweet gum tree and—luckily—bounce back into their own yard. At the same time, he noticed something brownish fall from the tree into the Pattersons' yard and assumed it was a leafy section of a branch.

6.3

The squirrel-machine hit the ground and Tackle pounced on it. What luck! This time, he decided, he would not risk sending it over the fence.

With ferocious determination, he tore through the fur and ripped the metal thing limb from limb, crunching each part into bits. Efficiently, he dug holes and buried the pieces separately. More than two dozen holes, sporadically placed around the yard. This machine would not rise again.

6.4

"You're a beast, Nana." Albert hopped down from the trampoline to get the ball.

She laughed. "I guess I'm stronger than I look."

"Good thing it didn't land in the Pattersons' yard. Tackle would probably have shredded it."

"All's well that ends well," Nana said. "Let's see what you can do."

As his grandmother watched patiently, Albert tried bouncing the ball as he jumped, hoping to get it bouncing high enough that he could try kicking it in midair. The first few minutes were chaotic, with the ball either not making it up high enough, or else bouncing away and hitting the net or hitting him.

After about ten failed attempts, he switched to holding it as he jumped and then releasing it and trying to kick it as they both fell. Of course, that wouldn't be the way it happened on a zee, but it would give him some practice connecting with a ball in midair.

After twenty more failed attempts, he remembered to focus on sending his energy out rather than on criticizing his failures. He finally got one kick in, and the ball sailed over the trampoline's safety net, bounced off the roof of their shed, and landed in a dirt-filled wheelbarrow near their flower bed.

"Goal!" Nana said, and they both laughed as Tackle howled.

Albert climbed down, so pleased that he gave his nana a huge smile before running to get the ball.

"I love this energy, Albert," Nana said. "When you work hard, work hard, but find the joy, too."

After lunch, he practiced clarinet. This time, he tried something different. He tried playing the hard song that he had been avoiding, the one that had three notes he couldn't play. He played it for about ten minutes, trying to stay positive, and on the final try, the song sounded almost not bad.

His Spanish homework was so easy he was actually able to get it done more quickly than he expected, so when Nana went into the den for her afternoon nap, Albert gave himself a new goal: to get started on the training tutorial. Between now and the first game, he was supposed to do the first three lessons in the program as many times as possible. They would help him deal with some of his shawbles, Kayko had said. If he got started on lesson number one, maybe he would feel ready for the next practice tomorrow.

Thinking he might need more space, he took his Z-da and his

phone into the garage, which had been turned into a gymnastics practice space for Erin. He sat on one of the mats and began the process of copying the training tutorial from his Z-da to his phone, which Unit B had said would make the program easier to use if he wanted to do a lesson at home or at school without arousing suspicion.

A light blinked, indicating the copy was complete. He opened the program and saw three options: audio only, which was beamed directly to the translation device in his ear; video, which could be viewed and heard on the phone; or "volumetric display," which required activating a "volumetric-display projector" app that was part of the download.

Since he was alone in the garage, he decided to see what the volumetric-display projection was all about. He set his phone on the mat in front of him and tapped the VDP button.

A beam of bluish-green light came out of the flashlight lens of his phone and a free-floating image jumped into three-dimensional form. It wasn't a personal trainer, though. Hovering over him was a horrifying monster with the muscular body of a Tev and the massive head of a Gaböq, wings like a dragon, claws like a tiger, and a thick, oily-looking tail. Its hands clenched and unclenched as it moved toward Albert.

Albert kicked the phone away as he scooted back on the mat. The garage had grown suddenly hot, as if the thing were radiating warmth. It's a projection, Albert told himself, and the heat is just my own temperature rising. But that glint in the thing's eyes and the undulation of that oily tail—

Albert scrambled to his feet and picked up a baseball bat.

They stood eyeing each other, Albert trying to work up the courage to leap forward and grab his phone.

Then the creature spoke, and the hushed, low growl stole the strength in Albert's knees. "This is your final warning, Albert Kinney. If you play, you will die." With a sound like the sucking in of air, the creature's wings unfurled, and thousands of spikes emerged from the stretched skin. The voice rose to a roar. "No one will be able to save you. Do you understand?"

Shaking, Albert swung the bat at the hologram and dove onto the mat for the phone. He pressed Off, but the program froze in a loop, the creature's mouth opening and the first syllable of a growl looping over and over. "No. No. No. No."

At that very moment, Albert heard the sound of a car in the driveway, and the garage door began to slowly rise.

He blocked the light with one hand and pressed the Off button again, but the light blinked against his hand and the audio kept going. The car stopped in the driveway, and Albert saw Erin and his mother preparing to get out. As he turned to hustle inside, he stuffed the phone in his pocket, which stopped the projection of the image and slightly muffled the growling chant.

"Albert, wait!" his mother called out. "I need your help unloading! I stopped at the garden center."

On the shelf next to the door was their mom's old boombox with music that his sister liked to play when she was working out. Panicking, he flicked it on and turned up the volume to drown out the audio coming from his pocket. Sweat was beading on his forehead.

"I hope you notice me, baby. I'm trying hard to be your man. I'm doing everything I can. Don't Go. Don't Go." The song played on.

A desperate instinct kicked in and Albert jumped into a series of aerobic exercises to the beat of the music.

Erin started laughing at him.

"You hate that song," she said, hopping out of the car with her gym bag.

Still shaking, he put everything he had into pretending that what he was doing made sense. "I'm exercising," he said, picking up the bat and lifting it up and down as if it were a barbell. Faintly he could hear the growl coming from his pocket, so he began to sing—loudly. *"I'm trying hard to be your man! I'm doing everything I can."*

His mom couldn't help laughing, although she tried to hide it. He knew he looked and sounded ridiculous, but there was no turning back. It was as if he'd jumped on an accelerating train and now he couldn't jump off.

"Nana said exercising would make me feel better and she was right…." He set the bat down and began doing jumping jacks. *"I'm trying hard to be your man! I'm doing everything I can."*

"You're officially insane." His sister laughed and walked into the house.

Albert kept going. "You can go in, too, Mom! I'll unload the car in a minute. I'm almost done."

"Well, at least it looks like you're feeling better," she said, and began to head inside. "Bring everything out to the back patio when you're done."

Albert kept the act going, jumping into a squat and singing even louder. Then he got a glimpse of someone on the sidewalk outside: Trey, staring at him with a smile on his face, having been standing there for who knew how long.

"Nice routine," Trey said. "But where's your pink sparkly costume and why weren't you at school?"

Albert turned his back and quickly hit the button to close the garage door.

"Wait! You look terrified," Trey called out. "What's going on with you, Albert?"

Although the door was closing, Trey ran forward. "Come on, Albert! Talk to me!"

For a moment, Albert thought Trey would make it in, and the thought of having to deal with him made him feel almost sick, but the door closed before Trey could duck under it.

As soon as he was alone, Albert pulled the phone out of his pocket, covering the front to block the image from reappearing. Fumbling, he turned down the volume and then finally powered down the entire phone. In a daze, he walked over and turned off Erin's music. The garage was silent for a few moments. A trickle of sweat ran down his neck. He breathed in, startled by the smell of his own fear.

If you play, you will die.

6.5

Much to report. First, another unexpected blow. Through today's earlier spybot footage, I saw Kinney happily exercising outside. Surprisingly the grandmother tried throwing him a ball. Of course she had terrible aim,

and it hit my spybot! Even after the fall, the camera
was still working, but then the canine pounced.

I initiated remote self-repair, but the bot is not
responding. I hate that dog. I should have eliminated
it upon first arrival. The squirrel was the first robot
I created based on an Earth life-form, and I had grown
fond of it.

Stop. Believe in your brilliance. You will succeed.

He pulled his robotic tarantula-like comfort pet from his pocket
and petted its head. It crawled up his arm and nestled against his
neck, purring.

Reframe.

The loss of the squirrel is manageable. The hologram
worked and will, no doubt, have an effect on Kinney.
Patience.

The botmaker closed his log and rubbed the top of his gheet's
head. His stomach hurt. He realized he had forgotten to eat.

7.0

"Albert! Hey, Albert, wait up."

Albert heard Trey's voice loud and clear behind him in the noisy hallway on the way to Spanish class. The hologram yesterday had shaken Albert completely. He hadn't been able to eat dinner. Hadn't slept.

"I'm just wondering if something scary happened in your garage yesterday," Trey said, catching up. "You can tell me, man. I mean, if there's something going on."

Albert stopped and looked at him. The sight of his old friend's face was confusing—a glimpse of the old Trey was definitely in there. Albert hesitated. "I don't know what you're talking about, Trey."

Raul's voice came next, calling out for Trey to wait for him. Jessica Atwater was with him. Trey gave Albert a look, then turned to Raul and adopted that new mocking voice. "You should have seen this guy yesterday. He was doing a dance routine."

Albert turned abruptly and walked on.

"Do it! I want to see it!" Raul called out, laughing.

"I don't see your necklace today," Trey said, following Albert. "Why aren't you wearing it, Albert?"

Albert kept walking, seeing Freddy Mills out of the corner of his eye, approaching from the right.

"I thought you got onto a soccer team, not *Dancing with the Stars*, Kinney," Trey called out. "Or are you going into gymnastics now?"

Raul said, "I think he's joining the Special Olympics Gymnastics Team."

Trey laughed.

Albert didn't look back, but he could hear Freddy. "You guys shouldn't make fun of Special Olympics. Those athletes are amazing." As Freddy continued to stand up to them, Albert rushed ahead.

After all that dancing around yesterday, there had been no way Albert could convince his mom he was sick again. I should have cut off my arm, he thought. Anything would be better than this.

Somehow, he got through his morning classes; at lunch, he was extra careful before sneaking into the boys' bathroom and locking himself in a stall.

His plan was to activate the Z-da and go to Zeeno and talk with Kayko one-on-one. Tell her about the hologram threat. Tell her about his fear. Tell her everything. Truthfully, he would have preferred to tell Unit B and then return to school without even making the trip, but he wasn't sure he could trust the robot. She was the one who had downloaded Kayko's lessons to his Z-da, after all.

He pulled the necklace out of his pocket and stared at it. There was one thought that was giving him hope, a thought that had occurred to him somewhere between fourth and fifth periods this morning. The Z-da could be malfunctioning. The threatening message could have been a fragment from something like a video game, a hologram training game that got out of whack. Maybe Tackle had damaged the Z-da when he had caught it in his mouth and there was no one actively trying to kill him. It was a thought. On the other hand, someone might have gone to the trouble to warn him for good reason. Glancing down, he thought maybe he should just flush the Z-da down the toilet and be done with the whole johka thing. He definitely wouldn't miss Vatria or the Tevs or the stress of wondering who he could trust.

Then he thought about Kayko and Ennjy and Doz and all the others. He pictured the way they connected with the ahn and the way their eyes turned gold. The right thing, the courageous thing to do would be to go.

You can do this, Albert Kinney, he said to himself. Just go and talk to Kayko. Hoping he wouldn't regret it, he brought the Z-da to his lips, covered the top left hole, and blew.

The szoŭ was initiated, and Albert felt the usual sliding-up sensation before blacking out.

But when he thumped into place, he was sitting on board an unfamiliar ITV. More of an empty, airborne closet, really, with one window, four blank walls, and one cold steel chair.

Albert stood up. "Unit B? Hello?"

A notification rang out from a computer that Albert couldn't see. Thanks to the device in his ear, it was immediately translated into English.

"Kidnapping of Albert Kinney complete."

7.1

Albert knew deep in his gut. This was it. He had made a fatal mistake in activating the szoǔ.

The whir of the computer in the front of the spacecraft and a faint rumbling in the rear was all Albert could hear. "Unit B?" he asked.

A few seconds of cold silence passed.

"Trajectory set for the event horizon of Black Hole 3275," the computer said. "Zero percent chance of survival."

With a strange detachment, he listened as the message repeated.

Ms. Holly loved black holes. Back in the fifth grade, his teacher played a NASA animation video that showed a cute cartoon alien traveling toward a relatively small black hole. As the cartoon guy neared the area around the black hole called the event horizon, he was pulled apart and stretched out in a process that Ms. Holly had laughingly referred to as "spaghettification."

A vivid memory popped into his mind of the fifth-grade Jessica

Atwater for some reason. She had just gotten a radical haircut, Albert recalled, and he had been aware how great it looked. They were in Ms. Holly's class, and after the NASA animation, Jessica raised her hand and said something extraordinary out loud. She said, "Sometimes I think I can feel a black hole in my soul."

There was a second of silence, and Albert remembered turning to look at Jessica, thinking that it was brave to say such a thing and wanting to know more about what she meant, but then a number of the kids laughed, and Jessica's face—framed by her cute new haircut—had turned bright red as she realized that her comment was a terribly odd one that she should have kept to herself.

In that moment, Albert remembered feeling her embarrassment *with* her, watching her face and yet aware that his own face was growing hot, almost as if he had made the comment himself. Probably because he had been in that position so many times— feeling that wave of shame at his own poor judgment. He remembered wanting to lean over and tell her it was an interesting comment, but that was a risk he hadn't taken.

For a moment, as the spaceship he was in careened toward destruction, he was quite calm, and a complex set of thoughts occurred to him. How amazing that back in the fifth grade, he had been able to feel Jessica's pain, as if some kind of invisible thread had connected her soul to his. And how amazing that he was remembering it so vividly now. And why hadn't he had the courage at the time to reach out to her? Was that a shawble? He flashed back to Raul's boneheaded comment about the Special Olympics and how Freddy Mills had stood up to him when he hadn't. Why didn't he have that kind of courage? Would he ever get that kind of courage? How?

The whole matter of life was a mystery. He imagined the entire timeline of evolution—from the big bang to amoebas to dinosaurs to hominids to people. He imagined those historic figures who started all the wars and he imagined the ordinary people, too, the people who built schools and made black-hole videos and got haircuts and laughed at or sympathized with each other. He imagined the fifth-grade Albert growing up to be the seventh-grade Albert who was now recalling the fifth-grade Albert at the most unlikely time.

How ironic, Albert thought. If he had taken the cowardly path of quitting by simply not initiating the szoŭ, he wouldn't be flying to his certain death. And this last thought punctured Albert's moment of calm. His certain death.

He was not ready.

He was so not ready.

He opened his mouth and what came out was like nothing he had ever uttered: a trapped animal's scream. The scream was long and loud and still going when another sound entered Albert's ear.

"Albert? Albert, can you hear us?"

Albert froze.

"Albert, this is Kayko. Unit B, Ennjy, and I are in your usual ITV. We are approaching and transmitting audio through your Z-da. Can you hear us?"

For a brief moment, Albert felt a rush of relief. He ran over to the window and looked out at the emptiness of space. "I don't see you. What's going on? Is this some kind of training exercise?"

Unit B's voice came through the Z-da. "This is not a simulation. You are in a rogue ITV that is programmed to fly into Black Hole 3275. Approximately seventy seconds until—"

"Get me out of here!" Albert screamed.

"We tried," the robot said calmly, "but the function to enable a szoŭ from your ITV to our ITV is not working."

"What?!"

Unit B spoke to Kayko, but the audio was clear enough for Albert to hear. "We are approaching the danger zone and risk also losing this vehicle, which contains two life-forms and a robot. It is most rational to abandon this rescue mission and set trajectory back to Zeeno."

The moment of silence that followed brought with it a horrible chill. And then, just as Albert was preparing to hear the worst, Kayko's warm voice came through. "Don't worry, Albert. We are not surrendering the fight."

Ennjy's voice came next. "We're with you, Albert. Take a breath."

A rush of gratitude flooded him and he blinked back the tears that were surfacing.

"Access a copy of the ITV1000 operations manual," Kayko said to Unit B. "There must be a way to gain control."

Another notification came from the ITV1000's computer. "Sixty seconds."

"Albert, listen," Kayko said. "We have information! The panel on the wall in the front of the ship will open if you tap it twice."

Her calm instruction gave Albert something other than his own panic on which to focus. "Which is the front?" He ran around thumping the walls until a sensor beeped and one wall slid open. A panel containing a bank of buttons and levers that looked somewhat similar to the controls on Unit B's ITV was revealed. "It's open," he said.

"Push the green button to remove autopilot," Kayko said. "You need to pilot the craft."

"Me?"

"Push the green button, Albert."

There were two green buttons. Albert pushed one and a ridiculous song, an orchestral thing, began to play. He pushed the other one and was notified that autopilot was now stopped.

"I heard that!" Kayko yelled. "Pull back on the black throttle firmly while slowly turning the white steering wheel all the way to the right."

Every feature of the complex panel competed for Albert's attention. "How am I supposed to know where those are?" he cried.

"Thirty seconds," the ITV's system announced.

Ennjy spoke again. "Take a breath, Albert. Listen to my voice."

Albert breathed in, and in that moment he noticed a steering wheel on his right and a throttle on his left. "Okay. I'm pushing the throttle..."

The ITV's speed increased.

"Pull, don't push!" Kayko yelled.

"Steer to the right at the same time!" Unit B said.

Albert pulled back on the throttle and then turned the white wheel all the way to the right. The ITV did a sharp 180, slamming him against the wall and to the floor.

"Whoa! Decrease speed, Albert!"

"I can't do this!" Albert said.

"You can," Ennjy said. "Put your hands on the controls and focus on Kayko's voice."

Albert got up and ran back to the controls. His life wasn't the only one on the line. They wouldn't leave him, which meant he had to get out. Shaking, he put his right hand on the wheel and his left on the throttle.

"Are you there?" Ennjy asked.

"Here," Albert said. "Ready."

"Turn with the right and pull back with the left," Kayko said calmly.

Albert listened to her words and turned the wheel slowly with the right while pulling back slightly on the throttle. The ship turned.

"Trajectory altering," the ITV's computer said. "Chances for survival fifteen percent."

"Excellent!" Kayko's voice was jubilant. "Increase speed slightly, Albert. Hold the wheel steady with the right and push forward slightly with the left."

Albert took a breath and pushed the heavy black knob forward, feeling the spacecraft respond.

"Exiting danger zone," the computer said. "Chances for survival fifty percent."

Through the window, an ITV came into view. "I see you!" Albert exclaimed, hope rising.

"Full throttle now," Kayko said. "We're both going to move forward at top speed. Push the throttle forward all the way with the left but do not allow the right to move. On the count of three. One, two, three."

Albert pushed the throttle forward all the way, and the spacecraft took off. As the force kicked in, he instinctively placed both hands on the wheel to steady the tugging, his eyes glued to the speeding taillights of the ITV ahead of him. "I'm doing it!" he cried out, and within seconds the computer's voice came through: "Trajectory reset to Zeeno."

"You did it!" Kayko said.

A wave of relief hit and ushered forth a burst of tears. Too nervous to let go of the wheel and wipe the mess away, Albert laughed.

"Follow us," Ennjy said. "And we'll lead you safely to Zeeno."

And then all three of the voices in the ITV yelled: "Decrease speed!"

Before plowing into his friends, he pulled back on the throttle.

"Much better," Kayko said.

"Yeah," Albert said. "Sorry about that."

"You'll need to stay engaged and attentive," Ennjy said. "But you can begin to relax."

Albert took another breath and relaxed his hands on the controls, accelerating slightly to catch back up and then keeping his speed steady, staying focused on the lovely gold taillight of his friends' ITV glowing in the vast blackness of space.

"Good. Good," he heard Ennjy say.

In the quiet, Albert noticed that the music that he had inadvertently activated by pushing the first green button was still playing. It was an otherworldly song, created by instruments that were different from anything he had ever seen or heard on Earth. Now that he listened, it was a beautiful piece of music, which had the effect of both calming down his nerves and lifting up his spirits.

His mind flew back to the marvelous mystery of life. How amazing that the universe had evolved in such a way that life created and enjoyed music on different planets with different instruments. How amazing that he, Albert, was able to appreciate that while hurtling through space.

"Thank you for coming to get me," he said, finally reaching up to wipe his eyes. "It was an amazing thing for you guys to do. I don't know—I don't know what to say."

"I advised against it," Unit B said.

Kayko laughed. "Don't listen to her."

"Based on your shawbles, I assumed you would not be capable," Unit B said. "My job is to calculate risk and make suggestions—"

"Which we don't have to follow," Kayko interrupted.

His life had been hanging by a fine thread, and his friends had chosen to take the risk.

The ITV ahead of him dipped to the right and he followed, starting to almost enjoy the action of piloting now that he wasn't hurtling. Specks of light twinkled into view.

"I have so many questions," Albert said. "How did you guys know I was in this ITV? How did you find me?"

"Unit B was expecting your szoŭ summons. When it didn't happen, we thought you had lost your Z-da. Earthlings are known to lose things, so when I first programmed your Z-da, I thought it might be useful to add a location mechanism, a *find-the-Z-da* alert. This is not a feature that we use here in the Fŭigor Solar System because we do not lose things. So, when Unit B notified us that she didn't receive a szoŭ summons, I activated the location mechanism and, thankfully, that worked. It notified us that you were in an unpiloted ITV heading toward Black Hole 3275."

"We are concerned that your Z-da malfunctioned and will investigate," Ennjy said.

Unit B said, "I recommend that this situation be viewed as a deliberate malicious intention, not a malfunction."

"What?" Kayko's voice was sharp.

"En route to the Opening, I successfully avoided a DRED and succeeded in tricking it into detonating at a safe distance," Unit B explained.

"What? Why wasn't I informed?" Now Kayko's tone was angry, something Albert had not imagined was possible.

"What's a DRED?" Albert asked, unable, of course, to remember the incident.

Unit B's voice came through as cool and crisp as usual. "A dedicated remote explosive device. My analysis determined that the threat was over and—"

"Withholding critical information from me is a terrible choice!" Kayko said sternly.

"Interrupting speech and blaming others are shawbles," the robot said calmly.

The swirling colors of Kayko's face flushed.

"As for my choices," Unit B continued, "my choices are yours, Kayko Tusq. You are the one who programmed me."

"You are correct," Kayko said. "My error."

Confused, Albert spoke next. "Wait. Did you say explosive device? We were targeted on the way to the Opening?"

"Based on my analysis," Unit B said, "it seemed reasonable to consider the event to be a discrete visual trauma, so I initiated a memory wipe of the event. Based on this new evidence, I am now concluding that the threat did not evaporate when the DRED exploded, but that the threat is ongoing."

The low growl of the threatening hologram replayed in Albert's mind: *If you play, you will die.*

Ennjy's voice came next. "We must face the truth. Someone intends to kill you, Albert Kinney."

7.2

"Did the Z-da signal the rogue ITV?" Feeb whispered, poised to record whatever Kayko had to say.

The team was huddled in a tight circle on the floor of the practice facility. Albert was sipping a nerve-calming smoothie that Ennjy had thoughtfully prepared. Kayko had brought a low bench to the circle to use as a makeshift table, and on it she and Giac were running a diagnostic on Albert's Z-da. Although the wall had been set to privacy mode, they were taking extra precautions by playing music over the speakers and talking softly.

"We don't know. We do know that the kidnapping of Albert was not the only act," Kayko said, and told them about both the DRED and the threatening hologram, which she had learned about from Albert on their way home.

Silence came over the circle.

"I was hoping the hologram was a mistake," Albert said.

Toben reached out and touched Albert's shoulder. "We are relieved to have you with us."

"I sent a message to President Lat," Kayko said. "She expressed her relief that Albert was not harmed and promised to launch an investigation."

"The Tev team did it," Beeda and Reeda said in unison.

"Perhaps not the whole team. Hissgoff?" Doz suggested. "That tactician is brutal."

"It could be Vatria," Albert said. "She said some nasty, threatening things to me."

"What? That is most unlike a Sñekti," Sormie said. "When?"

"At the Opening."

"Threats are a violation of FJF rules," Feeb said. "If there was a witness we could report it. Did anyone else hear it?"

Albert shook his head.

"Although Sñektians are usually verbally respectful, Vatria must have much anger toward all of us, given the history," Feeb said.

"What do you mean, given the history?" Albert asked.

"The Skell family has a grudge against the Zeenods and Lightning Lee," Feeb said. "Vatria's grandfather Paod Skell was a Sñekti Star Striker for Tev. Seventy-five years ago, he played against Lee in that last game before the invasion—and lost. Paod Skell felt as if his loss brought dishonor to his family name."

"But that was so long ago," Albert said.

"On Sñekti, family is everything," Ennjy said. "Now, his grand-daughter Vatria Skell has risen to be the best striker on Sñekti, and the fact that the Tevs have chosen her means that Vatria has a chance to restore honor to the Skell name." She shook her head. "That kind of pressure would be difficult for anyone."

"I tried to be nice to Vatria," Albert said. "After our first practice, I saw her being punished by Hissgoff and tried to sympathize with her."

"Emotional humiliation and physical punishment are common practices on Tev," Ennjy said. "I'm sure she cannot show that she is bothered by that."

Beeda and Reeda both made the same face. "We hate Tevs."

"It's not Tevs you dislike, it's the Tev philosophy," Kayko said gently. "If you were born a Tev and raised by Tevs on Tev, you would have that same way of being."

"To be pitied by another Star Striker would be viewed by the Tevs as added humiliation," Ennjy added. "Sad, but true."

"But—" Albert was about to say that he wasn't skilled or strong enough to be a real threat to Vatria or the Tevs. He was about to say that, from the start, he thought the Zeenods had picked the wrong player in choosing him. He was about to say that maybe he should step down and let whoever was their second choice take his place. He was never going to understand the ahn or be able to perform those tricks with the zees.

"Yes?" Kayko turned toward him. They were all waiting for him to speak, their faces open and trusting. Albert's heart squeezed. He didn't want to leave this circle or hear them say, *Oh, thank you for telling us! We have made a mistake, and now we can correct it.* He felt good when he was with them. Anxious about his abilities on the johka field, yes, but good.

"What is it, Albert?" Ennjy asked.

"I—I was just going to ask Kayko and Giac if they figured out how the Z-da was hacked," Albert said.

Giac spoke. "I found the code for the hologram. Ingenious," she said with admiration. "My guess is that the code was transmitted into the Z-da via its optical port at some point. There's no sign of any code that would serve as a signal for the kidnapping. I'm not sure how that happened. It's possible the two things are unrelated. We can wipe the Z-da clean and reboot it."

"Wait," Albert said. "It was Unit B who loaded the training tutorial onto my Z-da. She's the one who had access to it. What if she hacked it?"

"She is Z-Tev property," Feeb said, "but—"

"Z-Tev property!" Albert yelped.

"Let me finish," Feeb said. "Historically, robots were never a major part of Zeenod culture. As Zeenods, we value life-form intelligence over artificial intelligence so have always placed limits on the number and types of robots in use. We did create robots to serve in certain capacities, but not like the Tevs and Z-Tevs. They love robots and have created them to serve in many capacities— pilots, guards, educators, caregivers, street cleaners, waste removers, et cetera. And many other planets have followed."

Giac stepped in and got to the point. "When our team was accepted by the FJF, the Z-Tev government assigned us a robot chaperone that we had to use. So, yes, technically, Unit B is Z-Tev property."

"This is not making me feel better!" Albert said.

"Albert," Ennjy said. "Not to worry. Once Unit B was assigned to us, Kayko and Giac scanned, reprogrammed, and customized it."

"I understand your concern, Albert," Kayko said. "Just now, before we landed, Giac ran a systems check and updated Unit B's critical-thinking program. It's functioning well."

"It's Hissgoff!" Doz said. "I would bet my bottomest money on it."

Beeda and Reeda nodded. "It has to be a Tev."

"It could be Vatria," Feeb mused, his usual frown growing even deeper. "Whoever is responsible is growing more determined."

"But why?" Albert cried out. "It's just a soccer game!" The room grew silent.

Kayko stood. Although she was thin, there was something immensely solid about her. She knew herself. Every inch of her body and every synapse of her brain and every pulse of her heart. When she looked at Albert, as she was doing now, there was nothing in the way. No self-consciousness, no second-guessing, no posturing, no hidden emotion. "We need to show Albert what's at stake. Show him Zone 3."

175

"Let me," Doz said. "I'll take him."

Sormie shook her head. "Can't we just explain? It's too dangerous to go."

"He needs to see it," Kayko said. "Thank you, Doz, but you know the guards wouldn't allow any of us to leave. Albert, go back to the ITV. Tell the guards that you are not feeling well and that you are leaving practice early to return to Earth. I'll send a message to Unit B. I'll explain that that we want you to see the true Zeeno. Zone 3. I'll tell her to activate the cloak."

Giac's eyes lit up.

"But we haven't really tested that!" Sormie exclaimed. "What if it doesn't work? What if they're stopped by the Z-Tevs?"

Kayko put her hand on Sormie's shoulder. "Giac studied how to cloak an ITV so that we could have a tool for the revolution. A tool to help us to subvert the constant Z-Tev surveillance. It's time to test it out."

Giac nodded.

"Giac and I will be in direct communication with Unit B," Kayko said. "We'll adapt if necessary. Everyone else, resume the training. If anybody checks on us, we need to look as if a normal practice session is occurring."

Giac handed Albert the Z-da. "Fully repaired. You're ready to go."

Albert looked at Kayko.

"One step at a time, Albert. Are you ready?"

7.3

The guards seemed suspicious, but Albert made it into the ITV and they took off, following the typical protocol they would use if returning to Earth, which meant the window screens had to be engaged. Once they were out of range of the normal Z-Tev surveillance, the robot activated the cloaking mechanism, changed her trajectory to Zone 3, and descreened the windows.

Jumping into view in the front window was an approaching local transport vehicle with the official Z-Tev insignia on the front.

"We'll find out if the cloaking mechanism is functional," Unit B said.

Albert stiffened as the ITV grew closer. "What happens if it isn't?"

Unit B said nothing.

Holding his breath, Albert stared at the two massive torpedo-like DREDs mounted on the side of the passing vehicle.

A moment later, they were gone.

"Whew!" Albert exhaled.

"Cloak is functioning," Unit B said into the communications system.

Albert could hear Kayko's and Giac's cheers.

"The Z-Tevs have power and knowledge, but their behavior reveals that they have grown lazy and are underestimating the Zeenods," Unit B said.

Kayko's voice came over the system. "Activate the historic Zeeno view, please."

Unit B tapped a code into the computer and the blackout screen on the window reappeared and then morphed into a scene.

Albert brightened. Below was a view of Zeeno that he had

been expecting to see from the start. Tree-covered mountains on the right and woods on the left, and in the deep and wide valley between were the vast open fields, dotted with zeeruptions, their colors sparkling in the pink sunlight. The ITV soared over the mountain, descending low enough to see a village with houses nestled here and there, at odd angles and random distances, each wrapped as if anchored to the ground in flowering vines. The trees and plants were much more colorful than anything in those science documentaries about the "strangest creatures on planet Earth."

A flock of small multicolored winged creatures flitted up from one tree and Albert gasped.

"Those are the ahda birds," Unit B said.

"Toben was talking about them. They're beautiful."

"They're extinct. Before the Tevs invaded Zeeno, the planet had an abundance of healthy flora and fauna. Zees were also plentiful and vigorous. The Z-Tevs have destroyed habitats by overbuilding without respect for our ecosystem. The loss of plants and animals and fungi depletes the energy of the zees, and without the energy of the zees, the system can't produce new growth. The planet is dying."

"But—" Albert looked out the window.

"A simulation." Unit B turned off the hologram program and activated the window mode. The real Zeeno landscape appeared.

Bleak. Gray. Grids of buildings. Traffic. Z-Tevs and robots everywhere.

"After the invasion, Zeenods were sent to live in zones. We're traveling to the zone where the grandparents of your team were sent to live, where your team grew up, and where your team currently lives except when bused to their practices with you." Unit B turned toward the mountains.

"It's terrible," Albert said.

"Indeed." The robot's voice sounded almost sad.

Albert looked at her. "You know this?"

She blinked. "I have been programmed to know this."

They rode in silence for a while, passing dull, barren land. After a while, Unit B turned again and headed closer to the foothills. Around a bend was a large bleak village with row after row of humble shacks. The whole thing was surrounded by a large wall with a guard's station placed at the entrance. Unit B guided the ITV closer so that Albert could see the desolation of the scene below. His teammates were poor, he realized, poor and imprisoned. He tried to imagine what it would be like if the Tevs landed on Earth and forced him and his family to leave their homes.

"The grandparents of your team were all excellent johka players, and this zone is known for continuing to teach their children how to play the game even under Z-Tev rule." She zipped to the right, and Albert saw a small, scraggly field below, where a johka game was being played. To his eyes the children looked like they were about Erin's age. A handful of parents and grandparents watched from the sidelines.

Unit B contacted Kayko, informing her that they were at the field in Zone 3.

"Go ahead and take him down," Kayko said. "Tell my uncle that I want Albert to see a game."

"What?" Albert panicked.

"The guards are at the other end of the village beyond the wall," Unit B said. "And none of the Zeenods will reveal you."

"Trust them," Kayko added. "Oh, and none of them will be able to speak English, Albert. They cannot afford translation devices."

After Kayko signed off, they landed; and, since they were

far enough away from the front entrance, Unit B uncloaked. By the time they opened the hatch and walked out, the players had stopped midplay and all the players and parents had turned to face them, mouths agape.

One of the oldest stepped forward.

"What is the meaning of this?" the Zeenod asked in a dialect of the Zeeno language.

Unit B replied in the same language. "Kayko Tusq would like Albert Kinney to meet you."

Stunned silence. And then one of the young players said, "Albert Kinney!" Suddenly the kids were all around Albert, bowing and asking him questions.

The coach, Kayko's uncle, introduced himself warily. "My name is Keydo Tusq. We are honored to meet you, Albert Kinney." The older generation of parents and grandparents bowed.

"I am honored to meet all of you," Albert said, the dialect flowing out of his mouth, thanks to his translation device. He bowed.

Clearly anxious, Keydo addressed Unit B. "This visit is a grave risk to—"

"We are cloaked," Unit B said. "Kayko has taken every precaution and feels this is essential for the cause."

"Cloaked." A small smile appeared on the old uncle's lips. "Giac has succeeded."

"Kayko wants me to see a game," Albert said.

The jubilation was intense. The players, shoeless and dressed in rags, took their places on the field with an old semideflated ball, eager to show their beloved game to the Star Striker they had heard so much about. At first, the play was almost familiar. The kickoff, the passes, the defensive blocks, and the shots on goal were similar. A lovely buzz of energy seemed to be in the air.

Keydo leaned in and spoke as Albert watched. "In the old days, every Zeeno child grew up playing johka in whatever village they lived in and everyone in that village came out to watch." His dark green eyes were wistful. "Now, we are only allowed to play in small groups with a limit on the number of villagers who can watch."

"What are they afraid of?" Albert asked.

"When Zeenods watch a johka game, we don't just watch. We send our ahn to the players. Every game generates an astounding amount of energy."

"They're scared the game will make you stronger?"

Keydo nodded. "We have worked hard to keep the Zeenod culture alive. Kayko and the team are now taking great risks. With help, they were finally able to get a petition to the FJF asking for permission to play, and it was received and granted. Although the rules of the FJF have to be followed and although the Tevs and Z-Tevs are pretending that they are delighted that Zeenods are playing in this year's tournaments, in reality, they are frightened. They are worried that if we win, the Zeenods here on Zeeno and the Zeenods who fled to other planets will be emboldened. With the gathering of all our energy, there could be a Zeenod uprising."

A series of passes sent the ball flying across the field; and then, a beautiful interception by a defender stole the ball. The audience cheered.

Keydo's green eyes were starting to turn gold. "Can you feel it?"

Albert nodded as the game continued. "We have it on Earth, too. Sort of. It's a kind of energy. When the team plays well, you feel lifted up and everybody feels it."

As the game continued, the familiar scent of pine hit Albert's nose and he noticed a zee erupting midfield.

When the zee was an inch or so off the ground, a short striker with chubby legs spied it and ran toward it, calling for her team-mate to send her the ball long. Albert could feel the change in the energy of everyone on the field. As the girl, face bright, picked up speed to try a jump-over, Albert could feel the focusing not only of her energy, but of her entire team's energy. The geyser was weak, rising only two feet in the air, but it still would require tremendous finesse to use it as a springboard. You can do it, Albert thought. She hopped on it and was propelled a few feet down the field, where she landed and kept running, receiving the ball from her teammate, kicking it neatly past the keeper, and scoring a goal.

The team went wild.

"That's Kayko's cousin," the uncle said.

Albert smiled but felt a catch in his throat. There was some-thing so different about the way Zeenods played. They were so all-in. He wanted to play with that much heart. He wanted to win for them, and he had never wanted anything so badly in his life.

7.4

The botmaker's superior gave him an odd look when he logged out to take his midday meal outside.

"Who are you?" she asked as he walked past her station. "Did someone steal Mehk?"

Paranoid, he almost panicked, but then she laughed, and he

realized it was a joke. She was saying it because he always worked right through the day, eating at his desk.

He forced a smile and hurried out. The streets were crowded, but he found a secluded spot in one of the trash alleys where no one would bother him to write in his log. He had been as surprised as the Zeenods by the kidnapping and attempted murder of Albert. Glued to the surveillance feed in the ITV, he had watched the rescue with mixed emotions.

```
While I plotted to get Kinney to resign, someone else
plotted an assassination. Someone wants Kinney dead.
Someone with resources. Someone with determination.
Who? Whoever it is must be furious. Outsmarted by a
Zeenod tactician! The fact that Kayko had thought ahead
and programmed an old Earthling-inspired technology, a
find-the-device mechanism, into the Z-da was, I have to
admit, brilliant.
```

He looked up at the mounds of trash being compressed in the various compartments in the alley. Against the backdrop of the whirring machinery, he thought about how even careful plans could get squashed. Impervious to the stench of garbage, he took a breath and returned to his log.

```
Albert Kinney also continues to defy expectations. I
thought that my hologram threat would make him resign.
And then, when I heard the panic in his voice during the
kidnapping, I thought he would never be able to pilot
his way out. Life-forms will always be unpredictable and
therefore impossible to control. Zeenods and Earthlings
```

in particular, perhaps. Why? You need to think about this. In the meantime, keep your masterpiece in place and be patient. The first game is still weeks away.

1. Look for better psychological methods to frighten Kinney into quitting.
2. Brainstorm who is behind the DRED and the kidnapping.
3. Continue monitoring the feed in the ITV.

7.5

Unit B settled herself at the control center and called Kayko. "Albert is hibernating and we are now in autopilot safe zone. I can carry out the task."

"Thank you," Kayko said. "I'm grateful to the president for managing to acquire the new security drone. Detecting malicious interference in either the spacecraft or the Z-da is crucial."

"Message received. Initiating advanced security sweep F54732."

A panel door opened and a drone flew out and began a painstaking sweep over every inch of the vehicle.

Although it passed directly over the grayish stinkbug spybot wedged into the seam between two grayish ceiling panels, the spybot's sophisticated software prevented it from being discovered. No alarm was sounded, and Kayko was given the all clear.

8.0

"*¡Atención!* You have ten minutes to fill in the blanks," Señora Muñoz said. "You may use your book if you need to, but try to do it without looking up the translation first. *¿Me entienden? Muy bien.* Begin."

Albert looked at the two-page list of English words and knew all the Spanish words immediately. With lightning speed, he completed the work and then sat back and thought about the training tutorial.

Ever since returning to Earth, he had been avoiding the sessions. Following Unit B's instructions, he had deleted the hacked training program on his phone and had used his repaired Z-da to reload the correct program last night, but then he hadn't followed through. Yes, a part of him was worried that it wasn't completely fixed and that another threatening hologram would appear. But there was something else. A paradoxical effect was kicking in: the more Albert wanted the Zeenods to win, the more afraid he was that he would fail them. If he tried and failed to do the lessons Kayko had developed, his confidence would plummet, and he needed confidence if he was going to play in a high-stakes tournament in which someone clearly wanted him dead.

When Señora Muñoz wasn't looking, he pulled his phone out of his pocket, opened the training program, clicked Audio Only, and hovered over the Start First Lesson button. Unit B had assured him that he could use this in public, that the "audio only" feature would be beamed directly into the translation device in his ear, like an earbud, and no one else could hear it. Of course, the safest thing would be to test it first in private to make sure it actually worked, but…he glanced at the clock. Seven minutes. Seven minutes with nothing to do. He might as well face his anxiety over this and at least listen to a bit of it. Holding his breath and wincing in anticipation, he started the program.

Welcome to the first lesson: Thought Awareness.

Albert looked around the room. The other students were writing. No one had reacted or glanced over. He picked up his pencil, pretended to turn his attention to the already-completed paper on his desk, and listened to the voice in his ear.

The ahn begins with the breath. In this exercise we breathe in and out. But while we do this, a thought or emotion or feeling may arise and pull our attention away. We will

186

practice simply acknowledging whatever thought or emo-
tion or feeling we are experiencing without judgment. Then
the thought or emotion or feeling can come and go.

Albert gazed at the blank space at the bottom of his paper. Breathing in and out sounded easy enough.

While you are breathing, if fear arises, say to yourself, "I
see fear." If shame arises, say, "I see shame." And so on.
Find a comfortable posture. Close your eyes or allow your
gaze to rest on something neutral.
You will hear a bell to begin this exercise. When you
hear the bell ring again, the exercise will be over. This exer-
cise will last one minute.

One minute, Albert thought. I can do that. Piece of cake. Or as Doz would say, piece of cookie. The thought of Doz made him smile. *Ding…*

To begin, inhale one, two, three, four; hold one, two, three,
four; exhale one, two, three, four.

Albert breathed. *Inhale one, two…* The back of his right knee itched. Don't be stupid and scratch it, he said to himself…exhale one, two…he really needed to inhale. He tried to breathe in… one, two, three—he was off count and his lungs already felt full. He probably had smaller-than-average lungs, he thought, because he was so short. At ten, Erin was already tall for her age. She was proba- bly going to end up taller than him, which was so unfair. If he had to have a negative trait, why did it have to be shortness? Why couldn't he have something that no one could see…like a peanut allergy? Then he could just avoid peanuts, which would be hard because he really did love peanut butter toast in the morning. It was his comfort food. It just smelled so good and filled him up in the right way and—

Ding…

The exercise was over. Startled, he realized that he had completely failed. Failed to breathe. Failed to acknowledge his thoughts without judgment. Failed completely. Forgetting where he was, he cried out, "I'm such an idiot!"

The classroom burst into laughter.

"Do you have a problem, Alberto?" Señora Muñoz asked.

Mortified, Albert picked up his pencil and stared at his desk. "S-sorry."

Still laughing, Trey said, *"Alberto tiene muchos problemas,"* which won him another round of laughter.

8.1

After dismissal, Albert's phone buzzed. A text from his mom.

I'm in the east parking lot. Don't forget your clarinet.

He stopped at his locker, grabbed his instrument, and walked to the parking lot.

He was dreading the start-up of private clarinet lessons. Just when he needed every second to focus on his training for Zeeno, he had to take time for something as useless as clarinet lessons. He had tried to tell his mom that he didn't need them. He argued that he wanted to get a job after school, which she should encourage. But she went ahead and arranged the lessons. She was feeling guilty, he thought, for all the time and money she spent on Erin's gymnastics. At least the teacher had an opening on Thursdays after school, which wouldn't interfere with his johka practice schedule, and the guy's house wasn't far from school—just not in a section of the neighborhood he knew.

"It's probably not too late to cancel," he said when he opened the car door. "I really want to get a job."

"Hop in."

"If I have to go, at least let me walk," he said, wanting the solo time to process the day.

"I need to meet the guy, Albert." His mom gave him her look, and he got in the car. "I'm going to have to drop you off a little early because I need to pick up Erin and get her to her practice, but the teacher said you can wait inside."

"Who is he again and what am I supposed to do?" Albert said.

"The woman at the music store recommended him. Everybody calls him Mr. Sam. He's been teaching private clarinet for the past fifteen years. He's supposed to be good with kids."

"If he makes me play 'Twinkle, Twinkle,' I'm walking out," Albert said.

"He'll probably give you exercises to do and tell you what you're doing right and what you're doing wrong so you can improve." They drove for a while, listening to the GPS directions, and then she slowed down, peering out the window, as the road curved and her phone announced that they were arriving. "He said look for the painted door...there!"

All the houses on the block were identical—small, ugly brick boxes—except that one had its front door defiantly painted bright blue and splashed with yellow, green, white, and red. This was Mr. Sam's attempt to make the best of what he could afford, Albert guessed. When they knocked, it took a while for Mr. Sam to get there.

"Welcome! Welcome! I'm just finishing a lesson," he said, standing in the bright, messy living room, glancing quickly from son to mother. A big shaggy man with long, uncombed hair, a beard, and baggy clothes that didn't quite match, he looked vaguely familiar to Albert, yet Albert couldn't place him. The sound of someone playing the clarinet floated down from the hallway. Not "Twinkle, Twinkle" at all. Albert wasn't sure what it was, but it sounded good.

Albert's mom introduced herself and then Albert, and when Mr. Sam shook Albert's hand, he paused midshake. "Wait, you play soccer, right? You're a striker."

Albert was taken aback.

"The pickup game at the park." Mr. Sam pulled his hair back in a ponytail and grinned. "You joined us once. You were amazing!"

That was it, Albert thought. He knew Mr. Sam had looked familiar. The guy with the ponytail and huge smile who played keeper.

"I've still got fifteen minutes with another student," Mr. Sam went on. "Albert, you can wait here until I'm done." He turned to Albert's mom. "Catherine, right? Catherine, you can pick him up at four forty-five. Okay?"

"Okay then," Albert's mom said brightly. "Looks like we're in the right place. I'll be back at four forty-five."

"It's not far, Mom," Albert said. "And now I know where it is. I can walk."

"Great!" Mr. Sam clapped his large hand on Albert's shoulder. "A twofer. Get your exercise and let the lesson sink in."

His mom smiled uneasily. "You sure, Albert?"

"Yes."

"Text me when you leave and text me when you get home. Bye-bye, honey." To Albert's horror, she tousled his hair and left.

Mr. Sam gave him a smile. "I promise you, Albert. Someday, she's going to leave the hair alone."

Albert smiled back, and then Mr. Sam turned and raced down the hallway toward his other student, calling back, "See you in fifteen."

Albert sat down in the little waiting area by the door that consisted of a wooden chair that had been painted white with black musical notes on it and a small side table overflowing with books about music. He noticed gigantic muddy cleats under the side table and smiled. This Mr. Sam thing might not be so bad, he thought. Once a week, he could walk here after school, maybe do an audio training session along the way, and then have a nice walk home alone.

Now, he had fifteen minutes to relax. He pulled out his phone, opened up the training program, and hesitated. He knew he should redo the first lesson since he had failed at it so miserably, but he activated the second lesson, hoping it would be easier.

Welcome to the second lesson: Sending Ahnic Energy Inward. A shawble that is met with anger, shame, fear, or

denial will worsen. We must meet our shawbles by acknowl-
edging them and then directing ahnic energy inward.

    Stand up and take a few deep breaths to begin. Now,
close your eyes and think of a time when you made a mis-
take or you didn't perform as well as you would have liked.

Albert snorted. That's easy, he thought, remembering not only
the failure of the first lesson, but the heat of shame in Spanish
class when he had blurted out what an idiot he was. The Zeenods
had clearly made a huge mistake—

Good. Start by placing one hand on your chest and the
other on your abdomen. Feel your lungs and diaphragm
expand as you take a deep breath. Inhale one, two, three,
four...

Ha, Albert thought. I can't even do that.

As you exhale, pull your hands away from your body slowly.
As you do that, say, "I am removing negative thoughts,"
and imagine that your hands are pulling those thoughts out
of your mind and body.

Albert pulled his arms out. I look stupid and feel nothing, he
thought. I'm definitely not doing this right.

Next, spread your arms and imagine that you are collecting
ahnic energy with your palms. Inhale slowly, bringing your
palms to your chest, saying, "I forgive myself and deserve
to receive the ahn."

Albert sighed. Ridiculous. It's like preschool yoga or something. What next…was he supposed to sing, *"Everyone's special and I am, too?"* Why did Kayko give him this when the stakes were so high? How would this help him do a bounce-off or a jump-over or a ride-up with the zees?

If you are thinking that this is ridiculous, then it is even more important that you do this exercise as often as possible.

Albert opened his eyes.

Close your eyes and try again. With practice, you will be able to send ahnic energy to yourself without words or motions, but for now, do the exercise as instructed.

Down the hallway, a new piece of music began with two clarinets—Mr. Sam was playing with the student. One played a simple jazz melody that looped over and over. The second clarinet improvised around the melody, sometimes winding around it, sometimes soaring above it, sometimes almost laughing with it. That was what his nana had meant when she said she liked the sound of a clarinet. Played well, it had a great sound.

It must feel good to be able to play that well, Albert thought, and then he wondered if he could ever play that well. Am I capable? If I put in the time, could I get there? Was that all there was to it?

Maybe attitude was important. Maybe if he wasn't so hard on himself, he would have more confidence and that would help—with music, with soccer, with everything. He recalled the way Kayko had looked at him after that first practice, when Albert had been trying to think of a way of quitting. *Be kind to yourself,* Kayko had said. *Learning is difficult.*

He exhaled, trying to focus on the training session. Maybe his habit of putting himself down was a shawble. Self-loathing. That was what Kayko had called it. Maybe kicking that habit would be a key to connecting with the ahn and improving on the field. "Okay, I am removing negative thoughts," he whispered as he pulled his hands away from his body. And then he swept his arms wide, trying to imagine that he could gather the hum of the ahn through his palms. He pressed his hands against his chest. His palms felt warm. "I forgive myself and deserve to receive the ahn."

He smiled. It was ridiculous, but it actually felt kind of good.

The music was growing louder, which meant that Mr. Sam couldn't hear him. Eyes closed, he did it again. And again. By the seventh time, he had a lovely rhythm going, his body and breath in sync, his voice growing stronger. By the twelfth time, he didn't even notice the click of the back door opening and the soft sound of footsteps.

Pressing his palms against his chest with a huge smile, he repeated, "I forgive myself and deserve—"

And then a terribly familiar voice—

"Albert, what are you doing here?"

Albert's eyes snapped open to see Jessica Atwater standing in the living room, facing him, skateboard in her hand.

"What—what am I doing here?" he stammered. "What are you doing here?"

"I live here."

"You live here?"

"I live here. This is my house. What are you doing in my house?"

"This is Mr. Sam's house. I'm taking clarinet lessons."

"Mr. Sam is my dad."

"Your dad?"

"You're taking lessons? Since when?"

"Since today."

"But what are you *doing*?" she asked.

"What do you mean, what am I doing? I'm waiting for my lesson."

"No. What were you doing when I walked in?" She pressed her free hand on her heart. " 'I forgive myself.' What was that?"

Albert's face burned. There was something about the tone of her voice that told him that she was genuinely curious, but he didn't trust it. "I—I— It's—It's a line from a movie. I was just messing around." He forced a laugh. "It's hilarious. About a guy named Albert who is doing this yoga move. It's hilarious. I say it sometimes just to crack myself up." Albert threw back his head and laughed like a maniac.

"Oh." She didn't laugh.

Too far in to back out, Albert pressed his hands to his chest and hammed it up even more. "I forgive myself!" He laughed again, aware that he probably looked insane. "Oh! Sorry, my phone's buzzing."

As he whipped out his phone to answer a fake call, Jessica gave him a puzzled look and left him alone.

8.2

Tackle panted, choosing a patch by the front gate on which to sit and keep watch. Albert would be coming home from school soon, and he wanted to finally get a good sniff and a close look.

For the past two days, Tackle been kept indoors again, a punishment for the multiple holes he had dug in the yard. That had dampened his delight in finally triumphing over the squirrel-machine.

Luckily, this morning he'd been granted a little more freedom. Mr. Patterson had fastened a cable in the front yard from the gate-post to the metal railing next to the front steps of their house. To this cable, he had attached Tackle's leash. This new arrangement prevented the dog from roaming into the backyard and disturb-ing the new grass seed, but enabled him to stretch his legs, pee, and run back and forth in the front.

All day he had been patrolling from this limited vantage point. No strange scents. No squirrel- or bug-machines in sight.

He didn't like being tethered to the line, but it was better than being stuck inside.

8.3

The clarinet lesson was never-ending. Albert couldn't let go of the fact that Jessica had caught him doing that ahn exercise. What Mr. Sam was saying might have been interesting, but it was hard to pay attention to a teacher when Albert's inner voice was busy beating himself up about what he had done.

"We're going to improvise," Mr. Sam said. "So I won't be giving you sheet music or asking you to learn any specific songs. What I want you to do is listen to music and try to play with it—not necessarily playing the melody—just playing whatever sounds like it fits with what you hear."

"I—I can't do that," Albert said, scratching the backs of his knees.

"Yet," Mr. Sam said. "You can't do it yet. Have an open mind. I'll be giving you lots of tips."

"But—"

What Albert wanted to say was that he couldn't improvise knowing that Jessica was listening. She would hear every wrong note.

"But what?" Mr. Sam asked with a smile. "Is it scary?"

"No," Albert lied again.

"What do you love to do, Albert?"

"What do you mean?"

"I mean, if you had a free afternoon what would you want to do with it?"

"Play soccer," Albert said.

"Not surprised. You're super skilled on the field. Okay. What do you love about soccer?"

Albert was speechless.

"No one has ever asked you that?" Mr. Sam smiled.

Albert thought about the joyful expressions of the Zeenod kids playing in their bare feet with that deflated old ball in Zone 3; and then, surprisingly, that reminded him of those moments when he and Trey were younger and they were getting into the flow during their best games. "I love connecting. I love it when you want to make a run to the goal, but then a defender blocks you, and you have to change your plan. You see a teammate open and pass the ball, and your teammate receives it and sends it into the goal. And it's all happening in a split second."

Mr. Sam brightened. "I love it. That's improvisation, Albert! When I improvise with other musicians, I don't think about what I should do to sound great. I listen to what is being played, and then I focus on making whatever I do flow with what everybody else is doing. It's being a part of something bigger than yourself. Like being a part of a team. You might connect with music the way you connect with soccer, Albert. All I'm suggesting is to have an open mind while you're trying it out. It might not float your boat, and that's okay. Not everybody in the world has to play the clarinet, right?" He smiled. "But before you give up on something, it's only fair to try it for real."

Albert managed a smile back and he got through the lesson, albeit by playing as quietly as he possibly could.

As he left, Mr. Sam said, "Hey!"

Albert turned around.

"Whenever you're doing something you love, remember that it's something you love doing."

Albert wasn't sure what he was supposed to say back. "You're talking about the clarinet, right?"

"I'm talking about everything, Albert. Music, soccer, eating chocolate, whatever," Mr. Sam said. "Sometimes people miss out because their minds are somewhere else. If you love music, then remember to love it while you're playing music. If you love soccer, remember to love it while you're playing soccer. If you love to eat chocolate, remember to love it while you're eating it."

Albert laughed. "That sounds like something my grandmother would say."

"Wise woman. Feel free to join us for pickup at the park anytime." Mr. Sam smiled.

"Thanks," Albert said.

"See you next Thursday here," Mr. Sam said.

As Albert headed home, he felt his emotions pulling in two opposing directions. Although he intended to talk his mom into canceling the rest of the lessons, he liked Mr. Sam and actually found the idea of learning how to improvise interesting. But the lessons were too socially risky. Mr. Sam was Jessica's dad, after all. Albert would be horrible at the clarinet, and it would be too embarrassing. Jessica would tell Trey.

The moment Albert thought about Trey, his mind began to replay all the negative interactions he had experienced with Trey since the end of sixth grade, and then he grew angry with himself for caring so much. Trey isn't worth your time, he kept trying to repeat.

Deep in thought, he walked up the driveway, and Tackle flew at the front gate, yanking his leash along the cable, sending a trio of birds flying. Albert jumped back, dropping his clarinet case.

"Stop barking at me!" Albert yelled at the dog.

It was an understandable mistake to assume that the dog's enthusiasm was aggression, but it only served to make the dog try harder, bark louder.

Albert looked around to see if Trey was actually home to witness his fearful response, the more ridiculous given the fact that the dog was now tethered to the cable and couldn't possibly jump the fence. No, of course, Trey wasn't home. He was at soccer practice with the school team every day after school, which was where Albert would have been if the coach had actually given him a chance.

His phone rang.

"Albert, where are you?" His mother's voice was angry. "You were supposed to text when you left Mr. Sam's house. Did you get my texts?"

"I'm home. Can't you hear Trey's stupid dog? They've got him on a leash-thing now." Albert held the phone out, and the dog obliged with a *grrr*. "What happened to the idea of not texting so much?" He ended the call, picked up his clarinet, and rushed into his house, slamming the door behind him.

The house was empty.

He stood for a moment, shaking with anger. Anger at the dog. At his mom. At his classmates. Mostly anger at himself. And then he dropped his clarinet case and threw his backpack to the floor.

After he'd seen what was happening on Zeeno and learning how the Tevs and Z-Tevs were ruining the planet, Albert's determination to help Zeeno had felt solid. But the moment his feet touched Earth again, the confidence that he could actually offer help began crumbling. Determination didn't matter if he lacked so many other necessary skills and qualities.

To his horror, he felt tears rising as he walked through the living room. Tears. He wasn't even sure why.

A note was waiting for him on the kitchen table, held in place by a vase with a flower in it, and he read it first without paying attention. And then he read it again.

Hi, Albert, I was feeling sorry for myself today. So I rolled myself over to the park to do my physical therapy exercises by the pretty pond. Hope you had a great day. If you didn't, I totally sympathize. Take a breath in and let it out. See if you can turn your day around.—Nana

The breath Albert didn't know he was holding exhaled from him in a heavy sigh. He pictured the effort it took for his eighty-seven-year-old nana to roll her wheelchair all the way to the park. And her trip home would be uphill, Albert realized. Another sigh and a long look out the back window. It was a beautiful day, and he hadn't noticed. He heard Mr. Sam's question in his head. *If you had a free afternoon what would you want to do with it?*

He could sit here and beat himself up. Or he could grab a soccer ball, dribble to the park, keep his nana company while working out, and then give her a hand on the way back home.

Albert grabbed a soccer ball, steeled himself against Tackle's inevitable growl, and jogged to the park.

8.4

The day was warm enough that the botmaker decided to hang out in one of his favorite places to write and do some brainstorming: the rooftop patio of his building. When he arrived, a young Z-Tev couple were picnicking at one of the tables there—something he had learned to expect. Although they were facing away from Mehk, the eyes in the back of their heads blinked when he stepped through the doorway. Immediately, the male turned and pointed to a sign that read: THIS SPACE IS RESERVED FOR Z-TEV RESIDENTS ONLY.

"I'm so sorry to disturb you," Mehk said. "I am a pest exterminator. Someone reported a gheet sighting, and the office sent me to check on it."

"Ridiculous," the Z-Tev said. "Do your checking later."

Ignoring him, Mehk began an inspection of the various rest-pods on the patio while secretly releasing his robotic gheet from his pocket. As the couple bickered about which of them should make the "exterminator" leave, the tarantula-like machine crept around a pod and then under a table, and then reached the couple's feet. Swiftly, it began to climb up the leg of the male. Upon feeling it, the Z-Tev screamed, shook the creature off, and then ran inside, leaving his lunch and his partner. While Mehk scooped up the gheet, the female Z-Tev gave him a nasty look and left.

Helping himself to their lunch, he placed his pet on his shoulder and turned his full attention to capturing his thoughts in his log.

```
Kinney is training, and I find myself growing anxious.
The ahn is powerful, more powerful than most of the
small-minded beings in Fŭigor realize. I never thought
that Kinney would remain in place as Star Striker long
enough to begin this training! What if Kinney actually
learns how to use the ahn?
```

He stopped. A series of memories came back to him, times throughout his childhood when he had tried and failed to send and receive the ahn. When had he tried last? When he had been Kinney's age? Eventually he had given up, telling himself it wasn't important. But now, the thought that he might have to watch an Earthling learn how to use a power that he hadn't learned—He closed his eyes and tried to clear his mind.

Believe in your brilliance. You will succeed.

His eyes snapped open. He had two options. Try again to get Kinney to resign or wait to see if the mysterious assassin got to Kinney first. Or perhaps there was a third? Combine forces with whoever wanted Kinney dead? Whoever it was had resources he didn't have. He noticed a bug crawling on the arm of his rest-pod, one of the invasive species the Z-Tevs had introduced, and he flicked it away. But how could he find out who was behind the murder attempts? An idea popped into his head.

What about another bluff? A bluff with a little blackmail thrown in? Send a message from an encrypted address to a list of possible assassins and see if it strikes home?

To: X

The DRED was a bold move. It didn't work, so you planned the little detour to Black Hole 3275. Yes, I know who you are. Yes, I am watching your every move. Yes, I have evidence that incriminates you.

Do I have your attention?

Ha! We both want Kinney eliminated from play. I can make that happen without even the need for violence. Your attempts clearly show your lack of imagination. Seriously, your attempts

203

```
were old-fashioned and clumsy. I operate on a
micro level. I can avoid detection. You need me.
Signed, Anonymous


   Not bad. Make a list of those who want either the
Zeenods or Kinney to fail. Send it to all of them. It
just might work.
```

He scooped up his gheet and smiled. A blue sparkle lit up each of its six eyes.

He thought of another bluff experiment, another message he could send to Albert Kinney! That would take a little longer to deploy, but—oooh, he was excited.

9.0

Welcome to the third lesson: Sending Ahnic Energy Outward.

Albert had arrived at his first-period class a few minutes early and had decided to use his time wisely. Señora Muñoz was talking to another teacher in the hallway, and, as other students trickled in, Albert sat behind a propped-up book at his desk, his phone in the audio-only mode.

In sending ahnic energy, we lift up others and liberate our minds from our shawbles. We strengthen the ahn between us and create a profound ripple effect.

Jessica walked in and glanced at him. As she sat down, he found himself wondering if his face was flushed. He forced his attention back to his phone.

Think of someone with whom it is easy to feel a connection. Send ahnic energy to that person by saying or thinking, "May you be well. May you feel joy." This can be translated simply as sending a kind thought. With practice, you will be able to do this without words, but begin by doing this exercise as instructed.

Jessica unzipped her backpack and pulled out a notebook. The cover was full of her drawings done in black and purple marker. He had never noticed that she was into art. A black line drawing of a dragon brooded in the corner of her notebook, looking fierce and holding a skateboard in its claw. Albert leaned forward but pulled back when she shifted in her seat.

Unit B disguised as Jessica popped into his mind and the little scene replayed: the robot had looked at him with Jessica's brown eyes and said, "Based on my research, this body-form was determined to be one that you'd enjoy."

Recalling the exchange, he flushed all over again, and then he turned his attention back to the lesson.

Think of someone with whom it is easy to feel a connection. Picture that person in your mind.

Focus, Albert. Kayko wouldn't have given you these lessons if they weren't important. An easy connection. Albert thought about his grandmother. She was easy to connect with. She was probably doing her physical therapy or knitting right now. He glanced out the classroom windows at the leaves of three maple trees glowing red in the bright morning sunshine. Or maybe she had rolled out to the backyard and was working on her laptop. May you be well, Nana. May you feel joy.

He paused, unsure. Was that ahnic energy? Was his thought supposed to magically vibrate through the air and reach Nana's mind and make her feel good? Without the right physiology, without those bems and folds, how was this supposed to work?

But he had to admit that it felt good to send a kind thought to Nana. Maybe he should stop thinking and just do it. May you be well, Nana. May you feel joy. May you be well, Nana. May you feel joy. May you be well, Nana. May you feel joy.

Ding!

Now take another deep breath in and let it out.

Albert shifted in his seat as more students streamed in. The program continued.

Think of someone with whom you are in conflict.

Trey walked into the classroom with Raul, and Albert almost laughed at the timing.

Picture that person in your mind. Now, imagine sending ahnic energy to that person—

As Trey stopped at Jessica's desk to talk to her, Albert considered what would happen if he sent ahnic energy to Trey. Nothing, he thought. Trey wouldn't suddenly receive a warm fuzzy feeling and decide to be kind back. Maybe the Zeenods could influence each other through the vibrations of energy they sent out, but that didn't mean it worked for everybody. Albert recalled the moment on Zeeno in the parking lot after that first practice when he had witnessed Vatria being punished and he had tried to be kind to her. At the time, he didn't just think a kind thought. He actually worked up the courage to walk over and say something nice to her. And how did that end? With Vatria radiating ahnic love back to him? No. With spit. Albert felt anger rising in him as if the scene were actually happening in the moment.

Trey laughed at something Jessica said, and Jessica smiled and blushed slightly, an action from her that boiled Albert's blood. And then he asked himself, if Jessica liked Trey, why should he care? Anybody who wanted to be Trey's friend or girlfriend or whatever wasn't worth Albert's time. He imagined wadding up a tiny ball of paper and sticking it in his mouth and then spitting it at Trey's neck. Bull's-eye!

Ding! The lesson was over.

Albert stared at his desk. He'd obviously failed at that lesson. But really, he didn't get it. Sending thoughts of kindness to someone like Trey would not, could not make him a better soccer player. The lessons were a waste of time.

Suddenly Trey read a text on his phone and then turned and looked at Albert. "Hey, guess what, Kinney?" he asked.

Assuming some kind of joke was coming, Albert kept his mouth closed.

"You're going to be our new dog walker."

"What?" Albert was seriously confused.

"My mom texted. Because I'm on two teams now, I don't have

time to walk Tackle after school, and when my mom complained about it to your mom, your mom suggested that we hire you." Trey smiled. "She said you have plenty of time because you quit soccer."

"Hilarious joke," Albert said.

Raul laughed. "He looks scared. Is your dog mean?"

"I'm not scared," Albert said, reddening. Trey and Raul and Jessica were all looking at him.

"Did you quit, Albert?" Trey asked. "Or are you playing on a team?"

Albert met Trey's gaze. "My mom doesn't know everything I do, Trey. And I'm not your new dog walker."

Trey shrugged. "Check your phone. My mom said your mom texted you."

Albert looked down. Two texts from his mom had come in before he started the lesson, but there were always texts from his mom and he hadn't bothered reading them yet.

He opened the first.

Great news! You wanted a job and you got it! Cynthia is hiring you to walk Tackle.

And then the second.

She'll text you with instructions later this a.m. You start today right after school. Isn't it perfect?

9.1

Grrr. Tackle stopped pacing and scanned the trees again, the muscles across his shoulders rippling. Nothing. He resumed. Back and forth from gate to steps. Steps to gate. Pulling his cabled leash along the line. He stopped to sniff the slightly wet leaves in the grass. Moldy. Boring. The air was still.

Give up pacing. Give up patrolling. Give in to napping, dog.

He tried stretching out on the grass halfway between the house and fence.

A siren called in the distance, and his ears pricked. A deep longing to run rose up in his chest, and the muscles of his flanks twitched again.

Then a smell. He lifted his head and—oh!—Albert was approaching. Instead of walking toward the front gate, the boy put his hand on the front gate and began to open it.

Tackle couldn't believe his eyes. Nobody other than a Patterson opened their gate. Long ago the mailbox had been purposefully set up on the other side of the fence so that carriers didn't have to endure Tackle's protective response. And here was none other than Albert walking in! Walking in to see him!

Excited, he raced toward the gate. Startled, Albert hurried back out and slammed the gate shut, the smell of his fear hitting the air.

Fear? The dog wanted to cry out, Albert, you have no reason to be afraid of me! *Grrr.*

9.2

"That didn't exactly go well," Albert said as he stepped back. He was supposed to open the gate, unlatch Tackle's leash from the cable, and take him to the park. Last fall, he would have been excited to do it. Now, he was afraid to open the gate.

The dog kept barking, running in short bursts and then jumping up on the gate.

Both his mom and Mrs. Patterson always said Tackle was more bark than bite. What Albert wanted to hear was "All bark, no bite."

Maybe a bribe would work.

He walked into his house, set down his backpack, and got the biggest, fattest carrot from the refrigerator. Tackle had loved chewing on carrots since he was a puppy.

"Is that you, Albert? How was school? I'm on the patio," his grandmother's voice called out.

"Fine, Nana," Albert called back, trying to take the quaver out of his voice. Not wanting his grandmother to see how afraid he was, he tried to slip out the front door.

"Can you bring me an apple?" she called.

He tucked the carrot into his hoodie pocket, grabbed an apple, and walked to the den, where the sliding glass doors led to their back patio. Nana was sitting in the late-afternoon sunlight with her laptop and her knitting.

As soon as he stepped out, Tackle barked again from his spot in the front yard.

Setting down the sweater she was knitting and taking the apple, Nana said, "Thank you, sir. Gorgeous day, isn't it?"

"Yeah," he said.

"Your mom texted and said she got you a job walking Tackle."
Nana took a bite of the apple. Tackle barked again and she
laughed. "Sounds like he can't wait. Why don't you take a ball?"
She nodded over to an open bin that held a number of soccer
balls.

Albert scooped one up.

"You'll both benefit from the exercise," she said, and then she
added something that made Albert wonder if she had noticed
his new fear of his old friend. "Animals are like us, Albert. They
respond to the energy we give."

Avoiding her glance, he walked toward the driveway. "Yeah,
see you later, Nana." Call an ambulance if you hear me scream,
he wanted to call back.

"Enjoy it!" her voice rang out.

On the other side of the fence, Tackle followed as Albert
jogged to the front. Tossing the soccer ball into the Pattersons'
yard, Albert whispered, "Look. I'm here to take you for a run in
the park. So don't kill me."

The dog sniffed the ball.

Albert's heart was pounding against his chest and a trickle of
sweat loosened from the nape of his neck and ran down the center
of his back. He stepped to the gate and reached out for the handle.
Instantly the dog ran over, paws on the gate, a loud, sharp bark.

Albert's stomach clenched, a knot of fear.

"Okay, I admit it. I'm afraid of you, Tackle."

He thought about the first ahn lesson. Thought Awareness.
*Acknowledge whatever emotion or feeling or thought you are experienc-
ing without judgment.*

I'm feeling fear, Albert thought. Hello, Fear. Yep, you are definitely here. His heart rate slowed a little. He took a deep breath in

and out. And then the second lesson came to him. *A shawble that is met with anger, shame, fear, or denial will worsen.*

An insight came to Albert. Fear wasn't a shawble. Fear was a response. The shawble was in denying the fear or being ashamed of the fear or being angry with himself for the fear. He pictured Kayko's gold eyes. If Kayko were here right now, she'd say, *Be kind to yourself, Albert.*

Albert smiled. "It's understandable that I'm afraid of you, Tackle. You're a beast. But I'm tired of being afraid of you. Believe it or not, I'm not your enemy."

The third lesson came to him. *In sending ahnic energy, we lift up others and liberate our minds from our shawbles.*

"I am going to send ahnic energy to you now, Tackle," Albert said. He took a deep breath in and imagined sending shimmering vibrations of kindness to the dog. "May you be well. May you feel joy."

He thought about that silent sound that seemed to come from the Zeenods when they were sending out their energy through the ahn, and he began to focus on the vibration of energy he was sending toward the dog.

The dog stood panting, his front paws up on the gate.

Albert breathed. May you be well. May you feel joy. Albert's shoulders released and his heart slowed. He felt good. Calm and at peace. He opened his eyes, looking down to avoid challenging the dog with a direct gaze, putting his hand in his pocket and withdrawing the carrot. He breathed in and out. "May this carrot bring you joy." He took a step forward.

The dog pushed back and returned to all fours. Then he opened his mouth and barked; and a lightning bolt of understanding ran straight through Albert's spine.

This is unexpected, the dog said.

Albert dropped the carrot. The dog had barked—and he, Albert, had heard that bark as a sentence.

The dog barked again. *What's going on?*

Albert's comprehension was effortless and complete. It was the same thing he had experienced in Spanish class and on Zeeno when he wanted to find the words to say something in a language other than his own and the words he needed simply rose to the surface of his mind.

Through the slats of the gate, the dog sniffed and barked again. *What are you doing here? I don't know you anymore.*

Albert took in Tackle's speech, reasoning that the device in his ear that enabled him to understand alien languages was enabling him to understand dog language. He must have had this ability from the moment of his implant, but only today when he had approached Tackle with calm ahnic energy did he actually tap into it. Now, he wondered if he had the ability to speak dog language as well.

Still not looking directly into the dog's eyes, Albert barked. *Tackle, I understand you.* The sounds had simply come out of his mouth.

Tackle couldn't believe his ears. He blinked. He looked at Albert.

With growing excitement, Albert picked up the carrot and held it over the top of the gate. *May this carrot bring you joy.*

The dog looked at the carrot and then again at Albert.

Albert smiled. He remembered the secrecy clause in his contract with the Zeenods: he had promised not to tell any humans. The contract had said nothing about dogs. So, in a series of whispered barks, and yelps, and yaps, Albert explained. *I have a device in my ear given to me by an alien culture. It's making me able to understand and speak your language.*

Tackle backed up, barking. *Wait. What? You're talking to me? Is this happening?*

Albert nodded, raising his gaze to meet the dog's. *Yes. I know. It's a mind-blow.*

I knew it! The dog stepped forward, panting. *You've been disappearing! That strange light, that sound—a crackling. The squirrel-machine!*

What? What are you talking about?

A machine disguised as a squirrel has been watching you, Albert. I've been trying to warn you. And then I saw you disappear. And then the machine sent out strange bugs that wanted to attach to you.

Albert thought about all those times Tackle had barked so aggressively. *You've been trying to warn me.* A chill went through Albert as he took in the news about the squirrel and the bugs. Someone or something here on Earth was spying on him or worse.

Tackle barked. *Where did you go, Albert? Have you been hurt? Were you in danger? Are you in danger?*

Wait. That squirrel machine—Albert looked around and then whispered, *Is it here?*

I defeated it, the dog said proudly. *Ripped it and buried the pieces.*

Wow. Thank you, Albert said, and gave the dog a look of gratitude so warm it made Tackle weak in the paws.

Just in case someone is spying, let's go to the park, Albert whispered. *We can tell each other everything.*

Tackle looked at Albert. *If the Pattersons come home and I'm gone—*

The Pattersons hired me to walk you, Albert said. *Because Trey is so busy. Every day after school except Thursday, which is when I have a clarinet lesson. I'm supposed to take you to the park and give you some exercise.*

Albert waited for this to sink in. Then he offered the carrot again. *A snack and a run in the park. Not bad, right?*

The dog took the carrot in his mouth and then jumped back so Albert could open the gate.

Soccer ball in one hand, leash in the other, Albert walked out jubilantly. On the way to the park, the dog had a surprising amount to say, and Albert marveled at how many different sounds he made that he had never noticed before. Yes, there was barking, but so much more. Yips, yaps, yelps, gruffles, huffs, ruffs, whimpers, whines, snarls, howls, growls, snarls, yowls.

Albert wanted to know every detail Tackle could remember about the machine-like squirrel and bugs so that he could report everything to Kayko. In return, Albert told Tackle all about the johka tournament and Zeeno. Tackle was surprised to hear how many times Albert would be going back and forth and wanted to know how Albert knew whom he could trust. They talked like old friends, stopping only when another person was walking past.

Tackle, Albert said as they arrived at the park's entrance. *I'm sorry I thought you had turned against me. All this time you've been trying to warn and protect me.*

Tackle glanced up and then quickly back down.

It must be hard, Albert said as they took the path leading to the park's main field. *You're so much more intelligent than any of us thought.*

Tackle stopped and looked up at Albert, his brown eyes full of emotion.

What is it? Albert asked. *Did I say something wrong?*

216

No, the dog whispered, his brow wrinkling. *It's just this…to be understood. I've needed this.*

Albert crouched down. *It's huge.*

They looked at each other.

Are you going to cry? Albert asked.

Are you? Tackle asked.

Albert laughed and Tackle made a funny noise.

Yo, dog, was that a laugh or a cry or a sneeze? Albert asked.

A laugh, Tackle said, and began to trot.

Albert dropped the ball and began dribbling it as he jogged beside the dog into the open field. *I've got to get into really good shape, Tackle.*

The dog laughed. *Just try to keep up.*

They both took off running.

A long run, short sprints, push-ups, sit-ups, juggling, bicycle kicks…Albert did it all, with Tackle serving as both inspiration and coach.

On their way home, Albert felt that delicious rush that came from using every muscle in his body. *This is the kind of workout I need,* he said.

Me too, the dog said. *Same time tomorrow?*

I can't do it every day, but four times a week will be amazing.

By the way, why have you been so crazy about the trampoline lately? the dog asked. *I've seen you practicing.*

Albert told Tackle about the zees and how he hoped jumping would help him train. *I also brought out my sister's old springboard to practice jumping forward and I set up a smaller tramp on its side to practice bouncing balls off it.*

I wish I could go with you to Zeeno and see those zees and help protect you, the dog said.

Albert smiled and stopped to scratch Tackle behind the ears. *What I need is for you to keep a lookout here. I had no idea that the squirrel-thing had been planted in the yard. Now, you'll be able to tell me if you see or hear or smell anything suspicious and I'll be able to understand you.*

I will be on guard, Tackle said.

As they approached the house, Albert stopped again. *Hey, want to come over and give the tramp a try?*

A funny look came over the dog's face. *You have to ask?*

Together they raced to the Kinneys' backyard. Albert climbed onto the trampoline and asked Tackle if he needed help getting up.

The dog shook his head. *You realize who you're talking to?* He backed up, got a running start, and leaped. When his paw hit the rubbery dark surface, his weight sent a wave through the trampoline, which almost toppled Albert. *Whoa! The ground is moving!* Tackle yelled, bouncing, his feet slipping out from under him.

Albert laughed and jumped up and down, sending the dog up and down, too. *It's crazy, isn't it?*

Tackle laughed and got up and ran around, getting the hang of it, bouncing in a circle. *Whoooeee! Crazy!*

The two began to howl as they jumped, laughing hysterically.

And then came a voice. "Albert?"

His sister Erin was standing on the threshold of the patio door, staring. "OMG, Albert. You're just getting weirder and weirder."

Yep, Albert barked, and then he laughed and kept bouncing.

10.0

Albert's heart lifted when the ITV landed and Unit B deployed the stairs and he saw the entire Zeeno team waiting for him in the parking lot.

The officials went through the required routine and departed, and then Kayko led Albert and the team into the practice space. As soon as they were safely inside, the team relaxed, greeting Albert with their exuberant fist bumps and bows, and Kayko called for a huddle.

"Guys!" Albert said. "I've had a breakthrough and I have news!"

"You broke through something? That is bad," Sormie said.

"No, it's good!" Albert took a breath. There was so much he

wanted to say he didn't know where to begin. "First of all, seeing Zone 3..." The flood of images made him choke.

"You understand?" Kayko asked.

"I can't understand completely," Albert said. "But I understand more, and it makes me want to win."

A chain reaction of grateful smiles lit up the practice space.

"And I can see that the training sessions are going to be helpful. I have a long way to go, but the game isn't until November and I'll do the training sessions every day." Albert described how he'd already used the three lessons to deal with his fear of Tackle and how that had enabled him to discover that he could actually communicate. Sormie panicked on hearing that Albert had told the dog everything, but then Feeb reminded them all that the contract prohibited Albert from telling humans, not animals.

"That's because animals are not given the respect they're due by other cultures," Toben said, shaking his head. "Albert's dialogue with the dog proves what many Zeenods believe: animals have intelligence."

Albert told them about the squirrel-machine, and their alarm worried him. It sounded to them like a spybot, and they wondered who would have taken such a risk to place one on Earth. In the Fŭigor System, it was illegal to travel to and from Earth without permission of the Fŭigor authorities. The Zeenods had permission through the FJF to travel to and from Earth for the purpose of facilitating Albert's training as Star Striker. Would the Tevs or Gabŏqs take the risk of coming to plant a spybot? What did they hope to gain?

Kayko told them she would discuss the situation with President Lat, who would want to report it to the FJF.

"We are fortunate to have a trusted ally, now, in the dog called Tackle," Toben said. "He will help keep Albert safe on Earth."

Albert nodded. "Tackle will be on the lookout. It's funny. I must have been able to understand dog language the moment I first came back to Earth with the translation implant, but I was too wrapped up in my own thoughts to notice. It took me a little time, too, to be open to the training sessions. But I think I'm learning. I think the whole shawble concept is becoming clear. A shawble can hold you back, keep you from sending ahnic energy to yourself and to other people—"

"Or to other Zeenods," Feeb said.

"Or dogs," Toben said.

"Or Dozs," Doz said.

Everybody laughed.

"Well done, Albert." Kayko nodded and smiled. "A start of excellence."

Albert went on. "I'm excited about the whole mind-body-spirit connection and how the training sessions can make me a better soccer player. This week, I had a breakthrough in my backyard. I can't wait to show you."

Doz jumped up. "Let's roll and rock, as Albert would say!"

Albert laughed. "Let's roll and rock!"

They went onto the field; and as Kayko led a series of short exercises, Albert stretched and jogged, taking in the faces of the Zeenods, and imagining them being forced to grow up in the bleak and desolate Zone 3.

"Nice work, team! Let's begin the scrimmage," Kayko said, and divided the players into Team A and Team B. "Team B, please activate blue."

With a touch to their shoulders, the smart-fabric practice jerseys of the players on Team B changed from gold to blue.

"I'll never get tired of seeing that," Albert said. "I wish my clothes on Earth could respond to commands and do things like change sizes or colors."

"Yes," Doz said. "Earth technology is crud."

Albert laughed. "I think you mean crude. But *crude* and *crud* both work."

"Both teams, circle up for the ahn," Kayko said, and Albert followed Ennjy and the rest of Team A to their side of the field.

The players closed their eyes and began to breathe in unison. Albert joined. Okay, Albert, he said to himself. May you play well. May you find joy.

Albert took in another breath and let it out slowly. He was nervous, but he focused his attention on his breath. He pictured the faces of each player in the huddle with him. Hello, team. He focused his mind and heart on sending out his positive energy. May we all play well. May we find joy.

And there it was…a sensation of being both lifted and held. After a few seconds of increasing intensity, there was a whoop from Ennjy, and Albert jumped forward with his teammates, throwing one arm around Ennjy's shoulder on his right and Doz's shoulder on his left. Although the ritual occurred at every practice, Albert was awestruck and grateful each time.

He thought about the sadness that plagued the planet Zeeno and vowed to himself to do everything he could to be as supportive of the Zeenods as they were being of him.

Both teams immediately spread out across the field, and a rapid passing drill began on each side. Player to player to player, the ball went smoothly between Zeenod teammates. "We use the ahn to connect," Ennjy said. "To feel each other's impulses."

The scrimmage started with a kickoff from Heek to Wayt, two quiet players from Team B. About two minutes in, just as Albert got possession, he smelled that unmistakable aroma of pine coming from the left and knew a zee was about to blow. He scanned where the smell was coming from and saw the change in color begin in one part of the ground. Thrilled, he headed for it, kicking the ball just as it was rising. With a satisfying smack, the ball ricocheted off the zee and sailed toward the goal.

The Zeenods stopped playing.

"You did it, Albert!" Doz cried out.

"How did you know the zee was coming?" Ennjy exclaimed.

Albert sniffed. "The smell. Oh, wait. You guys can't smell."

Giac waved to get attention. "It's terpene! I did the research, and there is a chemical in Earth pine trees called terpene, which is also present in Zeeno's crust. It gets released in a chemical reaction that occurs right before a zeeruption. That's why it smells like pine to Albert right before a zee rises."

"Of course!" Toben said. "I knew that Earth animals used their sense of smell. You can smell a zee before we can see a zee?" Toben's eyes grew wide. "This is useful!"

"But is this a normal human ability?" Kayko asked. "Albert hasn't been technologically altered to achieve this power, has he?"

Feeb turned to Albert. "If you have been altered, we will need to report this to the FJF officials."

Albert laughed again. "It's normal," he said, and Toben nodded.

"It's a superpower!" Doz said.

"It's not exactly a superpower," Albert said, wrinkling his nose. "It's just a nose."

Toben grinned and looked at the team. "Albert can smell!"

"Albert smells! Albert smells!" Doz started chanting, and everyone joined in.

Albert laughed.

"Wait," Toben said. "Lightning Lee must have had this ability, correct? How could we not know this?"

They all looked at Feeb, who quickly called up Lee's johkadin on his Z-da. Feeb read for a minute and then looked up. "Seventy-five years ago, we used a helmet-based technology for Lee because we hadn't yet perfected the breathing implants, so—"

"Lee had to wear a helmet!" Beeda and Reeda said.

"Of course, which would cut off any ability to use the sense of smell on the field," Toben said.

"What a wonderful discovery," Kayko added. "Albert, we will use this superpower of yours to our advantage. When you smell a zee, give us a signal. If we know even a moment before our opponents that a zee is about to blow, we can be more prepared. Until now, the Tevs' superior vision has given them an advantage."

"If I give you a signal, isn't that cheating?" Albert asked.

"Every different race from every different planet in the Fŭigor Solar System has different biological advantages or disadvantages for the game," Feeb explained. "That is one reason the games are so exciting to watch. You may use your natural sense of smell as an advantage for your team just as we may use the ahn and just as the Tevs may use their vision. If you had no sense of smell and we added one with technology, that would be against the rules. No player's abilities can be enhanced with technology that is not FJF-approved, and the only things FJF approves are breathing implants, body-temperature-regulation implants, and language-translation implants."

"That's why robots are not allowed to play," Giac added. "Robots are basically all technology."

"What do I smell like?" Doz asked, and held his arm up to Albert's nose.

Albert laughed. "You smell like Doz."

At that moment, a large ITV happened to land near the rooftop garden of the capitol building next door, which would ordinarily not be worth noticing; however, this was the location of the vacha tree that Toben had pointed out at their first practice, and the force of the ITV's landing sent the tree's feathery blossoms flying toward the field in a graceful slow-motion dance.

The Zeenods stood still, watching the incoming shower of petals.

"Vacha petals," Ennjy whispered.

"This used to be common," Kayko whispered to Albert. "My uncle said that before the invasion, Zeeno was covered in vacha trees." When she smiled at the team, she had tears in her eyes. "Here they come!"

To Albert's surprise, the team ran toward the descending pinkish-white petals, catching them on their tongues like snowflakes.

"Try one!" Doz said. "The taste is yummery!"

Laughing, Albert watched one float down, a quarter-sized, feathery thing. Before it hit the ground, Doz lunged in and caught it. "Catch them before they melt."

Toben caught one and ate half and gave the other half to his gnauser, who nibbled it with such delight, everyone laughed.

With a wave, Doz sent a petal toward Albert. Albert caught

it. A lovely melt. Like candy. Like strawberries and honey and cream.

Yummery.

10.1

The botmaker was at work when the message scrolled across the interior of his smartgoggles.

I am watching you right now.

Startled, he pulled down his goggles and looked around. His coworkers and superiors were busy, as usual. Quickly, he logged out for a restroom break, and on his way another message appeared.

Do I have your attention?

With trembling hands, he pulled the restroom door shut and took off his goggles. He had given all of the recipients of his bluff an encrypted online address, which he had been checking hourly. No one had sent a message to that address, so he had assumed he had failed. But now, this. Someone had managed to hack into his personal online address and—

The moment the top of his head warmed, he realized that a szoŭ was occurring. After teleportation, he found himself in an empty ITV, an unmarked spacecraft with all the blackout screens on the windows activated.

A replay of Albert Kinney's kidnapping ran through his mind. Whoever was kidnapping him was probably sending him to a black hole. Unlike Albert, he had no friends who were aware of his absence, no friends ready to risk their lives to rescue him.

He lunged toward the control panel and was trying to override the autopilot when an alert came through the system. Another szoŭ was occurring.

Tensing, he watched the form take shape, ticking through the list of possible assassins he had sent his bluff experiment to and wondering who it would be.

When the form coalesced into the shape of President Lat, Mehk was shocked. The Zeenod president was the last on his list. Yes, she had to serve the Z-Tevs and because of that might be pressured into helping the Tevs win, but she seemed to walk a line between the Z-Tev occupiers and her fellow Zeenods. She was passive, if anything. She wasn't a warrior or an assassin, Mehk thought. Before she became president, she was just a professor of linguistics, one of the few Zeenods who were allowed to have a position of power—the Z-Tevs needed her language-translation expertise.

"I am recording this," she said. "Keep your hands where I can see them and sit down."

As the ITV hummed in its cloaked orbit, Mehk took a seat. He was more terrified than he had ever been, and he couldn't help being fascinated to notice how it was affecting him. The rapidity of his heartbeat. The constriction of his muscles.

Although her words were strong, he noticed that her voice wavered. She looked terrible, as if she hadn't been sleeping. Her face, which he was accustomed to seeing on-screen, looked tight and twitchy and there was a flickering of desperate anxiety in her eyes.

He blinked. "How did you find me?" he asked. "My message was encrypted."

"You're right. Impressive encryption," she said. "It wasn't your technology that gave you away. It was your language."

Startled, Mehk leaned forward. "Language?"

"Your message. The unique voice that emerges in your writing," she said. "An overuse of the holophrastic interjection *ha*. A tendency to employ anacolutha as well as a habit of writing to the self in the second person. An overuse of the exclamation point. Et cetera." She waved her hand. As she spoke, she seemed less anxious, more sure of herself. "I ran an analysis of your particular lexicon and your sentence-construction habits through my research and the government database and found matches. You've written a lot of letters over the years, haven't you, Mehklen?"

A rush of shame hit the botmaker, although he believed he had nothing to be ashamed of.

"Most recently you have been writing to my office demanding to speak with me about a new 'masterpiece.' Before that—"

"But I—"

"Before that you wrote under a series of different names demanding money to create your various 'masterpieces,' and it goes way back, doesn't it?" She called up a holographic display of a series of electronic folders and files and scrolled through them at random so that Mehk could see them. "I matched them with letters written over the years. I believe you sent the first one when you were seven. This one…"

She flicked open a folder, and there was a letter that Mehk had forgotten about. A letter addressed to the president of Zeeno at the time, outlining the technology to improve medical drones and demanding that the president send it to each of the presidents of the other planets in the Fuigor Solar System.

Seeing this artifact from his childhood made Mehk feel a little dizzy, as if the ITV had taken a sudden turn.

"It was an extraordinary idea," President Lat said. "And soon after you sent the letter, the Z-Tevs made those drone improvements and claimed them as their own."

He couldn't believe he was hearing this—the truth—after so many years of silence.

She went on. "Although you didn't begin speaking until the age of six, you began to solve complex mathematical equations as well as take apart and put together machines by the age of four." She opened another document, showing test results from his former education center. "You invented your first robotic mechanism at the age of five. At six, your coding skills were unmatched. You can speak fourteen languages without a translation device." She looked up and something like a smile crossed her face. "Your knowledge of linguistics is even better than mine; you've studied psychology extensively; and you seem to have a photographic memory."

To see facts about his life laid out like this made Mehk almost sick with exhilaration.

She smiled and flipped to another file. "You are the only child of Zeenod parents who were both convicted of theft shortly after you were born."

"They were—"

"I know. They were wrongly convicted. They were outspoken in their opposition to the Z-Tevs. The Z-Tevs in power were threatened by their intelligence and framed them. It's an old story. Both your parents were banished and died. You were raised in an orphanage, where you had to be routinely put into solitary confinement because of troublemak—"

"I had—"

"When you came of age, you were given the job you have now instead of being sent to a Zeenod zone because of your intelligence. But your bosses and your coworkers don't value you. They think of you as odd and annoying." She turned back to the first page of the overview document in his file. In bold letters:

This citizen is psychologically unstable; however, he is able to complete his work.
Keep this citizen in place. No promotions. No transfers.

As Mehk read the words, he began to burn.

She flicked the holographic display of the file closed and looked at him. "I know you're brilliant. I know you hold back at the fabrication facility. You deliberately give them second-rate work. You don't want to give anybody anything unless you get respect in return. I don't blame you." She leaned back. "I know a lot about you, Mehk. More than is in this file. That's because I know what it's like to be a Zeenod living on an occupied planet. We are oppressed. We're devalued. We're denied the opportunities we deserve. The Tevs and Z-Tevs are taking everything from us, and if we dare to speak out, we're labeled as criminals and banished. We have to find ways to survive."

"You survive by being a politician and following Z-Tev orders," Mehk said.

She nodded. "I do."

"But what does that have to do with Albert Kinney?"

Her jaw tightened. "I was given an order: his life or mine. I was told that, ultimately, it would be better for the planet—for Z-Tevs and Zeenods alike—to remove Albert Kinney. And that's all I can say." The president inhaled sharply and leaned forward. "What I can't figure out is what you have against Albert Kinney."

"I don't have anything against him. I just want him to resign."

The president's brow furrowed. "Why? Is someone paying you to do it?"

Mehk raised his chin. "I act alone. I want to use the tournament to showcase something I've created that will benefit the entire solar system."

She brightened. "Your masterpiece? The one you've been mentioning so mysteriously in your letters? Well, here I am. Tell me."

Now his jaw tightened. "I have given away my ideas before only to have them stolen."

Without shifting her position, without blinking, she spoke. "I ran a thorough analysis of your expenditures, your time, your transportation requests—all your business and personal accounts. You've broken the most serious laws in the Fuigor Solar System. You stole an ITV and made an illegal trip to Earth. You've stolen materials and resources from your employer and from the government, and I have enough information to incriminate you on all charges."

Something that had been tightly wound began to unravel in Mehk's chest. He was losing control. His muscles clenched. He began hitting himself hard on the side of the head.

The president adjusted both her position and her tone. Reaching forward, she tapped his knee, and when he stopped and looked up, she was smiling at him warmly. "Mehk, we are alike, you and me. We're both ambitious. We're both Zeenods and yet we're not Zeenods, are we? We are disconnected from much of what makes a Zeenod a Zeenod, perhaps because we have spent our lives surrounded by Z-Tevs. We are, in some ways, more Z-Tev than Zeenod." He was about to argue that he didn't identify with any planet, but then her voice took on a whispered hush. "I bet you're like me, Mehk. I bet you've never felt the ahn."

Mehk shifted uncomfortably. It was disconcerting—the way Lat seemed to know him.

She waved her hand. "I have no interest in stealing your secrets from you, Mehk. I'm here because we can help each other. We both want the same thing. I need to eliminate Albert Kinney, and, with my resources, you can make it happen without detection. That spybot you planted in the ITV—"

"You know about that?"

"It's undetectable, Mehk! The only reason I know about it is because, once I received the message and figured out who you were, I started spying on you."

He hit himself again. "I shouldn't have written that—"

"Mehk! It has brought us together. And now I know how impressive you are! Look at all you've accomplished! And with my help, you can accomplish even more. I can clear your criminal record and promote you to serve as my top technical advisor with the best resources available. No more making silly robotic toys. I want to help you get what you deserve!"

The dizziness returned.

"But before I can tell you how you can help me, I need to know what your mission with this masterpiece is all about. I have a file full of information about you, Mehk, but I don't know what it is that you're planning." She smiled. "My guess is that it is truly remarkable."

The vehicle was spinning, and he was feeling light-headed. The thought that he should have eaten something before he left for work flitted in and out of his mind. It was difficult to think clearly with so many words and smiles swirling around. Behind President Lat's chair, he noticed the control panel of the ITV blinking the words MAINTAIN HOLDING PATTERN, and he realized that the vehicle wasn't spinning. With one hand, he gripped the chair; with the other hand, he touched the thought-loop microbot embedded in the side of his head. Why wasn't he hearing his positive thought-loop? Was the roar of his own thoughts drowning it out? For a moment, he became lost, thinking about the complexity of the mind—how surprising and unpredictable it was. His thought-loop had been helping him, nudging him away from self-deprecation and toward positivity, but ultimately, his mind was too complex to be controlled.

"Does your masterpiece have to do with robotics?" the president asked softly.

He knew what she was doing. A psychological ploy of complimenting him, making him believe she was on his side. With effort, he focused and ran through the options in his mind. If he refused to work with her, he would be prosecuted and imprisoned—or sent to the gravespace. If he worked with her and revealed his secrets, she could steal the credit. The trick would be to give her what she needed and to find ways to protect himself and his intellectual property along the way. The trick would be to maintain control and strength and acquire power.

He straightened and looked her quite suddenly in the eye. "I have perfected robotics technology, and to prove it I have designed a robot to play as a Star Striker in the johka tournament, a robot that is so perfectly functioning, it cannot even be detected as a robot."

"I don't understand. You're telling me that there's a Star Striker in place who is actually a robot?"

Mehk exhaled. "Not yet. Mine is an alternate. I have secretly replaced the alternate choice for Kinney with a robotic replica of that choice. Once Kinney resigns, my—"

"Alternate? Kinney's alternate isn't even on my radar."

"Precisely! Choosing the alternate enabled me to get my robot in place without the usual scrutiny. And it has been functioning beautifully! Completely undetected so far. Surpassing all my expectations. And when Kinney resigns and the alternate is called to take Kinney's place, no one—not even the FJF—will suspect that it isn't a life-form. I've designed it to pass even the DNA test!" He leaned forward, emotion rising. "It will play without a flaw."

He caught his breath. For over a year now, he had been fantasizing about the moment when—after the johka tournament had ended—he would stride out during the victory celebration and reveal to the entire solar system that the Star Striker was a robot, his robot.

President Lat sat back, taking it in. "An elaborate stunt."

"Not a stunt! A public revelation. A way to make sure that everyone sees that the work is mine."

"But here you are—ready. And Kinney hasn't resigned. You've tried and yet—"

Again, the flush of shame. "I underestimated Kinney."

"If Kinney were out of the way, you believe your...robotic replacement could play and win you the credit you deserve. I understand. You want money and fame and—"

Mehk stood, tears suddenly rising. "You don't understand." He pulled something out of his pocket, and the president, thinking it was a weapon, stiffened.

"My apologies," she said softly. "Please. I'm listening."

He blinked and sat back down. His grip released slightly on the thing in his hand, and the president was astonished to see a gheet. Absent-mindedly, the botmaker petted the top of its hairy head. Although it looked real, she guessed from his file that this was one of his robotic triumphs.

"It's not about—It's just—" He stopped and took a breath. The gheet purred. Mehk looked up and said quietly, "Everything's imperfect. I can fix it."

They sat, silent, the ITV humming in its holding pattern.

"Mehklen." She touched his knee again. "You're a genius! What a brilliant idea to reveal your creation at the biggest event in the solar system. We can help each other and both get what we need. I can get you materials and access to—"

He brightened slightly. The gheet crawled up his arm and perched on his shoulder. "I planted a new bluff that I think will work to get Kinney to resign. And if that doesn't work, I have another idea, but I need certain resources that I don't have and—"

"Wait," she said. "What I want to propose is something beyond getting Kinney to resign. My orders have changed." Her voice reeled him in carefully, gently. "The order now is to create an explosion during the game, and with your ability—"

"An explosion to do what?"

She paused. "I know you're not a murderer, Mehklen. I'm not, either. If it were up to us, neither of us would resort to that. But this is an order. It's an order to eliminate Kinney on the field. I can't reveal the reason behind it. But after it's done, the tournament will continue and your alternate can be called into play for game two. You don't want to lose this chance to follow through on your dream, Mehklen. An explosion during the game. That's what we need. The problem is that the FJF controls the surveillance in the stadium. You, however, are the master of deception. You could get something in. Something creative and effective and—"

"Undetectable," he said.

"Exactly."

He looked down as the meaning of what was happening, that she was sweetly blackmailing him to do her dirty work, descended like a weight on his shoulders. The gheet responded to his sudden depression by nuzzling his neck.

The president waited. "You do that for me and I make sure your dream comes true. You'll have my full support."

He scooped the gheet off his shoulder and sat for a moment with it resting in his hands. "I don't have a choice, do I?" He looked up.

She smiled again. "It will be a win for all of us. I'll set the coordinates to take you home." She stood to leave and then turned. "By the way, how did you trace the assassination attempts to me?"

Something like a smile now crossed Mehk's face. He looked up. "I didn't. I bluffed."

A wince crossed the president's face, but she tried to hide it.

11.0

As the days and weeks sped by, Albert felt as if time weren't a series of moments that occurred one after the other, but rather that time was a path on which he was moving. And he wasn't moving on it of his own accord, he was being carried by the winds of what he was learning. Exhilarating.

Suddenly it was the sixth of November; the big day was in exactly one week, and he didn't want to miss a moment of the final preparation. And so, on this particular Friday, as soon as school was dismissed, Albert took off. The November sky was crammed full of gray clouds that looked impatient to release their torrents. Albert shivered and set his clarinet down so he could pull up the zipper of his hoodie, and then he looked again at the sky. He and

Tackle had to get in a training session at the park before the deluge hit.

The past seven weeks had been the best of his life. No question. Practices on Zeeno were hard but joyful. The danger seemed to have subsided. No more malicious spybots were detected either by Unit B in the ITV or by Tackle at home. The workouts with Tackle at the park were such an unexpected gift. The ahn lessons in the training tutorial—focusing on thought awareness and sending ahnic energy inward and outward—were harder than he'd have thought, but he was practicing all three. Both Ennjy and Kayko had noticed that each of the sessions on Zeeno had gotten more productive. He had moments when he was able to successfully complete a bounce-off or a jump-over, and the way the energy surged from the zee into the ball or into his own body was powerful. The way Giac had described the ahnic boost as something that happened to each cell was something he could feel in his muscles and tissues and organs. A physical and mental high. He still had failures, but there were moments of triumph, too.

Instead of begging his mom to let him quit clarinet or dreading the upcoming band concert, he decided to apply himself to practicing at least ten minutes a day—ten minutes with a laserlike focus on what he didn't know rather than what he was already good at; and in just three weeks he had improved enough to want to keep trying. Nana had noticed. Mr. Sam, too. And, thankfully, Jessica hadn't been at her house on Thursdays, so Albert had been able to focus on his lessons without worrying about what she thought.

His phone buzzed, and he pulled it out. A text from his mom:

*Don't take Tackle to the park today. Chance of rain 80%. Could
be lightning.*

Mom! Albert's eyes rolled and his breath exhaled in a huff.
And then he caught himself. Acknowledge what you're feeling
without judgment: Okay, I'm annoyed. Send ahnic energy outward. His mom meant well. He texted back:

I can tell you're afraid, but you can trust me. I'll be careful.

He was about to text a few cheerful emojis when he heard
Trey's voice behind him.

"Hey, there's my dog walker."

Albert felt the tension hit his shoulders. He took a breath and
looked back, intending a calm reply. But Trey wasn't alone. Jessica
was with him, and the sight of her caught him off guard. Catching
any boy and girl who weren't neighbors walking home together
was a noteworthy event among middle schoolers. She was on her
skateboard, as usual, having to go slow, of course, because Trey
was on foot. Quickly Albert resumed walking, closing his mouth
and picking up his pace, but now they were close behind. He
heard Trey explain to Jessica that Albert lived next door, making
it sound more like a pain than a benefit.

"Hey, Albert." Unlike Trey's voice, Jessica's was nice. "We're
going to Trey's to practice for the band concert."

Albert didn't want to look back, but he didn't want to be rude.
"Oh," he said, unable to think of anything else.

They had caught up to him now.

Trey, carrying both their saxophone cases, bragged, "Mr.
Chaimbers asked us to do a big duet."

"It's not a *big* duet," Jessica said, laughing and zooming slightly ahead of them on her board. "It's just a duet."

"It's *the* opening song for the concert," Trey said. "What's Beginning Band going to play—'Mary Had a Little Lamb'?"

In that instant, Albert's confidence evaporated.

"We played some good songs in Beginning Band," Jessica called back. "Remember?"

Trey laughed. "No."

A block to go.

Trey turned to Albert. "Where's your necklace?"

Jessica pushed forward. "Trey, which house is yours?"

Unwilling to follow her change of subject, Trey moved forward with his own. "So, Albert, are you playing on another team or did you quit soccer for good?"

Albert knew he should ignore him, but he couldn't. "I'm playing on a team. We have an important tournament next week."

"Really? Maybe I could come and watch."

"This is a fascinating conversation, guys," Jessica said, pushing faster. "Come on, Trey. I can't stay too long."

"Where's your tournament, Albert? You can come and watch any of my games," Trey said. "We're undefeated."

"That's great, Trey," Albert said. "I'll remember that."

"Why won't you tell me where you're playing?" Trey asked. "Why the secret?"

Jessica picked up her speed, crossing a quiet intersection. "Trey, I'm going to keep going straight unless you tell me where to go."

"No. Turn right. I told you I'm on Oak Street."

Ahead of them, she turned, and he called out, "Slow down. Second house on the right."

As their two houses came into view, Tackle put his front paws on the gate and began to bark.

"That's Tackle," Trey said. "Albert's afraid of him."

Albert stopped. "You know that Tackle actually likes me better than you, right?"

Trey laughed, jogged up to his house, and set down the sax cases. "Hey, boy!" Trey opened the gate and crouched down.

But instead of greeting his owner, Tackle leaped past Trey, knocking him over. With a happy howl, he ran to Albert.

Jessica laughed. "I guess Albert's right."

As she put out her hand to let Tackle sniff her, Trey stood, furious.

"I'll get his leash and take him for his regular walk," Albert said.

"He doesn't need a walk." Trey grabbed Tackle's collar. "Come on, Jessica."

Man, I blew it, didn't I? Tackle barked to Albert as Trey pulled him toward the house. *It was instinct! I wasn't thinking!*

Albert hurried inside.

A mere thirty minutes later, as Albert was doing sit-ups in his room, he received the text from Mrs. Patterson saying they had changed their mind about the dog walking. Albert was "no longer needed."

Trey's little jealous fit was to blame, Albert knew, which wasn't fair to him and wasn't fair to Tackle. The poor dog wouldn't even understand what had happened. Albert howled.

A moment later there was a knock on the door.

"You okay?" Nana's voice. "Can I come in?"

"I'm okay," Albert said.

His grandmother poked her head in. "You sound upset. Did something happen? You want to talk?"

"No, thanks. I'm fine. I'm doing core work. I was just getting through some sit-ups."

"No dog walking today?"

He shook his head.

She nodded. "Well, good for you for keeping up with your exercises. Hard work pays off, Albert. Look at me. I'm up and walking now." She waved her cane.

"Yeah. You're doing good, Nana."

The door closed and he heard her limp away.

His phone flashed. Another text from his mom.

Erin changed her mind about her birthday. Instead of bowling, she wants the girls to come for a sleepover next Friday. I said yes. Just so you know.

Everything was unraveling. Next Friday, at midnight, he was supposed to activate the szoŭ and meet his entire team at the hotel headquarters on Zeeno. The FJF had arranged everything. At the hotel, he and his team would watch the first game in the tournament, Jhaateez versus Gaböq, which was being played on Gaböq. The next morning, they'd be facing off against Vatria and the Tevs for their big game in the Zeeno stadium. Now, his house was going to be filled with Erin's friends.

For the past weeks, he had been able to deal with his twenty-seven-minute absences from Earth easily because the Zee-nods had let him choose the times and days, as long as they stayed the same. He had chosen lunch on Mondays and Wednesdays because no one noticed he was gone. And then he chose Saturday afternoons, because he really wanted something special to do on Saturdays, and because that was when his mom and Erin were at her gymnastics practice and when Nana liked to nap. The szoŭ time for the big event was dictated by the FJF, and it had already been stressing Albert out. Friday at midnight was risky. What if his mom peeked in on him at the moment he was beaming up? To be on the safe side, his plan was to stuff some pillows into his bed and then sneak outside for the szoŭ. Usually, his mom liked to go to bed early, which he had been counting on. A slumber party meant that the house would be full and nobody would be asleep by midnight.

Just as Albert was telling himself to breathe, his phone lit up and he received an unexpected message.

11.1

Albert picked up the phone, and on his screen was a text message.

Greetings, Albert. This is Lightning Lee.

Albert gasped. He couldn't believe it. He had been waiting for this moment, hoping the legendary player would contact him.

I'm sure you are delighted to be on the team, and I know that you have been training both your body and your mind.

Albert felt a rush of pride. He was dying to talk, to tell Lee everything that had been happening, dying to hear what the experience had been like so many years ago. He had a thousand questions and wanted to hear every word of wisdom. Maybe now that Lee was contacting him, Albert could reach out and meet in person. His mind raced into the future, but he caught himself and took a breath. He recalled Mr. Sam's advice to enjoy the present and turned his full attention back to the message.

As the final three practices and the first big game approach, I want to share my expert opinion.

Albert read on, holding his breath, and then the next sentence hit like a sledgehammer against his heart.

The Zeenods made a mistake choosing you.

The floor under Albert's feet seemed to shift.

You and I both know the truth, Albert. You are not who they think you are. You are not strong enough, skilled enough, or brave enough. Quit. If you leave the team, they will have a chance of winning. If you play, they will surely lose. The stakes are too high. Do the right thing.

12.0

On Saturday, the moment Albert teleported into the ITV, Unit B began going over the schedule. "Three practices left, Albert Kinney. On Friday, you need to—"

"Stop," Albert interrupted. He took a breath in and let it out. "I'm quitting."

The robot's eyelids blinked. "This is an unexpected statement."

"I didn't know how to get a message to you, so I'm here. I read the contract, and I *can* quit, so don't try to tell me I can't."

"You can quit, yes; however, based on your behavior thus far, I am surprised. Although you were not required by FJF rules to attend every practice, you have not missed a single one, despite attempts on your life. This indicates that you are fully committed to playing."

"Not anymore." He walked to the window.

"To be clear," Unit B said, "if you quit now, the Zeenods will play without a Star Striker until game two."

"They're supposed to have an alternate," Albert said.

"They do. According to security regulations, they cannot recruit or train the alternate until the first Star Striker has resigned and has been processed out. This takes time."

"Does that mean they'll be one player down during the game?"

"No. One of their own will step up to take your place."

"Then that's no problem," Albert said. "In fact, it's better. They're more likely to win without me for this game. And then they can train the alternate for the rest of the tournament."

In the window, Albert's reflection was superimposed onto the scene outside: to the left, starlight and a whirlpool of gases were sending a swirl of color through the vast darkness like a spiral staircase, so beautiful it made Albert's chest ache. He didn't want to think about an alternate taking his place. A part of him wanted to take back his proclamation, turn around and tell Unit B with a smile that it was all a joke, that he couldn't wait to see Kayko and Ennjy and Doz and Feeb and the others, couldn't wait to run on that odd spongy field and bounce off a zee. He took another breath, detecting that particular pine scent that was always lingering in the crevices of the spacecraft, the scent that was so Zeeno, and he almost broke down into tears.

"Albert?" the robot asked. Oddly, her voice sounded almost kind.

Albert closed his eyes. He didn't deserve any kindness. He was weak. From the start, he should have admitted that he wasn't good enough in any way—body, mind, or spirit; that was his real shawble. He had wasted everyone's time. "Just get the message to Kayko that I quit." He paused. "And tell her I'm sorry."

Unit B was silent for a full minute, and then she spoke. "My research indicates that if there is conflict between two parties, resolution is more likely to occur if the parties talk face to face. I suggest that we continue to Zeen—"

Albert shook his head. "There isn't conflict. Please turn around and take me back."

"I can request a video conference with Kayko and—"

"I've already made up my mind. Take me home."

Unit B walked over to the controls and began to adjust the ITV's trajectory. "Resetting journey to Earth. By the way, you could have sent a message and saved me this trip," she said, her back to Albert, her words crisp and quick. "Paragraph 523B in your guide explains that you can record and send an audio message to me through your Z-da."

"Yeah," Albert muttered under his breath, "I'll miss you, too."

Her head swiveled to face him, and her eyes flashed. "Pardon. Were you speaking to me?"

Albert lost it. "I'm so sorry that I didn't read every nanometer of the ten-thousand-page guide you gave me!" He began to remove his Z-da. "I won't be needing this."

She held up her hand. "There is no need for you to raise your voice or remove your Z-da. Fŭigor-issued equipment and materials can only be returned after the game is over, regardless of whether you play in the game."

"That's ridiculous. I'm done."

"If you read paragraph ninety-eight—"

"Whatever." Albert turned his attention back to the window.

"You can come down to Earth and get it after the game is over. I don't care."

"Is that a joke?"

"No."

"Albert Kinney, you must know that I cannot 'come down to Earth.' Have you not understood? My appearance on Earth soil is illegal, according to Fŭigor law. It could cause a major incident, and the ripple effect of that could cause widespread panic among Earthlings—"

"Yeah, yeah, blah, blah. Next time I'll text you." Albert pressed his forehead against the window. He knew he was being rude, but he couldn't see how it could possibly matter. Everything was over.

"The day after the game, I will activate a final szoŭ to begin the processing."

"Fine. Whatever."

"I will then retrieve the Z-da and remove the implants." Then she delivered the final blow. "At that time, your memory will be wiped."

He looked at her black eyes. "Wiped, as in I won't remember anything?"

"Correct."

"Do you have to do that?"

"Star Strikers who resign are considered unstable. So, yes."

He turned to the window and stared into the vast blackness of space.

12.1

The surveillance footage of Unit B receiving Albert Kinney's resignation came in when the botmaker was halfway finished with the fabrication of two microbots required for the assassination of Albert Kinney. When he heard the words "I'm quitting" in Albert Kinney's now-familiar voice, he leaped up with a squeal.

The facility was closed, so no life-forms were present. A robotic floor polisher, on its fifth lap, did not respond.

Mehk sat back down and sent a message to President Lat through their encrypted channel:

For your information, a tactic that I set in motion has achieved success! I crafted a fake message to Kinney as if from former Star Striker Lee, persuading Kinney that it would be best for the team for him to quit. My theory was that Albert would do anything to help the Zeenods—even if it went against his own desires—and I was correct. It worked! The power of psychology! I will stop work on the explosive device since it is no longer needed.

An image of Albert's face came to him, the look of sadness as he quit. Mehk had witnessed how hard Albert had been working and knew the sacrifice Albert was making, and a surprising ping of sympathy touched his heart. Perhaps President Lat was right, he thought. Perhaps he was more Z-Tev than Zeenod. Perhaps Albert was more connected to Zeenods than Mehk would ever be. For a moment, Mehk was flooded with admiration for Albert's team spirit, and he found it confusing, and then a kind of dizziness came on. He was hungry. He was exhausted. He hadn't eaten or slept much in two days.

The robot turned to make its sixth round, the whir of its motor drilling into Mehk's brain.

"You can stop. The floors are already clean," Mehk called out.

"I'm programmed for eight cycles," the robot replied.

"Well, whoever programmed you is an idiot," Mehk muttered. "A waste of energy."

A message from the president came in. Mehk looked at it eagerly and then froze.

Finish your work. The plan is to move forward. Do your best work on this—I know it will be brilliant—and you will be rewarded.

Mehk blinked, trying to understand. Wasn't the explosive meant for Kinney? If Kinney wasn't playing, who would the explosive be used on? To what purpose?

With dread, he looked through the scope at the chip he was working on. The work was beautiful. Creative. Impressive. Deadly.

13.0

Anger grew like a poisonous vine in Albert's mind that week. Unable to convince his mother he was sick, he dragged himself through the mud of each day, after school immediately locking himself into his room, where his thoughts grew even more toxic. A burst of anger at himself for not being good enough; followed by a burst of misdirected anger at Lee; followed by a burst of anger at the Zeenods for choosing him, for inviting him to be attacked, to be humiliated, to risk his life. I don't owe them anything, he chanted over and over. And the next moment, the sadness would rise like floodwater.

Nana tried to get him moving at the park or on the trampoline, but he kept saying no. His mother said she could tell that something was wrong but that she was having a particularly busy week and as soon as his sister's party was over, they had to sit down and have a big talk.

Whatever, he thought.

On the morning of the twelfth, Thursday, he announced that his clarinet lesson after school would be his last. The band concert was tonight, and he had been taking lessons to improve enough to play in the concert, which he had done. "Mission accomplished. The End," he said over his cereal bowl.

"But I thought you were enjoying it," his mother said.

"You've been improving," Nana added, her face creased with worry.

He shrugged. "I should probably just skip the concert tonight, too. I'm sure they're better off without me."

"Actually, with that attitude, it's true," his grandmother snapped back.

"Oh for heaven's sakes!" His mother gave Nana a desperate look. "We're supposed to be encouraging Albert to play. He *has* been improving."

"With all due respect, Catherine, encouraging him to play doesn't mean squat to me. Encouraging him to play with a good attitude is what's important." Albert's no-nonsense grandmother leaned forward and locked eyes with him. "When you are in a band, you are a part of a team and you owe the team the best, most positive energy you can give."

"I agree with the part about attitude, but let's make one thing clear. You're playing in the concert tonight, Albert," his mom said.

Albert stared at his plate. "I'm definitely quitting next semester."

"Quitter," Erin muttered as she reached for the milk.

Enraged, he stood and grabbed the milk carton and held it over Erin's head, and everyone in the room froze in shock.

"Albert," his mom said softly. "Put that down. Erin was wrong, but put that down."

He slammed the milk carton on the table, sending a zee of milk up, which splashed onto his sister anyway. She screamed. He grabbed his backpack and clarinet and walked out the door.

The minute he was out, Tackle barked and ran to the gate as he had been doing every day. *Albert, I've missed you! What's going on? Why aren't we talking? You're leaving for the big tournament tomorrow night, right?*

Tackle still didn't know that Albert had been fired from his dog-walking job. Albert hadn't told him. Saying it out loud would just make it worse, his brain reasoned. All week he had been making quick lame excuses to Tackle about having too much homework and needing to hurry off. Now, he did the same thing.

I'm late, he said to the dog, and headed to school, trying as best he could to block out the mournful howl behind him.

Albert? C'mon, man! This isn't fair.

13.1

Tackle watched Albert until he disappeared around the corner. Albert wasn't late for school. Trey was still inside. That meant Albert was deliberately avoiding him again, and why? The last week had been hard on Tackle. No workout on Monday, Tuesday, or

Wednesday, and this morning another snub from Albert. What had he done to deserve this kind of treatment, he wondered? The only mistake he had made was showing more excitement about seeing Albert than Trey last week. Not exactly a crime. In the meantime, the dog's loyalty and service were exemplary. He was guarding the yards, patiently keeping track of every flutter, every scent, every murmur.

Since the grass in the Pattersons' backyard had been repaired for a while, and since there had been no additional suspicious machines causing him to further disturb the yard, the Pattersons had given him full access. Now he took off and ran around the perimeter of the house at full speed, sending a real squirrel scampering up a tree. And when he came full circle, he ran around a second and a third time.

His muscles twitched. One day without real exercise, and he felt stiff. Three days in a row and he didn't even feel like a dog. And that wasn't even what was really bothering him. What was really bothering him? Albert's absence.

How could Albert not understand how important it was to spend time with him? Only one person understood him, really understood him, and that human was practically ignoring him. Maybe all humans were just stupid. Pathetic, really. After all, most dogs understood some human words. *Yes. No. Good dog. Bad dog. Fetch. Food. Outside. Park. Stop. Go. Sit. Roll over.* Even the air-brained Pomeranian who lived on the corner was able to learn some English. Did any humans ever learn Dog? No, they did not. Albert had been given the gift because of his alien implant. He hadn't really *learned* how to speak Dog.

In the cool November air, Tackle stood for a moment, anger and resentment rising.

13.2

That morning Albert didn't believe his mood could be darker. But then he arrived at school, and Señora Muñoz began the Spanish class with a cheer, in Spanish, of course, for the school's soccer team and for Trey because they had won yesterday's game against their biggest rivals and Trey had scored all three goals. *¡Viva, los Warriors! ¡Viva, Trey!*

Albert wanted to vomit.

His teachers didn't even seem to notice his depression, which he thought he would be happy about but which ended up making him feel invisible. At his clarinet lesson after school, however, Mr. Sam asked immediately: "What kind of face is that? Tonight's your school concert. Aren't you excited?"

Albert couldn't possibly explain. He just shrugged and walked down the hall into the little room for his lesson. Sitting on the painted wooden chair, he pulled his case onto his lap and began putting together his instrument.

"Let's talk before we play," Mr. Sam said. "I want to give you some performance tips."

Albert stopped, but he didn't look up. "I don't really need them. This is going to be my last lesson." His voice sounded as flat as Unit B's.

Mr. Sam sat back in his chair, silent for a few seconds. Then he leaned forward. "Lots of people get performance jitters. It's also called stage fright—"

"It's not that," Albert said. "I'm just not good at this, and I don't see the point."

"What? You've improved radically in the past six weeks, Albert. Last week you said practicing ten or fifteen minutes each day was making all the difference in the world and that you were enjoying it."

Still looking down, Albert shrugged.

Mr. Sam stood and walked over to the window and looked out. The back of his sweatshirt had a faded image of a turtle with sunglasses playing the clarinet. When he turned back around, he caught Albert's eyes and smiled. "Your mom paid for this lesson, so let's not waste it. As I was saying, stage fright is—"

"I don't have stage fright. I'm just not good enough to bother continuing."

Mr. Sam picked up his own clarinet and sat back down. "All the way into my twenties and thirties, I had an issue with confidence—"

"I—"

"Humor me, Albert. I'm a teacher. I need to be teachy for a minute."

Albert shrugged as if to say *Go ahead.* He knew he was being a terrible student, the kind of student a teacher like Mr. Sam didn't deserve.

But Mr. Sam just went on. "Okay, Albert. So imagine a much younger me sitting in the auditorium or the club or whatever, and I'm waiting to go on. And somebody goes before me. It might be another soloist or whatever. And I'm sitting there listening… and I'm getting really freaked out because they're good. And then I start thinking how bad I'll sound in comparison. And that freaks me out more. And then I start hoping they'll make a mistake so I won't have to follow something so good. And then I actually start hating them for being good. And then I start hating myself for hating them because I know I'm being jealous. And then by the time it's my turn, I'm filled with all these negative thoughts. And—I play terribly. And then I say to myself, *See? I'm no good.*"

In the quiet, Albert heard the front door open and the thud of a backpack on the floor. It was probably Jessica. He fast-forwarded in his mind to the concert, to having to sit there and listen to Jessica and Trey nail a saxophone duet. The cool couple. So talented. So popular. So perfect.

"But then I learned something from a very wise teacher," Mr. Sam went on. "Here's what I learned. It's simple. Think nice thoughts about whoever goes before you instead of jealous thoughts. If they're good, then send encouraging messages to them in your mind—*That's great! Keep playing! You sound good!* If they're fantastic, then say to yourself, *Wow, isn't this fabulous music? Aren't I lucky to be hearing it? How inspiring!*"

Albert stared at him, anger rising in his chest.

"Honestly, Albert, that kind of thinking has an incredible effect. You feel good and kind and generous. You radiate goodwill. And you end up playing better." Mr. Sam blinked. For a second, the openness of his face reminded Albert of the Zeenods.

Albert closed his case and walked out.

"Albert?" Mr. Sam's voice followed him.

Jessica, standing in the hallway, looked at him.

"Albert?" Mr. Sam's hand touched his shoulder. "What's wrong?"

Albert whipped around to face him. "You know what? I'm tired of everybody telling me to think kind thoughts. Kindness sucks. I don't need to hear any of this." He hurried past Jessica and ran out the door.

The sun was already low on the horizon, gold between the trees. His favorite kind of light; Nana called it the gloaming. Something seemed so wrong about feeling sad and angry in the midst of this loveliest of lights, and yet he couldn't stop the way he felt.

It would be a matter of moments until Mr. Sam called his mom and his mom called him. Sure enough, his phone buzzed in his pocket. He did not pick it up.

When he reached his driveway, he stopped.

Everything was unusually quiet. Even though Albert had been avoiding him, Tackle usually ran to greet him. The sight of the empty yard made Albert want to howl.

He walked up to the Pattersons' front gate and hesitated. Their car was gone. He opened the gate and walked around to the Pattersons' backyard.

The dog door opened and Tackle trotted out; and the sight of him was so welcome it made something catch in Albert's throat.

Tackle was not a dog who would grovel for attention, so he was trying hard to look as if he didn't care. Nonchalantly, he trotted over and sniffed around the trunk of the tree and peed on it, and then he walked past Albert, giving him a sniff. It was a beautifully protective sniff, Albert knew, a sniff to make sure he didn't detect anything suspicious lurking or lingering on Albert's clothes or skin or seeping through Albert's pores, because that was the kind of dog he was, the kind to serve even when he was getting so little in return.

Albert set down his clarinet case and his backpack and sat on the grass and the dog circled once and then also sat. Albert felt as if a sponge, heavy with both sadness and rage, was stuck somewhere in his chest, making it hard for him to breathe. Everything good that had been lifting him up had evaporated and what he was left with, the muck gathering in that sponge, was everything bad—and he had no one but himself to blame. On Sunday, Unit B was going to activate the final szoŭ and take back the Z-da and remove the breathing device in his lungs and the translation device in his ear. He would be ordinary Albert again. The Albert who did nothing. The Albert who had nothing. And he wouldn't even be able to talk to this magnificent beast who was waiting patiently with him in the grass.

You look like you need to cry, the dog said.

Albert gave him a quick glance.

What? You think dogs don't cry? I've been howling every day all week.

Albert tried to smile, but tears threatened to spill, and he struggled to gain control and then finally blurted out, *I got fired, Tackle. I'm not supposed to walk you anymore.*

Tackle sat down across from him, panting lightly. *Was it my fault? What happened?*

His eyes were so sad, Albert had to look away. *I have worse news.*

Tackle sat up tall. *Give it to me.* His muscled body, his glossy reddish-golden coat, the power of his animal nose, the strong symmetry of his face, those wet golden-brown eyes, rimmed with black, staring at him patiently, regally... He was a prince of a dog. Albert's friend.

Albert pulled up a few blades of grass and flicked them away. He couldn't say the words *I quit,* and so he whispered the only thing he could get out at the moment—a lie. *I can't play in the Fŭigor tournament anymore. I got disqualified because of some rule. No more Earthlings.*

Tackle's ears twitched and the skin between his eyes wrinkled. *That doesn't sound fair. I'm sorry, Albert.*

The tears welled up, and he couldn't stop them. *They have to take away the translation device, Tackle. After Sunday, we won't be able to do this anymore.* He looked at the dog, the tears now streaming. *We won't be able to talk...and...they have to erase my memories....*

What?

I won't remember any of this.

The boy and the dog looked at each other for another long moment, and then Albert buried his face in Tackle's neck and cried.

13.3

"Albert didn't come to my last meet," Erin said at dinner. "I don't see why I have to go to his band concert. There's stuff for my party that I want to—"

"You don't have to come. I don't want you to." Albert shoved a forkful of pasta into his mouth.

"We're all going," their mom said. "Erin, that's enough."

"I, for one, am looking forward to the concert," Nana said. "Music always makes me feel good."

"Me too." Their mom smiled. "By the way, Albert, you need to tell me in advance when you need something special like a white shirt and black pants. And I don't know why you put up such a fight about insisting that the clothes we borrowed wouldn't fit. They fit perfectly. You look very nice, Albert."

"In Trey's hand-me-downs." Erin laughed.

Albert snapped. Without stopping to think, he sent his last forkful of pasta at her face.

She screamed and scooched back, and, luckily for Albert, it landed on the table.

"Albert!" His mom couldn't believe it. She turned to Erin. "And you started it, Erin. This has to stop." When Erin was silent, she added, "If I don't hear a genuine apology, Erin, I'm canceling your party. A party is not a right, it's a privilege."

"I'm sorry, Albert," Erin said quickly. "That was mean of me."

Albert apologized for the food fling, but neither her apology nor his made him feel any better.

When they arrived at school, his family found seats in the middle, and Albert dragged himself to sit in his place on the stage with the Beginning Band. Freddy Mills, over in the tuba section, was wearing a bow tie, looking so excited it made Albert feel worse. Out of the corner of his eye, Albert could see Trey and Jessica standing offstage with their saxophones.

After the Beginning Band students were in place, Mr. Chaimbers walked to the center of the stage and gave a nod, and the curtains were raised.

The packed auditorium erupted into applause. "Welcome to tonight's concert! We're going to hear all three of our bands tonight—Beginning Band, Concert Band, and Jazz Band, in that order. But to kick off the evening, we're going to start with a jazz duet performed by Trey Patterson and Jessica Atwater." He turned and waved at Trey and Jessica to walk on.

The two of them looked fabulous, gorgeous and smiling, as they walked to the front of the stage, and jealousy began to bubble inside Albert's core. Instead of looking like a little kid in dress-up clothes, Trey looked adult in his crisp white shirt and his sleek black slacks. Albert wished Trey would look at him. He was ready with a glare of hatred so fierce it would knock him off his feet.

As Mr. Chaimbers introduced the name of the song, Albert continued to drill his glare at Trey's back, his jealousy a hot magma bubbling throughout his body. A series of fantasies fired through his mind: Trey tripping, Trey blowing a hideously wrong note, the audience laughing, the audience booing, the audience throwing rotten tomatoes, Trey having a panic attack, a legion of vampire bats swooping down from the rafters and chasing him off the stage, an army of Tevs marching in to take him prisoner.

Albert's stomach churned and his hands began to shake. Fail, Trey. Fail.

The chant inside his head began softly at first and then grew louder. He glared at the back of Trey's head, as if his chant could burn its way into Trey's brain and fry the synapses that told him which fingers he should press to get the right notes.

Fail, Trey. Fail.

Fail, Trey. Fail.

Albert imagined jealousy spilling out of him like lava and spreading along the floor, rolling toward Trey.

And then Jessica lifted her sax to her lips, and the stage lights sent a lovely little shimmer off her golden instrument, a gold that reminded him of the gold in the eyes of the Zeenods and the gold in the eyes of Tackle, and the gold of the lights inside the hygg, and the gold of the sun setting on the leaves of the maple tree, and he was pulled, for a moment, outside that dark place where he had been crouching.

He heard Mr. Sam's voice saying that if he sent silent words of encouragement, he would radiate goodwill. It was the same idea as the third lesson in his training. *In sending ahnic energy, we lift up others and liberate our minds from our shawbles. We strengthen the ahn between us and create a profound ripple effect.*

All the negativity he had absorbed from Trey, from Vatria, from Lightning Lee, from Unit B, from the hacked monster, from his sister—he was disgusted by it. And he was disgusted, too, by all the negativity he had generated. Much of it was directed inward, but a huge amount was directed outward. A shawble, he realized. He didn't want to be a person like Trey or Vatria or Lightning Lee, a person who put other people down.

An image of Tackle shaking the tension in his body out after a sprint on the field came to Albert, and suddenly Albert wanted to stand up and shake all the negative energy out of his body. And then another image came of Tackle, that moment when Albert had decided to face his fear and send positive thoughts to Tackle. Albert remembered that the moment when he intentionally sent ahnic energy to the dog was the moment they could understand each other.

Okay, Albert told himself. Just let go of all this negativity. Think kind thoughts. What do you have to lose?

He closed his eyes and felt the jealousy. I see you, Jealousy.

He heard Kayko's voice: Be kind to yourself, Albert Kinney.

He imagined himself in the middle of the circle of his teammates when he first received energy through the ahn. It's been rough lately, Albert, he said to himself. So give yourself a break. You're sad and you're wearing Trey Patterson's hand-me-downs. Eyes still closed, he noticed his heartbeat slowing down. He took a breath and let it out. May you be well, Albert. May you feel joy.

He pictured Jessica standing in the spotlight. She didn't deserve bad energy from anyone. He took a breath and focused on her with his mind and heart. May you play well, Jessica. May you feel joy.

It felt good to wish her well.

The music began.

May you play well, Jessica. May you feel joy.

The fire inside Albert began to cool.

May you play well, Jessica. May you feel joy.

He took another deep breath and let it out. He pictured Trey standing next to her. He resisted momentarily and then he told himself to try. You can do this, Albert. Be a better person than you have been.

He pictured the old Trey, his partner on the field. That friend had to be in there somewhere. May you play well, Trey. May you feel joy.

Something unexpected rose up from way underneath the hot magma: a tiny bubble of delight. He was shocked, but he actually felt better wishing Trey well than wishing disaster on him. He felt large instead of small.

May you play well, Trey. May you feel joy.

Eyes closed, he listened as the song continued. The two saxophones split into harmony. They sounded good. Really good. The jealousy began to rise again, and he felt its heat, and he said to it: Yeah, I see you, Jealousy, but I'm really tired of you. So take a rest because I'm going to focus on something that feels better. And then he turned his attention back to the music. Fantastic. You guys sound great. Keep it going.

It felt good. He imagined energy spilling out of him and traveling through invisible threads of ahn to Trey and to Jessica. He imagined that they could feel his energy flowing into them and that it radiated out through their fingertips into their saxophones and out into the auditorium. He imagined it traveling to the ears of his nana, his mother, his sister.

A smile spread across Albert's face. This was good. This was right.

He opened his eyes and watched Jessica and Trey finish their duet, take their bows. He clapped, hoping they'd look at him as they walked off the stage. If they did, he'd give each of them a genuine smile. Great music. Inspiring!

They didn't look at Albert, but Albert saw the glow in their faces and knew they were happy; and instead of wanting to rip the joy away from them, he felt good.

Mr. Chaimbers introduced the Beginning Band's first song, and Albert's bandmates turned their attention to their music stands. Albert lifted his clarinet to his lips and began to play. They sounded good. Tight. The trombones came in right when they were supposed to, and Albert felt happy for them and happy for Mr. Chaimbers, who had been trying so hard for the past month to get that part right. The audience clapped and they played their next song, which was even better. A swing tune with a fast beat. There was something amazing about joining his clarinet's sound with the sound of the others in the band. Like magic.

As Mr. Chaimbers introduced the last song, Albert looked out. Everyone beyond the first two rows was in darkness, so he couldn't see his family, but he found himself smiling. This is what an audience looks like from a stage, he thought, and there's something nice about knowing that people who love you and want you to play well are out there, even if you can't see them.

They nailed the last song, and then it was over. As the Concert Band entered from the left, the Beginning Band exited to the right and took their seats on the right side of the auditorium.

The Concert Band was good, but the Jazz Band blew Albert away. They killed it, sounding like total professionals. Every song seemed to seep into Albert's muscles and make him want to move.

After the concert was over, he made a vow to stick with the music, to practice harder so that he could make it into Jazz Band at the beginning of next year. He couldn't wait to tell his mom and grandmother.

When the concert was over and the students joined their families for refreshments in the lobby, Freddy walked by, and Albert caught him by the elbow. "Hey, good job tonight, Freddy. I thought we sounded good."

"Wow," Freddy said, stopping to give him a surprised look.

Albert smiled and looked him right in the eye. "I mean it."

A huge smile. "We did sound good."

Albert saw Jessica standing by the cookie table with a bouquet of bright yellow flowers in her hands. Trey was there, too.

Before Trey could say a word, Albert smiled and said with genuine warmth in his voice, "Trey, Jessica, your duet was fantastic." They both looked up, and Albert went on. "I loved the duet. And every song Concert Band did was great. You guys were really inspiring."

Trey gave him a funny look.

"Thanks, Albert." Jessica smiled, radiating joy.

13.4

That night, Albert tossed and turned in bed, waiting until he couldn't hear a single sound in the house. At around eleven thirty, he sat up, pulled out his Z-da, and activated the guide.

The section on how to send a message to Unit B was long and slightly confusing, requiring the use of both the Z-da and his cell phone. He read it three times and then copied the sequence of fingerings, blowing into the Z-da mouthpiece, to activate the signal for the message. Nothing happened for a few moments, and then his cell phone glowed. Albert picked up his phone and saw a text.

Unit B here. Albert Kinney, this is unexpected.

Albert's hands were shaking as he typed.

I want back in. They probably won't take me back, but I have to try.

He waited, holding his breath.

Albert, by "back in" do you mean that you would like the Zeenods to allow you to resume your role as their Star Striker for the Fŭigor Johka Tournament, even though you informed me six Earth days ago that you quit?

Albert sighed.

Yes.

Is this a joke?

Albert typed quickly:

No.

And then he hesitated and added:

267

Also, Lee sent me a message through my phone. A text message that disappeared after I read it. I didn't reply. I don't know if this counts as breaking the secrecy rule. I want to be honest.

A long pause. Albert had no idea if Unit B would agree to contact the Zeenods, no idea if the Zeenods would be able to trust him, really trust him, ever again.

And then the text came.

When you quit, I ran a diagnostic and determined an 80% chance that you would change your mind. I also ran a psychological diagnostic on the negative effect of giving the Zeenods news that you quit if there was a likelihood that you would change your mind. I determined it was best for all to withhold your message and allow them to infer that you had to miss the latest practices due to a scheduling conflict, but that you would be there for the game.

Albert blinked. He read the message twice.

Wait. Are you saying you never told them I quit?

That is correct.

Albert held his breath.

What about the text from Lee?

You had no choice in the receiving of the message and you sent no message in return. Technically there was no violation of secrecy on your part. I'll investigate what it means for Lee. Perhaps the assumption was that the device would be used by you only on Zeeno, in which case it may not be an infraction. At any rate, that has nothing to do with you.

Albert jumped out of bed.

So, can I play?

Only you can answer that. Do you mean: May I play?

Albert laughed.

May I play?

Yes, you may. The Zeenods are expecting you.

Grinning from ear to ear, Albert did a victory dance around his room. And then he ran over to his window and looked up at the moon and the black night beyond it. He, Albert Kinney, was going to Planet Zeeno tomorrow night. He and his team would be staying in the hotel near the stadium that the FJF had arranged. They would all watch and analyze the first game in the FJF series, Planet Jhaateez versus Planet Gaböq, which was happening that night on Gaböq. They'd be playing both teams later in the tournament, and Albert would have the chance to see what they were like on the field. Then they'd wake up the next day and play their game against the Tevs. It would be strange and dangerous and important, and he was going to be the Star Striker.

Albert looked out the window again. Somewhere up there a robot was hovering in a pine-smelling ITV messaging with him. He smiled and turned his attention back to his phone and typed:

I love you.

After a moment, Unit B's answer came back:

My internal processing system has not been configured for the action "love."

Albert laughed.
Another message came through.

Please confirm that you are aware that the FJF investigation of the hacking and kidnapping produced no results. With no arrests, the likelihood of another threat or attempt is high. You, the Zeenods, and I will need to be on alert every moment.

Albert sat down. It was so strange, really, that the universe could produce beings as peaceful and kind as the Zeenods and as brutal as Vatria and the Tevs. He took a breath and followed it as it entered his lungs. He thought about how much he had already learned from the Zeenods and how much he wanted their planet to thrive. Kayko and Ennjy had helped Albert survive the kidnapping. He wanted more than anything to help his new friends and trusted that they would help him deal with any threats that came his way. Yes, it was dangerous, but he was ready. He typed:

I understand and accept the risks.

Message received. Do you require any other information or would you like to end this communication, Albert?

Albert thought about Lightning Lee's message, and a flicker of doubt ran through his mind. The beloved former Star Striker thought he should quit, but then again, Lee had no idea what Albert was capable of. Albert would just have to prove himself. He typed:

I'm good.

From Unit B:

I don't understand. Behaviorally good? Morally good?

Albert smiled.

It means I don't need anything else. See you tomorrow, Unit B!

Unit B:

I'm good, too.

Albert typed:

Wait! If we win, will I get a trophy or a medal or anything to show for it?

Unit B:

Each player is given what you call a medal for each game won. An object such as a trophy is given for the tournament win.

Albert set down his phone and climbed into bed. A fantasy

popped into his mind: he would beat the Tevs, win a medal, and make sure that Trey caught a glimpse of it, if that was possible without breaking the secrecy rule. He stayed in bed for a few seconds, but then he hopped up and slipped on some socks and shoes, grabbed a hoodie, slipped an apple and a carrot into his pocket, and snuck out the back door.

The November air was cold and dry. No clouds. Just the almost-bare trees and a half-moon and the Big Dipper and the crunch of leaves underfoot. He crept past the trampoline, picking up a lawn chair, and went to the part of the fence that was closest to the Pattersons' back door. He stood on the chair and peered over the fence.

Softly, he howled out his question. *Are you there? Can you come out?*

He waited, worried that the Pattersons had locked the dog door. But after a few seconds he heard the unmistakable sound of the heavy flap opening, the jingle of Tackle's dog tags, and the rapid click of his nails against the wooden porch steps as he flew out. *Albert?* the dog called softly.

Delighted, Albert hopped down and ran around to the gate. The second he opened it, Tackle was on him. The two laughed at the unexpected midnight meeting and, not quite knowing what to do with the surge of energy, wrestled around before settling down and sitting down.

What are you doing out here? Tackle asked, sniffing him. *It's freezing, man. You're in your pj's.*

"I'm excited because I'm going to play in the tournament after all." Albert whispered the words.

The dog's ears pricked. *I only understand Dog, dude.*

Albert laughed and softly barked an apology. *I brought us a midnight snack to celebrate.* He gave the dog the carrot and, between bites of the apple, told the dog everything. As they nuzzled to keep warm and enjoyed their snacks, Albert was sure he couldn't be happier.

Thanks for the carrot, Tackle said. *Yum.*

Yummery, Albert said, and laughed.

13.5

The botmaker tapped off the surveillance video, took off his smartgoggles, and rubbed his face.

Kinney was back in. The number of twists and turns that were happening was making him feel ill.

Before he could fully process the new information, a message came from President Lat, who was watching the footage at the same time.

No matter. Stay the course for game one. You can put your plan into action for game two, which was our original agreement.

He stared at the robotic gnauser, to which he was adding a surveillance camera. In addition to creating the system for the explosion, he was also expected to get this new spybot in place at the hotel to capture video of arrivals and to infiltrate the hotel's ventilation system and spy on the team.

"I can't think straight," he muttered to his gheet, stretched across the top of his empty drink cup, keeping him company while he worked in the otherwise empty factory. The six blue eyes blinked sympathetically at once.

The image of the Earth dog popped into his mind. Albert Kinney and the canine had grown closer, an unexpected outcome of the Pattersons' hiring of him as dog walker. The two had a... what was it called... a friendship.

Mehk glanced at the sleek arachnoid. "Did you know that Earth dogs receive as much if not more of a dopamine hit—that's the 'joy chemical' in the human brain—when they receive praise as when they receive food?"

The gheet's head tilted in the listening posture.

"I learned this recently when I did more research on canines!" Mehk exclaimed. "Praise is as important as food!"

He stopped working and looked out the window, momentarily perplexed by a question. Did all life-forms need praise? Did he? Was the praise he received from President Lat genuine even though she was using it to blackmail him?

He thought again about the dog. While he admired Tackle for his loyalty, for his muscle and endurance, for his olfactory abilities, overall the dog had caused problems, and he could not risk any more surprises. There was too much at stake. It pained him now—was this the Zeenod in him?—but he had to find a way to eliminate it, remotely, of course.

"Life-forms are beyond control," he said to his gheet. "This is why you are preferable to a life-form."

The thing purred and wiggled.

14.0

Tackle knew about Erin's party—Albert had told him about it the night before—so the dog wasn't surprised to see the activity after school. The car zooming in with grocery bags. Balloons being tied to the lamppost.

Before dinnertime, when it was still light, girls began arriving. Mostly by car. Each girl loaded with a sleeping bag, a pillow, a backpack. Each girl greeted at the door by Erin with a shriek. A shriek of happiness, Tackle thought, but he wasn't completely sure.

Since the weather was warm for November, the girls spent most of the evening in the backyard. Screams on the trampoline. The smell of the barbecue grill. Hot dogs. Hamburgers. Toasted buns. Music thumping. Girls singing. Girls dancing.

In the midst of all that commotion, the Pattersons left—all three of them—and Tackle followed them out and watched the car leave and then he hung around the front and side yards for a while, hoping for a glimpse of Albert. But when he finally got around to wandering back inside, he noticed something strange. His dog bowl. Full. His initial response of excitement was quickly tempered with suspicion. Something smelled wrong. He sniffed again and backed up. Not wrong. Dangerous. Poisonous.

His ears flattened back against his head and his hair stood on end.

Someone had been in this kitchen. Someone had prepared this bowl of food, thinking, hoping that he couldn't detect the toxic scent. Someone wanted him to get sick. Or die.

He tore around the house, barking and growling as he entered every room, in case the interloper was still there. He didn't smell or feel a presence, but he wasn't going to take any chances. When he was sure no one was in the house, he sniffed around the kitchen, trying to pick up a stranger's scent, and when he couldn't find one, he ran outside to check the perimeter.

Tonight was the night Albert was going to the game. It was happening at midnight. Tackle had to warn Albert of this new development and was hoping to see him outside, but only the girls and the mom were out.

He stopped racing and stood for a moment, panting, looking from one side of the backyard to the other. Oak tree. Chew rope. Gum tree. Pile of leaves. Picnic table. Ball.

Three huge crows flew from the top of the Grangers' tree to the Pattersons' gum tree, cackling to each other and startling a real squirrel in the tree. Without moving, Tackle watched the squirrel's rapid and expert escape: a scamper along a branch, a leap to the fence, and another leap from there into the safety of the Kinneys' much smaller cherry tree. In the distance came the huff of a truck on the busier street to the north, the one that led uphill.

His muscles twitched. His ears flicked. He jumped on the picnic table and began to howl.

The girls laughed. He kept howling.

Albert's bedroom window opened, and Tackle barked out a command for Albert to come over as soon as possible.

The window closed, and Tackle jumped down and ran to wait by the gate.

A sour smell and a yap came from the left. The Pomeranian from the corner house, a small, talkative dog named Simba with a ridiculous mane of hair whose pee smelled like boiled cabbage, was walking by with his owner. *Hey,* the Pomeranian yapped at him. *You'll never guess what happened today—*

Busy, Tackle barked back, and sure enough, there was Albert rushing out of the front door of his house.

Rude, the little dog muttered as he continued past.

Tackle brought Albert to the backyard, and when he told him about the dog food and how he could smell the poison, Albert threw his arms around him.

You are such a smart dog, Albert said. *I'm so glad you were able to smell it and know to avoid it. I couldn't forgive myself if anything happened to you, Tackle.*

What does it mean, Albert?

It must mean that whoever is trying to stop me knows you're trying to protect me, Albert reasoned.

You shouldn't go, Tackle said. *You shouldn't play.*

They sat still for a moment, listening to the laughter of Erin and her friends.

If I quit, Albert said, *whoever is doing this will win.*

Tackle nodded.

Albert put his hand on Tackle's head. *I'm leaving at midnight. I'll be careful. My teammates will be watching out for me. We need to win this game. I'll come and tell you all about it when I get home. I'll show you my medal. Stay inside. Lie low and protect yourself, Tackle.*

The dog looked at him. *Yeah, that's not going to happen.*

14.1

In the dark quiet of the den, Albert was trying to meditate when a blood-curdling scream ripped through the house. Erin and her eleven friends were in the living room watching a scary movie, the volume turned up so high that Albert could hear not only the spooky soundtrack with its rumbles and screeches and odd pings and the inane dialogue of the seven teenage characters who had snuck into a house that was for sale, but also the heavy breathing of the alien creature that oozed between the walls, emerging in the dark to devour them one by one.

Focus on your breath, he said to himself. Inhale one, two, three, four; hold one, two, three, four; exhale one, two, three, four.

His grandmother, strong enough to walk now with only a cane, had left that morning for a weekend-long knitting workshop in Baltimore called Yarnia, and his mother had agreed to let Albert have the den—Nana's room—while she was gone. He had begged for it, arguing that it would enable him to watch television in peace during the party, but really it was because the den had sliding glass doors that led out to the backyard. He planned to sneak out at midnight and activate the szoŭ outside, which would be safer than activating it inside where someone could walk in on him. He had been worried about the party, but having all the commotion in the house was helpful. With so much going on, no one would be paying any attention to him.

As he breathed, he allowed an emotion to rise to the surface: anxiety. His life was in danger. Tackle's life was in danger. I see you, Anxiety, he said to himself. And then, instead of trying to pretend it wasn't there, he decided it would help if he went over the details of his departure, what he would do when it was time to go, and the questions he would ask Unit B and Kayko upon arrival. He was in the middle of thinking through his list when he noticed that the house had become silent.

He opened his eyes to a room that had grown darker. The moonlight that had been streaming through the sliding glass doors had disappeared—the sky choked by swiftly approaching clouds. Gone, too, was the crack of light that had been visible under the den's door to the hallway.

He held his breath and listened. All he could hear was the ticking of the old-fashioned clock on the wall. He checked his phone for the hundredth time: 11:33 p.m. He hadn't expected the movie to end so soon...or maybe it wasn't over. Maybe it was at that moment of suspense right before the climax—he had already seen the movie—when the mirror was going to crash and then the beast would break through the wall like a tsunami.

Albert waited for the sound of the crash, knowing the girls would scream again. But the solo clock ticked on.

Out of the blue, an image of Vatria came to him, the stare from her eye in the back of her head. *I can see that you are weak.* Another shudder ran through Albert as he remembered the terror of hurtling toward that black hole, alone in that rogue ITV. And then Unit B's admonition came to him…*the likelihood of another threat or attempt is high. You, the Zeenods, and I will need to be on alert every moment.*

A sound came, a brushing of something against the closed door.

Albert stood and, without making a sound, walked slowly toward the door. The clock's tick seemed to grow louder. The poisoning of Tackle's food made him wonder if by agreeing to be Zeeno's striker, he was endangering his family, too. What if whoever wanted to stop him from playing in the tournament decided to wipe him out here—on Earth—rather than on Zeeno and didn't care who else was hurt in the process? Or what if they wanted to deliberately hurt his family as a way of getting to him? He had thought he was being brave in saying yes to the contract, but maybe he had been reckless.

The sound came again. Albert stopped moving and held his breath. There was no way that Erin and her friends would turn off the movie before it ended, no way they'd quietly crawl into their sleeping bags and go to sleep.

Something was wrong.

He tiptoed all the way to the door and put his ear against it.

A whisper came as if from within the wood. *Albert…Albert…*

Albert froze.

And then from under the door something wet and cold touched his bare toes. He screamed and jumped back, falling on the floor. The door creaked open.

The light flicked on and Erin and her friends all crowded in to look at him, howling with laughter.

"I told you we'd get him," Erin said, throwing a wet sponge at his head. "He's a chicken."

With his heart still pounding against his chest, Albert threw the sponge back as hard as he could. Erin ducked, and it knocked the wooden clock off the wall. The clock hit the floor and broke into pieces.

Erin and the girls ran.

Albert slammed the door, rage flooding his system. Knowing that all this added stress was the last thing he needed, he tried to calm himself by taking a deep breath.

A few seconds later, the door opened. His mom brought Erin inside and closed the door.

"I've had it with you both," his mom said, her voice serious and strained. "You two need to talk. Work it out. Come to some kind of understanding. Because I don't want to live in a house where there's fighting." She looked at Erin, her eyes welling. "You know what your dad said when you were born?"

Erin and Albert both held their breath. It wasn't often that their mom talked about their dad.

"He said, 'I'm so glad now Albert will have a friend for the rest of his life.'" She wiped a tear from her eye and walked out and closed the door.

The siblings were silent. In pieces on the floor, the clock sat. The second hand kept ticking, but instead of moving forward, it thumped against the minute hand, bent upward, blocking it.

A truth came out of Albert in a voice that was surprisingly calm. "You have no idea what's going on with me, Erin. If you did, I don't think you would be so mean."

She blinked.

"It's true," he said. "Ever since you made your new team, you've been obnoxious and mean. Like Trey. You hate me and you think you're superior."

Her face reddened. "You have no idea what's going on with me, either. I'm actually really scared. Like, all the time." Her voice almost broke, but she went on. "I thought being on the team would be amazing. And it sort of is, and it's also really scary. Everybody on the team is perfect. And there's all this pressure on me to be perfect. I used to love meets, and now when it's time for one I just want to throw up." She looked at Albert, and he thought she might cry.

"Do you want to quit?" he asked.

"I'm kind of afraid to quit and afraid to keep going," she said.

He nodded. "I'm under a lot of pressure, too."

"What's yours?"

"It's…it's just middle school and…there's a lot of stuff going on. But it's big stuff."

She looked at him. "I think the pressure is making me a little crazy, and I don't really want to be that way." A smile broke. "But just so you know, the whole sponge thing wasn't even my idea. It was Mari's idea."

"Mari?" Mari was one of Erin's new friends from school.

Erin smiled. "She has a crush on you."

Albert was shocked.

"I think, like, five of my friends have a crush on you," she said. "It's disgusting." She smiled and punched him, and he punched back. "Just tell me if I'm right about one thing," she said. "A girl gave you the necklace, right?"

He smiled, thinking about how Unit B had chosen a "generic female" body-form, and then he nodded. "Right."

"Is she your girlfriend? Are you in love? Can we meet her?"

He punched her again. "None of your business."

"Okay. So, can I go out and tell Mom that we made up?"

"One condition," he said. "You have to swear to leave me alone for the rest of the night. I'm serious. I'm putting a chair against the door and I'm turning out the light and I'm going to sleep. And I'm not coming out until morning."

"Deal," she said, and they shook.

Erin left and he sat for a while with his hand over the Z-da on his chest, breathing. His phone dinged with a text message from his mom.

Proud of you two. Erin said you had a good talk and that we all need to give you your privacy for the rest of the night. Good night, Albert.

Thanks. Good night, Mom.

Albert texted back.

Over the couch hung the family photos. They had a tradition every year since Albert was born of taking a family selfie on January first and framing it for the wall. Nana's son, his dad, smiled from only the first four.

After a few deep inhalations and exhalations, Albert pulled out the sofa bed that Nana usually slept on, created a fake body out of pillows under the blanket, put on his socks, shoes, and jacket, turned out the light, checked his phone, and slipped out of the sliding glass doors.

The backyard was pitch-black. Glancing above the fence line, he saw no lights on in Trey's room on the second floor. Trey's parents' room and their TV room were both on the other side of the house, and the fence blocked any other view from the first-floor windows.

He checked the clock on his phone again. They had agreed that he could activate the szoŭ at any time between 11:45 and 12:15. It was 11:57.

Albert planted his feet on the ground and took another deep breath in and out. Then he lifted his Z-da to his lips and blew.

Thirty seconds.

Excitement rose in Albert's chest. He closed his eyes, picturing how happy his team would be to see him.

And then he heard that unmistakable sound...the heavy thwap of the dog door and the rapid click of Tackle's nails on the wooden porch.

I'm coming, the dog called.

No! As Albert felt the top of his head grow hot, he watched in shock as the dog sailed toward him over the fence.

14.2

As his paws cleared the fence, Tackle saw the sphere of tightly packed shimmering shapes descend from the sky and heard the sound like the crackling of a fire...*thump!* His paws hit the ground.

No! Albert reached out an arm, as if he could push the dog away, but Tackle was already leaping forward and jumping up to put his paws on Albert's chest.

Boom! The sphere hit them both, and Tackle shuddered. Before he could respond, the ground snapped away from under his paws.

He gulped for air, and everything went black...

Twenty-seconds later, when Tackle's eyelids opened again, Albert was shouting at a strange metal human-shaped machine that was pointing an object at him. Although confused and still dizzy, Tackle tried to rise to his feet. *Grrr! Back off!*

Albert looked at him. *Calm down, Tackle. Don't move. Don't bite. This is Unit B. She's just trying to protect me. I'm going to explain to her that you're my dog so she puts away her weapon.*

I understand, Unit B barked.

Tackle's eyebrows went up.

Albert yelped. *You speak Dog?*

Unit B opened a compartment on her thigh and put her weapon back inside. *I have been programmed by Kayko to speak all known languages. Not perfectly, but adequately. On Earth, that means all human, animal, plant, and fungal languages. If I were a robot designed by another engineer, a Tev or Z-Tev, certainly, my language system would be limited. Robots programmed by many engineers exclude animal, plant, and fungal because they do not believe those life-forms are worthy of attention.*

Tackle panted uneasily, adrenaline surging through his body, his legs shaking despite the fact that he wanted to appear unafraid.

Your file doesn't indicate that you have a canine, Albert, Unit B said.

He's not my dog. He's my friend, who happens to be a dog, Albert said. *The Zeenods know all about him. They know he has been protecting me on Earth.* Albert crouched down and stroked Tackle's head. *You're in a transport vehicle, Tackle. We're heading toward Zeeno. You shouldn't have come. I'm going to call Kayko and figure out what to do.*

Tackle struggled to remain calm and sniffed in Unit B's direction. *What is that thing?*

I can hear you, Unit B said.

A robot, Albert explained.

Tackle sniffed again. *Not human. Not animal.*

Kind of like a cross between a computer and a bicycle, Albert said.

Much more sophisticated than that! Unit B argued.

Like that squirrel-machine, Tackle barked.

Yes. But this one is good, Albert said.

As Albert and Unit B talked with Kayko through video transmission, the dog began to patrol the ITV on unsteady paws, sniffing. So many new smells and sights and sounds. Some that smelled foreign, some familiar. That pine scent was here somewhere, faint but lingering. He had to learn what was "good" and what was dangerous; he had to get his bearings, be strong, be courageous, even though he was confused and frightened. He licked a paw and tried to think through the muddle in his head. He was alive. He was with Albert. He was heading toward Zeeno. He would focus on his job: to help and protect Albert so that they could return home safely.

After a while, Albert ended his call and turned to him. *Okay, Tackle, we are both going to take a very nice nap in a thing called a hygg.*

A nap?

Trust me. You're going to love it. And then you're going to get a breathing implant—

What?

You can breathe in here because it is equipped specially for us, but once we arrive you won't be able to breathe on your own unless you have an implant. Unit B thinks she has one that will fit. I talked with my coach, Kayko, and she thinks it would be safest if you stay here with

Unit B. It's going to be a long wait, so she'll take you out to stretch your legs from time to time. I'll meet you after the game.

No, Tackle said. *You need me with you. I came to make sure nobody hurts you.*

For that the dog was rewarded with a hug.

Tackle! Someone tried to kill you! I want to protect you, too. Come on, you've got to check out this hygg. You're about to have the nap of your life.

Against his better judgment, he let Albert push him into the delicious-smelling tent; and then, happily, Albert remained there, snuggling up with him. Tackle was about to admit that the hygg was amazing, but he fell asleep before he could murmur a sound.

With a start, the dog woke later, as if no time had passed. He was alone, unsure where he was, and he panicked until the opening unfastened and Albert's face appeared.

Hey! We're almost there, Albert said. *Check out my gear.* As Tackle emerged from the hygg, Albert pulled on a baggy uniform and then pressed a button. Tackle watched the fabric tighten.

And this isn't even my johka uniform. Look! Albert pulled out another set of clothes and shoes. *Look at these cleats! They have built-in computers to record my plays! And super-powerful batteries!*

Preparing for landing, Unit B said. *I'll administer the breathing implant as soon as we're there.*

Tackle felt a change in Albert's energy, a building up of excitement.

With a barely perceptible thump, the vehicle landed in the lot of the hotel.

And then, without warning, another metal thing flew out of a compartment and zoomed toward Tackle's face.

One of the drone's arms grabbed Tackle's snout. Another shot filmy white disks of tissue into his nostrils.

Tackle gasped and struggled to break free.

Unit B! Albert screeched. *You should have given a warning!* And then he turned to Tackle. *It's your breathing implant. Try to relax.*

Relax? the dog started to say, but when he opened his mouth, another tissue was shot into the back of his throat. He looked at Albert, wondering if he had been betrayed, and then a warmth spread through his throat and neck. A moment later, he was breathing in and out.

The same thing that had attacked him blinked several lights at him and then spoke in a language the dog couldn't understand.

Your heart rate and pulse and blood pressure are all normal, Albert said, hugging him. *It totally worked.*

A complicated set of instructions came out of Unit B's mouth as she opened the ITV door and deployed a set of stairs. The ordeal that Tackle had just been through, coupled with the sudden influx of an entirely foreign set of smells and sounds and sights, flooded the dog's adrenaline system.

Overwhelmed, he did exactly the opposite of what he should have done. He bolted.

The mouselike gnauser that was sitting on its hind legs near a shrub in the hotel's parking lot took off after him.

"Tackle!" Albert screamed, and followed, too.

14.3

While watching the chase through the surveillance footage, the president and Mehk exchanged messages.

This is a disaster. I don't understand the appearance of this Earth animal. Albert was supposed to disembark the ITV and walk straight into the hotel.

I am surprised, too. I had a deterrent delivered to the dog. This was not supposed to happen.

Clearly, you failed. And the gnauser can't keep up.

I'll reprogram it to return to the hotel.

And neutralize the dog!

14.4

Albert knew that his decision to chase after Tackle was impulsive. Not only was it dark outside, but the unfamiliar city street was on a steep decline. The dog managed to keep his balance as he ran downhill, but Albert tripped on the spongy ground and rolled. By the time he got himself back on his feet, he caught only a glimpse of the dog turning down a side street, illuminated by the glow of a building at the corner.

There were no streetlamps in the Z-Tev–occupied capital of Zeeno, but the exterior of each building the Z-Tevs had built glowed eerily, made from a luminescent material that became brighter in the dark. These lights also emitted a dog-audible hum, so for Tackle, running through the streets was like running through a spooky kaleidoscope of sounds.

Tackle, Albert howled, but the dog's brain was overwhelmed.

One corner led to another and another, and after several minutes, Albert lost sight of the dog completely. Catching his breath, he slowed down, realizing how foolish he had been to take off by himself. Intending to make contact with Unit B, he reached for his Z-da, only to find it gone. Either he had failed to put it on after waking from his hygg or it had fallen off when he fell.

He howled Tackle's name again and waited. No howl back. The street he was on intersected with a busier street a block away. Several shops—what looked like restaurants—dotted the block. Screens were visible in many windows showing the pregame interviews with players of the Jhaateez-versus-Gaböq game that was taking place that night on planet Gaböq.

And then Albert saw a sign for something that reminded him of a hotel and he smelled the woody smell of a campfire. An open archway led to a corridor between two buildings, a kind of dark tunnel that flickered with light at the other end. As he walked closer he heard the deep wailing of an instrument coming from within. He knew that mournful sound. Pressing himself against the wall when he reached the end, he cautiously peeked around the corner and then quickly pulled back. The corridor opened into a wide courtyard, and occupying it were Tevs. Not just Tevs. Gathered in the center were Hissgoff and the Tev team, and although most were facing away from him, an eye in the back of each head maintained a lookout.

Heart pounding, Albert crouched down and cautiously peered out again. Under the moonlit sky, the players were gathered around a fire pit. The fire itself was small, but they were all glowing with bioluminescence. Between two Tev players, a musician was playing the same instrument that Albert had first heard at the Opening. As tall as an upright bass, the thing had just one thick string that wound through two holes in the instrument in a continuous loop. As the musician pulled the string, hand over hand over hand, at varying speeds and slightly different angles, the string vibrated against the holes, creating deep rasps and wails. It was like the sound a massive tree might make while being uprooted, Albert thought with a shudder.

One by one, the players were lifting up an object that looked like a heavy club. Each player hoisted it up and then made two sharp slices through the air with it, one to the right and one to the left, before passing it to the next. Some kind of ritual, Albert guessed. He noticed that Vatria wasn't there and wondered why she wasn't included. He couldn't imagine the Zeenods engaging in a pregame ritual without him.

Another sound entered the air, a sound coming into the courtyard from the street. A moment passed before Albert recognized it: Tackle's howl! The Tev music stopped and the courtyard went silent.

Albert made a break for it, running out, thinking they couldn't possibly see him in the dark tunnel. But two Tevs caught him by the arms before he could make it even halfway out.

"I'm just looking for my dog," Albert protested as they dragged him back to the courtyard. "I didn't even know you were here."

"It's Albert Kinney!" Hissgoff shouted. "The Earthling is a spy!"

"Call the authorities," another said.

A third player picked up the ritual club and said, "Wait. We can think of something more effective than that!"

A rumble came from the Tevs—a kind of deep-throated laugh.

"We can argue it was self-defense," the Tev said, hoisting the club and staring into Albert's eyes. "It is dark in this courtyard. We heard a sound and—"

Albert's throat went dry, and then suddenly a local transport vehicle appeared overhead, its hatch open. Kayko was at the controls and Doz and Toben were hanging out the doorway.

Doz yelled and tossed out a fist-sized helicopter-like surveillance drone, which flew down and hovered at face level in front of the Tev with the club, a row of blue lights blinking around its core.

Quickly, Hissgoff reached over and made his Tev player lower the club. He held up his hands and smiled at the drone. "There is nothing here to record."

An uneasy silence followed as the vehicle landed and Doz and Kayko hopped out.

"What is this?" Kayko asked.

"The striker was spying on us," Hissgoff said calmly. "We were having a team meeting and caught him listening to our strategies."

"I wasn't spying!" Albert shouted. "My dog followed me into the ITV and then jumped out. I got lost trying to find him and ended up here. All I heard was music. That's it."

"Dog?" the Tev tactician asked.

"Domesticated Earth animal," Toben said.

"I don't see a dog," a Tev player said. "We can't believe what this Earthling says."

"Albert, did they do something to your dog?" Toben asked.

"I don't think so," Albert said, trying to keep his voice from shaking. "I don't know where he is."

"We have no information about a dog." Hissgoff shrugged. "As for this footage you are recording, please do send it to the FJF. FJF officials should know about Albert Kinney's attempt at spying."

"Albert Kinney is telling the truth. His ITV driver confirmed the dog," Kayko said. "We received a call that the dog ran out and Albert tried to follow." She directed the drone to capture footage of the heavy club on the ground with a sweep of her arm. "Perhaps the FJF should know that you threatened our Star Striker with a weapon?"

"I don't see a weapon." Hissgoff shrugged again. "I see a Tev ritual object."

A Tev walked over to Albert and glared. "Capture this on video. I don't want this Earthling to be disqualified. I want to shred him on the field. There is no crime in wanting to be rightfully victorious."

The other Tevs laughed, and Hissgoff clapped him on the shoulder.

Kayko bowed, her voice remaining calm and polite. "We will see you next on the johka field."

Albert followed his teammates back into their vehicle with the drone, and as soon as the firelight of the courtyard was out of sight, he breathed a sigh of relief.

"We are pleased to see you alive, Albert," Kayko said as she headed back to the hotel. "Unit B notified us and we began the search." She withdrew Albert's Z-da from her pocket and tossed it to him. "If you had had this, it would have been possible to track you more quickly."

"You found it!"

"On the street," Doz said. "Outside our hotel."

"I'm sorry," Albert said. "And thank you." He told them about the attempt to poison the dog on Earth, which shocked all three of them.

"We will need to tell the team," Kayko said.

Albert leaned forward, looking out at the glowing buildings

below. Tackle was out there somewhere. Alone. And, as Albert had just learned, there were dangers lurking around corners.

Toben put his hand on Albert's shoulder. "You are worried about your dog. We will look for him."

Albert tried to say *Thank you,* but the lump in his throat made it too difficult to speak.

14.5

Staying close to the shadows, Tackle put his nose to the ground to try to smell anything that had a trace of Albert. He had heard Albert's howl at one point. He knew it. He had been close. But the streets were a maze.

A vehicle zipped above the dog's head and he looked up. If Albert wasn't on the ground, how would he ever find him?

As he turned a corner, he heard a strange shout. Three aliens with tentacles for arms ran toward him, their flesh jiggling, screaming at him in a language he didn't understand. He took off, knocking over a container of some kind. Another catlike being lunged toward him.

In a panic, he ran away from the lights and kept running until he reached an area with apartments and alleys. A residential neighborhood. He slowed and sniffed his way into a quiet dead-end alley that was filled with large garbage bins. Two small creatures nibbling something on the ground looked up, their eyes popping out and then retracting in. Tackle growled, and they curled into ball shapes and rolled away.

Cautiously he approached the bin in the darkest part of the alley and sniffed. It was high enough off the ground that he could crawl under it; and there, belly on the ground, paws under his chin, he panted until he calmed down. And then he fell asleep.

14.6

Albert wanted to spend the night searching for Tackle, and Toben and Doz insisted that they'd help, too, but Kayko intervened, deploying Unit B for that task and taking Albert, Doz, and Toben to the hotel so that the team could stay together and prepare for the big day tomorrow.

The FJF had provided several large adjoining rooms, and in the largest, the Zeeno team gathered with a specially catered dinner, also provided by the FJF, to watch the Jhaateez-vs.-Gaböq game. Albert felt guilty because he knew that the team ordinarily didn't get this kind of luxury—fancy food and a hotel room—and if he hadn't introduced this extra anxiety about Tackle, they'd be whooping it up.

To make it worse, the game was a shock. The athleticism of the Jhaateezian players and the brute strength of the Gaböqs were daunting enough, but then there was the whole Gaböq environment—a hot, cracked crust suspended over a series of water-filled underground tunnels into which players could fall. The fact that he would be playing in radically different environments hit Albert hard; he felt as if he'd had barely enough time to get a feel for the zees. And then Jhaateez won, an outcome that lifted the spirits of his teammates—Jhaateez was a peace-loving planet and an old ally of Zeeno—but dampened his spirits even more. They'd be playing their next game against the Jhaateezians, and Albert had been hoping the Jhaateezians would lose.

At midnight, with no news of Tackle, Kayko insisted the team get their sleep. While the players crawled into hyggs, a rotation of volunteers kept the search for the Earth dog going.

But several hours before dawn, the searches were called off. Everyone needed sleep.

14.7

The message that came through the botmaker's encrypted channel sent a chill down his spine.

If we fail tomorrow, we're both dead. Find the dog tomorrow before the game and take care of it.

I will.

You cannot be late.

I will not. Everything is ready.

15.0

When Albert crawled out of his hygg in the morning and saw Kayko already up, her face revealed the sad news: the dog was still missing.

As soon as all the players emerged from their hyggs, Kayko called everyone to gather in a circle. "We are about to leave for the first game of the tournament, and much is at stake. We want to play well and lift the spirits of the Zeenods still on the planet, as well as all those Zeenods who fled a generation or two ago to live on other planets. But let us acknowledge our anxiety. A dangerous force has been acting against Albert and against us. We acknowledge that we are afraid and we also vow to be determined and courageous. We will face the fear and do our best."

She walked from person to person, smiling into each set of eyes before moving to the next. "We should be safe. The FJF is watching. But be alert and report anything suspicious to me immediately." Turning her full gaze to Albert, she added: "If we do not find the dog before you have to return to Earth, we will continue the search."

Albert nodded.

"Kayko," Doz said. "Do you think those other Zeenods, the ones who left to live on other planets, will come and offer their support in the stadium?"

"I don't know what to expect," she said.

"At least your families are here, right?" Albert asked. "Zeenods are allowed to come to the game, right? The Z-Tevs and Tevs can't keep Zeenods away with the whole solar system watching."

"Restrictions are lifted," Ennjy said. "However, most Zeenods cannot afford to travel and stay here in the capital. Our families are not here."

Albert remembered now that he had seen many Z-Tevs and visitors from other places filling the streets and restaurants of the capital the night before, but no Zeenods. He felt his face grow hot. "That's not fair. If they were here, the power of the ahn would be greater, right?"

They all nodded.

"It means we have to try harder," Ennjy said.

"There is good news. A secret benefactor has assured me of special surprises for the halftime and end-of-game celebration," Kayko said brightly. "I am told not to reveal."

They all cheered, and Doz jumped into the same pose that Albert had chosen for his johkahin. "Let's roll and rock!"

Hidden behind the grate in the ventilation system of the room, a gnauser recorded the meeting through the lens in its right eye.

15.1

Albert was already on edge as he followed his team into the stadium amid the pregame hoopla. Some of the activity was similar to what Albert imagined a professional soccer game on Earth would be: staff and players and fans were arriving and food vendors were firing up their hovercarts and sending an intoxicating array of smells across the stands, all of which Albert enjoyed, even if his Zeenod teammates couldn't. But then television cameras rolled in and Z-Tev news teams began their live prestart interviews, and a robotic video crew and reporter made their way to their half of the field and requested an interview with both Kayko and Albert.

"I'm not the best johka player," Albert whispered to Kayko and Ennjy. "They should talk to you, Ennjy."

"Fans are fascinated by Star Strikers," Ennjy whispered back. "Not because you're better than the rest of the team, but because you're aliens."

I'm an alien, Albert thought, and smiled.

"Normally, the Z-Tevs would not allow us to speak in public,"

Kayko added. "But the solar system is watching so they have no choice."

The video cameras rolled into place, and Kayko went first.

"Kayko Tusq," the reporter said. "The Zeenods have not shown an interest in johka for the past seventy-five years, and now you're playing again. How can you possibly be prepared for this game against the formidable Tevs?"

Albert's jaw dropped. It wasn't a lack of interest that was a problem! It was oppression by the Z-Tevs that had kept Zeenod from playing. After what Albert had learned about the percentage of Zeenods who'd died or been imprisoned after speaking up, he was sure Kayko would explode and get hauled away.

Instead, Kayko's response was cordial. "The Tevs will be difficult to beat. But we're ready," she said. "Zeenods have always loved the game of johka, and we intend to make Zeenods everywhere proud."

The reporter turned to Albert. "How are you feeling, Albert Kinney? There hasn't been an Earthling Star Striker in many years. All eyes are going to be on you. How do you feel?"

Albert wasn't sure what to say. He looked into the camera and tried to sound confident. "I'm honored to be here with my teammates."

The reporter pointed out the VIP boxes, which were three sections of the stands surrounded by darkened screens. In the Tev box were President Tescorick and his guests; in the Zeeno box, President Lat and her guests; and in the FJF box, the FJF officials and past Star Strikers.

"The earthling Lightning Lee is here with other past Star Strikers. All are eager to watch the game. We know that you are not allowed to discuss the tournament with Lee while on Earth; have you had the chance to talk here on Zeeno? What advice has Lee given you?"

Albert froze.

"Lee and Albert have not communicated yet," Kayko said.

A stream of sweat trickled down Albert's spine. He had forgotten about Lee's message, and it seemed as if Unit B hadn't informed Kayko that Lee had sent it. Albert wondered if he should have told Kayko, but then he would have had to explain the content of the text message. Albert didn't want Kayko to know that Lightning Lee thought he should have quit.

Kayko said a few more words on camera about the team, keeping the focus on the game and not on the politics, and then the announcement came for the field to clear.

Relieved, Albert followed Kayko with the other Zeenods into their locker room—a round high-tech space with replay screens, massage beds, towels made of muscle-soothing fabric, hyggs, and hydrating stations. For security, no outsiders were allowed into the locker rooms, so official FJF maintenance and medical drones had been developed to tend to the players' needs.

"I thought you might talk to the reporters about the Z-Tevs," Albert whispered to Kayko.

"We need positive support for this game," Kayko explained. "When the time is right, we will speak out. Today, we focus on winning."

To begin the ahn ritual, Ennjy activated the command to put the various drones into rest mode. As the team formed a circle and began to breathe, Albert's mind jumped from anxious thought to anxious thought.

"Albert," Ennjy said gently. "You're jiggling your leg."

Albert opened his eyes, disappointed and ashamed, and met Ennjy's soft gaze.

She nodded. "I said this not as judgment, but as acknowledgment. I'm nervous, too."

"I'm always nervous," Sormie said, making everyone smile.

Then it was time. They lined up and ran out. Kayko first. Then Albert. Then the other members of the team. The energy of the stadium was intense as they lined up in the center of the field. The Tevs were called next and stood opposite, strong and tall, their faces impassive, their eyes locked on their opponents.

Albert tried to look at Vatria but found he couldn't hold the gaze. A terrible thought crossed his mind—that Vatria had the power to send some kind of muscle-stunning agent through her eyes that would enter into Albert and make his legs wobble even more than they already were.

Fear, he said to himself. I see you, Fear. He focused his gaze on the fans, wondering how many were rooting for them. Play for the Zeenods out there, Albert said to himself. Win for them. Win and then find Tackle.

An FJF official stepped forward and released two official medical drones. The drones zipped down the lines, scanning each player to make sure that no performance-enhancing technology had been embedded into bodies or gear.

The Tev anthem came first; and that piece of wordless music, played on that wailing instrument, sent a chill through Albert that seemed to strike the marrow of his bones.

The Zeeno anthem was played next, and the atmosphere transformed. Zeenods in the stands rose to their feet and began stomping a beat in unison. A small number compared with Tevs and Z-Tevs, but more than they had imagined.

"Look," Doz whispered. Others were standing and singing, too. Their old allies, fans from the planets of Liöt, Fetr, and Manam, were rooting for them. Even Jhaateezian fans, whose team they would be playing against next, were rooting for them.

Albert's teammates exchanged excited glances.

"Gather," Kayko said. They stepped in closer and put their arms around each other's shoulders, getting into the rhythm. Glad he had practiced and memorized the song in Zeenod, Albert lifted his voice with his teammates. A feeling of joy rose and filled his body, emanating out and joining with his team and all the fans. Joy multiplied by a thousand.

Kayko and Hissgoff stepped up for the Exchange of Crests, and then the Star Strikers were introduced. Albert and Vatria stepped forward to meet in the middle as their images were projected on the many screens around the stadium. Fans cheered, and they performed the customary ritual of bowing and saying the FJF vow in unison. "As a representative of my planet, I promise to play to the best of my ability, to respect you as my competitor, and to uphold the rules of the game."

Albert had practiced the vow, and, as a representative of Zeeno, he had also been coached to add a silent meditation directed to his opponent: *May we both play well.*

The words came into his mind, but he couldn't embrace them. He didn't want Vatria to play well. He wanted Vatria to fail. Miserably. He knew that wasn't how Kayko or Ennjy wanted him to think, but he couldn't help it.

As Albert finished and rose from the bow, he found himself looking straight into Vatria's huge reddish-orange eyes with those long, jagged pupils. Her gaze flicked up to his forehead and back.

"I see your beads of sweat, Albert Kinney," she whispered. "I know this is a sign of Earthling anxiety."

Anger ripped through Albert. Before he could react, a trumpetlike instrument sounded and a coin toss determined that Zeeno would have the first kickoff.

"Places," a voice boomed over the loudspeakers, and the crowd cheered.

With the back of his hand, Albert quickly wiped away the sweat, hoping no one else noticed.

15.2

Cautiously, Tackle made his way down the busy street, preferring to stay close to the side where ITVs were parked, instead of the wide promenade where most of the people—could he call them that?—were walking or darting in and out of shops and restaurants.

Exhausted, hungry, and thirsty, he stopped to sniff what he hoped might be the Zeenod equivalent of an apple, a round reddish thing, but it stood up on legs and hurried away. *Grrr.* If he could just find a little food and water and then Albert.

He had gotten through the night. Thank goodness for that hiding place. And thank goodness for that hygg on the trip here, he thought! If he hadn't climbed into that tent with Albert to get some rest and hydration during the trip, he wouldn't have had the strength to keep going.

Two aliens stepped out of an ITV just ahead of him, chattering excitedly, and he paused. They saw him and did something that seemed oddly familiar to Tackle. They took a picture of themselves with him in the background and then laughed and sped off.

Initially, he was puzzled by the fact that the aliens here didn't seem threatened by him. After all, he was a creature from another planet! But the more time he spent on the streets, the wider variety of beings he saw. Two-legged, four-legged, three-legged, one-legged, no-legged. Some, like the two just now, were curious about him, and some didn't bother looking. Perhaps they didn't even know which planet he was from.

He stopped as a thought occurred to him. All those different people on Earth, all the human beings who had before seemed so distinctly different from each other in his mind, he now realized were all one. The family of human being. All related. And all the dogs—the Pomeranian, the poodle, the Chihuahua, the retriever—they were all his family. The family of dog.

Remarkable.

Another group of excited aliens walked by, these bearing those hideous eyes in the back of their heads, all munching on something that they were pulling out of papery cups, the delicious scent of which made the dog feel almost dizzy with hunger. And then, to his delight, one of them tossed a cup onto the ground.

A purple globe about the size of a golf ball rolled out.

Sniff. Sour in a pleasant way. *Sniff.* Sweet, too. Worth a lick, at least. *Mmmm...* A bite. The surprise of juice. A chew. He swallowed and paused a moment. The treat didn't come back up. Delicious, actually. Enough substance to get him the boost he needed.

He stopped and looked up at the pink sky.

How strange to be here. How interesting it would be to explore it with Albert. But without him? He was lost.

Grrr. What a brick-head he had been for not listening to Albert! Getting spooked and running out the door? Exactly the wrong move.

He looked back toward the street, and then he noticed something he hadn't noticed before. The people—the aliens—were all essentially moving in one direction. Instinctively he followed the crowd.

Finally, he came to an intersection with a huge circular building into which the crowd was pouring. Albert's game was a big deal, and this had to be the place.

Tackle took off for a spin around the perimeter, hoping for some Alberty kind of smell.

15.3

The players took their places on the field, and Albert stepped into the circle.

As a hush descended over the stadium, Albert became hyper-aware of Vatria's presence, directly across from him. He felt as if he had a target pinned onto his chest and Vatria were focusing all of her attention on hitting it.

The ref walked to his position and let go of the ball, which floated to the middle of the field. The hush continued, as the ball settled in the center spot. The ref gave a nod, and then the trumpet blew.

Game on.

Albert passed the ball to Ennjy and all the players leaped into action.

The crowd cheered, and the enormity of what was happening started to sink in. I'm playing soccer on another planet, Albert thought to himself. Unbelievable. And then he told himself to forget all that and focus on the game. He saw an opening and ran toward it—the sprint helping to loosen him up. Sormie had the ball and passed it to him, but a Tev got possession and started the run to the other end. When Albert followed down the field, the fact that the Tevs were running forward and yet able to stare backward from their rearview eyes made him so disoriented he almost felt dizzy.

He knew he had to ignore it, and, finally, the strangeness of it began to wear off enough to allow his attention to sharpen. The Zeenod defenders managed to get the ball and send it to Doz, who delivered it to Albert. Immediately, a Tev attacked, so Albert sent it back to Doz. A good, solid kick. Doz had it, and then the Tev right midfielder took possession. As Albert and Doz both raced to get the ball back, the midfielder kicked it hard, a perfect through ball toward the Zeeno goal. Luckily Feeb was at the top of the box, running to meet it. But then, like a rocket, Vatria sprinted all the way to the ball with a speed that Albert couldn't believe. Vatria slid into Feeb for a perfectly timed tackle, and Feeb went down, tumbling across the field. On the sideline, Kayko cried foul, but the play didn't stop. Using her upper-body strength, Vatria popped back up. One solid kick from her and the ball zoomed past Toben's head and hit the net so hard, Albert thought he could hear the thing scream.

The Tevs and Z-Tevs cheered.

With Feeb still down, Kayko called out for a medic. As the medic took Feeb off the field to receive treatment, Kayko initiated the formal process to challenge Vatria's speed. "We have studied the Sñekti average running speeds," Kayko said. "No Sñekti can run that fast. It must be an enhancement."

The Tev tactician smiled. "You honestly think that between the opening ceremony and kickoff, we performed an enhancement?"

Kayko ignored him. "I'm calling for a scan and a replay analysis."

The tactician stepped back, holding out his hands. "We have nothing to hide. The speed is the result of Vatria's superior physical form and training."

The ref gave the signal, and, while the fans began to chant, a compact medical drone zoomed from the sidelines and scanned Vatria's body. At the same time, another ref conducted a replay analysis to check Vatria's speed.

The conclusions of both reports were broadcast over the loudspeaker, and the crowd hushed to listen.

"Unmodified Sñekti with two implants detected: one for breathing and one for language translation, both FJF-regulation devices. Speed replay of player: record-breaking, but within the realm of possibility for a Sñekti."

The Tevs and Z-Tevs in the stadium stood and cheered.

"We chose our Star Striker well," the tactician said, and clapped Vatria on the back.

Goal for Tev.

As all the players ran to take their positions for the restart of the game, Albert sensed that the entire team was shaken. Whoever got the first goal always had an advantage. For the next ten minutes, both teams played hard and fast, and Albert was stunned by the surreal ability of the Tevs to zip around the field, gaining the most touches. The speed of Vatria, in particular, meant that she was able to get from one end of the field to the other fast enough to play both defense and offense. He recalled Kayko explaining that the Tevs and Sñektis processed more visual information per second than they did, and now he was seeing what that meant on the field.

Vatria had two more shots on goal, but Beeda and Reeda blocked one, and Toben blocked the other.

Twenty minutes in, Albert caught the smell of pine. A zee erupted, but its position made it useless to the Zeenods. Surprisingly, a Tev player tried to use it for a jump-over. When she didn't approach it with the right energy, instead of jumping off it, she sank into the center.

Albert knew what that felt like, and, even though he was happy that it had happened, he empathized with the player. The Tevs and Z-Tevs, on the other hand, hissed and booed her as she, gooped and humiliated, was replaced by a sub.

Knowing that he could choke and experience the same predicament, Albert half wished there would be no more zeeruptions. Then, thirty minutes in, he began to really worry. The Tevs and Vatria were so fast and so tireless, the zees were the Zeenods' only hope.

And then, right before the end of the first half, things started to look up. The Zeenods got possession and used the ahn to complete a series of passes, bringing the ball down the field and putting the Tevs on edge.

Albert positioned himself and received a perfect pass. He headed it on target, but, to his dismay, their goalie leaped and caught it.

As soon as the goalie sent the ball toward the opposite end, Vatria took off and easily won it, sending it quickly to her left forward, who was waiting to strike, perfectly placed on the edge of the box.

But as the ball headed toward the Tev forward, Albert smelled pine behind him. He turned and saw the second zee of the day begin to erupt about twenty yards from the Tev's goalie to the right. This was their chance. If a teammate could get the ball away and send a long pass down to him, he could use the zee to make a goal. That is, if he didn't choke.

"Zee!" Albert called out, and ran back toward the scent.

The message caused an immediate reaction, stimulating the ahn among all the Zeenod players on the field, sending a burst of speed and strength to the defenders, who dove for the ball. One stole it from the Tev forward and sent it flying down to Albert.

Now Albert knew that every Zeenod in the stadium was sending ahnic energy to him. He stopped thinking about how he, individually, might fail or succeed and focused on the ahn of the team. In the next second, he received the ball and kicked it toward the rising zee. With a satisfying thwack, it bounced off the zee, picking up insane momentum, and then zoomed to the left of the goalie and plunged into the net.

A nanosecond later, the trumpet signaling halftime blew.

The Zeenods in the stands stood and cheered.

"Enhancement!" the Tev tactician called over the din. "Their striker knew the zee was coming."

Kayko and Albert both ran to join the ref.

Now it was Kayko's turn to smile. "We have nothing to hide. Albert is able to smell the zees; however, that is normal for an Earthling. Run a scan if you want."

The ref called for the drone, and the Zeenods kept a chant going. As the drone scanned Albert, he looked over toward the dark window of the VIP box, knowing that Lightning Lee was in there, watching. Albert smiled in that direction, elated.

As the Zeenods kept the chant going, pounding the stands with their feet, the scan was processed. And then a hush fell over the stadium as the report was announced: "Unmodified Earthling with two implants detected: one for breathing and one for language translation, both FJF-regulation devices."

Kayko gave Albert a huge smile.

1–1.

The Zeenods cheered and then the halftime music began. Six gold ITVs flew above the field and opened their doors. To the amazement of everyone below, vacha-blossom petals began to fall, the traditional Zeenod halftime confetti.

Breathlessly, Toben ran to Kayko. "How is this possible?"

Kayko beamed. "New vacha trees are growing somewhere— so many that a treat like this is feasible," she whispered. "I am not allowed to reveal more."

It was the most hopeful thing imaginable.

The Zeenods in the crowd went wild, tilting their faces to the sky, holding out their hands as the feathery, pinkish-white petals flew and floated and fluttered, filling the stadium and falling like snowflakes onto the hands, tongues, heads and shoulders of the players as they left the field.

In the swirling chaos, no one could possibly have noticed that one of the petals was actually a microbot in disguise.

15.4

The sensor on the underbelly of the microbot switched on and began its search for the target: the ball.

Although the FJF had surveillance drones and bomb-detector scanners as well as Zhidorian guards roving throughout the stadium, the chip in the vacha-blossom microbot contained no bomb or explosive materials, only code.

It acted just like all the other vacha-blossom petals. After appearing to float randomly, it landed on the ball as the players were leaving the field. Nothing remarkable in that. There were petals everywhere. Petals on food carts, petals on shoulders, petals on tails, petals on bems. There was a petal on the oily bald head of the president of Tev at that very moment.

It only took a moment for the bot to transfer a code through the optical port in the ball to the computer embedded in the ball's core. The code changed the control system of the ball, preparing two chemicals that were already present in the ball's automatic inflation system, sodium azide and potassium nitrate, to drop into the central chamber upon activation, which could be initiated by its maker via remote control. This would arm the ball. After that occurred, when the ball was kicked forcefully, the jolt would trigger such a rapid expansion of nitrogen gas that the ball would explode, and the power of that explosion would kill whoever had kicked it.

Unaware of any of this, Albert went with his team into the official locker room to catch their breath and listen to Kayko talk through their strategies for the second half.

15.5

Mehk was sitting several rows down from the VIP box where President Lat was sitting. Lat had chosen the seat so that she could keep her eyes on him, and he could feel them, now, on the back of his head. He had worked hard to prepare, and a part of him— he was troubled by this—was eager to see his technology unfold. He didn't want anyone to be killed, but he did want his devices to work, a paradox that was making him anxious. On top of this, there was the dog. He had tried and failed to get his hands on it and had decided to lie about it to Lat. Now, Lat was waiting for the message she wanted to hear. He typed quickly and hit Send.

Code transmission 100% successful. The ball is ready. I will activate the final step remotely when the time is right.

15.6

The crowd cheered as Albert and his teammates ran back onto the field, energetic after the surprise of the vacha blossoms and after their halftime hydration and ahn session. The score was 1–1. Albert's mind was on staying connected as a team; and, as he looked again at the VIP box, he imagined how wonderful it would be to prove mean old Lightning Lee wrong.

But from that fantasy, a new thought emerged in his mind, and with it came a wave of tension. Wait, Albert thought, could it be that Lee was the one who wanted him to fail? That it was Lee who'd hacked the Z-da and sent him hurtling toward the black hole? Did the old player resent a new young player taking over the spotlight?

Maybe Unit B and the Zeenods were worried about Vatria and the Tevs when they should have been watching Lee! What if Lee wanted to take him down? Maybe Lee was, in fact, planning something for the second half. An assassin who had his sights on Albert right now.

"Doz," Albert whispered as they jogged the last few yards. "What if it's Lee who is trying to harm me?"

Doz was taken aback. "Lee? Lee loves you."

"Loves me?" Albert exclaimed. Uneasiness flooded his system. He wished he had confided in Doz or Kayko or Ennjy earlier. He should have told them right away about Lee's message. Now, it was too late.

Doz gave him a slap on the back. "Let's roll and rock."

Albert tried to shake off his anxiety and focus on the moment.

A rhythmic stomping from the Z-Tevs and Tevs in the stadium began as the ref let go of the ball. It floated into place at center field, and then the trumpet blew.

Vatria passed it quickly to a teammate, and, just like that, the second half was on.

The Zeenods came out hot, and both teams battled back and forth for possession for the first few minutes.

Luckily, two more zees blew quickly. Albert called them and the Zeenods used them both, once to steal the ball away from the

Tevs and once to almost score. An incredible pounce onto the ball from the Tev goalkeeper kept them locked at 1–1.

With the renewed boost of energy from the zees, though, the Zeenods dominated for a while; but then, when Albert had the ball, he tried to go for a run instead of passing. Serious mistake. The Tevs got possession. Vatria passed the ball quickly to the right forward and took off toward the Zeenod goal. The Tev forward played a long ball into the box. Vatria got there and took a shot. Wincing, Albert held his breath. While the rest of his teammates were focused on sending their ahn to Toben, Albert's mind was seeing the worst. Then Toben slapped the ball away and out of bounds, and the Zeenods cheered.

The ball came to a stop in midair, and then, as the ref signaled for the Tevs to have a corner kick, it returned to the corner spot and landed gently. The Tevs prepared and the Zeenods took their marks.

"Albert," Ennjy called out. "Remember the ahn."

Albert took his position midfield and tried to ignore those back-facing third eyes and send ahnic energy to Toben and the Zeenod defenders. The left forward for the Tevs raised his arm and kicked the ball to Vatria, who dribbled past two defenders. But Feeb, back in the game, managed to steal the ball. A quick kick to Doz, who headed it in Albert's direction.

Wide open, Albert knew the ball was his, and then from nowhere, a Tev defender—the same one who had threatened him in the courtyard—appeared in his peripheral vision. As Albert jumped for the ball, he felt a slam to his face. Next thing he knew, he was on the ground, blood dripping from his nose, the Zeenods screaming foul.

The ref walked over and tapped the Tev's right shoulder with the foul-marking sensor. A yellow stripe appeared on his uniform, signaling a warning. If he received another, the stripe would glow red and he'd be removed from play.

The Zeenods in the stands cheered. The Tevs booed.

The Tev defender smirked.

Beeda and Reeda dove toward the ref. "It should be a red! That was a deliberate hit."

"Calm down!" Ennjy called out, too late.

The ref touched both Beeda and Reeda's shoulders. A yellow stripe appeared on each of their uniforms and the crowd went wild.

"You're bleeding," one of Albert's teammates said.

Reeling, Albert felt a trickle above his lip and wiped it. Blood.

"Whatever," he said. "It's just a nosebleed. It happens all the time. I just need to stop it and then I can keep playing."

But as play resumed, Albert's nose and throat filled with blood. The blow had caused vessels to break in the anterior part of his nose, which ordinarily could be stopped without much concern.

Brilliant, Albert thought as he tried to inhale. The Tev must have gone for my nose on purpose. I can't smell a thing!

The inability to smell was the least of his concerns. While the voices of the players and the referees dimmed, Albert's breathing implant, not programmed to handle a flood of liquid, became overwhelmed.

Albert struggled to inhale, and then everything went black.

15.7

As Albert was being carried off the field, Mehk received a message.

What are you waiting for? You should have activated it by now.

I've been waiting for a moment when Kinney is alone with the ball so no one else is injured.

That is not your concern. I have been given orders now to detonate before the game ends regardless of whether Kinney returns. Just make sure to do it when the Zeenods have the ball.

The botmaker blinked. Someone was giving orders to President Lat, who was giving orders to him. A bitter hatred rose within him. Weak, the president had allowed herself to be controlled, and because of her, *he* was being controlled, forced to perform like a puppet. Up until this point in his life, he had committed serious crimes, but none had involved ending a life.

15.8

Unit B parked in the stadium lot and scanned the area visually for signs of the dog. She had been searching—either in the ITV or on foot—ever since the creature had bolted. This had involved sneaking around the restricted areas, the places the Z-Tevs didn't want visitors to see, and dealing with checkpoint guards.

The huge numbers of visitors from other planets complicated the search. The dog would have stood out if the population had been mostly Z-Tevs, as it usually was in the capital and its surrounding zones. Now, the streets were teeming with beings and creatures of all kinds—many on four legs.

Now, as she passed by the service entrance to the stadium, she noticed that the Zhidorian guard stationed by that portal had fallen asleep—the eyes on both heads closed—with their portable scanning device, the newest advanced model, resting in a holster at their side, the kind of scanner that could identify hormonal and chemical signatures as well as irregularities in code.

Quickly, she performed an analysis to determine how much more effective her current search would be if she were to take that device. Technically the word was *steal,* but although Kayko and Giac had tried tweaking Unit B's moral-module program, there were still imperfections; so the robot simply walked over and took the device out of the sleeping guard's holster.

15.9

Albert woke, a mask around his face. As his hands reached up to feel the mask, he noticed they were both streaked with blood, as was his uniform. Some kind of portable tank was attached by a belt around his chest.

Freaked, he climbed out of the opening, breathing heavily, to see that he was in a small medical chamber inhabited by a Zhidorian medic. The tall, fluid alien turned one head toward him and reached two tentacle-like arms out to steady him.

At the plump, cold touch, Albert recoiled.

"Albert Kinney, you are alive," the medic said. "Your breathing implant was damaged; however, your oxygen levels, blood pressure, and pulse are now back to normal. The tank is supplying you with oxygen for the moment, but I will be able to administer another implant soon."

"Where am I?" Albert asked. "Is the game over?"

"The game is continuing. You are in a medical pod on the sidelines."

Albert looked at the medical supplies and the scanning drones surrounding him.

Paranoia rose. He didn't know who he could trust. The injury to his nose could have been a chess move to get him off the field and into this isolated pod. This supposed medic could do anything to him, inject him with poison…remove his oxygen—he looked down at the tank strapped to his chest—or replace his oxygen with toxic gas…Anything could happen in here, and the medic could simply say that Albert had died from his injury.

"I'm feeling better," Albert said. "I can go back out there." As he tried to walk to the door, the room tilted.

One of the medic's tentacles caught him while the other rolled a chair toward him. "Sit, Albert Kinney. You are not ready yet."

Refusing to sit, Albert braced one hand on the wall to steady himself. "I'm fine. I mean, maybe I can't play yet, but I can go and be with my team."

"I have orders to hold you," the medic said. "Someone is coming for a consultation."

A chill went through Albert. "Who?"

A knock sounded on the door.

"Lee," the medic said.

"No. Please—" Albert's knees gave out, and he collapsed into the chair as the medic opened the door. A certainty snapped into place in Albert's mind and he was suddenly quite sure that Lee must be an aggressive, hateful has-been who was out to stop him. Heart pounding, helpless, Albert watched the medic step out; and then, blinded by the light pouring in through the doorway, he shielded his eyes as a figure stepped into the room.

15.10

"Hello, Albert." A voice disruptor embedded in the face mask altered both the tone and the quality of the speech of the fully cloaked figure standing before Albert.

Albert blinked as the door swung shut and his eyes adjusted to the softer light.

"Please trust me. I'm keeping my identity from you a secret for a reason," Lee said.

Albert tried to stay calm.

The figure took a step closer. "I know from my own experience as a former Star Striker how tempting it is to want to talk with someone else on Earth about all of this. I fear that if you know who I am, you'll break the secrecy vow, and we both know that the penalty for that is too great a risk."

"Why did you contact me, then?" Albert managed to ask. "Why did you send that message?"

A moment's hesitation and then: "I didn't send a message, Albert."

"You told me to quit," Albert cried out. "You said I'm not strong enough, skilled enough, or brave enough. I'd never do that to anyone."

Lee sat down. "Albert, I did not send that message. It must have been a ploy to frighten you! Someone must have posed as me to shake your confidence. You have to believe that."

Albert struggled, not knowing what to think.

"I came to make sure you were okay," Lee said. "I had to see for myself."

Albert swallowed. It hadn't occurred to him that the message could have been from an imposter. Now he could see that it was completely possible that Lee—this Lee standing before him now—was on his side and had been all along. The Zeenods loved their Lightning Lee, Albert reminded himself.

"The game is important, Albert. I know you're aware of the stakes for Zeeno. But your life is important as well. You can quit without shame. I came to tell you that, too."

Through the walls of the pod, the roar of the crowd grew louder.

"How much time is left?" Albert asked.

"Fifteen minutes," Lee said. "Still tied at one-one."

Albert hesitated and then began to voice what was really haunting him. "The Zeenods believe in me. They risked their lives to rescue me. I want to get out there and prove to everybody that I'm worth it. But more than that, I want Zeeno to have the best chance of winning. So…" He winced, and Lee finished his thought.

"You're wondering if the Zeenods have a better chance with you or without you as their Star Striker?"

Albert nodded.

Lee reached out a gloved hand and touched Albert's shoulder. "I'm proud of you. That question alone shows that you've grown. Whether you will be a help or a hindrance depends on your attitude, Albert. Where you focus your energy."

A comforting image of his nana came to him. She had given him the same advice about playing in band, he remembered. He pictured her looking at him across the kitchen table back home. That suddenly seemed like a long time ago.

Lee continued. "On Earth, we call individuals with great talent or great skills or great beauty stars. If you're a 'star' on Earth, you try to shine more brightly than others; you surround yourself with mirrors; you focus on the self. All your light, all your energy keeps going back into the self, and eventually you burn out. This is why so many 'stars' on Earth are unhappy. But to be a star on Zeeno means to be a part of a constellation, a team. When you're a part of a team, the light and energy from one fuel all. Everyone grows stronger; everyone shines brighter. You were chosen as Star Striker because of your ability to be a part of this team, Albert. Focus on being part of a team, and you will be an asset."

Albert took a breath in and let it out. Then he stood. "I'm ready."

Lee nodded, and Albert sensed a smile behind the mask. Two strong hands touched his shoulders. "May you play well, Albert. Whatever arises, may it serve to remind you of the importance of ahn connection."

Before Albert could react, Lee called the medic back in and disappeared.

While the medic installed the new breathing implant, Albert thought about this turn of events. Although he had been terrified when the famous and beloved Lightning Lee walked in, Lee had given Albert the blessing he needed.

With a renewed sense of determination, Albert put on his cleats and ran out the door.

15.11

When Albert reappeared on the field, his teammates and the fans in the stadium cheered.

"Are you sure?" Kayko asked.

"I'm sure," Albert said.

There were ten minutes left in the game, and the score was still tied at 1–1.

"Back for punishment?" Vatria said with a smile as Albert jogged past.

"Back for the win," Albert said, touching his nose. "Never smelt better. Never felt better."

Doz, hearing, grinned.

When play resumed, the Tevs got possession quickly, and the Zeenod defenders were fighting hard to win it back from Vatria when Albert smelled a zee coming. Scanning the area, he saw the change in the ground. Unfortunately, it was perfectly placed for Vatria. If she kicked the ball right, it could easily bounce off the zee and into the goal. Albert called out for Reeda to block the kick, but Vatria was faster. Vatria saw the zee and sent the ball flying toward it. Amazingly, she got the force right, which meant that the ball bounced off the zee—a remarkable achievement for a Sñekti. But she didn't angle her kick correctly, and the ball zoomed back and hit her in the chest with such force, it knocked her onto her back.

The reaction of the Tevs and Z-Tevs—to hiss at Vatria—stunned Albert. Surely Vatria was hurt. That blow would have smashed Albert's rib cage wide open and sent his heart flying into orbit.

Beeda and Reeda each extended a hand down to Vatria, but Vatria slapped their hands away, rising to her feet before the medic could arrive.

The game resumed, and Doz had the ball, but Vatria came at him like a hurricane, stole the ball, and charged down the field. Doz couldn't keep up. She pushed past all the defenders and took a beautiful shot.

Toben jumped for it, but the ball was fast and high.

Helplessly, Albert watched it slice in just under the cross bar. And when it slammed into the back of the net, Albert staggered back, feeling as if the ball had hit him.

Goal for the Tevs.

The Tevs and Z-Tevs roared, and Toben dropped to his knees, face in his hands.

As the Tev players rushed to clap Vatria on the back, the Tev fans started up their rhythmic stomping.

No, Albert wanted to scream! That couldn't have just happened.

"Vatria is unstoppable," Doz said.

Albert was speechless, self-doubt flooding in. He had wanted to do for the Zeenods what Vatria was doing for the Tevs. She was succeeding.

On its own, the ball rolled out from the net and floated to center field in preparation for the restart of the match.

Somehow, the Zeenods had to score. But it seemed as if the atmosphere had changed. It was as if the Tevs had won the space of the stadium itself with their goal. The Tevs and Z-Tevs in the stands were chanting and stomping and raising their fists, drowning out the Zeenod fans. The Tevs on the field were elated, showing no sign of fatigue.

Albert struggled to take a breath. His breathing apparatus was fine, he knew; it was anxiety kicking in. At the edge of his mind, he could almost see a wave of exhaustion threatening to break over him. His legs and chest ached. He looked around at his teammates and almost didn't recognize them. Doz looked grief-stricken. Feeb looked pale and weak. Beeda and Reeda were scowling. Even Ennjy was affected. Instead of calling out words of encouragement, she was silent, her eyes to the ground.

"Stay focused," Kayko's voice rang out.

And then, just as all the players ran to take their positions, a sound came. The Zeenod anthem. Somehow, in the pauses between the Tev chant, the Zeenod anthem could be heard. Albert looked at Ennjy, whose face lit up. Zeenods in the stands were singing. Allies from Jhaateez, Liöt, Fetr, and Manam were all joining in.

"We have the ahn!" Ennjy yelled out, standing tall. "Let it be used!"

The trumpet blew.

Albert passed to Ennjy. Tevs attacked, but she fought them

off and sent the ball to Doz. In a series of beautiful passes, the ball went from from Zeenod to Zeenod to Zeenod. A feeling rose in Albert, the same feeling he'd had when he was playing in the band onstage, that feeling that they were all making something together and sharing it with people out there in the audience whom he couldn't even see but who he knew were joined with them in spirit. This was the ahn. Just as the ball was sent to Albert, he could see Ennjy dodge around a defender to put herself into a perfect position. Albert passed the ball to her. She touched it, rolled it away from another defender, and dribbled it straight for the goal. Two more Tevs attacked, but she danced around them and passed the ball neatly to Sormie. The ahn was flowing through them all, Albert could feel it, and Sormie gave it a powerful strike. The ball sailed past the keeper and into the net.

Goal! A rush of energy swept through Albert's system, like nothing he had felt before. Ennjy and Sormie embraced, and Albert ran in to join.

2–2.

Now it was the thundering cheers of the Zeenods and their allies filling the air.

The entire team was jumping and cheering.

"Yes!" Kayko's voice rang out. "This is for Zeeno!"

Play resumed, and now Albert was buzzing with energy.

Both teams fought hard, determined to break the tie. After winning and losing possession a few times, Beeda finally stole the ball and sent it to Doz.

Albert sped toward the goal to place himself there, knowing that the ball was going to make it all the way down. As he was running, three Tev defenders could see that the ball was coming, too, and gathered in the box. Ennjy ran to the right and received the ball.

And then the scent came. A zee. Right at the top of the box. Albert yelled to Ennjy. As the zee began to erupt, practically under the feet of two Tev defenders, the defenders instinctively shifted away; and Albert ran straight for it. He was going for the most difficult move, the ride-up, and the crowd seemed to take one huge collective gasp.

If he didn't have the right energy, he'd sink into the zee-liquid. If he gathered too much forward momentum, he'd accidentally perform a jump-over and be propelled into the net. Only with the help of the team's ahn could he hop upward to a point where he could play the ball above the defenders and slam it down into the goal. Think up, he said to himself, stay calm. Your team is with you.

Time seemed to move in slow motion as he made the leap. *Up, up, up.* His right foot barely touched the buoyant surface of the rising zee, and up he went, feeling a rush of intense energy through his foot from the zee itself and from his teammates on and off the field. Energy zinged through every cell of his body. Fatigue gone. Muscle aches gone. Anxiety gone. He threw his arms out, sensed the zee still rising beneath him, and prepared to bounce again. We're doing it! he thought. This will be the tie-breaking goal. Ennjy kicked it up to Albert. The ball was coming toward him! They were doing it!

15.12

Mehk was watching so intently, he had failed to sense the president approaching. Everyone in the stands was on their feet, jumping and screaming, and for the past few minutes, the president had been deftly moving down the aisle, cheering on the team, looking as if she were merely intent on getting closer to the action. But suddenly her hand was on his arm, gripping violently.

"Now," she ordered. Shocked, he pressed the button.

Just like that, he realized, the deadly plan was in motion.

In the next second, Albert's kick would cause the ball to explode and—

Just then, the same Tev defender who had hit Albert's nose came out of nowhere. He jumped up to try to intercept the ball on the zee. But instead of bouncing upward, he smashed into Albert's standing leg, sending Albert hurtling off the zee before either of them could connect with the ball. While Albert rolled onto the field and the Tev landed in the zee-liquid, the untouched ball kept going, sailing out of bounds until it stopped in midair just over the sidelines.

The crowd howled.

The botmaker gasped and felt the president stiffen next to him.

They had both assumed that the ball would be kicked immediately after he had armed it. Now, with the ball hovering on the sidelines as the ref made her call, Mehk's malicious hack in the ball's inflation system was vulnerable to detection.

Nervously, he glanced at the four sensor drones that were on duty to perform random security scans. The ones scanning the north and south entrances and the vendors' preparation area were not a problem. It was the drone scanning the stands on the east side that worried him. Right now, it was zooming over the rows on the topmost deck, but it was working its way down. If the scanner neared the ball, it would pick up the irregularity in it and signal an alarm.

He had no doubt that if the authorities discovered that the ball was armed, the president would blame him.

The ref signaled foul, gave the Tev player a red stripe, and sent him off the field. Then it was announced that the next play would be a penalty kick. Albert would get the honors.

The Zeenods cheered.

As the crowd took up the cheer for Albert to kick the ball, the ball flew back and landed gently in the ref's hands.

The president turned and gave Mehk a relieved and satisfied glance.

15.13

Just as Tackle started to cross a street on the side of the stadium, a transport vehicle zipped above his head. In addition to large vehicles like trucks that rolled on the streets, car-sized airborne vehicles created traffic patterns in the air. The first low-flying vehicle had freaked him out—sent him running and howling. Now, he just ducked and waited. Funny, how quickly a dog can adapt.

Once the thing was gone and he was safely across the street, he began sniffing his way along the stadium's exterior wall again. He had already trotted around the outside twice. As he rounded the corner to the main entrance, he was hoping the guards he had seen before would be gone. No such luck. Hugging the stadium wall, he jogged onward. Halfway around, when he got to the players' entrance—a gate on the west side of the stadium—he was finally rewarded. Both previous times, the gate had been locked, but as he approached this time, one of the planet's wheeled truck-like vehicles was arriving and the gate was opening.

Quickly, Tackle shadowed the vehicle, slipping in through the gate. Once inside, he saw the tunnel that led into the stadium. From it, the smell of pine wafted and, sure enough, a trace of boy. Albert had entered through this tunnel. Albert was in there, he knew it.

He barked loudly, calling Albert's name, and then he took off running.

Behind him, he heard the familiar voice of Unit B ordering him to stop. No way. Let her chase after him. With every ounce of strength, he bolted toward the arc of light at the tunnel's end, where the smells of pine and players and food were waiting.

15.14

Ten seconds left on the clock.

As the crowd chanted and the players assumed their positions outside the eighteen-yard box, Albert took his position near the ball.

The crowd hushed.

The trumpet blew.

The eyes of everyone in the stadium were on Albert.

As Albert prepared to run and kick the ball, the energy boost from the zee was still resonating strongly throughout his body, and he was also feeling the additional rush of energy streaming into him from every Zeenod and Zeenod ally in the stadium. All his fears and doubts melted away and he focused on one thing only: the ball.

The fans began chanting and stamping their feet.

Albert started his run...

The bark came first, but Albert was too focused on the ball to see the dog running toward him from the sidelines. He didn't see Unit B, either, who was running after the dog with a scanning device in her hand, a device that was, at that moment, sending an alert to Unit B's internal processing system about an irregularity detected in the ball.

In that split second before Albert planted his left leg to begin the kick, two things happened at once. Tackle, intercepted by the tentacles of a Zhidorian guard, was pulled off the field, his howls masked by the sound of the crowd. In the same moment, Unit B, fearing that the ball was dangerous, shifted her attention from the dog to it. She activated her thrusters and dove toward the ball like a rocket. As Albert's kicking leg began to drive forward, the robot pushed Albert away with one hand and landed on the ball.

The ball exploded, propelling the robot up into the air with a mighty boom and throwing the players who were nearby back a few feet.

Seconds later, Albert and a stunned stadium watched as

pieces of the robot's body and bits of the charred ball thumped onto the field.

As a roar went up from the crowd, officials swarmed the field. In shock but unharmed, Albert stared at one of Unit B's detached hands. The reality of what had happened was sinking in. He searched the faces of the opposing team surrounding him, assuming one or all were to blame. The Tev faces were stone. Standing among them, Vatria straightened her spine, lifted her chin, and didn't blink.

The ref and FJF officials met with the two tacticians and a flurry of activity began. While fans grew restless, replays were watched; the pieces of Unit B and the ball were collected and examined; Albert and the other players were given quick medical scans; security drones swept across the field; and a new ball was brought out, scanned, tested; Kayko and Hissgoff were consulted.

Arguments in the stands about whether the game should be called off or play should resume erupted, and the tension increased. Finally, the director of the FJF addressed the crowd. When the Zhidorian announced that it appeared that the ball had malfunctioned and no foul play could be detected at this moment, the Zeenod fans protested. "A thorough investigation will be done," the official said. "But, for now, since we have no actual evidence of any foul play, the game will resume. The replacement ball is safe to use. The ref's ruling will stand. The penalty kick will be redone. Ten seconds on the clock."

Kayko and Hissgoff bowed.

The fans in the stadium went wild, and Albert's mind began to spin. Suddenly, they were back in the game.

"Zeeno! Zeeno!" the chant rose.

All the players took their positions. The new ball sailed into the hands of the ref as he walked onto the field.

"Do you want to take the kick, Albert?" Kayko asked. "It is your choice."

A small voice inside his head told him to hand off the responsibility to another teammate, and he stopped for a split second to investigate. Was it the voice of reason? Would he serve the team best by letting someone else take the kick? Or was that fear trying to pull him down? Another voice rose up within him: *Use the ahn and you will be taking the kick as a team.*

He looked at his teammates. *We're doing this together,* he said silently, and he could see the united response in their eyes.

The chant grew louder.

This was it. One kick was all they had. The chance to show that they could not be intimidated. He took his position and breathed, sending out his ahn to his teammates and opening himself up to receive theirs. Powerful, ready, he ran and kicked. Albert knew it was good the instant he made contact. A strong shot. The ball sailed. With wide eyes he watched the graceful arc. The goalie dove for it, but the ball ripped through his outstretched hands and slammed into the back of the net.

Goal!

The trumpet blew, signaling time.

It took a few seconds for the reality to sink in. 3–2. They'd won.

The fans cheered, and a burst of joy ripped through Albert. Suddenly Ennjy was hugging him, her smile radiant. "We did it!"

The other teammates rushed in, jumping and hugging, and Kayko ran to join them as the cheering in the stadium increased.

After the huge group hug, Albert noticed that the Tev players had formed a line and were marching quickly off the field. He shuddered at the thought of how their coach would treat them after the loss, but the blaring of the trumpet shifted his attention.

"The victory ritual!" Doz exclaimed.

Six gold ITVs circled back over the field and hovered. From the open doors flew the beautiful multicolored birds that had once filled the skies of Zeeno.

"Ahda birds!" Ennjy cried out.

"It can't be...," Sormie whispered. "Are they simulations?"

"They are real," Kayko said, a catch in her throat. "We are witnessing the rising of hope."

The crowd hushed as the birds took flight, a thousand of them, initially in random paths. Gradually the individual birds flew together to form one large group and the murmuration began—a lovely pattern in the sky, the same pattern as the infinity symbol, Albert noticed, and the birds seemed to change color with every shift in movement.

Albert's teammates exchanged excited glances and then looked up at the birds again, their eyes turning gold. Something more was going to happen. Albert wanted to ask what, but the entire stadium met the birds' dance with a sacred, expectant hush.

And then, as the ahdas continued their symbolic dance, they began to sing. The birdsong was ancient and ethereal and Albert knew he could not have heard it or anything like it ever before, and yet he knew its melody. Deep in his core, somehow, he knew the song.

Gently, Ennjy's bem extended. All the bems were responding. Then, as if prompted by an invisible conductor, the Zeenods on the field and in the stands began to sing with the ahdas, a wordless meditative chant joining with the voices of the birds, and it was impossible to tell which sound was coming from the sky and which sound was coming from the field. In awe, Albert felt his own breath turn to song. Eyes welling with tears, he sang with them, and a great lifting up began to occur, as if the movement of the ahdas acted as a giant hand to pull him and everyone into a heightened state of joy.

He looked at his teammates and realized that they were actually being lifted—him, too—a few inches off the ground. When Ennjy saw that Albert was rising, that he was experiencing the full power of their ritual with them, she smiled, eyes shining.

It was extraordinary to feel nothing underfoot, to feel lighter than air.

And then, with a great joyful crescendo the birds scattered into the winds, and Albert and the Zeenods gently thumped back onto the ground.

Kayko wiped the tears from her eyes and looked at the fans cheering in the stands.

"What happened?" Albert whispered.

"This is who we have always been and who we are," Ennjy said. "This is Zeeno."

Albert was silent for a moment, feeling the vibration of the song still in his chest. "How did I know it?" Albert asked. "How did I know the song?"

Ennjy put her hand on his shoulder. "You'll discover that when it's time, Albert."

Toben looked up at the specks in the sky. "Our secret benefactor is working to save and breed the ahdas, and now, they're flying again. They'll repopulate! This is amazing."

Albert had a hundred questions, but the FJF officials began the medal ceremony; and when President Lat walked onto the field, the intoxicating spell of the ahda ritual was replaced with tension. Although the players had no idea of the president's role in the explosion, they wondered what she could possibly say that could please Zeenods and not inflame the Z-Tevs and Tevs.

Bowing to the president of Tev, Lat said, "President Tescorick, the planet of Zeeno humbly thanks the Tev players for a game well played."

The Tevs and Z-Tevs were silent, watching their leader, who stood, gave a nod of his head, and sat back down.

The Zeenod fans cheered, and President Lat placed a game one victory medal around the neck of each Zeenod player.

Albert gazed at his. The word *triumph* was engraved on its gold face, and just as he was about to wonder why it was in English, the letters morphed. The Zeenod word for *triumph* appeared and then the letters morphed again and it appeared in Zhidorian. Second by second, the word appeared in all the languages of the players represented in the tournament.

"Come." Doz elbowed him as Kayko began to lead the team in a victory lap around the stadium. The Zeenods in the stands were ecstatic, but so were their allies, those from Manam, Liöt, and Fetr. The Jhaateezians in the stands were waving and cheering, even though the next game would be played against them. But as the team ran past the sections of the stands filled with Tevs and Z-Tevs and their allies—Gaböqs, R'tinuks, Yurbs, and Sñektis—the silence was chilling.

When they reached the center, robotic reporters flooded the field to snap photos and record interviews, and the grins never seemed to leave the faces of anyone on the Zeeno team. Even Sormie looked happy rather than nervous, and Feeb was dancing around, giving everybody fist bumps.

When the celebration was over, the team followed Kayko into the locker room, exhausted but thrilled.

An official had collected Unit B's parts, and they had been placed on the bench.

Albert stopped and looked at the container of twisted metal. He knew that Unit B had saved him because of the way she had been programmed, not because her heart or conscience or affection for him had driven her to sacrifice herself. But still, he couldn't help the wave of emotion—gratitude mixed with sadness.

"Excellent service from an excellent robot," Kayko said. They had a moment of silence and then huddled together.

"With our efforts, we have helped Zeenods everywhere," Kayko said, her eyes turning gold. "I expected a high delivery of sportsmanship from each of my Zeenod players, and I was rewarded. As for you, Albert…" She turned her gaze to him and the other Zeenods followed. "We chose well."

"Jhaateez next and then Gaböq!" Beeda and Reeda said.

"Wait." Ennjy stepped forward. "I want to address the seriousness of the explosion. I believe an investigation will reveal that it was a deliberate, malicious act."

"I agree." Kayko nodded.

Feeb added, "If we do not determine who sabotaged the ball, there is a high likelihood that more danger will be deployed."

Kayko looked at Albert. "We will understand if, under these new circumstances, you want to quit the tournament. There is no shame in announcing that you are done."

Albert looked at the team. "Done? No way."

"As you say, full steam in the head!" Doz cried out.

"Full steam in the head!" they all cheered.

15.15

Tackle managed to take a bite out of a tentacled arm as the Zhidorian guard dropped him outside the stadium gate.

"Aiiiiyyyy!" the guard yelled, turning both heads to their damaged arm as they walked away. Within seconds, the wound was healed.

Tackle spat the oily piece of alien arm onto the sidewalk as he fled. He had been so close to Albert! He had to get back in.

Dodging alien pedestrians, he ran around the stadium until he reached the main entrance. Exhausted, he wasn't sure if he had the strength to push through the dispersing crowd. Halfway in, the river of bodies split, some continuing straight past him, which would lead them onto the street, and others veering into what looked like a large parking lot.

A small being with three eyes bent to examine him, and then a large one yelled, "Klab!" and pushed him to the side.

The dog lost his balance and tumbled hard as a huge foot crushed his rear left paw. Quickly, he pushed through the pain, scrambled to his three good feet, and dragged himself to the wall near the threshold of the entrance to the stadium. There, he stopped to catch his breath.

He had to face it. There was no way he could find Albert in this mess. Albert would return to Earth and he would be left behind. Foot throbbing, he thought about what he would miss most, the newest things, oddly, the trampoline, the park, the long talks with Albert. And then the smells of Earth. The leaves. His bowl. His bed. He looked around at all the aliens. Maybe he could survive here. If he was incredibly lucky. But what kind of life would it be? A lonely one, for sure.

And then a voice came from deep within the dog. Do not give up, he said to himself. Your nose is taking in smells. Your eyes are taking in sights. Your ears are taking in sounds. You are alive. You can do this.

This burst of determination caused his shoulders to straighten, his head to lift, his ears to flick; and it was precisely this hopeful movement that caused a set of eyes in the exiting crowd to look in his direction.

15.16

The botmaker couldn't believe it. Pressed against the wall of the tunnel threshold ahead was the dog, the dog that had mangled his squirrel, the dog that had destroyed his negative-thought-loop bot, the dog that had outsmarted him and outrun him, the dog that had remained loyal to Albert Kinney, the dog that had, somehow, boarded the ITV and then raced onto the field, the dog that had led the Zeenod's robot to—

"Keep moving!" a Gaböq behind him said, his hot breath radiating over the top of Mehk's head.

Quickly, he stepped aside. The multispecies crowd was so intent on exiting and so consumed with thoughts of either celebrating or groaning—depending on which team they'd been rooting for—that they didn't even notice the sad-looking Earth creature in the shadows. Overwhelmed, Mehk stared at the dog, trying to analyze the emotions the sight of him was triggering.

During those final moments of the game, a part of Mehk had wanted the ball to explode as proof of his abilities, but he hadn't wanted the responsibility of Kinney's death—or the death of any of the other players—on his hands. When the dog had led the charge with the robot onto the field and the robot had sacrificed itself, Mehk had been surprised by a surge of gratitude. The ball had exploded and yet death had been avoided!

Now, a fantasy popped into his mind. He would take the dog to Albert and Kayko. Tell them everything. Tell them that he had underestimated them all. Tell them that it was their own president plotting against them. And then he would flee to a planet in another solar system—Earth! Yes, Earth!—and he would hide and survive and get back to work and—

With a shaking hand, he sent a message to the president, who had been swept into a flurry of end-of-game duties.

I did my part. My service is done.

A message came through almost immediately.

Your service has just begun.

The crowd surged and he found himself pushed forward. After numbly walking a few steps, he stumbled into the back of a robotic stadium greeter that had malfunctioned and was now banging her hand against the wall while repeating, "Thank you for attending, attending, attending. Thank you for attending, attending, attending."

A cold pragmatism settled over him. He had no choice but to give them what they wanted. As for the dog, he was sure they would rather have him in their possession than find out that he'd died on the street or had found his way back to Albert. And so, he reached into his pocket, pulled out his gheet, and flipped a small switch on the bottom to set the mode to "stun." All he had to do was get close enough to drop the gheet onto the dog's back. One bite and the canine would be comatose.

15.17

When they walked out of the stadium, the Zeenod fans were waiting, including those from Liöt, Fetr, and Manam. To Albert's surprise, the primary purpose wasn't for the fans to cheer on the team; it was for the team to thank the fans for their support.

As the players traded bows and fist bumps, an FJF official arrived on the scene with a replacement robot to pilot Albert's ITV home. As an added caution, Kayko and Giac took the robot aside to run a quick security scan.

Knowing that Unit B had been thoroughly customized by his team, apprehension rippled through Albert. Sormie, too, looked nervous.

"Can we trust this new robot?" Sormie asked in a whisper.

"Don't worry," Doz said. "As they say on Earth, everything will be hunky-dorky!"

Albert had to laugh.

Giac and Kayko returned with the gleaming new robot—gender-neutral—walking between them. "The unit is functioning appropriately," Giac called out as they approached. "It's a new model, right out of the box. We'll want to do some fine-tuning later."

The robot stopped and gave a short bow to Albert. Then it straightened and said in a high-pitched, cheerful voice: "Greetings, Sir! Unit D3492778 at your service, Sir. I am designed to make every trip for you a delight, Sir! Your satisfaction is my success, Sir!" The blank face displayed a smile. "I shall prepare the vehicle!"

As Unit D marched into the ITV, Albert turned to say his good-byes to the team. Just then, Vatria and her family and extended family walked by on their way to their ITV. Unlike the Tevs, who refused to address their opponents after a defeat, the Skell elders, Sñektians to the core, stopped to congratulate them. Although fiercely competitive, they were verbally respectful. And so, in the next moment, Albert found Vatria's regal grandfather Paod Skell bowing to him and the team. To Albert's surprise, Vatria bowed, too, keeping her eyes lowered.

"We respect your achievement," Paod Skell said. "We hope to have the chance to play against you and redeem ourselves."

As they continued on their way, Vatria, passing close to Albert, whispered, "I will see you again."

A flurry of new fans approached for more holo-autographs, and for a while, Albert forgot about everything but the thrill of being a part of the winning team. But when he began to climb the ITV's stairs to start the trip home, a ripple of sadness stopped him.

Tackle.

How frightened and lonely and hungry and thirsty Tackle must be—if he was even still alive.

"What is it, Albert?" Ennjy asked.

Albert turned. "My dog. How can I leave without him?"

"We will keep searching," Toben said. "We will ask—"

"Earth dog?" A Liötian fan who was collecting holo-autographs nearby stopped. "I saw an unusual creature run onto the johka field right before the explosion occurred."

"What?" Albert's spirit rose.

"I believe the robot that was destroyed in the explosion had been chasing that creature, but it was restrained by a Zhidorian," the Liötian said.

"Tackle was here?" Albert ran to the top of the ITV stairs to see over the crowd.

Beyond the Zeenods who gathered around his ITV, he could see the Tevs marching into their waiting ITVs. Beyond them, way in the distance, the mountains of Zeeno glowed a pinkish orange.

"Tackle?" he called out.

Nothing.

Albert took a deep breath and howled.

Toben knew his purpose instantly. "All for the howl," he said to the team.

In unison, each Zeenod took a deep breath and lifted their face up and amplified Albert's howl by matching it with their own.

Everyone and everything stopped—the Tevs marching into their vehicles, the paranj vendors guiding their hovercarts out to make their last sales, the robotic lot attendants, the pack of

Jhaateezian fans arguing about which of their opponents had the best skills, even a group of Z-Tev children who had been chasing a lizardlike animatron. Everything stopped.

And in that great pause, from the shadows of the main tunnel's threshold, just as the botmaker was about to release the gheet, Tackle heard the familiar howl and took off.

A nanosecond later, Albert heard the most joyful bark. And then he saw a flash of a reddish-brown coat of hair as a muscular Ridgeback burst through the crowd and began hobbling toward him.

"Tackle!" Albert cried. He was halfway down the stairs when the dog jumped on him. Albert laughed and cried and crouched down, hugging Tackle tightly.

What happened to you? Where have you been? Albert asked.

I've been looking for you, Tackle said. *And I found you and—*

You brought Unit B to me! Albert exclaimed. *If you hadn't found me, Unit B wouldn't have saved me.*

They stared at each other for a moment, hardly believing they were reunited, and then hugged again.

All around Albert, his teammates cheered.

Toben, Kayko, Ennjy, and Doz ran forward to meet Tackle.

"What a glorious beast," Toben said, crouching down.

"This is Tackle," Albert said. "He is intelligent and loyal and funny and brave."

"We are most pleased your dog is back!" Doz said.

Albert smiled. "I'm most pleased, too." He looked up at them and then back at Tackle's joyful face.

A vacha-blossom petal that had been floating over the stadium wall, dancing this way and that as the crowds were leaving, came to a rest on top of Tackle's right ear.

The dog sniffed it, grabbed it with his paw, and licked it up. Albert laughed. "Yummery, right?" Doz asked.

"Yummery," Albert agreed.

It was at this moment that Albert stood up and looked first at his teammates and then at the scene in front of him, and a feeling came over him. A premonition.

Although he didn't see the figure of the botmaker against the wall, although there was no way for him to know that in that very moment the botmaker was receiving a shocking message, a message that would guarantee a larger-than-life-or-death struggle for Albert and his team, Albert sensed the danger ahead. Without a scanning device, with nothing other than intuition, he felt it in his bones. Tackle felt it, too, and he rose to his feet to stand by Albert's side, ears perking. It was as if, for a brief moment, a curtain on this joyful scene had lifted to remind them both that unimagined difficulties would come, to remind them that, in life, the worthy did not always win and suffering was inherent in the risk. But, just as surely as they both sensed the struggle ahead, they also felt the rising of a quality that no robot has ever had the privilege of experiencing: the courage to face those risks.

"Albert!" Beeda and Reeda called out. "You have more fans here wanting your autograph."

And so, Albert gave Tackle a reassuring rub and turned to his friends.

That's the way life works sometimes. You are experiencing a moment of profound complexity on a planet that is spinning and hurtling through space, and, at the same time, you are called upon to give your attention to one small, specific task.

As Albert signed, he began to think about what it was going to feel like to return home. He couldn't tell anyone there that he was a Star Striker here; he couldn't show off his medal or tell the stories of all the extraordinary things that had happened. He had survived attempts on his life, had learned how to feel the ahn and ride the zees, and had become a part of the most remarkably compassionate, passionate team. He couldn't brag about the adventure to Trey or his sister or use it to impress Jessica or to make his mom and Nana proud. But Tackle was back, and Tackle would know it all.

"Come on," Albert said. "The medical drone on board probably has something to fix your foot."

As he waved a final goodbye to his friends and then began to help the dog into the ITV, Albert felt a rush of emotion, too big for him to name. Gratitude that Unit B had sacrificed herself. Gratitude that Lee had encouraged him. Gratitude that the Zeenods were continuing to place their trust in him. Gratitude that Tackle was alive. He knew that whoever had tried to kill him was still out there, but he had survived—and he and the Zeenods had won.

Albert looked at his hands guiding Tackle up the final two stairs and had the odd sensation that they weren't his hands. Likewise, his body walking across the threshold with the dog didn't feel like his body. His face, glancing at the new robot, didn't feel like his face. Perhaps I am transforming at this very moment into someone else, he thought. He knew it wasn't true, but he couldn't quite pinpoint what was happening. He couldn't put into words what he would learn later: that this extraordinary experience wasn't turning him into someone new; it was enabling him to become who he was always meant to be.

What now? the dog asked.

Albert smiled. *The next game.*